FORWARD AS ALWAYS

Olan Rogers & Jake Sidwell

Published by
Gungnir

Original Title: Forward As Always
First edition: October 29th, 2024
Edited By Jim Krueger
Designed By Voodoo Bownz
Publisher: Matthew Medney
First print run: 8000 Units

CONTENT WARNING
-Discussions and descriptions of death and dying
-Anxiety and panic
- Violence against children and elderly
-Graphic, detailed descriptions of injury and/or bodily harm
-Suicidal ideation

Printed in China
ISBN: 978-196-2594-20-2
Printed & Published by Gungnir

TABLE OF CONTENTS

JAKE'S ACKNOWLEDGEMENTS

Olan Rogers, my writing partner and closest friend, for being one of the few who stood by me as my health declined and my life fundamentally changed. It took more than seven years of you waiting for me to recover and countless thoughtful reminders of the worthiness of this story, but it's finally been realized.

Amberle Phillips for distilling the central problem of the earliest manuscript into: "This is a story by boys for boys." She didn't pull her punches, and now her fingerprint is on every page.

My dogs, Tillie, September, and Astrid, for keeping me company during the seven-year interim in which I was unable to write or spend time with people.

My immediate family for reminding me what the word 'family' means (when I most needed it and least deserved it). Few are so lucky.

My family-in-law for filling the gap left in the distance between my first home in Indiana and my new one in Oklahoma.

Our editor, Jim Krueger, for discovering the key that was already hiding in this novel. He'll know what that means.

Our publisher, Matthew Medney, for taking a chance on a couple of doofuses who simply love storycraft as much as he does. Our book was the immovable object in need of Matt's unstoppable force.

Dr. Ted J. Miller MD for being the first physician (after far too many) who listened to me, validated my concerns, and whose thoughtful medicine improved the quality of my life enough to make the writing of this book possible.

My D&D groups over the years. I attribute much of my happiness to the stories, characters, and worlds we've built and traveled together. You made the pain worth enduring.

Most importantly, my partner, for being the lighthouse on the shore when the waves grew too tall and too dark. Whatever goodness or meaning could charitably be extracted from this book, at least as far my contributions are concerned, let it be known that she improved them tenfold. All the best parts of who I am and what I make are stardust from her universe. I love you, Bee.

OLAN'S ACKNOWLEDGEMENTS

Jake Sidwell, you'll always be the Wiz to my Half-Pipe. Ever since I met you in Indiana during a freak blizzard and then being forced to ride in your Ford Taurus with broken heat, in fact you had to blast the AC so the windows wouldn't fog up! Oh yeah, and we had to have the windows down too! Fun times! I read your acknowledgment before I wrote mine and want to say, through thick and thin, I'll be there; you've always been probably one of my truest friends—those are in rare supply for me these days. As Gimli would say, "Smoked beef off the bone!" The funny thing is that I can hear your laugh as you reads this, and that's why I put that in there.

Amberie Phillips, you read our book at its worst and helped me hype Jake back into this story. Thank You!

To my Mom, Dad, and brother Chris, thank you for always being so supportive of whatever I do.

Our editor, Jim Krueger, you don't know how long we looked for an editor and for one to just jump into this story and believe in it. Really appreciate you!

Matthew Medney! Brother, we bonded over our love for Lord of the Rings, and here we are, making a book together. I can't thank you enough for believing in this book.

To the Starscreamers! You helped make this possible by believing in something that didn't exist yet. I can't thank you all enough. Thank you!

To my supporters, through the many years, you see the challenges I've faced, a constant uphill climb, and the many times I've been knocked down to the bottom. At any moment, you could have left, but yet you stayed. Thank you!

Ladybaby, year after year, we fight the unwinnable battle that is life. Stress seems to fill the cracks in our lives, and even though we try so hard, we don't get many wins. But the wins we do get are only worth it because I get to share it with you. We've been through a lot together, especially the last few years. I don't know what the future holds, but there is no one I would rather have by my side. Thank you for putting up with my chaos. Me and You till the end! Love you!

PROLOGUE

They came with fire. I know now that I couldn't have stopped them. But I was only eight at the time. The others were even younger.

It was late that night, during the tidal storm. Iris told us she'd be home before the next cycle, but the rain had already started. So I squeezed inside the oven, deep behind the kitchen wall. My safe place. You would've liked it, apart from the smell of charred clay.

Lightning flashed outside. Thunder trailed far behind. At that age, we hadn't learned to count the seconds yet or regard the drops in pressure, so the Tempest was still an enigma—a frightening one. All we could do was play games and pretend it wasn't coming.

"Eight…nine…ten!" Saph counted. "Ready or not…" She skipped past the oven in her poorly darned, black-bottomed socks that had spent too much time outside her shoes.

I shuffled farther inside the flue. It was a tight fit; that's what made it a good hiding spot, but I couldn't see much.

"Found you." Delight danced on Saph's voice from the bedroom. You know, she never complained about being the seeker. She always made her own fun. You two would've been fast friends, I'm sure.

Maksy slipped out from underneath her bed in protest. "You cheated."

"Nuh-uh," Saph said. "Or I woulda found Gaius."

Maksy considered it. "I guess."

"You better not be outside," Saph yelled to the room, though I knew it was for me. "It's off-limits."

Maksy whispered something in Saph's ear. There was shuffling. Then giggling. The two of them were dripping with guile as they slinked out of the bedroom toward the den. Saph wasn't much of a schemer, but Maksy brought out the worst in her.

Saph pounced on something I couldn't see. "Got you," she laughed.

"Not fair. I saw that, Mak." Little Rile was crying as he crawled out from his hiding spot. Always so sensitive. "You told her where I was. Now he's gonna win again."

"Not tonight," Saph said, sniffing the air. "Don't you smell it, Rile? Stinky feet. He's close." She always knew how to cheer him up. "We'll find him."

I wish they had. I wish they'd climbed into the flue with me right then and there. Or that they'd escaped, even into the storm. At least they would've had a chance, however slim. And I still wonder how different things might've been if Iris had come home before the rain. But we weren't so lucky.

Instead, a man in a fitted red jumpsuit kicked in the front door of our little Nest—the hole in the ground we called home. He stepped through the threshold and peered around. The other kids just stood there, quiet and confused, waiting for him to give a reason or apology. The man started violently shoving them into the dining room. They tried to fight back, but it was no use; he was more than twice their size.

He pushed them into chairs. They were crying, pleading. He wouldn't listen. When they didn't do as he asked, he hit them. I remember his voice was so eerily calm. He never yelled.

From my spot behind the oven, I could only see their legs, hear their terror. They were shaking. Rile was crying.

"It's gonna be okay," Saph said, trying to console them.

"Saph, it hurts," Maksy said.

"Saph?" the man asked. He leaned forward and inspected her more closely. "Huh. The intel was good for once. Get up."

He yanked Saph out of her chair. Maksy screamed, and he struck her so hard she fell to the floor. Her nose was bleeding, hair a mess, and she had marks on her arms and face. To this day, I can't recall the shape of her face, but I remember she was scared and crying. I was scared too. I didn't want it to happen to me.

Maksy saw me, my perfect hiding spot finally revealed. I scooted back, but it was too late. Her eyes grew wide. She pleaded with me silently. I slowly shook my head and shuffled back as far as I could in the flue, both hands over my mouth to stifle my own labored breathing. The man ripped her up by her hair. She screamed as he shoved her back into the chair. I heard him smack her, and he told her to stop crying.

When I think about it now, I get so angry. At him, yes, but more at myself. Because I remember thinking, please don't tell on me. Please, don't tell him I'm here.

Another man entered. His uniform was black but otherwise identical to the first's, and he carried two canisters of metal and glass that splashed with a viscous, dark liquid. He opened one, and a pungent and stinging odor, like fermented fruit and wet clay, stung my nose. You've smelled it before too. Ferno. I bet you hate it more than I do, with your sensitive beak.

"Renner…they're kids," the one in black said.

"Orders," Renner replied.

There was a deep sigh. Then, after too-short a pause, I could hear and smell the sloshing canisters—dousing every room inside the Nest. Maksy and Rile screamed as sticky liquid pooled around their feet. He'd soaked them with it too.

"That's all the extra ferno we have." The man in black had a lilting accent I'd never heard before. "I don't know about this."

"Put this one in the piercer," Renner said, pointing to Saph. "And tell Varic, the key is in hand." He seemed to shrug off the man's other concerns.

The other paused, leaning on one boot. "Do we really have to—"

Finally, Renner turned toward the man in black and stepped into his face. "If you're unhappy about the work, I can always have you transferred to the Cistern and find a man who asks less questions."

There was palpable tension between them.

"As you say, sir," the man in black replied, and he led Saph away. I can't explain the feeling exactly, but he took her like she was just a thing—not a person.

In a final act of defiance, Saph turned back to Maksy and Rile. "It's gonna be okay," she said, still sweet and full of courage, even at the end. You really would have loved her. She probably would've spoiled you.

The last I saw of her was a silhouette in the doorway outlined in a hot flash of lightning. And then she was gone.

Renner crouched down in front of Maksy and Rile. Only the bottom half of his jaw was visible. He was chewing something. He had a short black beard, well-groomed, except for two scars on the left side of his face where the hair grew in stark white. Whatever he was chewing on, he took it out and stuck it to Rile's shirt. His boots squeaked as he leaned in. The little ones leaned away from him. He examined them curiously, as one might look over an animal carcass.

"I don't get it. What are they so afraid of?" he muttered—not saying it to them, just at them. He stared, like he was waiting for an answer to materialize. After a moment, he stood, walked out, and shut the door behind him. It was quiet for a while after that.

Maksy whispered something to Rile. I heard my name but nothing else. She was scared, though. Her legs were trembling, and I could hear her sniffling. She was still trying not to cry. Rile hugged her, consoled her. He told her it was gonna be ok. That only made her sniffling worse. But the Nest seemed safe again. They'd been gone for half a minute already.

When I started to scoot forward to get a better look, I heard a snap and felt a sudden rush of hot air as the front door blew off its hinges.

And that's when the fire started.

And the smoke.

And the heat.

And the screaming.

When I was that young, I didn't have the context to understand. I knew something bad was happening. There was this feeling under my skin—a tightening and tingling, telling me to get up and run. But at eight years old, I didn't know what to do with that feeling, where to go, who to run to. So, I did the only thing I could think of: I closed my eyes and covered my ears, and I did as we always did when things were bad. I pretended it wasn't happening. Just a game. Hide and seek. I counted. I counted until I couldn't count any higher, and then I started again.

I don't know how long I stayed in the flue like that before the raincoats found me, but the storm cycle had already passed, and the sun was high in the sky.

"Luminator, there's a survivor!" a voice called.

A one-armed man, another raincoat, pulled me out of the rubble. He didn't speak at all, and his face was obscured by one of their customary tinted masks, so I couldn't tell if he was angry with me or not.

At the time, I kept thinking I didn't want to get in trouble. I didn't want to be sent to another Nest. We were happy. Iris, Rile, Maksy, Saph and me. We were content. I thought they'd let us stay if I could just convince them. I hope you won't judge me too harshly, but my prevailing thought was that I was a good boy, and I needed them to understand, so they wouldn't take me away.

"Iris is coming. She's just late." The words kept spilling out of me. "But she always comes home on time, and she taught us to cook, and I eat all my dewroot even though I don't like it, and I don't bring bugs in the house anymore."

I remember thinking I should cry. Adults tend to be more forgiving when kids cry. But I couldn't manage a single tear. It must have seemed odd to them. Now, I wonder…do you think it started that night, or have I always been like this? Sort of dulled at the edges, muted.

Anyway, a severe-looking woman in flowing graycloth robes knelt down in front of me. She wasn't a raincoat like the others. She was thin. Her face was wrinkled and starting to sag, and her wiry silver hair was pulled into a tight, unceremonious braid that hung behind her shoulders.

A golden symbol was embroidered into her clothes, just

above her heart—two stars, crossed one over the other. I recognized it as the symbol of Commonhope, so I knew they were good people. Our people.

The old woman took a cloth, wetted the tip of it on her tongue, and wiped the soot from my face. It wasn't gentle.

She barked orders to a dozen of her people, all raincoats. I'd only ever seen one before then: Iris. But these raincoats weren't like her. They were older, domineering, and quiet, hidden beneath those characteristic full-face oculums and wide blackcloth stormbreakers—masks and mantles that made them look otherworldly.

Whatever the old woman ordered, they obeyed. Some rummaged through the burnt rubble, looking for what, I didn't know. Others sent their hawks off in different directions with distinct whistles. None as fast as you, though.

There was a trio of raincoats discussing something in a hushed circle, sometimes gesturing to me. I thought I heard Iris's name. But eventually they dispersed.

That awful old woman finished cleaning and appraising my face. Then she checked the rest of me. Squeezed my legs. Nudged my feet. I didn't know what was happening. It felt like I should be doing something, but she gave no instruction. She grabbed my arms and jostled me back and forth like she was checking wobbly furniture. I almost fell, but she steadied me on the ground with her hands firmly on my shoulders. I couldn't tell whether I had satisfied some unspoken condition as she stood up and towered over me.

"Do you know why you alone survived?"

I didn't answer.

"That wasn't rhetorical," she said, looking at me and waiting for an answer to a question I didn't understand.

"Do you know Iris?" I was still trying and failing to cry. "She's a raincoat too, and—"

"—Iris is dead," she said. It was so matter of fact. Perfunctory, like a machine. Just three words strung tightly together and punctuated with the crumbling of my entire world. I dangled from her next words, which have held me in limbo for more than a decade.

"There were sixteen fires. Sixty-eight dead in total. Men, women, children. Seemed on its face indiscriminate—no discernible pattern, purpose, or declaration of intent...yet it was clearly targeted. We don't know what they wanted or where they came from."

Obviously, you and I know that wasn't true, but she was as convincing a liar back then as she is now.

"We have no effective method of tracking them and no way to determine if this will happen again, so we assume it will. They also left no trace. No shred of evidence. No survivors." She leaned forward and pushed one sharp finger into my chest. "Except one. One who hid. That's what I'm looking for. For hiders. Survivors. Runners." She held out her hand for me to take. "I want you to run for me now. Will you do that?"

That was the day I started my fifteen-year war of wits with Luminator Eloanne, the Lady of Steel and leader of Commonhope. But it hasn't been all bad. After all, she's the reason you and I met. Isn't that right, girl?

CHAPTER 1 - RUN

Dead black smoke rose through the rain and early dawn overcast. I'd seen it before.

"Just keep running, Gaius," I huffed.

The smell of petrichor had carried in before the rain started, but I knew where to bunker down, and I had a good estimate of how far out the storm was. I knew this route like the back of my hand. By now, I'd run it a hundred times.

My boots squished from the inside; El had warned me more not to tuck my pants into them. "It's moronic. You'll end up with trench foot." She was right, of course, but there was something about the way she gave advice—it always made me want to do the opposite.

Just keep running. Don't get distracted. El's voice repeated in my head. Look straight ahead, and do your job, packbrat.

After delivering my final commission to the sub-granary, I was supposed to head straight back to the mountains of Commonhope proper, but I just couldn't ignore the smoke. If it was really happening again...I had to see it for myself. Home could wait.

I ran through most of the night, several hours at least. I was tired. Agitated. And I couldn't even remember if I'd given a proper goodbye to Kwendani, the granary foreman. I just took off when I saw the smoke, and before I knew it, I'd run over fifty kilometers. I'll have to sneak him a book next time I'm through, as an apology.

Far above me, Raindrop soared and screeched in response to a streak of distant lightning, but it wasn't the Tempest she was worried about; she'd seen countless storms. Rather, it was the kilometer-high gravestone of smoke that had our attention.

Her red tail feathers twitched impatiently, awaiting my command. I whistled short and high, and she dove with her wings tucked back and away. Her gray plumage repelled the rain as she cut through it.

She lived up to her namesake every storm—swift as a raindrop. In a blur of cinder feathers, she came to a sudden halt, caught the air beneath her wings with a spray of rainwater, and landed gracefully on my forearm.

Her dark talons dug a little too deep for comfort into the green canvas of my stormbreaker, but my mantle was overdue for a repair or swap anyway. It hung too tight at the shoulders and broke too high above the knees. A definite misnomer, as far as stormbreakers go. The thing barely kept out the cold and rain at all.

"Careful now." I shook my sleeve. "I need this arm to feed you."

She loosened a bit and hopped up toward my shoulder. Those sable eyes of hers saw everything as they darted around—not just the rocks and dirt and tasty little critters scrambling to escape the storm. She'd seen the fire from above. I wondered what she would have told me. How bad is it? Did anyone make it? Was it them? She was certainly trying to tell me something as her head swiveled about, beak clicking.

"I know, girl. I'll get a closer look."

As she nestled into my neck, I held out a sliver of dried meat and scratched under her hooked beak. Covert white feathers excitedly flared from her chest as she plucked the morsel from my fingers. For the briefest moment, as she swallowed with head-rearing gulps, my mind drifted from the smoke. She almost managed a rare smile out of me. Those were precious on Galilei, worth stealing when I could.

I studied the silver-iridescent cipher bound to her leg. A pretty device—made primarily of low-conductivity bismuth. I pulled up the cylindrical shielding, spun the four numeric locks to 1-5-0-9, and resealed them, twisting the little cylinder shut. I extended my forearm toward the Commonhope mountains in the north and blew a loud descending whistle through my forefinger and thumb.

Raindrop took flight with a screaming kee-ee-ar. Her wings

whomped at first as she ascended toward the heavy clouds, then she suddenly whipped up through the rain like a loosed arrow, aiming to get above the storm. I pulled away the visor of my dirty oculum to watch her disappear into the clouds. She was gone in less than a minute.

Ciphers were clunky in execution, but there wasn't a quicker or safer way to get sensitive messages back to the northern mountains than a well-trained, red-tailed hawk. At least, not since the engineers fried our last pair of radios a decade or so ago in a bad storm cycle. I never got to see one myself. Even back then, they were barely functional relics of the old world, but I heard the signal could travel hundreds of kilometers in less than a second. Someone could be as far north as Welkin Vale and be talking to dewroot farmers at the edge of the Titan's Grave, clear as day, as if they were standing right next to you. So they said.

But now we ran, and our hawks flew. And we crossed our fingers, hoping the messages would be quick enough to matter. A better pair of boots would help.

The loose rubber of my heel flicked the bottom of my foot with every hurried step. I'd have someone patch it along with my stormbreaker when I got back, or I'd trade them in for one of the men's pairs. My gear in general was getting pretty shoddy, because I'd been gone longer than my monthly route allowed. Even the pack at my back bounced with the swish of too-little water at its base, and my rations were dangerously slim. All more reasons for El to chastise me.

I over-tightened the two straps across my chest, and the bouncing in my pack stopped.

As I came to the edge of the gorge, flashes of lightning illuminated the expanse below me. Patches of blue-green lichen clung to loose stones between shallow pools of muddy water. Above that, canopies of ruddy stone jutted from either side of the gorge, curling up like ribs housing a heart of flame and smoke.

"There you are."

Part of me felt like that kid from fifteen years ago, pretending the worst wasn't happening. Even though I wasn't plugging my ears or covering my eyes, I was still hoping to find strangers, beasts, maybe an accident—a precarious candle or an especially poor cook. But it was doubtful. I need to get down there.

A brave packbrat is a dead packbrat. Don't get distracted. Run. Hide. Survive. El and her little phrases had built a Nest in my head and never left.

In the distance to the east, the hands of the Tempest were moving in clouds of zealous black, and the increasing intensity of rain was a sure sign of her ire. She was coming. Right on time.

When lightning flashed, I counted. One-one thousand, two-one thousand, three-one thousand, four-one thousand…

Eight seconds passed before a low rumble rippled the muddy pool at my feet. Take a few minutes to survey, then shelter. The fury of the storm could paint a new landscape into the world, and I wasn't keen on becoming another crimson stroke on her canvas.

After I scaled over the slick precipice, carefully watching my steps and counting the seconds, I cut a trail down the steep incline into the depth of the valley. A piece of blistered skin popped inside my boot. Shit. Trench foot indeed. El sure had a nasty habit of being right.

Lightning flashed again. I counted. Thunder cracked in response as my tattered stormbreaker whipped about in the wind. Seven seconds that time. She's moving fast today, must be pissed about something.

The spongy lichen was a welcome relief from the kilometers of rocky terrain behind me. It had been a long night. I pulled the retractable hose from my pack and sipped the last of my water. The thing still tasted of rubber after all these years.

Smoke whirled in every direction, sometimes shifting with a mind of its own. I lifted my scarf over my nose at the stink of it. I knew the smell, pungent and stinging—a chemical stench. Like fermented fruit and wet clay.

Ferno. That confirms it.

It wasn't an accident. And I could only assume they weren't done. They were gonna hit others. It had been a couple years since the last one. I was starting to wonder what was keeping them.

I choked and coughed through my scarf. The smell brought up unwelcome memories. Same thing happened every time someone lit a hearth, or a stove burned too hot, or a campfire was doused. It didn't make me shake anymore, but it was enough to get my blood pumping.

The Luminators wouldn't be happy if they saw what I was doing, but I just couldn't do nothing. Even if my heroics had never helped.

"Hey," I called out, inching closer and counting the seconds between each flash of lightning. The fire was still raging, even through the night. That chemical sure loved to burn. "Anyone still here?"

I approached the Nest cautiously, focusing on my peripherals. Though, I couldn't see much through the cloudy lens of my oculum, which was long past due for a good clean and polish.

As I came upon the curling wall of the gorge where the Nest burned, there was a symbol of a four-armed giant carved into the shale wall, just outside the cave mouth.

"The old man," I muttered. My throat tightened. Please, no. Not Nat.

The fire still raged inside, though there were only dying embers at the entrance, sizzling at every drop of rain. They'd trapped the residents inside as they set it. Just like our Nest. And every other Nest that followed. Renner. Had to be.

It's not a packbrat's job to mourn or avenge, the Luminators would say. The raincoats would hold our enemies accountable, fighting clandestine battles, far from home, where things were supposed to be improving. That lie was easier to chew when I was eight. Whatever was happening, whatever they weren't telling us, I was only sure of one thing: We're losing.

The flames were just a couple meters away from me, and I could feel the heat and hunger of their tongues lashing at me. The Nest, just big enough to house a family of four, was reduced to nothing but wet ash. One of twenty or so faux-burrows Nat had dug around the base of the arching valley. He'd done the same thing when I lived with him—a deception to avoid this very thing. Futile.

"Give 'em a hundred holes to search through, and they'll never find you," he said. I'd believed him too.

He ran his own Nest for orphaned kids like me and wasn't a kind or cruel man. We were fed, and we had a place to call our own for as long as he could keep us. When someone's stomach got too big, he'd send them north to the mountains to join the packbrats, or raincoats. I heard he recently took in three others. I meant to visit and show him what I'd become. I really meant to visit.

I could imagine the children pulling on his droopy gray mustache or chalking his walls with images of their false little family like we used to. Did he still pretend not to see anyone sneaking extra food in the night? I swallowed the smoky dryness in my throat.

The rain was starting to go sideways. I needed to pick it up.

The only movements inside were specters in the dying flames, and the hot incandescence of Nat's hand-carved furnishings. I couldn't imagine what he traded to acquire that much wood—one of the rarest resources on Galilei. Trees couldn't survive the storm. Nat was a lousy craftsman too, with those knobby old fingers. He could only manage two bed frames, a couple mismatched chairs, and a table that wobbled if we didn't hold up the short leg with a book. Now it was all just fuel for the fire. No ferno needed.

And then I saw them. Two small bodies.

I'd seen enough. My stomach turned, and I could taste bile on the back of my tongue. I held it down, only just.

Lightning flickered and thunder followed only a couple seconds after, cracking over the whipping sound of wind and flames. The storm was on me. Gotta find shelter.

I took one last look at the Nest. Empty poultry cages dangled from the ceiling inside. No bones, no ash. They took the hens? Somehow that made Renner seem colder and crueler than everything else. I could only imagine it was him—the kind of person who'd spare birds but not children.

But I was out of time to reminisce or fantasize vengeance. I needed to get below the surface.

My boots sunk further into the deepening mud as a thunder wave shook the air. I pulled up my hood, tightened my oculum, and squinted through the figure-eight lens of the visor, plodding against the slinging mud and rain to get a better vantage. Too much smoke.

Don't get distracted, packbrat. El's voice forever rebuked me about the training I ignored.

It was raining upwards as I pushed through the muck, and I was being forcibly pushed back by the wind. I struggled to breathe through my scarf.

Just keep running.

The hand of the Tempest was on me, and as I looked upward, I could see her swirling funnel clouds forming, anxious to reach those fingers into the dirt and pluck me from the world.

"Not yet," I screamed. I slammed my hand on the firing mechanism around my waist. The internal torsion spring clinked pathetically—jammed with mud and sediment. My anchor was a no-go. Uh, shit. I barely had any footing.

Lightning struck the gorge behind me, and the deafening thunder rang in my skull. I ducked as flying debris stung like insects. I rolled the extra fabric of my gloves up my arms to protect my exposed skin. None of that would matter if I couldn't see; my oculum was getting caked with reddish clay.

Is there nowhere else to go? Amid the storming chaos, I saw a tiny blue glow southward. I'd just come from that way. Is someone following me? Is it Renner? I couldn't wipe the onslaught of mud from my visor fast enough.

My ears popped from the sudden change in pressure, and the temperature dropped. Along with my stomach.

Oh, no. Run, Gaius.

I plunged my feet through ankle-deep sludge, struggling to gain any momentum, whipped around by my stormbreaker. My boots were being sucked away from my feet with every step. I promise, I'll never tuck my pants into my boots ever again.

I leaned down on all fours, feeling around for solid ground. My fingers ran over a patch of lichen. I crawled to it slowly with my murky gaze fixed forward.

There! One of Nat's false Nest's nearby. Thank you. I could

make it if I could just gain some momentum.

The maelstrom had cleared up the smoke, but in its place was a white and brown threshing of torrential rain and crumbling landscape, like a smeared oil painting.

My back tensed with urgency at a familiar vibration inching closer behind me. The hammering of an avalanche of hail drowned out my swearing. I'd heard this many times, but I'd never been stupid enough to be stuck outside with it. I dared not look back.

Look straight ahead and do your job.

It was as though I was running in a dream—moving forward only enough to keep my pursuer at my heels. The wet ground peeled away beneath me as I crawled, exposing the dry underbelly of the terrain. I was being pushed and pulled as the cyclones dipped their swirling limbs through the cloud line.

Look straight ahead, and—

I turned and looked over my shoulder.

Descending from the sky like a maw of teeth opening to crush me was a wall of fist-sized chunks of hail. Lightning weaved in spasms through the falling mass like thread through cloth. I instinctually jolted up and away, trying to run but only stumbling backward.

My foot slid out from under me, and I was torn upward by the wind. I twisted uncontrollably before slamming to the ground, face up. Every muscle in my back tensed with pain. I could feel the hail drumming the ground as I tried to roll myself over.

My vision was fading as the reaching cyclones tugged my stormbreaker toward the sky. The Tempest was stealing the very breath from my throat as I screamed obscenities at her. I couldn't hear them over her bellowing. The mud slung up around me into the sky, slowly lifting me with it.

I could only think how disappointed El would be. The I-told-you-so's she would never be able to tell me. Even the memory of Saph and Maksy and Rile was too distant to hold on to. This is it. You win, El. I ignored you, and it killed me.

Just on the periphery of my vision, a broad figure loomed in the debris with two blue lights in its head. Those blue lights slowly went dark.

Then there was nothing.

CHAPTER 2 - CLARK

I awoke to the sound of a familiar voice, though the inflection had a mechanical warble, which tarried in a low hum at the end of every word.

"To err is human," the voice called, facing away from me. "But that does not mean one should seek it out."

Blood rushed to my head as I slowly sat up. The figure turned and clanked toward me.

"Clark?" I grumbled.

The Secondhand Jack towered at a full two meters in height, and he carried himself like he knew it. Much of his rusty, chrome-paneled frame was exposed under a patchy, green stormbreaker, but the sun-bleached mantle still helped to broaden his shoulders. The hood was the only part not in tatters, and it suited him.

"Good afternoon, Gaius." His wide-set eyes illuminated the rim of his hood in azure, rotating subtly as he looked me over. "Have your wits returned, or should I hand you back to the Tempest for another lesson?"

"I should've known it was you." I rubbed my forehead. "Thanks."

We were in one of the faux burrows—a short cave made mostly of scalloped, dusty shale. It echoed with the sound of the retreating storm and smelled of dust and stagnant water. Not unlike most Nests.

"Seems we both saw the smoke." He turned toward the light. "Much too late."

"It was Nat's place," I said. My voice was groggy.

"They targeted another orphanage. I cannot imagine why," Clark said, mostly to himself, an inquisitive hand on his chin. "Today will be a solemn day. I would have liked to see the little ones again."

"Me too." It wasn't the first of these conversations we'd shared over the last fifteen years—such things happened often enough to warrant an unfortunate shorthand. Nods, glances, brief funerals, and dignified silence. We didn't dwell, at least not outwardly. 'Forward as always' was the Commonhope maxim for a reason.

Outside, midday had broken, and the burrow was flooding with warm light. Chalk drawings shined on the dusty walls—an image of four small figures holding hands with a larger, four-armed man. Nat and his little ones, I imagined.

The gorge outside was drizzling with rain, though the hail already passed. The worst of it was long over. I sighed. I know better than to get caught in the storm. Can't always count on Clark to come to my rescue.

My pants were almost dry, and my boots had been removed. "How long was I out?" I asked, looking around for my gear.

"Long enough to miss the grand finale." He reached out with one arm to help me up. "But not long enough to miss the ghosting."

He could crush the bones in my hand with little effort, but Clark was always cautious with me, overly so. With every movement, the flux of gears, the buzz of kineticism, and the hum of electricity belied his humanity. He was the last of the Secondhand Jacks, although I couldn't imagine there was ever another like him. Others might think of him as zeros and ones—just a machine that ran on solar energy. But that didn't change the fact that Clark still felt like flesh and blood to me. He was, for better or worse, a friend.

In his right hand he held his prized weapon, a glaive pieced together from random detritus. He called it Toothpick. At the top, a curved blade was honed to a razor-thin edge on one side, which tapered down into mismatching alloys—welded to a long, heavy haft of solid iron. Only Clark could wield something like that. The weapon was covered in dents, scratches, and stories, just like him.

A single red and white feather hung from the blade's housing like a trophy, tied with rusted copper filament. And four translucent marbles, an equal number of blue and red, clinked next to the feather. I still didn't know their story. He told me they were gifts. Except the hawk feather, which he refused to discuss.

After lifting me to my feet, he crumbled bits of dried mud from between his fingers. I couldn't exactly see his displeasure, because of the iron grin permanently bent into his rounded face, but I knew him well enough to recognize it.

"Procedure would dictate a return to Commonhope proper to share our findings."

I nodded slowly. Then sighed. "El's not gonna be too happy with me."

"Then her disposition toward you will remain unchanged. Now, with the storm almost settled, let us prepare to spend what is left of those legs, packbrat."

"Sounds good to me—" I felt my anchor line snag behind me as I stepped toward him. "What the—"

Clark had anchored me to the back of the cavern while I slept, and the straps of my pack were also tighter than I preferred (though at least he'd refilled my water). A commonly fraternal act with him. Irritated, I released the steel grapnel from the wall behind me and rapidly cranked the retractor. Seems to be working again.

In a shriek of dust, the carbon tether coiled back into the bismuth gadget on my belt until it clicked as the torsion spring reset. Some esoteric words were written on the nautilus-shell frame of my anchor, and though I couldn't read them, every packbrat knew what they meant. We are the stars that guide. We are the common hope of the people.

"Raindrop's on her way to the mountains," I said, loosening the straps on my pack. "Sent her off last night with a message, but I can't say how long the Nest was burning before we caught it."

"I have little confidence in the bird." He stroked the feather at the end of his glaive. "The message may not be enough to incite the appropriate caution. This attack was frightfully close to the mountains. They may be zeroing in."

"I didn't have much to work with. It's four numbers, big guy. They'll know a Nest was hit, and they'll know it was hit by fire. I gotta believe that's enough to set some response in motion."

He tapped his polearm on the ground and his internal mechanisms zipped aggressively. "Perhaps, with permission from the Luminators, we can finally pursue the horror out there ourselves. I would like to bring home some answers."

"We both know answers won't come easy. But maybe a little retribution is in order. I'm hoping El finally reconsiders my raincoat status."

I pulled my brela from its sheath and flipped the straight, five-inch blade haphazardly back into my palm. It looked just like Iris's did back in the day, though mine was dull, and it always felt awkward in my hand, since I'd never been trained to use it.

The double-star symbol of the Commonhope was set into the blade in gold, and the hilt was tightly wrapped in cloth and tanned leather. Normally, packbrats weren't allowed to carry one. I was the exception. Not that it matters. Without a whetstone, it's a glorified letter opener. Just a symbol. For now.

"I'll convince her. You'll see." I re-sheathed the blade at my hip.

"Curious. I assumed you were shuffling off your mortal coil when you lingered inside a developing storm...against procedure."

I'm sure Clark would have raised an eyebrow at me if his face could move.

"You got me there. Just don't tell El. Always a step in the wrong direction," I said in my poor imitation.

"Then let us take a step in the right direction." He climbed to the exit. "This is our terrain, and we should make it known."

Thunder rolled far off to the west, and the rain had all but ceased. Summer storms were the most severe, but they were also the quickest. Heat moved in from the east as a gust of wind rushed into the burrow. The warmth settled comfortably on my skin, but as with everything on Galilei, comfort was an illusion.

Clark climbed to the opening and poked his head out, hood flapping against the swirling heat.

"Shall we?" I asked, hitching up my gear and climbing up behind him.

He turned back to me with that iron grin beneath his cowl. "Into the elements."

The exposed gears under his rusted knee plates spun to life as he thundered off into the canyon. Rocks powdered and spat under his feet. I breathed deep. Seeing Clark do his thing never failed to bolster my resolve. And after my little nap, I was ready to set the pace.

My eyes quickly adjusted to the gray light outside, as we sprinted through the gorge. Tendrils of steam floated upward like wisps of white hair from puddles of evaporating mud and hail. Ghosting was exclusively an early morning phenomenon after summer storms, so you were fortunate to catch two or three a year. The more superstitious folks regarded the spectral threads as spirits of the lost, but I didn't fancy the idea of passing through the leftover spirit-stuff of my friends and family.

The great ribs of stone hung as a canopy on either side of us. I was impressed it had survived almost completely intact. Stubborn structures like that always ended up as landmarks for us—anything the Tempest couldn't destroy.

Hail crunched beneath my boots as Clark cut through the rising steam ahead of me, swirling ribbons of vapor trailing behind him. His size was no indicator of his speed, and the echoing thud of his footsteps hinted at the power behind his every move. Glad he's on our side.

I caught up to him sooner than I expected, already sweating from the humidity. I could hear him mimicking breathing. I hid a smile.

"You are leaking." He pulled slightly ahead of me.

As I contested Clark's lead, I could just make out the burnt remains of Nat's Nest a hundred meters off.

"Do you think anyone made it out?" I paused, recalling the scene. "Only saw two bodies."

We ran without speaking for a moment, and I wanted to believe he was calculating the possibilities, but I knew better.

"Pick up the pace, packbrat."

Within an hour, we scaled the edge of the gorge and headed into the green moss fields at the foot of the northern mountains. Of the sparse flora that grew on Galilei, moss was my favorite. Springy, spongy, great for running. And it blanketed the entire base of the mountain range like a soft celadon sea leading into Welkin Vale—the only pass through the mountains. Unfortunately, the valley meandered more often than not.

"What do you think, Clark? It'll add an extra day or more through the pass, and the storm's been coming early the last couple weeks. I don't wanna get caught in it again if I can help it."

I took a long drink from my pack as we stopped near the base of the first snow-capped mountain.

His eyes flared blue as he scanned the thickening mist—a trick I envied. After a minute of silent surveying, he pointed Toothpick at the peak in front of us. "Up and over."

"Up and over then," I sighed.

It was a rough climb at first, sloshing through warm mud and impenetrable fog, but we eventually reached some spotty patches of moss. It still clung to the mountainside despite the Tempest's best efforts. Resilient stuff. Almost seemed an offense to clean my muddy boots on its otherwise spotless sheen.

By sunset we reached the midway point of the first mountain where the air thinned and fog dispersed. The neighboring mountains cut a silhouette against the cloudless, marigold sky like hunched old men competing for a breath above the surface. Always a pleasant sight, returning to these silent guardians. No matter what the storm threw at them, they remained steadfast and vigilant. Our most reliable landmarks. Home.

"Quick break." I slumped against the barren slate wall in a shaded gulley and sipped water from my pack. There was little room for chatting between drinking and wheezing.

"Very well." Clark pretended to breathe heavier.

I didn't appreciate the patronizing, but it was always better to ignore Clark's mimicry than make note of it. "Much obliged," I heaved.

Sweat dripped from the tips of my hair in cloudy droplets. I steadied my breathing and focused on rehydrating, like I'd been taught. After a few minutes of rest in the cool mountain air, I was ready to plod upward and onward.

Clark never pulled far ahead of me, and I was keeping pace, to my own surprise. Maybe I was selling myself short. If only The Lady of Steel could see me now. Keeping pace with the last Secondhand Jack as if I'm made of steel myself. I allowed a smirk to creep across my face, as we climbed beyond the clouds and into the snowline. The peak was less than forty meters above us.

A couple minutes later, I vomited watery orange across the snow below. That dewroot was definitely spoiled. I spit the rot and sipped on the siphon from my pack to wash out the bile and El's judgment. She doesn't need to know about that.

The air, if there was any to spare, was cold and unforgiving. Welkin Vale looked still and empty from that height. Not even a single red-tail soaring. I'm sure Raindrop made it. She's fast. Me on the other hand...

As usual, I was late, probably the last to return this month from delivering my commissions. Sidetracked again. At least I'd have Clark to accompany me for the tongue-lashing while Dim and Kai eavesdropped around the nearest corner. Little imps. Still, I was looking forward to seeing the twins. It was a long month away this time.

At the summit, Clark stopped. The marbles hung from his glaive, clacking in the breeze and glinting in an amalgam of purple. The feather was flitting and spinning like a lure dropped into a rapid river. He turned and pulled me up over the summit without a word. As I looked ahead to the next mountain, I saw only billowing smoke in hideous black.

CHAPTER 3 - LUMINATOR ELOANNE

"Again," Luminator El said. "Your time is worse than yesterday. Fifteen minutes and twenty-six seconds? You can't rely on a hawk to do everything for you, Gaius. Speed. Direction. Consistency. Cleverness. Survival. That's the way of a packbrat. A commission delivered, unopened, in immaculate condition, to the recipient, in the time allotted, against all odds. Is that too difficult for you to remember?"

"My memory's not the problem," I heaved through a flop of sweaty hair.

It was the tenth day in a row she had me running trials up the valley—down through the aviaries, around the training grounds, and back up again. Three kilometers of nothing but uneven rock to run on, with an uphill return. My feet throbbed, chest burned, back ached, and leg muscles twitched. The same as yesterday. And the day before.

"If not your memory, then what? Even the twins outpaced you in every trial. Dim and Kai are four years your junior. Should I put in a request for the sub-granary? I hear Kwendani's work is easy for the elderly. Might be a better fit for you."

"Just give me a minute, you old—" I stifled the last part under my breath.

She played with the green ring on her finger. "Would the Tempest give you a minute? What about the fires?" She paused. "Heaven forbid you run into Skavers."

Skavers? Now she was mocking me. I stopped fearing monsters when I saw what men were capable of. All my indignation bored into the hole I'd been chewing inside my cheek.

"You could always tend the library, join the scriveners. Anansi would be happy to have you. Much easier to catch your breath from behind a desk."

"But not the raincoats," I said.

She didn't respond. I hated that. I wanted to fight with her, even if she always won. I felt my face getting flush at the pompous all-knowingness of it. Always acting like she saw right through me.

"Fine," I continued. I'll show you just how little you know me. "Set up the clock. What's the time to beat?"

She cocked an eyebrow and scoffed. "The time to beat? You're sitting at dead last. How about beating your own—"

"The time to beat." I stood up, stretched my legs, and glared a decade-worth of bullshit back at her as I sipped water from my pack.

"Shanna did it in eleven minutes, eight seconds."

The siphon fell out of my mouth with a gasp. "Eleven? No goddamn way. Since when?"

"As I always tell you, Gaius, aim for the stars and—."

"—you miss the path in front of you. I know." I stared down the long route I'd been running all week. Eleven minutes. Shit. I took a deep breath. "I can do it."

She sighed. "Sure. Tell you what. If by some miracle, you beat her time, I'll hand over your first commission myself. Today. Right here." She pointed to the spot where she stood, unconvinced. "Along with a brand new brela." The words had a sing-songy arrogance.

I didn't enjoy being mocked, least of all by her. But a brela? It was odd she'd even consider disrespecting the legacy of raincoats who'd earned their blades the proper way. I hadn't even passed any of the written exams for packbrat certification.

"Don't say it if you don't mean it," I said.

She pulled a dagger from under her cloak, the wax of the sealed sheath was unbroken. A true brela.

"The veracity of my word isn't the issue," she said. "You've yet to break fourteen minutes, flitfoot. Eleven is a distant dream. Very distant. You're unmotivated, distracted, slow. Not to mention, overconfident. I'm offering you the impossible, because you've shown me nothing of the sort."

True. But I knew something she didn't. I'd been half-assing my runs—and everything else she asked me to do—everything but falconry, which I'd excelled at, because it was the only overlap with raincoat training.

I'd committed to giving Luminator Eloanne nothing but mediocrity on the packbrat front until she submitted my name for consideration to the rank of raincoat. I needed their resources to get to Renner.

Every chance I got, I told her that I wasn't made for running errands, that I wanted to fight. And after ten years of mediocre performances, second-rate trial times, and countless failed exams, she still rejected the notion, insisting I wasn't raincoat material. The irony wasn't lost on me. I knew I should give more effort to prove my skill, but El wasn't just any Luminator. She was always one step ahead of me. I had to outthink her, wear her down.

Now she was offering me a brela. I could jump the line and carry my own, even as a packbrat. One step closer.

My second wind kicked in. "You're gonna eat your words. I'll show you impossible."

"Oh, I estimated your worth the day we pulled you from that oven," she said dryly. "I know precisely what you're made of."

The hole in my cheek started to bleed. Say nothing. Don't give her the satisfaction.

El pulled out her timepiece, clicked it twice, and motioned for me to get into position. I hopped from foot to foot, waiting for the third click.

She really made me wait. I could hear the ticking of the little clock in her palm.

Tick-tick-tick-tick…

Click.

I bolted down into the valley. Speed and consistency were my focus. Pacing. I knew the trial like the back of my hand.

I started counting every other footstep in my head, like I'd been taught. One, two, three, four. Eleven minutes. It won't be exact—the count never is—but it'll give me a decent estimate of where I need to be in the run. I have to round the training grounds in the northern alcove in just under five minutes to stand a chance. That halfway point was crucial. Too quick, and I'd likely peter out on the uphill slope heading back. Too slow, and I'd never make up for lost time. Just under five.

The craggy mountain range on my right blocked out the early afternoon sun. That was good. But it also covered the valley in shadow. I had to be mindful about every step. One twisted ankle or stumbling misstep, and my time would suffer.

Did Shanna really run this in eleven minutes? I should've confirmed the board before I left. Maybe El was playing me. Is eleven really possible?

The air was cool and crisp, and I was keeping a good pace, even if my feet buzzed with overuse. Maybe I should've waited a day. Rested. I just couldn't let El have her way. Especially not with a brela on the line.

Thankfully, the birds were nesting in their aviaries—squarish, perforated dwellings made of gray mortar and stone, only a couple meters in height—so I didn't have to worry about getting shit on. I could hear them chittering as another aviary came into sight around the next bend. Five of their roosts in total before I'd reach the training ground.

Fifty-five, fifty-six, fifty-seven…I counted.

After about two minutes, I took a small sip from my pack. Half empty. Feels light. Could be lighter. Could I push it without the extra water weight?

I took the hose between my lips and siphoned the water from my pack, one mouthful at a time. Once it was empty, I did feel lighter. Was this how Shanna managed it? No. She's fast, but not particularly bright. This isn't even all that clever either. And it'll probably only buy me a few measly seconds.

Fifty-eight, fifty-nine, three minutes, two, three, four…

As I came around the second bend in the valley with three minutes behind me, I could just make out the top of my destination ahead: the hawk training grounds.

Thin, fraying tethers slung up high between two neighboring

mountains in a tangled mess of rope. It functioned as somewhat of an obstacle course, rigged with small metal rings and ribbons of varying color to be retrieved.

Any bird with an affinity for the ropes was trained to accompany Commonhope proxies—packbrats, raincoats, and some rare exceptions for others. They made great companions and even better messengers, but you had to keep an eye on them, even after extensive training. The birds were too clever and had a thing about food. Raindrop was no exception on that account, but she was a favorite among the trainers and probably the best flier in the group. Oh, I wish I could fly right now.

Anyone who says running downhill is easy never did it for ten days in a row. The pain starts in the shins, with muscles that often go unused. That's where the weight sits. The tips of the toes and the top of the feet go next, a sort of pinching pain followed by a constant dull throb. It isn't all that dissimilar to walking on a broken bone. The lower back holds out the longest, but it gives eventually too. The instinct is to lean backward, away from the slope, but that's wrong, and it puts pressure in all the worst places. And when one does something wrong for five straight days, it doesn't matter how day six goes. Or day seven. Or…

Forty-nine, fifty, fifty-one…

I was surprised to find myself running underneath the canopy of swinging rope in just under five minutes, as planned. At least I knew the first half was possible—the easy half.

The twang of taut cords bounced off the walls beside me. Strong winds conducted a chorus of chiming metal rings and flitting ribbons. A pleasant song, more so because I was alone. No bustle of the trainers whistling and calling—no squawks or shrills. And best of all, no petty guilt trips from Luminators named El. Peace. A rare thing.

The alcove stayed several degrees cooler than the surrounding area, cut off from the sun where the mountains on the east and west met in an arch of cold stone. I welcomed the coolness. I did not, however, welcome the uphill battle ahead of me—an especially difficult climb after nine straight days of grueling physical activity.

I couldn't figure out why El was pushing me so hard.

Typically, when trials showed diminishing returns, she would send potentials to the other Luminators for education and testing on a broad range of subjects—Galileian botany, survival, interplanetary history, cryptology and ciphertext, sewing, cooking, food preservation, navigation, geography, topography, cartography, atmospheria, triage, falconry, and more. The list was as comprehensive and esoteric as Anansi's library, a veritable rabbit hole of mysteries to discover.

But not a single piece of text on the history or culture of Galilei. I could recite facts about the rise and fall of the great cities of Earth and Ganymede, but I knew nothing about what was beyond the Thrash Sea, a mere five hundred kilometers southwest. I was competent in charting stars and tying knots, but I didn't know how or when or why we settled on Galilei. The Luminators told us vaguely frightening stories about Skavers—some indefatigable, unkillable monsters who'd chased us from our home planet.

They said the Titan's Grave, the canyon far to the south, was now all that stood between us and them. But I didn't care about that. I wanted a true monster. Renner. To find him, I needed information. Privileged information only a raincoat could access. Not folktales or bedtime stories about bogeymen. And—shit.

El was standing next to Luminator Doran at the top of the hill. Doran looked deeply disappointed. Not good. How many minutes have passed? How did I lose track? Damn it. I could hear El in my head, chiding me for getting distracted. She's wrong about me. This was just a lapse. Idiot. Maybe I hadn't beaten Shanna, but I definitely beat my own record. She'd at least have to admit that.

The taste of iron in my throat came in waves with every breath. It wasn't a matter of picking up the pace, but simply surviving the hill. I plodded along with defeat and shame sloshing in my gut.

As I passed Luminator Eloanne's smug, unbothered face, she clicked the timepiece with no fanfare. I collapsed next to her in a pile of sweat and disappointment. Idiot. Idiot. Idiot.

She stood above me with her hands resting on the small of her back. I could feel the smarmy I-told-you-so's oozing from her.

"Just say it, you goddamn sadist."

"Did you even bother counting the seconds?" she asked.

"Not in the mood, El."

"Indulge me."

I balled my fists to stifle what I really wanted to say. "Because you just need to hear me say it? Don't you?"

"By all means, packbrat."

"No! Okay? I got distracted halfway through. Are you satisfied? I'm wrong. You're right. You know everything. All my worst impulses. Does that make you happy? Do you take pleasure in…did you just call me packbrat?"

I sat up, confused.

She turned the timepiece to me. "Ten minutes, fifty-four seconds. A new course record."

I studied her face. "Are you playing me?" I looked around for Dim and Kai. "Did the twins put you up to this?"

Luminator Doran approached and handed El a small, nicely wrapped box. He seemed put off.

"You win, Eloanne." He ruffled his graying hair. "Again."

"I warned you never to bet against me. I know my pupils."

El took the little box in one hand, pulled the brela from her cloak with the other, and held them both out to me. "Your first commission and brela, as promised. Keep in mind, a brela is only a symbol. You are not a raincoat. But wear it well. Luminator Doran is acting as my second to observe your certification."

"And to be humbled by the Luminator's foresight," Doran muttered. He avoided my gaze, a bit embarrassed. "I hope you're not offended, Gaius. You hid your talents well. So well, in fact, that I didn't realize you had marked your study materials with footnotes that disguised your impressively average test scores—until Eloanne showed me. You should be quite proud. That obfuscation was a clever bit of survival. It'll serve you well in the field. You're just as she said. A packbrat through and through."

El…bet on me?

"I don't get it," I huffed. "What is this? You spent two weeks running my ass into the ground. I'm not even at my best today. Not to mention the last decade insisting I'm not 'raincoat material.' You never hid what you thought of me. You never believed in me. I mean, you just said—"

"—that I estimated your worth the day we pulled you from that oven? That I know precisely what you're made of? Something to that effect? Yes. Well. I meant it. Just not in the way you inferred. You'll have plenty of time to look up the meaning of tongue-in-cheek after you've delivered your first commission to the training grounds." El smiled. "After all, if you're to traverse the world at large, Raindrop will need her cipher."

CHAPTER 4 - COMMONHOPE

Five black pillars of smoke billowed through the clouds. Beyond the next mountain, somewhere beneath the gloom, our largest settlement was surely burning. We wouldn't reach them for another day.

Clark removed the hood of his stormbreaker in solace. I did the same and held my oculum against my throbbing chest with one hand. This can't be happening. The raincoats would have stopped them. Did they get deployed yesterday when the fires started? I could only hope Raindrop reached them in time.

The mountains were the center of our civilization. They held the disparate threads of Commonhope together—the farms, granaries, fisheries, scroungers, and Nests.

The Luminators always picked up the pieces after every disaster; without them we were lost. They directed raincoats to harbor refugees, investigate the fires, or provide protection. They managed the packbrat routes where we'd carry the weight of impossible words across vast expanses of dangerous terrain. And they raised new proxies year after year.

We were evidence that the system was working—that people weren't being forgotten or left behind. No matter how small or how few. And few we were. As long as Commonhope stayed connected and the Luminators endured in the mountains, we could survive together.

The sun had disappeared behind the snow-capped mountains to the west. If there was moss beneath my feet, I couldn't feel it. I didn't feel much of anything. I couldn't process what I wasn't sure of. There was just a heaviness, pulling me down the mountain. A confusion. We climbed down the side of the mountain into the eclipsing night.

My eyes couldn't focus on any one thing. I just watched my feet, trying to recount my mistakes, then trying to think of nothing at all. Neither worked. My mind was both violent and dull.

I'd never met my parents. Didn't even know their names. In some ways I counted myself fortunate, because I hadn't lost them either, but there was also an unanswerable question. Who would I be if they were still here?

Commonhope was there for me. The packbrats were my siblings. The raincoats and Luminators were my protectors and teachers—something like parents, I imagined. The scriveners and engineers too. We were a kind of family; we fought, loved, misunderstood, and showed up for one another. Who would I be if they were gone?

"We rest tonight," Clark said. "Tomorrow will be difficult."

I couldn't argue. I was exhausted, and it felt like any words would be too much and too little. Like everyone I knew would slip away if I admitted my fears aloud, or I'd jinx them if I expressed any hope.

We made it down the mountainside beneath dueling moons of pale crimson and spotted gray. For much of that night I was restless, somewhere between too tired to sleep and too anxious to be tired. Just as I'd drift off, my body would jerk awake, my heart pounding in my throat. It happened a dozen times over the course of a few hours. But eventually my eyes stayed closed.

As quickly as I'd fallen asleep, I was startled awake again. Clark had his hand on my shoulder. The world felt foreign, hostile. The smell of smoke hung in the air.

"It is early," he said. I expected more—some philosophical waxing to ease my anxieties, but he didn't offer any. I couldn't give anything to him either.

I equipped my gear and ghosted like the tendrils of steam after a summer storm, pulled up the next mountain in weary silence. Without the fog and mud to slow us down, we were able to climb to the frozen peak before midday. The smoke was still rising through the clouds below us, but it was thin and pallid, dispersed, having lost much of the blackness from the day before. It looked less severe too, but that only meant everything solid had already burned.

I rinsed out the filter at the bottom of my pack with melted hunks of ice and snow. Despite being empty, I swore it grew heavier with every passing hour. I wanted to drop it in the dirt.

We sank into a frothy sea of clouds and smoke—the final descent. The smell was mostly chemical and stinging. Ferno. I made use of my scarf and oculum as Clark pulled farther ahead of me. I wondered if he could actually see the horror below us.

"Quickly, Gaius." He hurtled down the mountainside.

I didn't have his vision or his finesse, so it took me a few minutes before I finally settled at the base of the mountain. I bent down to get a look beneath the wisping smoke, warm dirt between my fingers.

I was home. What was left of it. Commonhope proper was nestled in the intersection of two valleys, like one of the great thoroughfares of Earth. Except instead of cities and gleaming lights lining our paths, we lived in hovels and caves under the mountains between roads of natural stone and moss. No evidence of our settlement was permitted outside, except scant carvings in the mountain rock to denote ownership. At night, no one would ever know a soul lived there. That was by design.

However, it was the middle of the day. It should have been lively and vibrant—packbrats training, food cooking, clothes hanging, birds squawking, Luminators complaining. But it was quiet. Screams would've been less haunting.

But there were no screams. No cries for help. No wailing children. No panicked hawks. Only the crackle of dying flames.

The smoke ebbed and flowed with the breeze, revealing the horror in waves as I stood.

I stumbled back, nearly falling over a blackened corpse I'd missed on the way down. Dozens of charred bodies were scattered between the valleys. They were utterly unrecognizable. There were birds too. Raindrop…I couldn't tell if she was among them. The smell was rancid, like urine and scorched meat. My stomach knotted and churned.

A crashing spurt of fire startled me as Clark barreled through the caves, one by one, in a mad dash for survivors, tossing aside flaming furniture and kicking in crumbling doorways.

I waded forward through the bodies, studying each one for any features that hadn't been burned out of them. God…at least five of them were Luminators, the dual-star pendants still hanging around their necks. Most laid face down, arms outstretched, like they were crawling toward something…or away from it. They'd tried to escape. Where's El? There were no tight braids; no hair left at all. Some had been incinerated down to their bones, teeth exposed, lips pulled back over their gums in black and red bubbling skin.

My mouth sweated and tongue curled. I'd witnessed plenty of death before, but nothing like this.

Beyond the Luminators were twenty or so packbrats, all dead—bodies twisted and warped. They'd converged for the monthly observance. Someone was graduating? I didn't even know who. Goddamnit. Were they waiting on me? If I hadn't been late again, would I be laying next to them? Could we have stopped this?

Then I recognized two identical heads of curly hair, unburned—Dim and Kai. The twins had been strung up by their feet and hung from the cave above Anansi's library. Dim's head was smashed in, and Kai's throat was cut.

My head went dizzy as I tried to swallow the rising anxiety in my throat. I leaned over and threw up. There was nowhere I could look for relief. Even the inside of my eyelids flashed with the images of my dead brothers and sisters. I wanted to run, to scream, but there was nowhere to go. This was my home.

Clark didn't seem to notice my wobbling—or anything that wasn't right in front of him. He just continued ripping through the roaring flames and compromised foundations, going deeper and deeper into the mountain.

I knew he wouldn't find anyone. We never did.

But none of it made any sense. What the hell happened here? Where were the raincoats? Didn't no one fight back? This was a slaughter. In our home. I saw no other sign of our enemy. Not a single casualty on their side.

The mountain radiated like a colossal oven. Almost every inch of it was destroyed. The intricately hand-carved, wooden doors were nothing but charcoal on metal hinges. The library chamber, deep at the end of the talus cave, was worse off. The books, maps, history, and wisdom of Anansi—all gone, except for what remained in my head.

I backed away toward the valley where I'd run countless trials. I needed to get away, to find familiar ground. As I rounded the first bend, smoke fanned out from the perforated columns of the aviaries. No red-tails in the sky either. Were they all dead? Nothing survived?

"Raindrop," I muttered. I tried to whistle for her, but my trembling lips couldn't form the shape. I'd sent her back—No. She's fine. She has to be. She's fast. Smart.

A distant, mechanical hum resonated ahead of me, somewhere beyond the bend of the mountain. It wasn't Clark. He was too deep inside the flames.

I moved on my own, sneaking along the warm mountain with my palm on the cold pommel of my brela.

As I peered around the corner I saw an onyx vessel with a crested pod of tinted glass atop its frame; it had sharp edges and was clean and sleek. Perfect blocky white letters were painted on one of the narrow wings: COLONY 6.

A middle-aged man stood in front of the vessel, dressed in a pale red uniform and black boots, clean and form-fitting. He faced away from me. Is that him? Tall. Dark hair. Dark beard—though, longer than I remembered, and more gray. But it's been fifteen years.

Was he always that big? Maybe it's not him. I need Clark.

I tried to shuffle back, but my legs wobbled in place, and I nearly fell over. Calm down. I counted breaths and held out my jittery right hand. Get it together. For Maksy, Rile, Saph, and Iris. For Dim and Kai and the others.

I cinched around the corner. He was holding Luminator Eloanne by the throat. She was in rough shape—burned, and bleeding from the mouth. He shoved her against the hull of the ship and whispered something into her face, which made her turn away in disgust. She noticed me.

I'd seen a face like that before—one who wouldn't reveal me in my hiding spot. A brave face who begged for help without speaking. One who was about to die.

I put a finger up to my lips and nodded at her. She looked back at Renner, presumably to not give me away.

Her instruction rang in my head like a warning bell. Just keep running. Hide. Survive. Run, Gaius.

I stepped out. Quietly. I knew this valley like the back of my hand. I held the goddamn course record. My legs steadied. My hand too. He was only twenty paces away.

"Just tell me where Dex is, and all this stops." He dropped El to the ground. She didn't make a sound besides the thud of her back onto the charred dirt. Tough woman. Our Lady of Steel.

I moved a few paces closer.

"You'll never find him." El spit a bloody tooth onto the ground. Her voice was shaky. "I'll lie. If you make me talk, I'll lie. You can beat me, pull my teeth, flay my skin. I'll make you chase down a hundred false leads before I ever give him up. And you'll never understand why. Because all you people have is Varic's resentment. We pitied you."

Five more steps. Slowly.

"If you really believe that, you don't know Varic at all. Besides, look around, Luminator. There is no we. Most of your people are dead. Those who aren't, we'll find—the Breacher too. There's no one to perform your infamous steel courage for. It's just you and me. The least you can do before you die is assure the survival of colony six."

At the recognition of his voice, my blood boiled. It is him.

My arm, possessed by the vengeance of a hundred dead, lifted my brela to strike. I saw his full reflection in the side of the ship—a long black beard with two scars on the left side of his face where the hair grew in stark white.

Renner.

I brought the dagger down to skewer him, but he must've caught me in the reflection, as he dipped his shoulder just in time. My weapon rebounded off his scapula. I should've sharpened this damn thing. I stumbled forward, almost tripping over El with my momentum.

He backed away, and I turned to face him.

"Clark!" I yelled.

No response. No heavy footsteps coming to save me. I shouted again, louder.

There wasn't a hint of pain or concern on Renner's face as he touched his shoulder and inspected his hand. Blood. Though, not much. He wiped it across the breast of his uniform.

His eyes were sharp, like glassy obsidian, and he had a wide stare. It was unsettling, uncanny in a way. Some of his features seemed less human than Clark—colder and unmoving. He didn't regard me with any excess caution. He barely regarded me at all. Is he looking… through me? At El?

"Eloanne, is this the result of your training?" He calmly gestured to my brela. "Kid. That's not how you hold a knife. Look at your hand."

As the words left his lips, I felt it. A cut. No. Worse than that. Shit. The hilt must've slipped through my grip when I'd struck him. I was holding the blade with my bare hand. I dropped it, and my hand instinctively squeezed shut, shaking, blood dripping between my fingers. Sharp enough to slice my hand but not pierce him in any meaningful way.

"Run, Gaius," El said gruffly.

I stepped in front of her. "I haven't listened to you for the last decade. What the hell makes you think I'm gonna listen now? Just sit there and watch, and when I'm done, you can tell me how this son of a bitch knows your name."

I squatted down for my brela and carefully took it into my hand. The open split in my palm was dizzying, but I gripped my weapon firmly and held it toward Renner. He wasn't even looking.

He held a finger to his ear and was staring absentmindedly. "Understood, Luminator. I'm still interrogating the—of course. Tail-up by twelve-hundred—no, sir. Yes, sir—eleven-hundred then. No, that's not necessary. As you say. Forward as always."

As those words, our words, came slipping out of his vile mouth, the vessel behind us began humming and buzzing with swelling electricity. And all on its own, it hovered just above the ground as the glass pod hissed open.

Renner was flexing his fingers outward repeatedly. He seemed somewhat irritated.

"I wanted to finish my work here," he started. His eerie dark eyes fell on me like an eclipse, and my skin prickled. "But I'm suddenly in something of a rush. It's obvious the Breacher isn't here. So, you've got a choice…Gaius, was it? You can either drag your half-dead Luminator out of my way, and I'll leave you to bury the dead…or I can spend the next few minutes teaching you how to use that knife."

"I'm not moving," I said. "Fifteen years I waited for you to make another mistake. Just like before." He looked confused as I continued. "Do you want to know why you don't remember me? How a little packbrat caught you off guard? Cause you forgot to check the fucking oven when you killed Maksy, Rile, and Saph."

He arched an eyebrow, regarding me sincerely for the first time. "Saph?" He paused. "Oh, I see. You were there that night. I was less thorough back then. My apologies. I don't usually remember their names. But Saph, I remember. The captain's kid wasn't scared like the others. She was—"

"Shut up." Blood dripped between my clenched fingers. I shook my head. I didn't want to give him an inch. "Doesn't matter. She's gone. You can't hurt her anymore. This still ends the same way."

He wet his lips. "You have about thirty seconds before that piercer takes off for the canyon without me. You don't want that to happen. You don't want to be here when I've got nothing but time. Isn't that right, Eloanne?"

The canyon? Is he talking about the Titan's Grave? Was that a misdirect or a mistake? And who's the captain? Focus. Kill him.

He loosely held his hands up and shifted toward the ship, which was buzzing with more and more energy every second.

"Don't," I urged him, unconvincingly.

A weak hand slapped on top of my boot. I looked down. El shook her head at me, her tight braid singed and frayed.

I pulled away, ignoring her. He's right in front of me. Finally. Flesh and blood. I have him. Unarmed. It would be so easy. I gripped the blade tighter.

El tugged on my pant leg.

"What?" I snapped at her.

I could count on one hand the number of times I'd seen El burdened by fear, few that cracked the Lady of Steel's facade. But in that moment, with everything she knew about my ability and Renner's, the woman who trained me was telling me to stop. This is a mistake. I can kill him. Can't I? Is she telling me he can kill me without a weapon? Is he really that dangerous?

I begrudgingly motioned with my weapon for him to go by. "I'll find you. And next time, I won't miss."

"Better soldiers have threatened me with worse. They're in the same place as Saph." He stopped and got a good look at me. "Gaius, was it? You've survived me twice. It won't happen a third time."

"Tell that to your shoulder, jackass," I spat. "You'll make another mistake. And I'll be there when you do." I lifted El's arm over my shoulder. She grunted as we shuffled away from the piercer, my free arm still holding the brela toward him.

Then, without an ounce of tension, the man who killed everyone I ever knew hoisted himself onto the wing of his ship and climbed inside the pod.

"This planet only has eight months anyway," he gave a lazy salute.

"What the hell does that mean?" I yelled.

The glass lid closed over him with a hiss and click, and the craft lifted in distorted heat waves and high-pitched humming. I equipped my oculum and protected El as smoke and debris escaped in all directions. The vessel exploded up over the mountains, disappearing above the clouds in seconds.

"Clark," I shouted again. I knelt and gently held El across my lap. Her silver braid was intact but scorched on the left side of her head, just cauterized flesh. Her left eye was half shut, bruised and scalded. I tried not to show on my face how bad it was. Even the charred cloth of her robes was indistinguishable from the flaking skin on her left arm. Thankfully, the rest of her body had only suffered minor injuries. It could have been worse. But she was old. Older than I remembered.

"Clark's here too," I said. "He'll help. You need to just hang on. Okay?"

She wheezed in response. The stern face she'd maintained for Renner fell away into anguish. Her mouth hung open, bleeding. Renner had removed some of her teeth. I didn't want to think about it. She looked up at me with glazed eyes. If they ever had color, it was gone—replaced with frantic, bloodshot exhaustion. I searched for the source of her pain as if there was a thorn I could simply remove.

"Gaius." She reached for my face with her curled, burnt fingers—her green-stone ring had melted between two of them. "You're late again."

I shook my head, somewhere between laughing and crying. "Shut up. Just stop talking. Save your energy." My face flushed with shame. I knew what she meant, but if I had been here, if I'd come back on time, maybe…

She shushed me, as if she could hear what I was thinking. There was a lightness to her. It didn't suit her. Like she was gonna disappear in my arms.

"Packbrat," she wheezed, her humming inhales growing shorter.

I nodded several times, to make sure she knew I was listening. Her mouth fell slightly open as I lifted her closer to me to listen. All her commanding presence was gone, and all my years of petty resentment toward her were transmuted into begging the world not to take her.

I longed for her harsh voice again—to call me to action, to tell me what to do. Her hand slid from my face to my arm, and she weakly pinched me.

"You're…still here…" she muttered, falling unconscious.

She was breathing, but not well. I carried her back through my dead brothers and sisters and laid her down near the other Luminators, my empty pack behind her head.

Hot embers flooded through an arched doorway, illuminating the corpses outside in frenetic red. Clark's shadow stalked within another hovel, continuing his futile search for survivors.

"There's no one else," I yelled at him. He didn't deserve my contempt, but it needed to go somewhere. Better Clark than El.

My chest was so tight I thought I would split in half. *You're still here*. She was our Lady of Steel, harsh and cold and immutable. Renner thought he broke her, but he didn't know the first thing about Luminator Eloanne or the people she raised. She'd live, and we'd find him.

Clark's footsteps thudded and clanked toward me, though they were heavier, slower. His legs were red-hot, and his whole silver frame was exposed, rust and all. Two dead bodies were draped over his shoulders, unrecognizably burned.

I stared at him with a furrowed brow, El at my feet.

"Is that the Lady of Steel?"

"She's alive." I stood up. "I called for you. Twice."

"I…apologize." His voice was quavering. "Something took hold of me. I wished to save them. I thought perhaps there was another like you, hidden in the wall."

"It's just us now, isn't it?"

Clark shook his head as he laid the two bodies next to their comrades. "I found them, Shanna and Anansi, in the dormitory together. Something must have fallen against the door and barricaded them inside. They suffocated."

So Shanna had made it back after all. Of course she did. Goddamnit. First to go out, first to come back. The very best of us. I'd beaten her course record, but never her commission time. I was nothing like her.

I looked back at the twins, still hanging. "Can you…?"

He nodded.

Despite their levity and general incompetence, Dim and Kai

were loved. And they cared deeply for Commonhope. They were inseparable and delivered every commission together. Yet they'd died hung from the feet that carried them to every corner of Galilei. Why can't I cry for them? Did I care about them at all? I just felt confused. Sick.

Clark took up Toothpick and cut their bodies down, catching them with his gentle strength. He laid them next to the others.

"What about the raincoats?" I asked. "Where the hell were they?"

"Two were inside. I found them huddled over the engineers in the workshop. I imagine they did what they could until the end."

"Which amounted to nothing." That came out more hostile than I intended. I wasn't angry with them. But I was angry. "El must've deployed the others. What was she thinking? Leaving us defenseless…?"

Clark had no answer.

Any surviving raincoats were now disconnected, my fellow packbrats were dead, and the Luminators had been reduced to one unconscious, horrible old woman. I didn't want to think of the kids. It was all too much. I couldn't do a damn thing for them.

Renner was right in front of me, but I'd sliced my own hand worse than I'd cut him. The shame was too heavy to bear—the failure. Too many lives snuffed out at once. But no tears fell. My jaw was aching with tension.

Colony Six, whoever they were, would account for everything they'd done, and I'd make sure Renner understood his sins. If I had to brand it into his eyelids, he'd remember their names. Every person. Every home. Every child. Even the birds. No one would be forgotten.

"I think you were right." I was tightly gripping the brela at my hip with a crimson palm. "We pursue the horror out there ourselves. Or we become it. We pay them blood for blood. Every drop."

Clark donned his stormbreaker, and his mechanical eyes flared bright within the hood; steam effused from puddles beneath his white-hot feet, swirling up the two-meter glaive in his right hand.

"The four of us will have much to do," he said.

I nodded. Then raised an eyebrow. "Four?"

He pointed Toothpick into the sky. I looked up and squinted. Hawk tail feathers waved a red war flag in the cloudy morning sky.

A sharp inhale hitched in my throat.

Raindrop.

CHAPTER 5 - THE PLAN

El weakly attempted to push me aside with her good hand—the other was wrapped and slung, along with the left side of her head. She was lucky, relatively speaking. Her burns were external, so there was no major infection and no need for amputation. But she'd still been unconscious for nearly two days while Clark and I tended to her.

Upon waking, El was already giving me commands and demanding to see the bodies of the other Luminators. I blocked the doorway.

"Move," she said.

"Not today," I insisted for the fifth time. "Tomorrow. You need rest. Clark prepared the burial. Just be patient."

She waved her hand in protest but ultimately sat down in a fit of coughing. I handed her a cup of water, which she sipped through mismatched teeth, as if the pain was simply a problem she would deal with later.

We'd set her up in the burrow with the most structural integrity. The space was nothing more than a half-charred bed, table made of stacked debris, and a stone ceiling—along with what few supplies and items we could scrounge from the fire. It wasn't pretty, but it would keep out the coming storm.

"You need to let me work," she said. "I can't sit here, doing nothing. Made prisoner by a stubborn brat."

"That's exactly what you're gonna do. Clark has his eyes on the horizon, so they won't come within ten kilometers of this place unseen. You can rest."

"Rest," she scoffed. "If you're going to bully me into it, then you better apprise me of the situation. The whole of it. I'd rather be dead than ignorant."

"Apprise you? El, I still don't understand what the hell happened here. How did they find us? Weren't we careful?"

She took a moment to recount the events in her head and scratched at her bandages. "Perhaps someone talked. It isn't relevant. All you need to know is they flew over and doused the area in ferno. The people outside panicked and scrambled inside the mountain. Fools. I tried to warn them. Renner wanted us trapped. Only Dim and Kai listened to me. Can you imagine that? The twins—"

She stopped to see my reaction, like we would share a smile at the irony. When I didn't react, it was like the memory of their absence rushed back across her cheeks.

"I was knocked back by a blast and lost consciousness. Next thing I knew, I woke up with that man's boot on my head. When I refused his questions, he went to work."

She paused again, mouth half open. Her tongue played in one of the new recesses in her mouth where a tooth used to be. "Then he pulled Dim out and forced him to his knees. The poor kid had been tied and beaten already. He begged me not to talk, not to give anyone up—as if he needed to. The idiot was very brave. Renner honored that bravery with a brutality I won't soon forget." She started to crack.

I put my hand up. "I saw the rest for myself."

Her eyes went steel again. "My turn. How many Luminators?"

El stared at me with the same matter-of-factness as when she told me Iris had died. She wanted numbers, not names. Clarity, not grief. Maybe she made me like this.

"Just you," I said.

"Packbrats?"

I struggled to half-shake my head. The briefness of her pause was somehow worse than dwelling. Neither of us wanted to think about it. And dwelling betrayed our maxim.

"Raincoats?"

I looked expectantly at her. "El…you're the only one who

would know. Even for Clark, some of the bodies were…unrecognizable. We've maybe identified three, based on clothing, but it could just as easily be six or zero."

"Mm. If we assume three are dead…nine may still be deployed."

Twelve total?! Twelve raincoats? That was all we had. After all these years, the Luminators had let us believe we had a host of soldiers, fighting the good fight. So it was always hopeless. And that was it. No tears. No thoughtful epitaph. No reminiscing. Subtract the dead from the living and move on. Forward as always.

I needed answers. "Why send out so many? Even Kai could tell the fires were getting closer. Didn't you notice? Weren't you paying attention? Isn't this your job?" I didn't notice I was getting louder until I saw her shrinking away from me. Very unlike her. I lowered my voice. "I'm just saying. We could've prevented this. Planned for it. Something. You left us completely undefended."

El studied the water in her hand. One finger traced the wet rim of the cup. "Do you remember when we found you? Who pulled you out?"

I crossed my arms and leaned against the wall. "I don't know, El. A raincoat? Big guy with one arm."

"Lars. You only met him once. One of about thirty I deployed that day. I can still feel it, smell it." She danced a hand in front of her. "The heat and the smoke. The anticipation on their faces waiting for answers I only pretended to have. The way you're looking at me now."

She spit out a sliver of enamel and continued. "It took our group—maybe ten of us—a full day to reach the first fire. All dead. We passed four more fires on the way to your Nest. We hadn't found a single survivor."

I already knew the story of that night. She loved to answer simple questions with vaguely related anecdotes—get me thinking about something else so I'd forget what I'd even asked.

"We weren't used to the losses back then," she continued. "So when Lars found you, he was beaming, waving his big arm in the air to get our attention. The other raincoats were ecstatic. We'd sent so many hawks back and forth during the night and early morning—nothing but more dead.

"And you need to understand, he pulled you out of an oven, Gaius. An oven. I was expecting another corpse. And we all knew Iris was raising children. I had braced for the worst, up until the moment he set you down. And you just stood there on two little feet like a toy soldier, covered in soot. You didn't even cry. I remember thinking, he's like me."

Hearing her say it aloud made me wonder if other people noticed there was something wrong with me too—if they'd kept it to themselves or talked about me when I wasn't around. So, I've been like this for a long time. She never even tried to fix it.

And I was tired of her bringing up that night—mostly the way she talked about it, like I was a paragon of strength for hiding. I hadn't done anything useful, hadn't survived by ingenuity or skill or cleverness. I'd climbed into a hole in the wall and stayed there while my friends burned to death.

Give me a real answer. For once.

El looked up from her bowl. Her left eye was still swollen shut. "You want to know why I always sent so many out? Why I would leave us undefended? Why we always followed the smoke to the source, no matter the cost?"

I waited, but her furrowed brow said I should know the answer, that I was a fool for not knowing.

"Because I had to try." Desperation cracked in her voice. "To find more like you. Survivors. Clever, selfish things who would bite down on the world and never let go—who would scratch and crawl and dig and hold on, even as it all burned. Even if we never found another one. I had to try. I had to try…"

I thought she had a plan, that it was all leading to something. The truth wasn't as satisfying as I'd imagined. I'd done the same thing every time I saw smoke, even knowing the futility of it. I wanted to blame her, to have a target for my anger or a reason for why it all went wrong. But if I'd been in her position…maybe she was right. Maybe we're more alike than I want to admit. The thought chilled me.

She looked past me, presumably at the unsettling stillness outside. "But now, it really is just us and a handful of raincoats chasing smoke. Somehow, you and I keep surviving."

"Then use me." I held onto my resentment. We needed to change. "I never wanted to just survive. I wanted to fight. I've been telling you that since I was eight. Don't you dare keep asking me to bite down. Not after this. No more attrition. No more hiding. Point me in the right direction and let me loose." I knelt in front of her, took her wrinkled hand in mine, and squeezed. "He bleeds, El. You saw it."

"Oh, Gaius." Her hand didn't squeeze back. She shook her head with that quintessential Luminator disappointment. "You have always overestimated your ability and underestimated your potential. I tried to push you, but half an effort only makes you half a man. The way you are now? No. Renner would turn you inside out."

Like hell he would. "I'm better than you give me credit for," I continued. "And I heard him mention the canyon." She failed to hide her anxiety. "Yeah. You know me well enough to know I'm headed there with or without your help. So if I die because you withheld something—because you didn't try—then it's on you."

Her cheeks relaxed, dropping some weight she was carrying, and formed almost a smile, coy and prying at the corners of her wrinkled eyes. She gently laid her bandaged hand on mine, and like dross falling away from forged metal, her face pulled tight and severe. For the first time in three days, I recognized the whole of her. Luminator Eloanne. The Lady of Steel.

"Very well. If you're going to do this, you'll need help. Lots of it." She thought aloud for a moment. "I didn't like Renner's comment about us only having eight months. That didn't come from nowhere. Varic is planning something. Might finally be time to see how far along Dex's project is." She nodded, as if to confirm the plan forming in her head. "As soon as I'm self-sufficient, you two will head for the Looking Glass to find him. Clark knows where."

"The salt flats? You always told us never to go there. Remember? Nowhere to hide from the Tempest. It's a death trap. Blah blah blah. There's nothing out there."

"Glad some of the lessons rubbed off on you." She grazed the skin on her neck and winced. "And your caution is warranted. Even with things as they are, I can't risk telling you why or how he's there—communication with Dex has been inconsistent for good reason. But that's where he said he'd be. Just make sure you arrive between storm cycles."

"That goes without saying. What about you?" I pressed a finger into the doorframe, and it fell away like rotten tinder. "We can set you up in a better spot with some more supplies, but you're in no shape to travel. Certainly not that far southwest."

"I have a place nearby. Can't risk telling you that either."

I let out a dramatic enough sigh to tell her I understood the need for secrecy, given what had just happened, but also that I was truly tired of being left in the dark. And honestly, it was her dismissive tone that bothered me the most.

She continued, ignoring me. "From there, I'll gather the raincoats. As many as I can. There may be more survivors too—other Nests. If the sub-granary hasn't gone up yet, that's twelve more warm bodies. Kwendani will want to fight." She put her hand on my shoulder to steady herself. "Help me up for a moment."

Once she was on her feet, she studied the sky. Her thumb and forefinger rested on her bottom lip, and she whistled loud enough to echo across the mountains. I was impressed.

An old, mottled brown hawk came soaring down the valley moments later and landed at her feet. More survivors indeed. El whistled two short ascending notes, and it hopped up on her good arm. Well trained, that one.

"Good boy, Derecho." She pulled a bundle of thin, colored twine from her vestments and held it out to me. "Gaius, the purple one. Show it to him."

I waved it in front of the hawk. He turned his head to one side, squawked, and smelled it. El slid his cipher open, rotated the four numeric locks to something I couldn't see, and blew a long and low whistle until Derecho took flight southeastward.

"What's with the string?" I asked.

She hesitated. Another secret, no doubt. "Suppose it doesn't matter if you know now. We trained a few birds to associate colors and smells with raincoats."

"So, who's purple?"

"Andica. I'll need the best by my side for what's to come. And she's the best."

A raincoat's identity was kept secret, but Andica's exploits were well known—taking on gravehounds at Reaper Springs, collecting ghost wood for her brela handle from the beaches of the Thrash Sea, and even traveling beyond the Titan's Grave. I couldn't tell how much of that was rumor, which was probably the point.

"Suppose you'll meet us in the flats after that to take on Renner?" I asked.

"The only thing you need to worry about is getting to the Looking Glass. Renner comes after that. Don't go getting excited either. He's more dangerous than you know. You won't win a fair fight, so you'll need to be clever. And sharpen your brela."

"About Renner. You two knew each other. He even called you Eloanne."

She started to speak, but reconsidered. Her lips searched for some other tale to spin. She sighed. "Why did it have to be you? If Shanna had survived, I wouldn't be answering half these damn questions. Look, the whole of it…it'll be too hard to accept, coming from me. You wouldn't believe it anyway. Yes, we knew each other when he was young. Leave it at that."

"Leave it at that? That's flimsy, even for you. If you're gonna keep lying to me, at least put your back into it."

She seemed surprised at that. Does she really think so little of me?

I continued. "I might not have known what the lies were, but yeah; I knew. And it's just us now, El. You gotta give me something substantial to hold onto, because I'm dangling by a thread."

She massaged her finger where her ring used to be, replaced now with marred skin. "You have to understand. I didn't want it to be this way. It had to be. Ignorance kept us all alive, more than you'll ever know. I simply did what I could with what I had. I knew going in that it would be an impossible task.

"You'll learn most of it soon, with your own eyes and ears. It's better that way. Everything you want to know—I believe it's all beyond the Titan's Grave. And I see that glint of mischief in your eyes at the mere mention of the canyon, so hear my caveat before you go flouncing off to your untimely death."

"Spit it out."

"Prioritize whatever Dex asks you to do. And I don't mean you pretend to prioritize it, and then go do whatever you normally do. I mean actually prioritize it. If you want to build a future, one that works, if you don't want to be half a man, we have to support him fully in finishing what he's been working on for the last two decades. That's the plan. Your answers come after that. All of them."

"If it leads me to Renner, I'll do it. But I'd be less annoyed if you just told me what you know and your plan wasn't so half-assed."

"Unlike you, I never take half measures." She waved a hand. "Just do what I ask. For once."

This was nothing new. El was a vault, and even at the end of the world, she wouldn't loosen her tongue. "Fine," I said. "But you're not allowed to die until I get back and get those answers. I'll follow you into hell if I have to."

She laid down, clearly in more pain than she was letting on. Her movements were slow and labored, and she made noises in her sleep that she was likely suppressing while awake.

I kept one eye on the sky and the other on El as she rested. Clark came thundering down the mountainside a few hours later, Raindrop tailing above.

"How's it looking?" I called.

"No vessels detected," he huffed, pretending to be out of breath from his mountain trek. "But more smoke is rising. I spied a new fire approximately forty klicks southeast, and several more beyond that."

"That could be Ginko or Dallan's place," I said. Raindrop swooped down and was digging in my pockets for loose food. "Maybe we should stop over—"

"No speculation or deviating," El said. She rolled over and sat up. "That's what gets you into trouble. You have your course of action. Stick to it with no distractions. Just let me worry about everyone else."

"Fine." I was surprised to find a large part of myself still trusted El to manage the rest of the world. She'd done it my whole life, even if unsuccessfully.

"You two will be going together," she said. "Clark. Do not let him out of your sight."

Clark lifted his chin. "Of course. Glad to have the company. What is our objective?"

El filled him in, and he seemed giddy with the idea of getting to see Dex again. Apparently, he was Clark's creator. I suddenly wanted to meet him too.

We settled in for the next storm cycle that night. The noise and chaos were preferable to the stillness. Too much room in my head to reminisce.

The following day, we held a silent funeral. I buried four extra stones for Nat and the young ones. We didn't speak to each other about the fallen. There weren't enough words in all the fluttering ashes of our library to properly honor them, so we agreed not to try. It was over quickly. No time to waste in mourning. Forward as always.

Instead, we focused on getting El stable and self-sufficient, at least enough to make the trip to her new location (which she still refused to share), and we gathered food and tools to prepare for our long and dangerous journey.

I'd taken Kai's boots before we buried him. They were in better shape than mine and Dim's, and it felt right to keep their feet running. Honestly, I just wanted a piece of them with me, something to bring to Renner. Maybe I'd give him a kick from Kai.

Raindrop did some hunting for a few pink-eared stirige—fuzzy little mountain dwelling rodents—a favorite of hawks. It wasn't exactly a feast, but the little meat they had on them cooked up nicely, and the fat worked well enough for seasoning vegetables and greasing my anchor.

Four days after that, in the late afternoon, Derecho came flying back into the valley. El opened the cipher around his leg. This time El showed me: 0-0-2-9.

"Home, two days out." I nearly jumped out of my skin. "Andica's alive."

"Okay." She exhaled a sigh of relief. "It's time for you to head out. I've got work to do."

CHAPTER 6 - REAPER SPRINGS

Clark, Raindrop, and I took Welkin Vale back through the mountains. The soft, snaking spine of moss added more time to our trip, but to arrive at the Looking Glass between storm cycles, an extra day was needed anyway. We'd head south for three days, take shelter, let the storm pass, and continue southwest to Reaper Springs. There were a couple Nests nearby, so we could check for survivors before crossing south into the Rustyard desert, again taking shelter at the next cycle. Finally, straight west of that would be the salt flats of the Looking Glass and hopefully Dex. That left us plenty of time to search, all things considered.

El didn't say goodbye; she was busy prepping for Andica's arrival. I wanted to wait and get a chance to meet the legendary raincoat, but our schedule was already tight, and more fires would be rising every day.

I felt naked departing with no commissions in my pack. No letters, parcels, or supplies to deliver. Just a destination and two names. Dex first. Then Renner.

The first three days passed uneventfully as we moved southward through the mountains toward the gorge. When the images of burnt bodies began to press into the periphery of my mind, I struck up conversation with Clark, and he told me about his creator.

I learned Dex was, as Clark put it, "an unparalleled genius whose mastery of systems engineering and computational navigation would illuminate your dim comprehension of the world and put even the most proficient work of his peers to shame."

Given the fact that Clark's programming was wholly a result of his creator's design, his biased estimation of Dex's ability made me question whether El had gotten all her information from him. Or perhaps Dex really could create a solution to all our woes—build an army of Clarks, all singing his praises. I wouldn't hate that.

In the hours of silence between those conversations, I passed the time playing sling-and-snatch with Raindrop for as long as she would indulge me. It took a deft hand to challenge her, so the game demanded concentration, and I was happy to give it.

Most falconers only used one sandbag, two if the hawk or trainer was clever. We used three—one white, one brown, and one blue—for her to snatch in specific sequences. None of the other falconers could hold her attention, and no other hawk could hold mine. I imagine that's why they let me keep her.

I developed a distinct whistle for each finger-sized bag, and they all had a unique heft, so they'd fall at different rates. When we got in sync, throwing was like second nature. I could target difficult patterns, anticipate her movements, delay the toss or the whistle until the last second, and she'd have to predict the sequence like she was in my head. High short tone, ascending note, pinky finger trill. Brown, white, blue—a quick low snap, a high arching curve, and a fast straight.

Normally, we'd be at it for days, trying new sequences or incorporating the terrain—tossing through erosion holes in the tall granite outcrops or arcing over the hoodoo spires around Harrow's Nest. But today, she gave up after just a few hours. Maybe she could tell my heart wasn't in it.

Clark claimed her disinterest was more evidence for his theory that hawks were innately deceptive and selfish, only obeying when it suited them.

"Trusting such a creature may cost you someday." He twirled the feather dangling from his weapon. "Perhaps when it matters most."

"Now's a good time for that story. Don't you think?"

He brushed off my question. "No distractions. El's orders."

I'd pull that out of him someday. Another reason to keep going.

The Tempest reared her ugly head on the third day, right on

schedule, and we took shelter at the foot of the ribbed gorge. I slept well, which felt wrong—like a betrayal of some kind. The nightmares never came either, and I hadn't cried at the funeral or any day since.

That sense lingered, that there was something wrong with me, that I wasn't feeling or acting how I should. And in that sense, I kept finding my mind drawn to Renner and my childhood—not just the disgust and anger, but the way he asked, "What are they so afraid of?" That cavalier curiosity. The morbid detachment. I'd been thinking about it more and more, and I wondered if I was capable of the same—if something had made him, or if he'd always been monstrous. Was it under the skin or worn more like a shirt or a pair of boots? A choice? I buried the thought.

As we traveled that morning, Raindrop brought up the rear with sulking squeaks and a weary flight pattern, not at all in her normal flair. She deserved some meat. I'd treat her to it later.

We passed by Nat's Nest—just a gaping hole—and I considered how greatly he must have suffered before divulging the location of our settlement; I could only assume it was him. Though, it was hard to imagine a scenario in which he'd break. I didn't want to. The old man was a veteran of saving lives, specifically young, troubled ones, and Renner had stolen even that from him in the end.

"I'm sorry, Nat." I wondered if I would have been a better man in his position. Am I like Dim or El, ready to die for my convictions, or would I beg for mercy, telling all I knew? Thoughts like that were poison, but I had to believe everyone on Galilei imbibed a bit of self-doubt privately.

We continued hiking southward out of the gulch. At the top, I could just barely see the horizon where putrid yellow steam was rising from the collapsed caldera that comprised the Reaper Springs. Still a day off.

I only hoped the geysers and creatures living there would be more forgiving than the desolate flat rock between us and the springs. But I had my doubts. Even if the central volcano was dormant, plenty of horrors subsisted, organic or otherwise.

That evening, we made camp under a shaded tor we packbrats

used as a waypoint, a stone outcropping visible from a few kilometers in all directions. Decent cover from the storm, when needed, and it worked as a reliable signpost.

I split some of the rations I'd scrounged with Raindrop—twice-baked thunderfruit seeds and raw taproot. Worse than it sounds, but it was food. And I slipped her a sliver of meat when Clark wasn't looking.

He didn't have much to say when Raindrop was nearby. Maybe he thought she was listening, using his secrets against him. Instead, he just stared at me over the campfire as I snacked on some smoked stirige and overly ripe tubers.

"Not hungry?" I joked. As soon as the words fell out, regret flushed over my cheeks. I knew better than to poke that sore spot. The cruelty I was saving for Renner was starting to spill over the edges.

"No, Gaius. I won't be eating." He stood up.

"Ah, sorry. I didn't—"

He rested a hand on my shoulder. "I'll survey the path for tomorrow. It will be quite difficult. Gather your strength. Rest. Eat up."

"Clark…big guy, I'm sorry."

He walked off, and Raindrop just stared up at me with her glossy eyes. Judging.

"You could've stopped me, you know. Clark might change his mind about you if you made an effort to—" She hopped up in my lap and snatched the meat from my hand and a pinch of my finger with it. I yiped and whiffed at her; she flew off.

I watched her soar as I nursed my finger. The moonless night sky was freckled in stars. I couldn't see much else besides what our tiny bonfire illuminated, but I still felt at home. I'd been in the area many times, and I knew which caves and crags to avoid.

While my route never led directly through the steaming crater, I'd seen some bizarre critters on the outskirts of the springs. Had a run in with a family of mongs a few years back—hairless pink varmints, maybe half a meter in length with lidless, cloudy eyes and broad fleshy nostrils like ten limp fingers mashed into the end of their snout. They're mostly blind and nocturnal, but when I mistook their den for a refuge from the storm, I realized how vicious they can be.

Might've gotten myself killed that night if it weren't for the rations I'd tossed them—took nearly a whole pack to satiate the four of them. A raincoat would have had the whole family of mongs strung up and roasting before they so much as picked up a scent. A raincoat I was not, despite the brela at my hip. Even with the collapse of Commonhope proper, something in me still itched for that title.

As the stars nestled in the heavens, I caught the distant glow of two orange eyes, and I remembered it was the connivores we really had to watch out for. Fossorial little devils and barely the size of a boot when they stood on their hind hands. Bugging eyes waiting for you to fall asleep.

They had some kind of anesthetic chemical in their saliva that left you unaware and snoozing as they picked at you. You might wake to find nothing left of yourself, if enough of them were in on the hunt. Raindrop usually held them off, but she wasn't always with me.

One night, a pack of ten had followed me around. Waiting. Watching. Those big eyes blinking in the moonlight, disappearing, then appearing eerily closer. I'd heard the stories, and I had no intention of becoming another cautionary tale, so I made an example and kicked one into the distance. The others scattered and shrieked. I thought I'd taught them a lesson, but that night I awoke to find one face-first in the flesh of my thigh. A lesson of my own.

That creature didn't survive the night, but I still had a scar to remember it, like a shallow canyon running down my leg, just above the knee. Whenever I slept out here, I had nightmares about it. And whenever it rained, the scar ached.

The next morning, Clark was breaking camp and swatting Raindrop away from his head. He seemed to be in good spirits. I needed to apologize, but fresh wounds weren't for poking. Later.

I gripped my right leg, feeling the crease between the muscles. The key to managing pain is just to not think about it, but that option is rarely available. Thankfully, we had bigger troubles ahead.

The volcanic caldera that comprised Reaper Springs was host to a much worse variety of creatures than mongs and connivores. Insects and beasts thrived in the unforgiving heat and sulfuric-rich air. They'd grown savage and grotesque, feeding off one another, living and mating underground near the collapsed center of the dormant volcano—many-eyed and appendaged to excess, disfigured from the harsh environment and poisonous subterranean gases.

That route was ugly business for the unlucky packbrats assigned to the Nests on the other side. But the rich volcanic soil was supposed to be worth the trip. The people who lived there grew the most fragrant and juicy thunderfruit one could ever sink their teeth into. The beasts didn't favor it; they preferred warmer flesh.

I would've been more nervous if I wasn't accompanied by a Secondhand Jack. Although, my anxious brain kept imagining him leading us into a bloodbath just to quell his annoyance at yesterday's jabs. He had better sense than that. We'd get to our destination in one piece. Probably.

We continued southwest all day, right into the melting sunset. By the time one moon had half risen, Clark advised we rest for the night and take on the springs in the morning. Time was essential, and I wanted to avoid another night in connivore territory, but he argued, "Rest will find time for you, if you do not find time for it." That sounded like El wisdom, so I only slept begrudgingly.

I awoke two times that night, having sweat through my clothes. First, I dreamt about connivores, eating my guts while I laid there, paralyzed. Then I dreamt of my old Nest. I couldn't remember the details of the nightmare, but Iris lingered in my mind when I awoke. She used to make me feel safe. In the space between waking and sleeping it was easier to admit the fact that I missed her, still needed her.

Raindrop had nuzzled up beneath my chin during the night. Her company didn't go unappreciated.

The next morning was colder than normal, and we were up just before the sun. Above us, Raindrop squawked and clawed at her beak. She could smell the sulfur long before I did; she flew higher and higher as we went.

"No surprise. The bird will provide little support," Clark was far too happy to report. "You should familiarize yourself with such circumstances."

"She could still do us some good from up there." I drank deep from my pack.

"Unlikely," he continued. "The insects will be free to cause irritation, and I doubt her vision will be of any use through the gases. Moreover—"

"Clark," I said, with a parental tone. "Please."

"Right. It will be an arduous advance. Keep close and follow the wall." He pointed to a ridge inside the caldera where a crest of jagged, shining obsidian snaked through the steam.

"But that takes us west—almost northwest," I said. "We should be heading straight southwest. Saves a lot of time."

"If we pass through the center, as you propose, we accrue nine hours from the descent in slope alone. More importantly, the obfuscating gases and precarious terrain may set us wandering in circles." He pointed two fingers at his face. "Even these eyes have their limitations. The most practical compromise is to follow that wall to the chasm beyond, which will then lead us straight south into the Rustyard."

We'd lose an entire day not cutting straight southwest toward the desert. Any moment lost could be potential lives on the line. It could mean Renner was continuing his massacre. More children lost. More Nests destroyed. More—

"It is my aim to reach Dex as soon as possible," Clark added. He gently unfurled the fingers of my squeezing hand. The wound had opened back up and was bleeding through my bandage. "And we will. This route was part of my initial estimation. Trust me, Gaius. We have the same goal."

I breathed deep for a moment, trying to reconcile the damage our delay would cause. "Dex better be worth it."

"He did build me, after all," Clark reminded me, tapping his polearm on the ground with his chin held high.

"I admit that inspires some confidence."

"You will see." He squatted and twisted his body, stretching and loosening muscles he didn't have.

Raindrop circled and soared, waiting to see whether I'd be sending her in with us. I whistled a shrill tone through two fingers, instructing her to follow above, and we all headed toward the Reaper Springs.

We reached the slope of the crater just as the sun rose on our backs. The rim of the caldera, several kilometers in diameter, looked like the chapped lip of a sickly stone giant. Black, gray, and cracking.

During the winter months, purple flowers would rarely bloom along the lip. It was the only place I knew on Galilei where anything like that grew. Iris used to make trips to collect them for flower crowns. Took her days to return, but she always came back beaming, and Maksy and Saph loved them.

Today, it was barren.

Scattered springs of unnaturally blue water emitted amber steam in bubbling throats of hot, toxic fumes. The odor was mineral and sour even with my scarf wrapped tightly around my nose and mouth. At least the gas couldn't penetrate the air-tight seal of my oculum. What I wouldn't give for a full-face, raincoat respirator.

Clark pointed toward the volcanic glass wall. Instead of speaking, he swirled his hands at me in big circles. I shook my head and cocked an eyebrow.

He reluctantly stepped over to me and whispered, "The steam will grow denser as we proceed." He motioned his hands again. "So follow the obsidian, or we may lose one another. From here, we practice silence. Do not disturb those who slumber."

The sun was near its highest point, lighting the world around us in odious gold—hot above and wet below. My sweat coalesced with the condensation on my clothes. After only a few hours, I was soggy down to my socks in a vile effluvium not unlike sour eggs and dried vomit, and my throat was throbbing and dry. I didn't dare sip from my pack anymore, because even swallowing my own saliva started to feel like guzzling sand.

The oxygen-deprivation headaches and chest pain were preferable to the smell, so I was only taking short breaths. Extended exposure could be lethal to humans, so I couldn't imagine what kind of creatures were surviving in the vents below the surface, let alone thriving.

For most of the trip, I could barely see a meter in any direction, but where the haze was at its thickest, the space turned liminal, disorienting. I couldn't see my feet or my outstretched hand on the wall beside me. Felt like I might just disappear. I understood now why Clark didn't want to make a straight shot through it. Neither did I. It was fatiguing not knowing where I was.

Clark actively skirted us away from the larger pools. Something must be down there. The ground was a spongy pumice that sometimes crumbled and belched hot gas beneath our steps. From what I could tell, we were on top of old lava tubes. I kept imagining myself falling through into the dark or the maw of some shadow monster.

At times Clark led me with only a couple waving fingers, wading through the haze in front of me like a body bobbing in and out of water. He was also right about the insects. Thankfully, they were gathered around the pools in humming swarms, and they only grew loud or aggressive when the geysers gurgled or erupted. My stormbreaker would've kept them at bay if it actually fit. No such luck. All the spares had burned back home.

Just before sundown, Clark stopped, holding his arm out in front of me. His eyes were rotating wildly, struggling to focus. What is he seeing that I can't? Or what is he not seeing? I listened closely. Raindrop gave a long screeching call. Then there was silence, as if the world had fallen away. No insects or gurgling pools. Nothing.

The sound that followed seemed to emanate from the ground beneath us—a bellowing, deep and enduring—almost like the magmatic groan of a less-than-dormant volcano.

Shit. "Clark. Clark! It's supposed to be inactive."

I stepped back, eyes wide and fixed on the edges of Clark's stormbreaker ahead of me. I turned toward the direction we'd just come. There was no way we could outrun it. We were standing in the middle of a massive shield volcano. I could hear violent splashes all around, echoing off the obsidian on my right. The insects were agitated.

"It is not the volcano," Clark whispered. "It's…" He stepped forward slowly and held out a hand out for me to wait. He held Toothpick in front of him and scanned the springs. "Gaius. Follow the ridge. Go now." He dashed away from the wall into the cloud of swirling steam.

I started after him until I heard vicious snarling and crunching metal, which stopped me dead in my tracks.

A high-pitched yelp cried out, and Clark yelled, "Run, Gaius! Gravehounds!"

A pool splashed behind me, and padded footfalls followed. I reached my right hand out for the cold, smooth obsidian and sprinted. Just keep running. Don't look back. I could barely hear my crunching footsteps over steel clashing with bone and teeth and Raindrop's anxious calls overhead.

An imposing figure was running a couple meters beside me, growing in size as it closed the gap between us. It's shadow halted unnaturally and was yanked into the air. Then it slammed to the ground with a yipe, a ripping sound, and a great howl.

I'm okay. As long as Clark is with me, I'm okay. I stayed the course, keeping the wall on my right and my eyes locked on the ground through my oculum. Just keep running. Just keep—

My foot punched straight down through the pumice with a crunch, and my stomach jumped into my throat as I fell waist-deep into a scalding spring. My ribs smashed hard into the edge of the pool, knocking the wind out of me. Green and black dots speckled my vision, and my legs were burning. Something slimy brushed against my leg, and I struggled over the edge, lifting myself out of the blistering water in gasps and groans of pain. Steam rose from the boiled meat of my legs.

I blinked hard and scanned my surroundings for whatever was in the pool with me, but amid the green specs I only saw an umbra of violence and blood spurting through vapor.

My legs were sweltering, but I clambered to my feet. A bloody, bald canine limb—larger than my own leg—splashed into the pool next to me. Something snatched it and pulled it under. Horrified, I hobbled away toward the stone wall again, wincing with every step.

I grabbed my brela.

The beasts weren't likely to respect the symbol of Commonhope, but they might respect a few inches of metal in their gut. The whole dagger was only the length of my forearm, and the blade itself only comprised half of that, but I knew which direction to point it.

Shit. I forgot to sharpen it. How did I forget to sharpen it?

I staggered along the obsidian, more careful to watch for crumbling terrain or surprise pools. A six-legged beast appeared before me, deceptively large with the sun setting behind it. It was nearly my height on all-sixes, growling low and heavy. I readied myself with my weapon.

It leapt at me. As I brought my brela up, blood sprayed across my oculum. I stumbled backwards and frantically wiped the blood on my sleeve. Did I kill it? I didn't feel anything. Through a smear of red, I saw the tip of Toothpick pushed through the back of the hound's skull and out through its mouth, dripping in front of me. Clark withdrew his weapon, dropping the beast to the ground with a thud.

"The rift is not far." He lowered my shaking dagger from his face. "We may lose them on the other side."

"The other side? How wide is it?" I huffed through my muffling scarf. My legs were shaking.

"Just go." He was distracted by something nearby. His head swiveled back and forth. "Now, quietly before—"

A jaw snatched his shoulder and jerked him back into the roiling steam beside me. His gears were straining and whirring as he wrestled it alone. "Go!" he called again through the snapping and snarling.

Howling erupted from the ground again as more padded footfalls came crawling out of their pools. I reached the chasm in less than a minute. It was over four meters. On the other side, an elderly woman, covered from head to toe in a colorful knitted shawl, was waving me across the gap.

"Jump," she called with an aged rasp.

"Are you crazy?" I yelled back. "I won't make it—"

A crescendo of snarls and clanging metal thundered behind me. Several dark shapes burst from the fumes, chasing Clark. He barreled toward me, picked me up, and launched himself across the gorge. Hot air was blowing up from the rift as we arched over. I couldn't see the source. Or the bottom.

Please, don't drop me.

The sediment shattered beneath Clark's monstrous landing on the other side, and I felt something crunch in my ribs.

He gingerly set me on my feet. His hands recoiled. "Are you hurt?"

"Damn it. I think I broke a rib." I pulled away my scarf to take a stinging gasp of fresh air and inspected my chest. Nothing felt broken, but it could still be fractured.

Clark looked down at me, apologetically templing his fingers.

I reassured him. "Don't beat yourself up. Imagine if you hadn't grabbed me. Much worse."

"You're not safe yet," the old woman said. "The hounds are still hunting."

Back on the other side of the chasm, a pack of six, soaking-wet gravehounds stalked back and forth at the edge. They were ruddy and hairless except for a ridge of gnarled fawnish fur down their spines, and they had gills cascading down the underside of their necks. Their six legs were muscles stubby—made for running, not leaping.

Two of them prowled the gap on webbed feet. Swimmers. Shanna never mentioned that. Would've been good to know. Their pupilless eyes blinked white inside long, angular heads.

Behind them, a massive hound emerged through the haze, older than the rest. Twice their size. The beast snipped at the others as it passed. They cowered and backed away. Its left eye was gashed and bleeding, and its one good eye was locked on Clark.

Clark pulled off his hood and stared right back. They matched pace back and forth. The creature reared back its head and flexed its throat, gills flaring as it howled into the sky in dissonant tones—that same eruptive bellow I'd heard from beneath the caldera. The others yiped and barked, circling behind. The elder gravehound slipped back into the springs and the others followed soon thereafter.

Clark roared back at them, pounding fists against his chest. His stormbreaker was in shambles—more so than before, and he'd acquired a slew of fresh scratches and dents. No easy feat to damage that metal frame. I could only imagine the power of those jaws. Thankfully, imagining was all I had to do.

"Do you think we scared them off?" Clark asked.

I exhaled through my nose, shaking my head in nervous laughter. "Definitely."

The old woman cracked me in the knee with her cane. "This is precisely why I requested a woman. You men always stir the damned pot. Shanna has enough sense to follow the gap on this side. Now, come along. My Nest isn't far."

CHAPTER 7 - HOLLIS

On our side of the rift, it was as though we were looking through glass. The venting air kept away the smell, the sticky condensation, the stinging irritants. No gas or bugs at all. Even the noise of the springs felt distant. Though, my throat was still dry. I envied Clark in that moment. The need to eat, drink, and breathe was proving to be a consistent problem. He'd hate the thought.

"Are you Hollis?" Clark asked.

"Don't dally." She turned on a makeshift metal cane—a rusty old Secondhand Jack leg. "Worse things out here than gravehounds."

A shiver went up my spine as she said that. Night was falling on the Reaper Springs, and any visual of our pursuers went down with the sun.

It looked like there had once been calcium pools here on the other side, but they were dry and hollow now, made of multicolored mineral deposits like shimmering melted wax.

Farther in, a dozen long rows of thunderfruit had been planted, maybe half a kilometer from the chasm. Everything was tilled and cultivated. Skillfully. Even the vines were trimmed and trellised in even rows. None of the fields I'd seen could compare.

The actual fruit was swollen with ripeness. Their glossy ribbed skins had already turned a deep red, bordering on violet. Even when they're still green, thunderfruit is perfumy and sweet, if a bit tart, but these were practically falling out of their hard tawny shells, and the vines were sagging with juicy sweetness. I wanted one. Hell, I wanted ten. But not without the lady's permission.

"You can have as many as you like," she said, unprompted.

That obvious, huh. If I wasn't eyeing her crops with an open, drooling mouth, I might've thought she was listening to my thoughts. Stranger things had happened.

There were alarms cobbled together from rusty scrap, chains, and busted poultry cages—all hung and staked into the ground around the fruit.

The old woman tapped the alarm, and it jangled and creaked obnoxiously. "If there is an ounce of clumsiness in even one of those beasts, we'll hear it. Just don't expect it from the smart ones."

Raindrop picked at the chains between little squawking hops. Her breast feathers ruffled.

"The bird disapproves of this security measure," Clark said. "Once again, it seems our survival is in conflict with her nature."

"She just doesn't like cages." I squatted next to her and blew an abbreviated whistle. She pecked at the apparatus once more before hopping up my arm. "Don't take it personally."

"Of course not," Clark replied.

"I was talking to Raindrop," I said, scratching her neck.

Just beyond the rows of fruit, a hovel was nestled inside a rocky hillock. The ovate entrance to the Nest had no enclosure and was totally open to the elements. But it seemed nice, welcoming even. There were glints of metal and a few poultry cages dangling from the ceiling inside, though they were empty (most were these days). Raindrop hopped onto my shoulder to get a better look.

A hieroglyph of a ten-eyed woman with flowers growing from each palm was carved into the sediment outside. I couldn't recall if the woman's name was Hollis, but I'd heard rumors she knew things she shouldn't and that she had a way of seeing inside you. Shanna said the worst part of the trip wasn't surviving the springs. It was the old woman's stare.

I picked a few pieces of fruit until my pack was filled to the brim, stuffed down around my blanket. I clapped my hands as loudly as I could and watched the thunderfruit shells snap shut as the vines curled and retracted to the surface. Saph used to love running through them clapping her little hands.

"None of that nonsense." Hollis gave me a stern look. "How would you like it if I clapped in your face? They're alive, and because of them, so are we. Show a little respect."

"Sorry," I said. She's gonna be fun.

"Keep your apologies. Just don't do it again. And keep your hands off my furniture until you've had a wash. You're filthy."

My fingernails were impacted with dirt and grime, and my knuckles were covered in half-dried cuts and scrapes. I was a mess. I started to apologize but stopped.

Clark ducked inside. The ceiling hung too low for him, so he stayed bent at the hip. He inelegantly removed his stormbreaker, exposing his broad back where there was no tinge of rust or scratches or dents; it was clean and smooth like molten silver—brand new in contrast to the rest of his battered frame. He looked like someone else from behind, someone gentler.

"The door, if you're able," Hollis said. She pointed to a rickety pulley system attached to a frayed canvas tarp. The whole apparatus was ramshackle at best. Charitable to call it a door.

"Can do," I said, pulling until the tarp shut off the entry. Barely.

The rest of the Nest was clean but disorganized, housing the remains of what was once a cozy little home. More people used to live here. Whether they died or abandoned her, I didn't know. But she'd left all their belongings as they were: an unmade bed with an imprint in the sheets, the spine of a book cracked open and laid down on its pages, an empty glass of water with cloudy minerals left behind. The whole place felt like a picture, suspended in time.

The Nest also reeked of old smoke, which was considerably less offensive to my nose than the caldera, but it wasn't associated with great memories either. The old woman took out a pipe, packed it with some dried plant, and sparked a lighter. I hadn't seen a working one in ages.

"Do you mind?" she asked before lighting it. That surprised me. She seemed the kind of person who would do as she pleased.

"Not at all," I said.

She looked at me for a moment before snapping the lighter shut with a sigh. "No point in lying if you're no good at it."

Shanna was right. This old woman could see straight through me. I needed to keep my mouth and my mind shut.

Say something, Clark. Say something.

"Was I correct in identifying you as Hollis?" Clark asked.

"One for one," she replied, voice husky and indifferent.

"I see." Clark sat down cross legged. "I have some unfortunate news to report. Commonhope has—"

"—nothing to do with me." She settled into a blanketed rocking chair, put away her pipe, and pulled a quilt around her. "Used to be four of us, working the fields. Yurik, Dessi, Mattis, and me. Soon there'll be none. I'll till the fields until I can't, and then I'll die with no one left to bury me. And that'll be that.

"Just a carving in a wall no one will know how to find. The gravehounds will pick my bones down the marrow if the mongs don't get to me first. I've witnessed it three godforsaken times."

She shut her eyes and took a deep raspy breath. "But you think Commonhope cares about an old green-keeper? Hm? We arrived in ruin, and that's how we'll meet our end. Whatever happened, just let me die in ignorance. They owe me that much."

I understood how she felt. Part of me wished I didn't know. No. That's not quite right. Ignorance isn't the same as wishing it never happened.

"You've fed two generations," I said, sitting down next to Clark. "As far as I'm concerned, you've earned the right to die however you want. It's not like we take our regrets with us."

She peaked one eye open, "See, now that's the truth. Glad you understand. Here's some more truth: I'm tired. I was tired before you dolts stirred the hounds. Let me get some sleep while you two keep an ear out."

Barely a moment later, she was snoozing away. Not a care in the world. I felt something between envy and pity for Hollis. On one hand, she was utterly alone except for the odd packbrat here and there.

But on the other, I'd never seen anyone sleep so peacefully on Galilei. I wanted to learn her secret.

I scooted back against the far wall where the ground was warm and pleasant. My chest buzzed with exhaustion and my legs twitched restlessly. I untied the laces of Kai's boots and slipped them off. Dried pus had soaked through my socks, but no blood. No trench foot. And my ribs were only bruised, not fractured. I wouldn't suffocate in my sleep or drown in my own blood. Small victories. El would approve.

Clark sidled up next to me with his hands behind his head. His eyes dimmed as he stared up at the speckled ceiling. Shadows in the room danced as dull lantern light flickered. I glanced at him out of the corner of my eye.

His lanky arms had tiny lights hiding inside joints and under metal plating. It was harder to see them during the day. More obviously, he was covered in dents and bloody scratches, some more recent than others.

A finger-sized hole in the left side of his chest—where a heart might have been—was flaked with rust at the edges like the petals of an umber flower. Within that hole, the exposed gears, blinking mechanisms, and pumping machinery all slowed nearly to a halt as his general hum fell quiet.

If Dex had really built Clark, I assumed he must have given him that signature grin. I'd seen pictures of Secondhand Jacks in Anansi's library, and none of them had any such peculiarities. They were identical, all painted in dispassionate white. But with Clark, there was a warmth stirring in the cold mechanics.

"Do you recall when we first met?" he asked. His eyes were fixed above.

"Worst day of my life. Apart from meeting you, of course."

I could hear the faint mimic of breathing as he continued. "I do wish we had met under different circumstances. The others—" he paused, shifting his weight against the wall. "The little ones at the Nest, they were dear to many of us. So I hope what I say next does not undermine your grief." He turned to face me. "I am glad you survived."

I winced at the thought. It always made me uncomfortable

when people expressed gratitude for my survival. It felt cruel to the ones who didn't make it. "Clark—"

"—I know it is difficult to be the last of your people, to be alone, to outlive them." He looked at Hollis. "She probably wishes the others had lived instead. Perhaps she wonders why only she remains, lamenting her worst qualities and indulging in nostalgia about theirs. This way of thinking helps neither the dead nor those they leave behind."

I tried to recall any details of Maksy's face, staring at me inside the flue—how scared she was. But I still couldn't. Not Rile's either. Not even the color of his hair. I could remember Saph's socks, though. There were days I thought she should've survived instead of me.

Then I'd think, why not Maksy? Why not Rile? I wondered if they would've become packbrats or engineers. Maybe Saph would've become a Luminator, someone to lead. I closed my eyes, trying to picture her face, but all I could remember was a single bottom tooth, slightly amiss, like one packbrat snoozing during roll call. It was barely a memory. Might not even be true.

Clark was right. It didn't do any good. They were gone. Even Iris, our raincoat caretaker, was lost in the storm or fire or otherwise. I thought of her less and less as I grew older. It was easier when I was a kid, believing she would just pop in one day, scoop me up, and tell me everything was gonna be okay. The longer her absence went on, the more I resented her. I'd think, maybe she doesn't want to come back. Maybe she hated us. That resentment kept her alive in my head, but she deserved better. The truth, just as Hollis could see it, was that Iris was gone like the rest.

No. Not just gone.

"As they say, it is not the dead who suffer." Clark scratched a non-existent itch on the back of his head. "I admit to thinking, if I had arrived sooner, before the raincoats, perhaps—"

"Don't do that. It's not on us. Renner and Colony Six are at fault. Whatever peace we're after, we'll find it in stopping them. You and me."

"We may not be so alone. Luminator Eloanne mentioned nine

raincoats as well as refugees. If Hollis can survive in this hostile world, there must be others."

"I wouldn't count on it. At this point, I think we can confidently say, raincoats aren't the invincible soldiers that Commonhope would have us believe." I curled over on my side, trying to remember Iris's face or her hair or her smell. To give her a better shape in my mind than one of resentment.

"Perhaps not, but their motive was well-intentioned. Hope is worth the risk."

"Hope is great when it's not being used to obscure a lie. I'll rely on what I can see for myself."

Clark lifted his arms to yawn, elbow joints overextending, fists clenched. "Fair enough. Time to rest."

There was a sense of peace as slumber came. Just the electric buzz and slow clicking of a Secondhand Jack and the sleepy chirps of a red-tailed hawk. But peace, in my experience, is portentous.

"Rile, you gotta keep stirring or the dewroot's gonna burn," Iris furiously stirred a pot of simmering food. "Grab a stool and look at this. You can't just leave food to cook. It takes patience."

Iris's hair was tied up loosely behind her head, and she had a cloth hanging from her waist, which barely obscured the brela underneath. She pulled Rile up onto his stool.

"See how they're stuck to the bottom now?" She pointed into the pot.

"Sorry," he said. "Gaius caught a glutter, and I wanted to see."

"No, I didn't," I shouted from the den.

"Well, that's great. Bugs in the house and burnt lunch. Is this how I raised you boys?"

"No, ma'am," we said in unison.

"Gaius, you get your butt in here too. You're gonna learn to boil water if it kills me. And leave the glutters outside unless you want me to toss them in with the stew." She wiped her hands and the sweat from her forehead on the cloth. "Where are the girls?"

"I don't know," I said. "Saph's probably in the fields again."

"Agh. I told her a million times not to play there. I'm guessing Mak is with her?"

I shrugged.

"Great. Like raising mongs, I swear." She grabbed my wrists and flipped my hands over. "Oh, Tempest, strike me down. Gaius, your hands are filthy. Go wash up."

I looked down, but my hands were spotless. "Nuh-uh. They're clean."

"You know that's not true." She sounded distant. Moving away.

I tried to look up at her, to see her face and show her my hands, but my head wouldn't turn, like I was stuck in mud. I tried to look at my hands, but they were pulling away from me, on the edges of my vision.

The front door blasted off its hinges, and I was suddenly on a chair next to Dim. He was barefoot. His head was smashed in. I was wearing his boots.

Renner crouched right in front of us. I couldn't see his face either. Couldn't look up. I only saw his beard and the two scars of white hair. He was chewing something.

I tried to cry out for help, for Iris, but I could manage a meek whisper. Iris either couldn't hear me or didn't care. I tried to scream. Run. Move. Anything.

"I don't get it. What are they afraid of?" Renner took a canister of ferno and splashed it on my face.

CHAPTER 8 - THE ELDER

I was startled awake in a pool of sweat. A one-armed man stood over me with a single finger held up to his tinted oculum, which covered his whole face. I scrambled back to the wall behind me and reached for my brela. My heart was pounding from the dream.

The man's hand was calloused, bandaged, and colossal. He had a wide, black stormbreaker, covered in fresh blood, and at his hip, a well-used brela embossed with the two-star emblem of Commonhope.

I hadn't seen one like him since I was a child. "You're a raincoat."

He turned to the entrance where the tarp had been pulled back and Hollis was brandishing a broom in her hand. The cages and chains by the thunderfruit field clinked and rattled. The man's hand was on his brela in an instant. Hollis didn't react. She had the calmness of someone who'd been here before.

Clark was elsewhere, and Raindrop was perched on a metal shelf above, grinding her beak and waiting for a command. I was surprised she hadn't reacted to the raincoat, whoever he was. Had he gotten the drop on her?

While we slept, a shallow stream of yellowish miasma had flowed into the Nest, pooling mostly at a dip in the entrance. The chasm must've abated. I donned my scarf, oculum, and boots, but my atrophied muscles and thundering heartbeat meant I'd gotten the worst possible sleep—not enough to feel rested and too much for a reset. At least the sun was up, and it was cool and dewy.

The man motioned for me to stand and come to the opening. He took his brela and scratched a rudimentary gravehound on the dusty floor, pointed to it, then outside. He held up five fingers and moved them one at a time, counting. I nodded.

Outside the Nest, an amber fog had rolled in, lit by daybreak. Everything felt undisturbed. Quiet.

The cages rattled again. Raindrop chwirked with unease.

I stared wide-eyed through the opening and shout-whispered, "Clark." Only the distant cages rattled with response to my call. The raincoat waved his hand at me and shook his head, again holding a single finger up to his mask to shut me up. He pointed to Raindrop, then to the sky.

She was practically on her tiptoes as I whistled for her to scout above, and she spun out through the entrance with great speed. Swirling ribbons of gas followed her up into the clear sky.

As she soared above, I hunkered down at the entrance with a shaky hand on my brela. I really need to sharpen this. We waited, hearing nothing but the far-off spurts of active geysers and seeing nothing but sulfurous fumes.

"What's your name—" I started to whisper.

"Down!" Clark's mechanical voice bellowed.

The raincoat shoved me to the dirt and ducked. A whistling sound rocketed over my head. A young gravehound staggered out through the fog and fell over, limp and twitching, with Toothpick planted between its eyes. Raindrop shrieked in alarm as vicious snarling sounded off from the springs. Several thudding, padded footsteps bounded in our direction.

"The elder is here," Hollis said. "You brought the beast to my doorstep. After all these years. I'd rather die in the storm."

Clark thundered out from the fog and yanked Toothpick out of the dead hound. "That's Lars," he said, pointing at the raincoat. "He doesn't speak."

Lars nodded at me.

Lars? That name sounded familiar. El had mentioned him. "You. You…were the one who—"

"Gaius." Clark moved my hand to my brela and brought his

face near mine. He smelled of rust and coppery blood. "We're being hunted."

"So it ends like this." Hollis slid down the wall, broom still in hand.

Lars squatted down in front of her, took the broom, and rested it against the wall. He put his giant hand on her knee and squeezed gently.

She stared back at him for a moment. With a sigh, the tension in her shoulders seemed to melt away. "In your hands then, raincoat. You better honor that title. Cause the old carry grudges beyond the grave."

Lars got up and stood beside me. He waved us forward, and the three of us slinked outside. We moved cautiously, keeping an eye and ear out for rattling cages. First, through the thunderfruit field, then out toward the chasm.

We hadn't gone a hundred meters from the Nest before five snouts and ten rows of snarling teeth poked through the fumes in front of us.

"Do not do anything unnecessary," Clark said. "Be clever. Not brave."

I scrambled to unsheathe my brela. Lars pulled his out, flipped it expertly around his finger, and held the blade downward and in front of his face, opposite how I held mine. I switched to mimic his stance. The gravehounds circled us.

Clark aimed Toothpick in front of him. "The elder refuses to show itself. It is waiting."

"Waiting for what?" I asked.

"I do not know. Perhaps the bird."

I shook my head. "What do we do?"

The gravehounds formed a semicircle around us as we backed into each other with our weapons ready. Clark was buzzing and warm, every gear alive and spinning with anticipation. Lars's arms felt like a sack of rocks. Nothing but muscle. My head barely came up to his shoulder.

"No running this time." Clark leaned back against me. "Forward as always." He fired into battle. The hounds responded in kind.

With Clark and Lars behind me, I ran forward without looking back. The wild mutt before me was uncompromising in its advance, though easily the smallest in the bunch. It leapt, foolishly, claws-first.

I dropped, slid beneath its bare belly, and slammed my blade into it. I pushed with all the force I could muster as it dove over me. My blade barely went in halfway, but its body fell on top of me, shaking in death throes. As I shoved it aside, its innards splashed onto the dirt along with my dull, bloody brela. I'm gonna tie the damn thing to my hand.

I turned back to see Lars slash a hapless gravehound across the gullet, stopping its growl in a gargling hiccup. Then he tossed the brela ten meters away in the haunches of another and immediately charged it down to retrieve his weapon and continue the attack.

Clark speared the largest one in the chest. It fought against him, pushing back a full meter.

The last one dashed around Clark and was headed straight for me. "Gaius!" he shouted, utterly preoccupied.

I clawed through the filth where my brela had fallen, keeping one eye on the approaching beast. It bounded into the fog, disappearing. I stood up and stumbled backward. "Clark!"

"Run!" he shouted back.

The wild creature skulked back out, gas trailing from its open mouth like fire. I had nothing. No brela. Not even a stone in my hand. I definitely couldn't outrun it. I slowly retreated as my hands went to my belt, searching for a blade I knew wasn't there. But something else was.

Please, work this time.

The gravehound's legs tensed as it prepared to leap at me. I punched the firing mechanism on my anchor and launched the grapnel straight into its chest. The beast yelped and bucked backward as the sharp metal connected. The cable recoiled, going taut and screeching with resistance as the animal snapped at the small rod in his torso.

A smile swept over my face. I did it. But the smile quickly faded.

The gravehound bucked backward and yanked me hard to the ground, then took off running. It dragged me over sharp cracking rocks as I spun uncontrollably. I reached out desperately and barely got a fistful of thunderfruit vine. I held on for dear life and came to a strained halt. We were locked in that tug of war for several seconds. I could hear the squeak of the vines snapping, and my arms were about to give out.

Lars's brela thwacked into the dirt beside me. His face was obscured behind his visor, but his one big arm was wrapped around a hound's neck, squeezing with incredible might as the creature coughed spittle and phlegm, furiously kicking its six legs. Raincoat indeed.

I grabbed his brela and drew the blade across the anchor cable, and to my surprise it sliced through with no resistance, and the creature went tottering backward, off-balance. I stood and charged, holding the brela as tight as I could with both hands and plunged up to my wrists into the hound's chest cavity. The beast fell dead, and my hands sloughed back out like two bloody organs.

"It's coming," Clark shouted, his foe weakly thrashing at the polearm in its ribs.

I ran over and searched through the muck again, tossing aside wet viscera and blood-soaked mud until a glint of steel exposed my dull little blade. I grabbed it and stood, searching for Lars. A moment later, he collapsed through the fog on top of another dead gravehound and got up, his ragged breath fogging his oculum.

"Lars!" I held out his blade for him. He nodded and started toward me.

Clark ran over and stood guard in front of me, Lars close behind.

"The elder is unlike the others." Clark held out his weapon like a shield. "It tried to draw me away before you awoke. A cunning beast."

"It's also really big," I added, hurriedly wiping Lars's grimy dagger across my pants before handing it back to him. "Thanks. And...sorry."

He pointed his chin toward the springs.

A snout with mismatched whiskers poked through the haze, which ebbed with its breath. That one dead eye came into view, and then the rest of it—a muscled crag of solemn disposition.

As Clark mentioned, it wasn't like the other feral beasts. It was something else entirely. The elder was easily three times my size, dwarfing the pathetic weapon I held in my hand. Never had I been so keenly aware of the blade's intended use than in that moment, holding it with one trembling, blood-soaked hand.

The beast split its jaw to the sky, exposing mountains of snow-capped teeth, and released a dual-throated howl so deep it seemed to shake the blood from my veins. Then it glared in my direction with an awareness that unnerved me—one that said: you're the weak one. I knew, and it knew.

I became quite conscious of the blood splattered across my clothes—the blood of his pack. I stepped back.

"Put those opposable thumbs to good use," Clark whispered as he pulled my other hand up to steady my weapon. "That may be our solitary advantage."

Clark faced the gravehound. I could see my reflection in the untainted, smooth chrome of his back. I'm still here. I'm alive. That relieved some of my tension. He was always in front, after all. Always facing forward.

The elder beast lowered its head with its eye still on me, teeth exposed just enough to remind me they were there, and its matted spine of fur stood on end from crown to stubbed tail.

An explosive burst of steam hissed from a far-off pool.

Clark went right and hurled his glaive as Lars went left. The monster dipped, and the weapon disappeared into the fog, barely scratching its shoulder. Clark and the elder charged one another, head-on. It brought the full weight of its paws down on Clark's shoulders and sent him crashing into the dirt. The Secondhand Jack skidded and somersaulted backward, then leapt to his feet. All the while, I was planted right where I started. I didn't know what the hell to do, how to help. They were monsters, all three of them.

Lars was quick for his size. He didn't move like Clark. No bravado. Everything was intentional. Shallow cuts—leg, ribs, chest, neck, one after the other, dodging clawed swipes in between.

Clark charged again, ducking a sharp swing as he shouldered the beast in the ribs. The hound gnashed its teeth in snarls and bites. Clark growled right back.

I could only watch, mired in fear and amazement and the paralysis of my own ineptitude. There was nothing for me to learn from Clark's straight forward onslaught. But Lars had technique. He was fighting thoughtfully. No machine-like momentum. He ebbed, back and forth. Shifted, retreated, learned, adjusted. He used Clark's brashness as openings for his own methodical attacks. I can do that.

But Lars's movements were also slowing down. Raincoats were human after all. He needed my help. I started to shift around to the gravehound's blind side.

With a squatting thrust Clark slugged the monster in the chin—the full power of his legs behind the blow. The beast recoiled and shook its head in a daze. Clark darted forward and wrapped both arms around its neck and squeezed. It whipped about, jaws snapping. Lars jammed his brela hard into its flank, but he went careening into the distance after taking a back leg kick to the chest. Clark barely hung on.

After I'd slipped to the elder's left, hidden by its bad eye, I flitted forward on light steps and forced my dull brela between two ribs, where I imagined some important organs might be.

It howled and swung Clark about its neck, blindly nipping at my legs as I held onto my brela with slippery hands. I could feel the blade sliding against bone and flesh, and the creature thrashed. It battered Clark left and right until his grip loosened. The elder bucked and turned. Clark took a wild-legged blow and was sent clattering into the fog.

I was lifted off my feet as my blade slipped out with a bloody spurt and the monster took my leg in its mouth, tossing me into the fumes.

I skipped across the ground like a spinning stone on water, grunting in pain with each impact. As my shoulder slammed against a wall of obsidian, my breath went out all at once.

When my lungs inflated, I gasped a mouthful of toxic air. I

reached down to touch my leg. Searing pain. My hand retracted. Shit. Not good. My shin wasn't broken, but the skin was ribboned in bloody wet flaps beneath the shreds of my pant leg. I'd bleed out in a few hours without staunching it. If the elder didn't finish me first.

At least I hadn't dropped my brela. After sheathing it, I crawled on my dysfunctional limbs, fighting the urge to scream in pain. The last few days had already been a hell of a beating.

Clashes of metal and teeth bounced around the rock and dried pools. I couldn't tell where they were coming from. I kept crawling. Can it see me through the mist? Smell me? I heard steel crunching, dragging. It sounded like Clark was losing. Where's Lars?

For nearly half a minute, I lugged my weary body toward the sounds of waning violence. I eventually came through the fog next to the chasm. Subtle bursts of hot air were pushing the fog away. It wasn't as strong as the day before, but the air was clearer.

I ripped one of the shreds of cloth from my pants and tied it tight around my thigh. My foot was starting to tingle. Not good. Not good. A moment later, Clark came tumbling through the fog. As he laid on his back, his right arm was barely hanging by wires and warped plates of steel punctured by bite marks.

I pushed myself up on one foot. "Lars," I yelled. "We're by the chasm."

Clark tried to roll off his back, but the elder leapt onto him and picked at his right arm like a bone. Its front paws rested heavy on Clark's shoulders, pinning him, drooling with satisfaction.

I pulled my brela from its sheath and leaned on the obsidian for support as I wobbled onto my good leg. With one eye closed, I steadied my aim and held the blade between my forefinger and thumb. If Lars can do it, maybe I can too. Just like sling-and-snatch. Come on.

I instinctually whistled for a straight throw and lobbed the blade with what I realized was a dislocated shoulder, dizzying me with the kind of pain that shocks straight behind the eyes. I heard a yipe, as the elder stumbled sideways. I could hardly believe it when I saw my little knife sticking out of its front leg.

With the opening I created, Clark brought his knees to his

chest and launched the monster back over his head toward the chasm. Its short legs flailed in the air before it came slamming down on its side with a thud. A cloud of dust plumed around it.

It huffed through a bloody nose as it stood, wobbling and bleeding from dozens of cuts and gashes. Then it yanked my blade from its front leg and spit it in the dirt.

Clark clambered onto his feet and ripped his barely-hanging arm from the socket. The two of them lurched toward one another. He whipped his metal arm from side to side, scattering broken teeth and flesh. The gravehound reared its front paws in the air and slammed down on Clark with all its weary weight, smashing his head into the ground.

"R-report. Detritiv-vore...growth...n-nominal. Autotrophic… germination…s-sixty percent b-behind estimations," Clark warbled in unfamiliar tones. "M-m-meteorological anomaly inti-intimates…"

"What's happening, big guy?" I yelled. His eyes waned between dim and dead.

As Clark continued incoherently rambling, the monstrosity turned its knowing, bloodshot eye on me. I looked around for something, anything to defend myself. My brela was in the dirt beside its matted paws. When I looked at the knife, so did the gravehound. It didn't move. Like it was daring me to try.

Blood and rust were smattered across its smiling snout, and it was covered in purple bruises around patches of missing fur. I pulled some excess tether from my anchor and wrapped my shaking hands with it and hoped for the best.

The beast's legs were twitching, anticipating, as it growled deep behind missing teeth, blood dribbling from its mouth. It jolted forward at me.

A winged figure descended from the sky with a kee-ee-ar. In a flurry of cinder feathers and talons, Raindrop tore at its last good eye. She must've heard my whistle.

It thrashed, backing away in snarls and cries of anguish, but her talons were stuck in its flesh. She pecked at it, squawking and flapping to get away.

Lars came barreling out of the yellow haze and collided with all his might into the elder gravehound. He pushed it toward the open fissure and over the edge.

"Wait," I screamed, as it tumbled over the edge of the chasm, Raindrop still attached. "No…"

I stood for a moment, throbbing in pain and listening for a crash, but I heard nothing. I whistled high and shrill through bloody fingers. Nothing. I shuffled closer and wheezed another whistle. Nothing.

"Raindrop! Come on, girl!"

I hopped to the lip of the chasm, whistled, and waited. Come on. As I put my fingers into my mouth a third time, I was greeted by a flapping assault of feathers and toppled backward into the dirt. She nuzzled my neck.

"That's my girl. You did good. You did real good. You're getting meat tonight. That's a promise." Then she hopped up onto my shoulder. "Lars, you okay?"

Lars wearily nodded, though blood dripped from beneath his stormbreaker and his oculum was cracked. He stood over Clark whose eyes were dimmer than usual. There was still subtle motion inside the rusted hole in his chest. He was trying, though still muttering nonsense.

"…c-cataclysmic meteorological events. S-survival… prob-bability low. Skaver threat…d-detected on surface. How sh-shall I assist, keeper…?"

Skaver threat?

I mustered the fortitude to stand. My arms were battered, hands shaking, ribs bruised, shoulder dislocated, and my calf—when I was brave enough to peek—looked like the bloodied gills of a hard-fought gravehound. White exposed bone was hiding just under the skin.

I ripped off the rest of my shredded pant leg and wrapped it loosely around my wound. Then I bit down on the hilt of my brela, closed my eyes, and pulled the bandage tight. A scream whispered through the back of my throat. That should buy me a few more hours, but I'm gonna need proper stitches.

I wasn't sure who was in worse shape, though. Me or Clark. Raindrop and I wobbled over to his prostrate body. He was still gripping his busted arm. I leaned in close, listening for any signs of life.

"G-Gaius. I m-may have f-fallen victim to a concussion." Clark's voice wavered in dithering intonations. His eyes rotated in and out, struggling to focus.

"Can you stand?"

"Better than y-you, I am certain," he replied, sitting up. "B-but that is not the issue in question."

"Yeah. Looks like it knocked something loose." I rapped a knuckle on top of his head. "If it weren't for Raindrop and Lars, you might be even worse off."

"Lars fought well. To the b-bird, I give no credit. I had the elder r-right where I w-wanted it." He was on his feet a moment later and handed me his broken limb.

I smiled with relief. "Well, I'm glad you're—" A rumbling rolled in from the eastern sky. No clouds yet. But I counted the seconds before it died down. "Damn. She's early again."

While I was distracted, Clark grabbed my elbow and shoved my shoulder up and back into the socket. The pop echoed down the rift, along with my wailing.

"What's the matter with you!" I thwacked him with his own arm. "Maybe I should try shoving this back into place."

"D-Dex is more suited to that s-sort of work. Which you will see, w-when we reach the Looking Glass. At our c-current pace, we are less than a w-week from our d-destination."

"Current pace? I don't mean to spoil your optimism, but we're not exactly at our best." Raindrop squawked on my shoulder. "Not to mention, the Tempest is breathing down our necks. I think it's safe to say we're off schedule, Jack."

"We will m-m-make it." He walked by me, ignoring the scraps of metal dragging from his leg and picked up my brela. He handed it to me hilt-first and stumbled into the fog without explanation.

Lars removed his oculum and ran his hand through a flop of

sweaty, long hair. His eyes were light, almost gray, and he had a young, hairless face, with a square jaw and thin lips. He looked so calm, almost unaffected by what just happened. The corners of his eyes tilted up. He must make a habit of smiling behind that mask.

"So, you're the one who pulled me out of that oven," I said. "Back when this all started."

He smiled, nodded.

"I never got to say thank you. Honestly didn't think I'd ever see you again. It's rare to see one of you in person."

Lars just looked back at me.

"Oh, right. Thank you," I chuckled and held out my hand. He shook it. His thick, rough fingers felt like pumice. "I assume you know what happened. At Commonhope."

He furrowed his brow and shook his head.

Oh. Of course he hadn't. The raincoats always seemed sort of other-worldly, like they knew everything and could be anywhere at any moment—but seeing the confusion and concern on his face reminded me what he was: just a person, like me, with loved ones. He deserved to hear it straight—if I could manage it.

"I'm sorry. We lost the mountain, and everyone in it. It was fire. Again."

His lips parted slightly, forming tiny silent words.

"Um…El's alive—uh, sorry, Luminator Eloanne. We held a funeral for the rest. Buried them in the valley. She can show you where when you see her. It was…nice. Peaceful. I think it's what they would have wanted."

The words just kept spilling out, filling the void between us. "Oh, and the Luminator is trying to gather what's left of you guys. She's in contact with Andica. Probably found others by now too. You should check in. They're planning something. I don't know what, but I bet they'll be glad you're alive. I sure was. These days, we don't have a lot of—"

He reached out and rested his massive hand over my chest. His eyes locked with mine, and he held me there. He was crying. His hand moved to my shoulder. A gentle squeeze.

I continued, not knowing how to respond. "Um, she said…"

Then he pulled me in and wrapped his one big arm around me. I could feel his quiet cries against my chest. At first, I didn't know what to do, but I'd seen others hug. I wrapped my arms around him and squeezed back.

I suddenly felt safe. Warm—as if everything was going to turn out okay.

Then, some other foreign feeling bloomed in the center of me as I held him, like a new star. Heat rushed up through my chest and behind my eyes. I swallowed the rising anxiety. I wasn't ready for it. Didn't want it. I pushed against it, away from him.

"Right," my voice cracked as I shifted out of his embrace. I cleared my throat. "Uh, we should probably get to it. You know? Storm's coming. And the Luminator needs you."

Lars gave my shoulder one more tight squeeze, smiling half-heartedly. I never would've imagined such a soft face behind the mask. He stole one last knowing look, slid his cracked oculum back on, and jogged northward into the haze.

"Give the Luminator my best," I called.

He waved his one big arm behind him and disappeared. I had a million questions for him, but I was still trying to shake off my discomfort. I'd get a chance to see him again eventually. I'm sure he had a few incredible stories he could tell. Once all this was over.

Clark came jangling back with Toothpick and Hollis. The polearm had been crinkled in the middle by a massive bite mark.

"You three did it. The elder is dead." Hollis twirled her cane around her arm. "I'm going to smoke, eat, and sleep all day to celebrate. Care to join me? Storm will be brewing in a few hours anyway."

Clark marched up to me, bent low at the knees, and held out his hand for me to climb onto his back. "Unfortunately, we m-m-must be on our w-way. Tight schedule."

I was reluctant to be carried, but the thunder put a skip in my step. I put my arms around his neck, and he hoisted my good leg with the cradle of his hand.

"Headed to the Rustyard," I said. "Hopefully, by nightfall."

"Rustyard?" Hollis shook her head. "Do all men have a death wish? The Tempest'll swallow you long before then. If you're set on leaving, you better stop at Harrow's till the storm passes."

"I w-would rather be th-thrown into the Thrash Sea and left to r-rust than suffer th-their company." His two quavering voices vacillated between angry and deeply monotone.

I bopped him on the head. "You know she's right."

He just stood there, staring into the fog.

"Clark," I said in my most matronly tone.

He sighed and craned his neck to crack the bones he wished were there. Then he hitched me up higher on his back, and we said our goodbyes to Hollis. She seemed surprisingly melancholy about it. At least with the gravehounds taken care of, she could more peacefully tend to her crop.

We disappeared into the golden glow of the gaseous springs alongside the rising sun and followed the chasm southward toward the parched stone barrens where we'd meet a peculiar man and his peculiar children.

CHAPTER 9 - HARROW

Clark carried me out of the caldera slower than I anticipated in his condition. What use am I if I can't even do the one thing I've been trained to do?

As a three-armed mechanical abomination, we hobbled for a full day through the desolate karst—a sea of uneven, jagged limestone formations and deep interweaving streams. If I was running alone, I'd be careful of the sinkholes in that area, but Clark could see things I couldn't. At least, when he was fully functional.

"Should we be worried about the sinkholes?" I asked.

"I am s-still intact." He was clearly annoyed that I had to ask, but better that than both of us tumbling fifty meters through the substratum into an unsuspecting mong nest.

I was annoyed too, though not at him. I didn't like not being able to run. My leg was swollen, hot, and stinging with sweat by the end of the day. The swelling wasn't a great sign, but I was more worried about it going numb. If it hurts, there's a lower risk of sepsis until we clean the infection and dress the wound. Fingers crossed.

As storm clouds darkened the dusk sky, and I exchanged some worried words with Clark, he reminded me the Nest was only a couple kilometers away. I knew that already, and he knew I knew that, because I'd sent Raindrop ahead that morning with a cipher code for Harrow. 1-5-0-1. Burn. Hide. Maybe his memory was affected in the fight.

"M-my hood," Clark said as the pitter-patter of drizzling rain pinged against his head. I pulled up both our hoods and settled in for what would likely be an unpleasant few minutes. We were going to arrive before the storm. But not dry.

Clark jangled like a tin full of loose screws with every step. The sound was hypnotic. And I was tired—so tired that I only realized I had fallen asleep when I jolted awake to the crack of thunder and my arms slipping off Clark's neck.

He set me down gently into a shallow puddle at the bottom of a wide impact crater. "C-can you walk?"

"I'll manage," I said, knowing full well my leg needed stitches immediately.

We had only flashes of lightning and the glow of Clark's eyes to guide us, but I knew the area well, because Harrow's Nest was a regular stop on my commission route. Dozens of columns of storm-cut hoodoos surrounded the crater, standing guard over the various caverns below. It was almost shrine-like—perhaps dedicated to some unknown subterranean deity. And only one cavern glowed with dim yellow light, which seemed, amid the night around us, a beacon.

"Harrow!" I called into the howling wind. I heard the screeching of his children inside, but no answer from Harrow. Raindrop's voice was distinctly excited. Did he get my message?

Clark stopped at the sound of the birds. "I w-will remain h-here," he said. "To keep guard while you sleep and stitch the leg." He was only convincing himself.

"Suit yourself," I said with a wave. "Say hi to the Tempest for me."

I hopped on one foot toward the hollow. Clark would follow soon enough, despite his reservations about the birds.

The rock wall outside was crudely carved with the symbol of a man with four wings and hands held over his ears.

There were dozens of candles sitting on deep recesses along every wall of the inner chamber. Birds of all kinds were resting in open cages or on swinging perches. Their candle-lit shadows danced on opposite walls in the shapes of winged, horned devils. I wondered if that image was what Clark saw when he thought of them.

The birds themselves were as diverse in color as they were in shape, beautiful down to their last molting feather. Dozens were tiny—

green, blue, and gold. In the back were two caged speckled owls with wide aureate eyes, unblinking. The red-tailed hawks were a variety of glossy black, mottled white and brown, sheer gray, and mixes of all types. Their polymorphism helped us differentiate them, though I'd never mistake Raindrop for another hawk.

And there she was. Raindrop. Still the second-most threatening bird in the room, with her long talons, hooked beak, and sharp eyes. She flew to my shoulder, and I scratched her chin. "Glad to see you made it, girl."

Finally, sitting on the edge of a crudely-carved stone table, front and center—the cantankerous caretaker of the establishment—was Crumb, an old hawk. Blind, deaf, arthritic, flightless, and a damned enigma of the avian community.

The other birds mingled and caused a general ruckus with one another, but Crumb just sat alone, head slumped into his shoulders, too bent from years of hardship to even grumble a complaint about his miserable existence. All the color of his coat had dulled, and half of his tail feathers were nothing but frayed quills—more suited to writing than flying.

From crest to tail, Crumb was missing parts of himself. A chip in his beak, a crooked left wing, one missing toe, and a scar branching down his breast in the shape of an arc of lightning. Because he had, in fact, been struck by lightning.

He was the product of stubbornly living too long in a world that wanted him dead. Truly the meanest, ugliest creature I'd ever seen. And though I loved him with all my heart, he was also Clark's least favorite bird on Galilei.

I cautiously raised my hand to his nostrils. His cloudy eyes squinted. Then, his beak stretched open. The other birds went silent as he squawked like the creak of an ill-oiled door swung on rusted hinges. His beak softly closed over my finger.

"I missed you too." I scratched his head. I'd been here nearly a hundred times, and my fingers were covered in the scars of earning his friendship—a rite of passage he only allowed in blood. "Where's your dad gone off to, Crumb? Did he get my message?"

I looked around the room for signs of Harrow. It was quieter than normal. Some of the fledgling red-tail cages were empty, as were the incubators. In fact, it seemed most of the birds were gone.

Clark poked his head through the door and recoiled at the sight.

"I thought you were gonna wait outside," I said.

"I w-was," he started, "but I f-found him wan-wandering about in the r-rain."

A heavily cloaked man walked past Clark in a sopping wet fluster. He pulled back his feathered hood to reveal a balding head of wispy white hair. An acute overbite, hooked nose, sunken bulging eyes, and fuzz-filled ears may have been why his children felt so akin or why he started to tend to the creatures in the first place.

Either way, Harrow was no stranger to outside reactions to his appearance, and he only removed his hood for birds or friends—the former comprising most of the latter. Clark was a fringe beneficiary, because Harrow considered the Secondhand Jack a friend, even if it wasn't mutual.

He'd hatched and raised every fledgling red-tail that went to train in the Commonhope aviary—each one a unique child to him. Even the message system was of his own design. We'd survived so much because of him, so I just couldn't gather the courage to tell him what had happened to Commonhope. Harrow was the reason I excelled with Raindrop—the reason we understood and trusted one another. I couldn't imagine he'd respond the way Lars had. That conversation would have to wait.

"Master Gaius," he wheezed, shaking his head many times as he spoke. "I feared you were them. Your message. An appreciated vaguery. Burn. Hide. I could only decide on one."

"Uh, right. Well, it was all one message, Harrow," I said. "You do have somewhere to hide, don't you?"

"Mmm. I do," he said. "We all do. But now the fires find us where we hide. So I cannot hide where I would hide. I must hide where I would not hide."

"Good thinking, Harrow. Let's do that. Let's find somewhere

they wouldn't expect."

He looked around the room at the birds with a quivering bottom lip and hid his wrinkled head inside the flaps of his feathery coat. "Perhaps they don't expect me to be where I'm expected. Perhaps hiding is what they expect."

Clark mocked in two-warbling voices. "The g-great Harrow."

"I am not great, Clunk," Harrow muttered from the muffled layers of his dripping cloaks. Two little birds fluttered from the confines of his coat and perched near the ceiling. "I try only to protect my little ones."

My leg ached, and we needed to move fast. Our enemy was zeroing in on us, and they liked to attack just as the storms hit. If Harrow's Nest was in danger, we couldn't spare a minute.

"Do you have a suturing kit around here?" I asked.

"Yes. Supplies and hatchlings where you wouldn't expect," he said.

He effortlessly whistled a collection of bird-like tones and cadences while extending his arms. The little birds flew back inside his coat. Others found perches on his shoulders or roosted in the frizzled hair hanging from the back of his head. Every perch-able inch of him was taken. He seemed unaffected by the whole affair.

Only the two owls remained caged in the back as Harrow hunched down next to Crumb and lifted a hand to the hawk's beak. The creature's head bobbed as he lifted his shaking, three-toed leg. It took a few tries before he was able to grip Harrow's hand and pull himself up.

When Crumb was steady, Harrow whipped around and shuffled outside covered in birds, his hands held out before him. "To the unexpected."

With Clark as my reluctant crutch, I limped after Harrow into the pouring rain beneath flashes of lightning. He disappeared into a cavern opposite his home, and we followed him into the dark.

Clark's eyes faintly lit everything in steel blue. It was shallow and empty—smooth stone beaten by wind and water—and not nearly enough protection from the storm or fire. At the back of the cavern was a small hidden alcove which hooked deeper inside. I squeezed through with ease, but Clark cracked and popped the wall into shards and talc, displeasure growing with every step.

On the other end, in a vaulted chimney of rock perforated with hundreds of pinholes, Harrow was tending to a host of birds and eggs on a bed of feathers and linen. He had already moved almost all of them inside along with some supplies. Only the owls remained. Every flicker of lightning shot spines of light through the walls.

"The wise ones are last," he said, setting the birds down. With Crumb still attached to his arm, he scurried back toward the alcove. Clark grabbed him by the arm and held him in place. Harrow looked up at him as though he'd been betrayed. "Master Clunk?"

Clark held a single finger up to his mouth and slowly turned his head up toward the ceiling. I hadn't heard anything at first, but there was a hum hiding in the thunder and howling wind. Deeper. Constant. Mechanical.

The birds were growing anxious. Harrow's eyes grew even wider. Then he lifted Crumb above his head, and the bird let out a throaty call. There was all but silence among the lesser creatures. Even Raindrop lowered her head.

"It is…them," Harrow whimpered. "They will hurt the wise ones."

Clark moved his finger closer to his mouth and waved us over to the north-facing wall. We pressed our faces against the cool rock and peered through the pinprick holes.

On the other side, a shadow descended. The buzz rattled the loose stones at our feet as it settled in the crater outside. After a moment, the sound was gone, lost somewhere in the Tempest's groaning thunder.

A silhouette obscured the glow of Harrow's Nest behind it, creating a halo of orange. I recognized its shape—the sharp onyx features, the pointed nose, the glass pod at its apex. A piercer.

My muscles tensed, and my heart thrummed inside my ears. Before I'd noticed it, my hand was on my brela, and the pain in my leg changed to the twitch of anticipation.

It has to be Renner. Finally, I'll kill the monster.

A short, lean man with greasy, red and white curls hopped out into the pelting rain, illuminated by frequent lightning and the candlelight of Harrow's Nest. He stretched his arms with a sigh of relief then boxed at the rain. A much larger man stood up inside the pod and threw down a familiar canister to the red-haired man. The same stuff they'd used to set fire to my Nest.

"Much obliged, Vikas," the red-haired man shouted with a jovial wave.

If they were concerned with being seen or heard, they made no show of it. I put my brela away. Renner wasn't with them, but that just complicated things. Who are these people, and how many are there? Why are they being so cavalier now? This isn't like them. Renner said something about only having eight months. Are they getting desperate?

"Place is eerie as hell," Vikas yelled back. His voice was deep and slow. "Just make it quick this time, Deek. Tired of you messin' about."

"Where's the fun in that?" Deek replied. He strolled over to Harrow's Nest with a skip in his step, poked his head inside, and whistled a long dramatic whistle. "The lights are on, but nobody's home."

"Come on. Just light it, and let's go. Storm's kicking up."

"We should really find the geezer. He's gotta be hiding in one of these holes." Deek cupped his hands to his mouth and yelled, "Ain't that right, Harrow? Your neighbor sure has a big mouth. Well, had."

Harrow didn't budge, and he kept Crumb above his head to keep the peace.

"We don't have time for this, old man," Deek said. "I guess we'll just take the owls. I heard they taste like chicken."

Harrow turned to us, pleading for help. I grabbed my brela again, but Clark stayed my hand.

"No," Clark warbled. "W-we are in no condition to en-engage, and w-we know little of the enemy."

Harrow said nothing. And though his eyes fell to the floor, he kept his arm high, silently protecting his other children. He turned his back on the wall and refused to watch the scene unfold.

I kept watching. Any clues, anything, could be useful—could lead me to Renner. Vikas took the owls from inside while Deek emptied the liquid contents of two canisters at the foot of a dozen caverns, including Harrow's Nest and the one we had come through.

They didn't take the time to search them all, and I was sure he didn't think he needed to. I'd seen the sort of fire he was about to light. This would be the second time they overlooked me. That mistake would come back to haunt them.

"I'll count down from three," Deek started, "which is two seconds longer than I'm used to, and three seconds longer than any of you dirt-dwellers deserve. Come out, and I promise to listen to every word you know about Dex. I'll accept any information: physical description, location, embarrassing anecdotes—where the Breacher is. You know, fun facts. Oh, and one more thing. If you tell me what I need to know, the owls live. If you don't…well."

Harrow remained where he was, staring at his feet. His upheld arm was beginning to shake. Clark approached and gently held the bird keeper's arm up, still refusing to look at Crumb.

"Master Clunk?" Harrow whispered.

"It is n-not for you or him," Clark turned his head away.

"Three," Deek called out.

The Tempest was the only one to respond, and she responded with blinding violence—egging him on.

"Two," he called, playfully.

Harrow closed his eyes as the wind howled through the cave.

"One."

I peered through the wall as Deek pulled a smooth black baton from his waist. The baton crackled with electricity as he struck the ground with it. Sparks scattered, and a wicked flash of purple flames engulfed the area in a circling wave.

I reflexively jumped away from the wall as the heat expanded, and we all fled to the far end of the room. Raindrop crawled into my shirt, grinding her beak.

"I'm off to find a bird more willing to sing," Deek called. "You stay warm out here, Harrow."

After a moment, chemical smoke billowed in through the tunnel. We scrunched together against the far wall. Before I could panic, the smoke rose, swirling and venting through the ceiling holes. Only the people who didn't know him would suggest Harrow wasn't clever.

The vessel jettisoned off into the night in an explosive thunderclap. Harrow's arm fell, and the birds all cried out in response. "They will kill the wise ones." Little birds flew to roost in his clothing, chirping and hopping with worry.

"No, they won't," I said. "We'll get them back. We just need to get out of here first."

"The s-storm and f-flames are all that await us on the oth-other side of that wall. No harm will r-reach us here t-tonight. We w-w-wait till sunrise."

"We're safe. Then I guess we owe Harrow our lives." I scratched Raindrop's head.

Harrow slicked back the few strands of hair on his head. "Hiding where I would not hide is not what they expected."

"That's right. We're all safe because of you, hawk master."

"And Crumb," he said.

"And Crumb," I repeated, expecting Clark to scoff. But he just lowered himself in the corner farthest from the birds, near the smoke.

"Tomorrow we r-reach the Rustyard where sh-shelter will be s-scarce. Dex is just b-beyond the desert in the L-Looking Glass where sh-shelter is non-existent. Rest while we c-can. The d-days will be harsh."

"Right. Then, Harrow, I need your steady hands," I scrounged through the supplies and pulled out Harrow's suturing kit—gauze, alcohol, stitching thread, and a couple curved needles.

Shanna usually stitched me up when I needed it. I told the other packbrats I let her do it because she liked the work, but if I was honest, my hands just weren't built for delicate tasks. I could throw sling-and-snatch sandbags with precision all day, but holding a needle and thread made my fingers shake.

Harrow bent down and snatched up the thread between his agile fingers. He was more familiar with avian anatomy, but the skill had translated well enough to humans in the past. When that connivore had its way with me, it was Harrow who sewed my thigh back together.

He removed Kai's boot and rolled up my pants. I couldn't see much, which was probably for the best. The brief glimpse I'd gotten during the gravehound fight was bad enough.

It didn't take Harrow long to thread the needle and get to work on my leg. Even though I knew the alcohol was coming, nothing could prepare me for the pain of disinfecting such a deep, open wound. Besides losing consciousness.

When I awoke, my leg still hurt like hell, but it was stitched, gauzed, and no longer weeping pus. If I weren't suffering from nasal fatigue from Reaper Springs and ferno smoke, I would've checked it for bad smells.

Fires crackled faintly outside, and hatchling hawks chirped inside. The pinholes illuminated the hanging smoke in threads of soft morning light. We'd survived the night. Harrow obviously hadn't slept a wink, though.

We helped him gather up the eggs and get them into warm, protective places in his cloak to incubate. He said the adolescent birds were better off without us for now, that they were clever enough to survive on their own. Of course, Clark was more than happy to accommodate the suggestion, though he wasn't thrilled that Harrow was bringing Crumb with us.

We squeezed back through the passage from the night before and took a silent last look at the still-smoking burrows. Most of the whys in my mind had been driven out by other questions. Why mattered less with every fire, every dead child. Renner, Vikas, Deek, Varic. Who are they, and how do I get to them? None of that would be answered by standing around. We left as the first sliver of sun burned its yawning head above the eastern horizon, and we headed for the Rustyard.

CHAPTER 10 - LOOKING GLASS

The first day was difficult. Running across the barrens on a bad leg wasn't optimal, but I got into stride by midday. Just before sundown, we reached the rolling, vermillion sand hills of the Rustyard. The dunes stretched out forever, like tanned, calloused knuckles, long toiled in the heat of an endless summer.

Everything was still, silent, and dry as we traveled at a pace to keep Harrow in tow—easier with Clark carrying me every few kilometers. My leg was holding up, and we only had to restitch once on the second night.

But I'd been dreading this part of the trip. Running on sand was hell, even on a good day.

The Rustyard wasn't expansive like an ocean but more like a river of sand. You could pass straight southward in two days' time. But the dunes flowed east and west—starting from the edge of the Looking Glass—for a thousand kilometers or more to the east. We still hadn't mapped all of it yet.

I'd never been commissioned out that way either. Anything to stay out of the shadeless leagues of heat and freezing nights was okay by me. Back at Commonhope proper, the twins used to say the Rustyard could sap the moisture from your feet if you were foolish enough to take off your boots. An exaggeration, no doubt, but I wasn't about to put it to the test.

In comparison to the blinding-white ocean of salt that comprised the Looking Glass, the Rustyard was practically an oasis. In late summer (which we were rapidly approaching), the air would get hot enough to make your gums sweat and dry enough to crack the skin under your fingernails. The utterly barren landscape would plate you up for the Tempest like morsels on a spotless dish.

The Looking Glass was the bane of any packbrat. We were told never to go there. Never. I grew up with cautionary tales and nightmares of being stuck in that empty void with nowhere to run or hide. It represented everything our instincts taught us to avoid. To my knowledge, there'd never been a single commission delivered there in all the years I'd been a packbrat. Yet here I was, heading straight for it.

Somewhere beyond the flats—far from where the eye could see—were steep mesa walls that held back the Thrash Sea. But between those walls and the other edge of the Looking Glass, there was nothing. There was also no reason to believe we could reach the mesas or what was beyond them in the three or four days—before the storm returned. So what are we heading toward?

Clark reassured me repeatedly, insisting we'd reach Dex before the next storm, but he always seemed to take pause when he noticed how far Harrow was trailing behind us.

The old bird keeper had hidden his face beneath that feathered hood—atop which Crumb was perched, happily baking in the sun, looking as unfazed as the day I'd met him.

It didn't feel right to leave Harrow to wallow in his grief, but there wasn't much I could say to put his heart at ease. Like any honest father, he had favorites, and the owls were high on the list of his most beloved children. I shouldn't have told him we'd get them back. That was a cruel platitude. Maybe he could tell they were empty angry words, meant for me more than him.

Clark had become focused, single-minded. More machine-like. His movements lacked precision, and he had none of his famous bravado.

"You alright?" I asked.

"N-n-no-no talki-ing." His voice was more warped than before.

"You sure?" I clung to his back.

"Cons-serve con-conserve energy. Temperature f-f-falling."

"Suit yourself." I was worried about him, but he was right. The temperature was dropping rapidly with the daylight.

At sunset, we tread down the slip face of one dune and into the slack of the next, relieved to accept the coolness of the shade cast between them. We slept there before the night crawled in, and we were up again while the stars still hung in the early twilight sky.

The chill of the desert dark had snuck down into my bones. I was shivering and exhausted, as though I hadn't slept at all. I could practically hear Clark's told-you-so stare as I limped to the head of the pack, trying to walk off the cold.

Harrow had done what he could to salvage my leg, but not even the most skillful stitcher could give me what I needed the most. Time and rest. Two things I was plumb out of.

The next day passed much the same as the first—painfully hot and then painfully cold with little sleep. But a change of scenery was a welcome sight as we reached the desert's namesake: a sprawling graveyard of Secondhand Jacks.

First, at the peak of a distant sand dune, we saw an arm poking through the sand, waving slightly in the wind. As we came closer, more arms, faces, cogs, and internal parts were half buried, oxidizing in flaking bronzed rust. Any exposed parts were slowly crumbled by the elements into granules of brown sand, becoming part of the Rustyard. Hollis got her cane here.

Not only did Clark seem to pay no mind to the extinction of his kin, he seemed to relish walking among them, above them. He was the last. He'd survived. Outlived them—in that way, we were similar. But I didn't share his pride, and he didn't seem to share my guilt.

I was doing everything I could not to think of what I'd seen back in the mountains. I'd taken to counting steps and playing sling-and-snatch with Raindrop. It wasn't helping.

There was a worse problem too, one that I was keeping to myself. The water in my pack was making a worrisome sound—that of silence. When Clark wasn't looking, I shared what was left with Raindrop. If a few droplets were going to make the difference, it wouldn't matter anyway.

By sunup on the third day, we began to see more smoke rising far off to the northeast. Three of them, including Harrow's still-smoking Nest in the distance. We didn't speak of it. There was nothing to say. Nothing to do. We could only plug onward. Forward as always.

Clark bobbled in the sand for a moment and started walking in place. A moment later, he continued on. He was getting worse. Slowing down. That, or Harrow had blossomed with newfound energy—enough to overtake Clark. The former seemed more likely, considering the wheeze that spilled from Harrow with his every step.

Either way, it was midday before we saw the edge of the Looking Glass a couple kilometers due west of us. The sand of the Rustyard ended like a copper shore upon a glassy sheet of salt rock—as far as the eye could see and beyond.

Above us, dark clouds rolled in with the cool wind of an approaching storm. It would be on us within the hour. My leg bandages were sopping wet with blood. I'd overdone it again, but Clark didn't seem to be in a state to carry me.

This is going to be bad. We should've waited. What was he thinking? I was practically dragging my leg behind me. At least the wind is at our backs. I sheltered Raindrop in the safety of my stormbreaker. She wouldn't have the strength to rise above the storm.

Neither did I.

I stopped. The pain was too much. Clark leaned down in front of me to get on his back.

"Just give me a second," I said.

"N-no com-complaints-s-s."

I looked out across the flats. "This is suicide." I licked the resentment from my cracked lips. "Sky's already going dark. We undershot it, Clark."

But apart from the grinding of sand between his gears, Clark stayed quiet. He just waved his hand for me to climb on. I wanted to hit him. If we'd just taken another day, waited out the storm—

He waved his hand again. "U-up-p, G-G-Gaius."

It was hard to stay mad at him with his pitiful voice. "Okay...I trust you," I lied through my teeth. Every instinct was telling me not to do this. Every lesson. We could still turn around and find shelter.

I climbed on his back as thunder nipped at our heels and whipping gales billowed our stormbreakers. I breathed in ozone and breathed out a frustrated sigh I wanted Clark to hear, but he continued trudging on without looking back.

Harrow was a good distance ahead of us as Clark pushed through the last stretch of the Rustyard. Clumps of wet-caked desert fell off his heavy feet as we crossed into the flats.

I turned back to catch lightning flashing above the reddish dune horizon. The storm was on time, but we weren't. As usual, I'd shown up late. My guess was that our injuries were an unquantifiable calculation for Clark. It wasn't worth the energy to blame him.

A cold front pressed in as the sky cracked open with rain. Clark picked up speed. He was gawky, but the Tempest was always a good motivator.

"Th-ther-e," Clark shouted over the wind. "D-dest-tination."

I saw nothing at any distance that resembled a destination of any kind—just empty white beneath a growing shadow over the flats. Is he hallucinating now?

But then I caught a glint of silver, fine as spider's silk, nearly imperceptible. Then another. There were dozens—maybe a hundred—lustrous spires slowly cracking through the crust like pristine icicles or heat distortions, extending from somewhere below the surface.

Each spire was composed of three chrome ribbons curling around each other to a point. When they stopped climbing upward, they reached about four meters in height, thin as my forearm.

But the thing I noticed most about them was they were not made of bismuth like Raindrop's cipher or my anchor, which meant we were running through a cage of highly conductive lightning rods. I could only assume they were traps to kill anyone who got too close. Dex, or someone, had to be here, likely underground.

A uniquely brilliant engineer...or a mad scientist.

Clark limped us through the massive field of spires which were arrayed in concentric circles—closing toward what, I couldn't see—but we were definitely heading into the center of...something.

Lightning struck behind us, and the bolt arced like lattice from one rod to the next. It snaked down below the surface and superheated the ground around the spires into shards of shattering black glass, until finally dissipating a few spires away. We were either going to end up as roasted meat and scorched metal, or we'd get sliced to ribbons by shattering fulgurite.

"We're running out of options!" I could barely hear my own voice. Clark replied, but I couldn't make the words out.

Lightning flashed again and something stung my shoulder blade. Then it started burning, throbbing. I leaned into Clark and tried to make myself smaller as the pain radiated down my back.

"Clark, we gotta go!" I reached back to feel a large piece of glassed salt sticking out of my back.

The swirling fingers of the Tempest were reaching for us, but my shouts and cries were carried away by the screaming cyclones and cracking thunder. I could no longer tell the difference between pelting rain or sand. It all just looked and felt like a bloody mess—droplets of crimson wet sand spraying in all directions, sometimes painted with splashes of lightning. My back was getting riddled with sharp pain every few seconds. But I could still breathe, so the glass hadn't gone deep enough to puncture my lungs.

Then came the sound of the hail—a thousand icy hammers, pummeling salt crystals into dust. A reminder from the Tempest that the worst was yet to come.

My arms tightened around Clark in anticipation, as a mechanical screech cut through the chaos. I'd never heard anything like it before, and I knew well enough that it didn't belong to the storm. Clark shifted his head so I could see our destination.

Harrow was a few meters ahead, struggling with Crumb tucked away in his coat. Beyond them, at the very center of the smallest circle of spires was a flat, square hatch made of iron, roughly five meters across. It was loosely covered in discolored salt.

The ground shook as the hatch slowly extended upward and flung crystals of salt into the air. A figure stood beneath the hatch, waving us below. They were shouting something inaudible. Harrow hunkered down and crawled inside. I hung on as Clark stumbled his way to the opening, and we tumbled down into the darkness below.

CHAPTER 11 - DEX

As the dust settled and my eyes adjusted to the dim light and shadowed corners inside the hatch, a calloused hand lifted me to my feet.

His booming voice reverberated from the iron quarters around us. "What in the world were you thinking?"

Beneath the unkempt twirls of gray and red in his beard was a gap-toothed smile, white and happy. His broad shoulders strained a pair of frayed suspenders, which careened around his stout belly. He smelled of oil and rust. His undershirt was yellowed with the sort of old sweat that suggested years of hard labor, and the sleeves of his button-front shirt were rolled to his elbows.

Almost every inch of his exposed skin was covered in freckles and smears of umber grease. He reminded me of the engineers at Commonhope—always with their fingers in some kind of ancient machine trying to get the old world to light up again. Atop his thinning orange hair was a pair of circular wire-frame glasses with an amalgam of gadgetry bonded to the sides.

"El sent us." I heaved for breath. "Are you Dex?"

He leaned in—one pupil misshapen and larger than the other—as he studied me through his glasses. "El?" His tongue pressed up behind his teeth as he asked. "Ah. You mean Eloanne? I'm an old friend of the Luminator, yes. She sent you, huh? Things must've turned for the worst if she's taking this kind of risk."

He had no idea. I wobbled and winced in pain. My hand went to my shoulder and came back bloody.

"Whoa. Take a seat there." He motioned to the stool beside me as I teetered in place. He spun me in the chair and sucked air between his teeth. "Ouch."

"That bad?" I asked.

"Nothin too deep. Lucky. You'll live, lad."

Clark came forward and steadied me in the chair. "D-D-Dex," a tinge of pride in his warbling voice.

"Clark!" Dex shouted with joy, embracing him like a long-lost brother. "When the alarms went off, I hoped it might be you. Been some time since we—oh, yeesh. Look at the state of you."

He peered down the bridge of his nose, inspecting what was left of Clark. He immediately began meticulously snipping free-hanging wires and dislodging loose plates of dented steel. Tools seemed to materialize from the weathered, leather pouch sagging at his waist. He rushed over to a lopsided table welded to the right corner wall, rifling through various oily tools in sagging wooden drawers.

My vision was adjusting to the dark. I could tell we were surrounded by heavy metal walls—especially from the iron tinge on the back of my tongue. It was more metal than I'd ever seen or smelled. The hatch, which comprised most of the ceiling we'd fallen through, was framed in a series of tiny, slow-blinking lights.

Raindrop popped out of my shirt and flew up to perch in the struts above us. One warm, cloudy bulb dangled by a single cord below her. Everything was covered in dust or sand or greasy smudges, especially the collection of tools hanging from the wall behind Dex, several of which were well past their prime.

There were also two bulkhead metal doors with handwheels on either side of us, both sealed shut. We seemed to be in some kind of bunker. He had resources here I'd only read about. Resources he hadn't shared.

"Dex," I started, frustration building in my voice, "El told me you had a plan. Do you? Have a plan? Respectfully." I eyed the door to my left, wondering what solutions might be behind it.

He halted his search, turned, and looked down at me through his glasses. "Aye. I've got a plan, lad. Greener pastures. Been prepping our escape for almost two decades. That plan…you're standing in it." He went right back to the drawer.

"Right," I said, understanding nothing. "I'm gonna need more than that."

Harrow squatted down in the corner beneath the hatch with Crumb perched and preening on his hood. "Patience and rest, Master Gaius."

"Is that the old bird too? I didn't even see you," Dex laughed, peering into the corner where the bird keeper sat. "What are you doing here? Hiding the whole aviary in that cloak of yours I bet."

"Only Harrow and Crumb." Harrow lowered his head.

Dex frowned. "Ah, I see. Well, unfortunate circumstances aside, it's good to have guests. Can't tell you how long it's been since I've seen anyone else. Just me and the angry lady these days."

"Lady? You h-have a n-new assis-assistant?" Clark asked indignantly.

"Oh, that's right. You two never met," Dex cupped his hands over his mouth and shouted. "Bring me a drink, would you, Iris? My tank's bone-dry."

I sat up. Iris? It can't be. No. It won't be her. El told me she was dead.

Heavy stomping echoed from all directions like a metal avalanche. The handwheel on my left spun rapidly and the metal door flung open with a vibrating clang. Out stepped the angriest woman I'd ever seen. Her chin was scarred on one side and all twisted up in annoyance beneath a stubbly shaved head.

"I'm not your mother—" she stopped in her tracks and shot us a sharp glance. "Who the hell…?"

I breathed a sigh of disappointment. It's not her. Of course she isn't.

"Surprise?" Dex chuckled. "Come on, now. Say hello." He rubbed her head, and she swatted his hand away. "Show our guests some proper hospitality. This is a rare treat."

Iris approached on bare feet, no less saturated in the same sort of sweat as Dex, and she was dressed for heavy work. Definitely not her.

She was adorned in raincoat fatigues—black canvas pants and a matching, unbuttoned jacket—rigid and fashioned for weathering the elements. On the left shoulder of her jacket, where the double-star symbol of Commonhope should be, there were just tattered patches of new cloth, cut out and resewn.

Her heavy boots were tied and hanging from her neck, and they were caked in half-dried mud and flaking salt. She didn't seem to mind the dirty smear across the white undershirt beneath her jacket.

It's not her. That's no raincoat. She probably stole the uniform along with the name.

"They're friends, Iris." Dex extended his arms to present us.

With her boot laces tight on her thumbs, she ignored us and turned back to Dex. "It's supposed to just be us. You and me. That was the deal. No rusted scrap heaps, wrinkled nutsacks, or spineless Commonhope props."

"Iris—" Dex started.

"You got a problem with Commonhope?" I was breathy, weak, and embarrassingly non-threatening.

"I wasn't addressing you. Why don't you run along and give Commonhope a commission from me."

She rummaged in her pockets with both hands, then politely extended her middle fingers. Her hands and wrists were covered in long-healed burns that disappeared inside the cuffs of her sleeves.

I looked past her at Dex, who was leaning back in his chair with his arms crossed over his chest. He shrugged nervously. He clearly wasn't going to rein her in—or perhaps couldn't.

She moved her face into my vision and opened her eyes wider. "Skedaddle. It's an important message. Timely too."

With my teeth clenched, I breathed hard. "Deliver it yourself. While you're at it, give back the uniform. It doesn't belong to you."

"I'll wear whatever the fuck I want. Go tell it to your little mountain." She pushed a finger into my forehead and shoved me backward. I almost toppled out of my chair.

Clark caught me and squeezed my shoulder with a warbling sigh, then turned to her. "Th-there is n-n-no mountain. Commonhope p-proper was d-d-destroyed.

First, she shot him an incredulous glance and scoffed. Laughed. But as she looked back and forth between us, her smile faded, brow furrowed, and her neck tightened. She backed away on the balls of her feet, catching herself on the table behind her.

Dex unfolded his arms and suddenly squeaked forward in his chair. "Is that true?"

Clark kept his hand on me. "This is the l-last p-packbrat."

"What—the last…?" Iris asked.

But there was nothing to say and no one to say it. It was the truth. The packbrats were gone.

After a moment of regret and aimless staring, her face scrunched back up, angrier than before. "Long past due."

"Iris," Dex warned.

She stormed back the way she came, slamming the heavy door behind her. We sat in the uncomfortable tinny echo of her retreat.

Dex sighed and wiped his glasses clean. "I'm sorry for that. Should've warned you. Discretion isn't one of her virtues. She still hasn't learned how to say what she means. Forgive her, if you can. And please, tell me what happened."

Dex came around my back and started removing the pieces of salt glass. It hurt worse coming out. I stared at the floor, trying to recount everything I knew.

"It was Renner. The same man I saw fifteen years ago. He mentioned another. Varic. El says he's probably behind everything. I don't really know. It was too late when Clark and I got there. They'd already burned the mountain and everyone with it. The raincoats, packbrats, Luminators. Even the aviary. Everything except El who only barely survived.

"Sweet Sunday…" He stopped pulling out the glass. I gave him a moment to take it all in. Stole a moment for myself too, to just breathe. But the thoughts started flooding in.

They were all gone. Dead. Buried. Just like Maksy, Rile, and Saph. Like my Iris. So many others whose names I'd never learned.

When Dex removed the last piece of glass from my back, he

slumped back into his chair. "So, the Luminator's alive…well, thank goodness for that. What in the world has she been doing all this time?"

"Yes." I could feel heat rising in my cheeks. "Like I said, she's the one who sent us here. And with all due respect, what the hell have you been doing? Where were you when the mountain was on fire?"

He choked up at that. Then he looked around the room with wet eyes and extended his arms, barely managing to exhale the word, "Here. For more than twenty years."

I tried to hold back. "El trusted you—enough for your name to come up as the only solution to our impossible problem. But we find you here doing what? Hiding?"

My back stiffened with guilt as I accused him of my own worst moment. I didn't like the way he was questioning El, but my hypocrisy felt worse.

"G-Gaius, that is n-not the wh-whole story."

"Did you say Gaius—" Dex sat up and looked at me with wide eyes. "Can't be," he whispered to himself. He crossed his arms and itched at his sides. "Curious. When that girl showed up here, some fifteen years ago, she was in rough shape. The skin on her arms was… and her hands."

He held up his own hands, imagining some horror we couldn't see. "She must've dug through the embers of that Nest for hours before giving up. I mean, she was just a kid back then. No more than fifteen. It would've been too much for anyone."

My stool squeaked as I leaned forward and held my breath.

His voice cracked as he looked at me. He sucked air through the gap in his teeth. "She blames herself, you know. And goodness did the Commonhope brass toss her to the wind for it—your Nest that is."

"Are you telling me—" I stopped. My mind raced with questions. It is her. She's alive? And she came back for us. I was wrong. Did we only just miss each other? Did she get there before Lars pulled me out or after? She doesn't know I'm alive either? This whole time.

"You're sure? It's really her. My Iris?"

Dex nodded.

Clark leaned against the wall for support. "S-so another raincoat l-lives."

"But why," I started. "Why didn't she say anything when she saw me?"

Dex gestured to me generally. "It's been fifteen years, lad. You're practically a man grown. You didn't recognize her either. That fire twisted up more than her skin. You kids were her charge. By the time she got home, you were all just…gone."

He ran a hand through his hair and shook his head, incredulous. "So, I imagine she wandered down here, hoping to die in the worst place she could imagine. A place no one would go. The Looking Glass."

I'd seen firsthand what the salt flats could do to a person. She really meant to die.

"I found her passed out, dying. She wouldn't even speak to me once she was stable, like she resented me for saving her. Just locked herself up in the lower deck and screamed like a mother in labor. The same four names, over and over. I know them now as if they were my own children. Maksy, Rile, Saph…"

He pointed at me. "And Gaius." He smiled softly. "Wasn't till Clark uttered your name but moments ago that I knew. Eloanne kept you two apart. It'll be hell making any sense of that. Maybe it was punishment or resentment or some kind of calculation, who knows. But my goodness if she isn't the coldest woman on Galilei."

My heart was pounding in my ears, my breath short. "El knew? She knew…how could she not tell me?"

"I can probably count on one hand the number of times that woman told me the truth. It's a cruel task to lead on Galilei." He put a calloused hand on my knee. "But don't you fret. Now you've got time to tell Iris everything. Just…be patient with her. She might have muscles where her brains should be, but she's a whip of a woman where it counts," he said, tapping two fingers in the middle of his chest, eyes sharp.

"I just can't believe this. She's alive. I have so much to tell her. I—" I stood up to go to her, but nearly fell flat on my face. The room was spinning. Blood loss. I was honestly surprised it didn't happen sooner.

"Whoa. Slow down, lad," Dex replied with a laugh, steadying me. "I see you've got an appetite for conversation, but let's take a minute to gather yourself, okay?" We settled back into our chairs. "Thatta boy. Tell ya what. I'm sure you've got questions. And I've got answers. Catch your breath here with me for a bit."

I perked up at that. "Renner," shot out of my mouth.

Clark muttered something indecipherable—almost like another language.

"Clark's right," Dex said. "It may frustrate you to hear, but Renner is inconsequential. He's a lapdog. Only does his master's bidding, nothing else. Varic keeps him busy, so he doesn't inflict his worst vices on the wrong targets—his own people."

"You haven't seen what Renner is capable of," I argued. "I have. I wouldn't describe it as inconsequential."

"Don't misunderstand. Renner is dangerous. But Varic is the one in control, and he's the reason I'm here—why I rarely leave this place and why Eloanne sent you."

He fiddled with some dark controls on a handheld device on his workbench. "Very little room for error and even less time. And it was sensitive work, twenty years of it. We knew what it would take to keep it under wraps. Especially from the young ones—anyone who might spill the world's best kept secret."

"What work? What secret? What are you doing?"

"R-reaching f-f-for the st-stars."

"That's right, Clark." Dex's eyes were filled with wonder and pride. Clark garbled the same words again. "You're sitting inside the buried remains of the only Breacher on all of Galilei. Not even Varic knows where it is. It's why he's been burning us all into the ground. He's been looking for it. For the only ship off this world."

"This is why Varic is killing us?" I looked around. "Some sort of…ship?"

"That's right. Only one that can break the atmosphere. She's gonna take us home." He stroked the wall beside him like it was his sleeping child. "As many as we can fit. Back to Heaven's Vault."

I shook my head. Heaven's Vault? Was that one of the early colonies? A city on Ganymede? Years in the Looking Glass had obviously given him delusions of grandeur. He wasn't a genius. He was insane.

"I see that look in your eye. Skepticism is the first sign of a good scientist, so you and I will make fast friends. But I assure you, this ship will fly. I've been prepping our launch with Iris for some time. Only problem is…"

He nervously cleaned his glasses. "We're uh…gearing up to head south of the Titan's Grave, because we can't launch without the key to Heaven's Vault. And my intel says Varic's got his filthy hands on it. Once we snatch that pretty little apparatus, it's nothing but dark skies, bright stars, and blue worlds for us."

I sat forward. "A key? Renner mentioned something like that fifteen years ago."

"Then you must know what it looks like! Incredible. That's the missing puzzle piece I've been trying to find for some time. Go on, lad. Elucidate us."

"I don't…" My head was dizzy with confusion and blood loss. I was being flooded with new questions, but he hadn't even answered the ones I already had. "Sorry, I don't know. He just said, tell Varic the key is in hand."

He snapped his fingers and stroked his beard. "Darn. Too vague. But that's not nothing. Maybe we can go over the details again when you're feeling better? Think of something you missed."

I needed to slow down. He still hadn't told me the plan exactly, or my part in it. And I wanted—needed to talk to Iris. "You're headed beyond the canyon. What about Skavers? Isn't it supposed to be swarming with monsters? Or, let me guess, that was a lie too?"

Harrow covered his ears.

I sighed. "Hell, for all I know, Varic's a Skaver himself."

Dex shook his head solemnly. "No, lad. Make no mistake. Varic's a man—as rotten as they come, but still a man. What's been done to you is monstrous, and his most zealous supporters deserve a shallow grave. But don't compare the unpleasantries of men with… well, better not to recount the specifics. But the short answer is no.

He's no Skaver."

Harrow nodded with emphasis. "Not a Skaver. Just a man."

Dex continued. "But you're right. To my knowledge, there's no Skavers past the Grave. We should be grateful."

"Grateful. Right." I pictured the bodies of the packbrats back at the mountain. The young ones at Nat's.

"Ah, an admittedly poor choice of words." He scratched at his sides again. "Look. What you got were half-truths. Commonhope kept you in the dark for good reason, but I think it's time to start finally turning the lights back on. Sometimes light can be disorienting. For now, just remember it's men that snuffed out our people and men that set those fires."

"I won't have trouble remembering that," I seared Renner's emotionless, unnerving visage into my mind.

Dex appraised me for a moment. "I imagine you won't. And I'll be sure to relay your hostility when Iris and I make our move on Varic. I suspect she has a two-fingered message she wants delivered in person."

"Wait. If you're going, I'm going," I stood up, steadied myself as best I could. "That's why El sent me."

Dex eyed me cautiously for a moment, choosing not to argue or agree.

Clark cut the tension as he clanked over and sat down cross-legged, reaching for the crates of clutter beneath Dex's worktable and rummaging through their contents. With obviously little interest in our conversation, his mutterings warbled mechanically.

"You won't find what you're looking for under there, Jack," Dex said, sitting forward and looking down at Clark from the opposite end of the table. "At least nothing you deserve. Oh, don't make that face. I'm not gonna send you off to the Rustyard, old friend."

Dex got up and cracked his fingers. "Suppose we should get you two on your feet. Though, I'll leave the stitching to Iris." He pointed at my leg and the bled-through bandages, then wiggled his calloused fingers like ten well-oiled pistons. "Don't wanna be mixing blood and oil. We've already got one too many abominations on my ship."

He knowingly gestured at Clark with a wink and a smile.

Clark fell backward with a moan and cast his remaining limb across his face with dramatic aplomb, "S-s-soon, I w-will be back to one-hundred percent, Gai-Ga-Gaius."

"Looking forward to it," I said. "Hang in there."

"Come on, lad," Dex waved. "I'll take you to our resident seamstress."

"Hopefully, you're hiding someone else back there—somebody with soft hands and a gentle demeanor?"

He shook his head. He was already spinning the spoked hand-wheel on the door Iris had come through. "Just remember. Anything ugly she says, it's not about you. Mostly it's about Commonhope." He paused. "You know, I am somewhat relieved we still have the Lady of Steel. Steel is reliable, even if it's cold."

"Then you'll be happy to hear she hasn't changed. She's mobilizing what's left of the raincoats."

"I'm guessing she didn't let you in on the specifics—what she's planning on doing with her little militia?"

I shook my head. El never let me in on anything. Even after we lost the mountain, she was still hiding basic truths from me. Like flying ships and her familiarity with mysterious killers.

As Dex helped me through the doorway and into a corridor, Raindrop flew down and nested on my shoulder. There was just enough space for us to walk side by side across the metal grating. Dex became my crutch when I needed him.

Hanging in half-loops from the ceiling were a clump of tangled wires and orange bulbs. On either side of the hallway there were beveled metal doors with ascending letters and numbers written in chipped paint. S1, P1, S2, P2. A few meters ahead, the corridor ended with three short stairs leading up to another heavy door with the word CONTROL written in bold letters above a round glass window too dusty to see through.

I realized I couldn't hear the storm. In fact, since we'd been underground, I'd heard little but buzzing lights and the occasional wane in power. The Tempest was probably raging right above us, but my only indication of that was my internal clock. Experience.

The musty odor and subtle stench of ammonia was an easy price to pay for some genuine peace, but it felt unsettling to be so safe in a place like the Looking Glass, as if I wasn't paying close enough attention. I knew safety should be viewed with a certain level of suspicion.

I also wasn't fond of the stale heat, and the stitches in my leg were bulging and itching from sweat. I must have torn a few during the storm. At least the pain hadn't changed—just constant and burning, unless I applied even the smallest amount of pressure, which caused blinding agony. I wouldn't have walked on it so much if I'd had a choice.

Dex led me to the last door on the right before CONTROL and knocked. "Need your pretty little fingers, Iris," he said with a somewhat higher tone. "Boy needs some stitching. You decent?"

"Depends on your definition," her voice shot back through the door, rife with inattention.

He looked at me and laughed nervously, then pushed the latch up and away from the lock position.

He stopped and whispered through his oily mustache. "Sometimes I rub her head for good luck, but maybe don't, in your case. Oh, and before I forget, you'll need to leave the bird with me. Don't worry, kiddo. More company for sad old Harrow."

I whistled a swoop up to Dex's shoulder, and Raindrop hopped right up, like she'd been there before. Good girl. Dex pulled the door open with a grunt, and it swung wide ajar.

Then, with that gap-toothed smile, he patted my back into her room as though he was feeding me to the gravehounds. I stumbled inside, and the heavy door slammed behind me.

CHAPTER 12 - IRIS

The room was small. There was just enough area for a bed and some small furnishings, though it looked like Iris had no intention of livening up the dull gray space. It was well-lit from above—a couple bright panels—and cool enough for comfort.

On my right were three recessed shelves, one on top of the other, spanning the length of the wall. There was a black stormbreaker neatly folded on the top shelf. Next to it were two straight razors, closed and lined up across a clean folded cloth.

On the middle shelf, slid just out of its sheath, was a brela—same as mine, except the two-star adornment had been chiseled from the hilt.

There was also a wrinkled piece of paper, creased along dirty seams. It was pushed back away from everything else on the bottom shelf, not quite hidden but not within easy reach either.

However, the most important feature in the room, apart from Iris herself, was the fist-shaped dent in the metal wall beside her. It was still wet with blood. I tried desperately not to look at it or let her know that I had noticed anything at all—anything that might remind her of why she'd done it in the first place or that my face might be a more punchable option.

Iris herself was at the edge of the bed against the wall in front of me. Her knuckles were bandaged and dappled with blood. The room suddenly felt much too small.

I needed to tell her, but standing there, staring down at a person I didn't recognize, it was hard to parse what I was feeling. In my memory of her, she was so much older than me, bigger too. But we were barely a few years apart. Dex was right. She couldn't have been older than fifteen back then. Maybe thirty now. They had children raising children? What else did I misremember? Were things always so desperate?

She'd shaved her head, and there were extensive burns on her face and neck. The scar tissue tugged at the corner of her mouth on the right side. Opposite Clark, she'd been burdened with a permanent frown. She had plenty of reasons to wear one. Hopefully, what I was about to tell her would change that. Even if only a little.

"Iris—"

"Let's get the blood out of your boot." She chewed on some sweet-smelling, dark root as she spoke. The anger had faded from her voice, but it was deeper than I remembered. She gestured to a spot on the bed beside her. "Sit."

I did as she asked while she pulled a medical tin out from under the bed.

"I uh—" my voice quavered. I'd lost a good deal of blood, and I was on edge. How do I tell her? Just say it. I'm Gaius. I'm your Gaius. Will she believe me? I looked at the bloody dent in the wall again.

She rummaged through the tin and laid out what she needed in the same fastidious manner as everything on her shelf—neat, perpendicular. The bed was soft and clean, along with everything but Iris herself, and the room was practically sterile. Smelled like nothing in particular. The dust, grime, and ammonia that plagued the rest of the bunker was gone here. I was certain she'd accomplished that with no small effort.

As she leaned down to grab my leg, I reflexively grabbed her wrist. A mistake. She twisted my fingers up behind my back.

"You want this hand stitched to the bed?"

"No, ma'am." My voice squeaked out smaller than I intended.

"Then keep it to yourself." She released me. "And while we're at it, keep your mouth shut. We're not here to reminisce about your sad life."

"Yes, ma'am," I replied. Yes, ma'am? What the hell. It was like I was back there again. In the kitchen, at the oven, with her teaching me how to shallow fry thunderfruit seeds in stirige oil.

She took off her jacket, folded it, and knelt in front of me. Her burns went up to her elbow on the left side and up to her shoulder on the right. She really did try to dig us out of the still burning ashes. I could see it all right there on her skin.

Why didn't El tell us? How could she do that to us?

Iris gently untied my laces. Every wince I produced was repaid with a hush until she managed to slide the boot free. My sock was black and sticky.

She took the boot to a water basin in the corner and tipped it upside-down for me to see. As the goop slopped out—first clear and watery, then in red drips, and finally like old pieces of dried fruit—she shook her head.

"Commonhope's fallen pretty far." She tapped the bottom of the boot like she expected the rest of me to come tumbling out. "It's no wonder they're all gone if their best is a little flitfoot."

"Fastest maybe," I mumbled. Didn't she just tell me to keep my mouth shut? Now she wants to talk?

"What's that?" She turned her ear toward me.

"I said I was the fastest," I avoided her gaze, "but I wasn't the best."

"Well, no one left to compete now. You're alive, and they're not." Her voice trailed off. "That's all that matters."

I remembered what Dex told me. She doesn't mean it. With what Commonhope did to her, she had every right to direct her anger at me.

Peels of brittle dried blood sloughed off my boot, as she rinsed it from top to bottom. When she was finished, she took a cloth and bucket from below the basin and ran it under a spout of water.

Her arms and shoulders tensed with wiry muscle as she lifted the bucket. If it came to it, she could snap me in half without breaking a sweat. She was still a raincoat, with or without the insignia on her shoulder. Would've been good to have her in the fight with those gravehounds.

"Besides, you do know the time trials were bullshit, right?" Iris said. She must've caught my skepticism. "You didn't? Come on. Use your head. It was just motivation for any packbrats who needed a push. The times were fixed. So maybe you were the fastest, but looking at you, I doubt it."

"That's a lie." I doubted my words even as they fell out. "I saw the time myself."

I beat Shanna's time. I had the record—saw the clock. Didn't I? Was Shanna's time fixed too? I should've counted the seconds back then, made certain.

"I don't know why you care," she said. "You still weren't fast enough."

It shouldn't matter. But I couldn't help feeling betrayed. Of course El fixed the damn times. Even that was a lie. I tried to turn my face, my shame, away from her.

Iris's bare feet were silent on the metal grating when she returned to inspect my leg. She took great care removing the sock, wiping away the sweat and sand and coagulation. When the still-clinging stitches were removed, there were three open gashes underneath—down to the bone—and a dozen scratches or so. I sucked air through my teeth to stifle the pain I felt looking at it.

"It's gonna heal ugly, but at least it'll match your face," she lifted my chin to appraise some of my other long-healed scars. She started to say something, but her mouth fell open as she stared at me for a moment too long. Her brow furrowed in confusion. She suddenly released my chin, almost like it was hot to the touch.

Did she recognize me?

She swallowed and turned away, clumsily grabbing a glass bottle from the cabinet above the basin. "Anyway, it's your own fault for not stitching it right the first time." She turned back and shoved a pungent clear liquid at me. "Drink."

"Uh. What is it?"

She mimicked drinking, "Do it."

I took a sniff and instantly recognized the acrid, vinegary smell. The engineers called it dragon's-milk—some distilled fuel that made the old machines start smoking again. Or they'd drink it for setting bones and amputations. Rarely for recreation. It was even sourer and more offensive than Iris.

She insisted with a look that said, or else.

I only sipped at first, but she pushed the bottle back, and I was forced to choke down several heavy gulps of the dryest, most vile poison I'd ever had the displeasure of swallowing. I pulled away as my throat practically burst into flames, some of it splashing down my chin. Every inhale was hell.

Iris took some string into her mouth and spoke through her teeth, "This is why they teach you to run."

She threaded the string through a curved needle. Even quicker than Shanna with her fingers. I was desperately trying not to cough in her face, but the dragon's-milk had me in fits. The size of the needle didn't help either.

When the thread was tied and ready, she rested her hands on my knees, looked me in the eyes, and gave me a stern nod. It calmed me. Or maybe it was the dragon's milk. I was sweating as I nodded back.

She spent the next half hour suturing the gashes and salvaging whatever hanging pieces of flesh were still attached. Of course, she still found time to mock my grunts and twitching. For the first few minutes, I felt every tug and pull on my skin. More than that, I felt the pull of an impossible conversation. What did she see when she looked at me? A stranger wearing the face of someone she'd rather forget? Or was I just another Commonhope packbrat? I needed to tell her, but I didn't wanna get slugged.

After a few more minutes of useless introspection and cowardice, I felt warmer. Bolder. I couldn't feel the needle at all. Then, I started to feel good. It was getting harder to hold onto a thought. I kept forgetting why I was in the room, who I was with. But I liked it. I focused on my breathing and studied the door behind Iris with ritual focus.

Handle, frame, lock, hinges, threshold, open, shut, slam, leg, needle, teeth.

"You should try this stuff." I blew through my lips as if smoke was going to come out. My throat was still hot.

"Sit still," her voice was short.

"Yes, ma'am," I joked.

"Don't call me that," she took the thread into her teeth again. Then she took out a pair of shears and cut the thread. "There."

It was over sooner than I expected. The wound was bandaged, but the room was spinning. My hands hadn't left the bed for fear of being stitched to it, and I had squeezed the life from her sheets for fear of falling over. I was wobbling like a toddler, head too big for my body.

"You survived." She slapped my knee to help me confirm the pain. "Run next time, and maybe you'll keep surviving."

"The one thing I know how to do," I said. "Survive." My eyelids were heavy. I could see the throb of my heartbeat in my peripheral vision. It was hypnotic.

"You'll want to stop talking now." She stood and stretched out her arms.

I blinked slowly in response. I was tired. Why is she staring at me?

"What are you looking at?" I asked. My eyes were unfocused. Everything seemed to be fading further away. I didn't like the way she stared. She doesn't know me. What I've done. What I've been through. My head and fingers tingled.

"Get some rest." She started toward the door.

I shook my head. Wait. I'm supposed to tell her something. I couldn't remember. Everything was cloudy. What was it? It was important. I tried to remember the most important things I could.

"Renner." Did my lips always feel so puffy? "If I just got there first. Oh—but I stabbed 'im good with this."

I went to pull out my brela, but it clattered to the ground. She picked it up before I could and held onto it.

"El's okay," I continued. "I saved her. Even though she told me not to. She's always telling me what to do. 'Run, Gaius. Do your job, Gaius. Pay attention, Gaius.' But I don't listen to that hag."

She dropped my brela. Her eyes were on me, her lips parted. Why'd she drop it? Is she mad at me? I couldn't tell. But I know her.

That's Iris. I reached out to her. Oh, right. I wanted her to tell her. She deserved to know.

"I was there," I said. Yes. That's it. My words were like soup, though. "It was Renner. I saw 'im do it. Saw 'im burn Maksy and Rile. Watched 'im take Saph. But I'm gonna kill 'im for it. Put 'im in the ground."

Then, I was suddenly cascading backward toward growing darkness. I fell into it, like warm water washing over me. It was so nice.

A hand cupped the back of my head, holding me up. Iris? But I was sinking, falling through her fingers.

"You little shit." There was a crack in her voice. "How are you alive?"

CHAPTER 13 - BREACHER

I woke in the dark to the sound of a bulkhead door scraping closed. The clang reverberated in my head, but my leg was better. At least, it moved the way I wanted, even if it hurt like hell. Raindrop was cuddled up underneath me.

"Who's there?" I was groggy and raspy.

The shelf hummed with warm light behind me. I rolled my head to see Dex's silhouette leaning on the water basin, his arms crossed.

"Seems you get to keep the leg," he said. "Good, good. Though, you should know it nearly cost my head. Iris thinks I should've given her fair warning about your uh, identity, as it were. Just thought it was your peace to speak."

He rubbed his jaw with a wince and laughed nervously as he continued. "Anyway, she slugged me good and isn't too keen on letting it slide. I'm not suggesting you owe me, but a good word with her might go a long way. Just lay off the sauce this time around."

"What are you talking about?" I rolled back over and closed my eyes again. I could barely remember how I got there.

His laugh echoed across the bunker walls. "I'm saying you could've delivered the news of your resurrection with more finesse. Though, I s'pose that's not the point."

"And what is the point, exactly?"

He held up his hands in surrender. "I see your bleeding has made you a bit testy. I'm just here to tell you we're gearing up for some cloak 'n' dagger south of the canyon. We'll be off soon."

I shot up. "You're going after Renner?" The blood rushed to my head and spots formed in my vision. I nearly passed out.

Dex bent down and grabbed a folded towel to wipe his hands. "I know how you feel, and we'd welcome the help, but it's gonna be ugly business. Dangerous, even for a raincoat."

I swung my legs off the edge of the bed and stared him down. "I've seen ugly. I want in. I know Renner. I've fought him once already and—"

"—Slow down now, lad. You're eager, and I hear you. But there's still the unfortunate matter of your leg to tend to. Iris is good, but don't go thinking there's magic in those stitches. You need to stay put, or she's gonna be poking you again in a couple days."

Even if he was right, I wouldn't miss my opportunity. "What can I do?" I asked with as much desperation as I could muster. Don't go without me.

With clean hands, he walked to the shelf and picked up the wrinkled piece of paper I'd seen the day before. He held it for a moment, eyeing it with a soft smile, then handed it to me. "For now, you can rest. And you can ask questions. You have a lot to learn. But most importantly, you can set the story straight with Iris, if you feel so moved. We're not leaving for a few days yet."

The paper was faded and yellowed from having been overhandled—unfolded and refolded numerous times. Something small, white, and delicate fluttered out as I held it. A single petal.

Inside was an old, wilted flower crown, flattened with time and pressure. I recognized it. Flowers from Reaper Springs.

Underneath the crown, the paper itself was a messy painting of four children standing around a taller girl with long hair. There were exaggerated smiles painted across their faces. It was us. The Nest where it all started. But there were no flames. No suffering or fear or death or signs of what was to come—like time had unwound, and we were still together. Iris, Maksy, Rile, and Saph. I was there too, standing just to the right of Iris and shorter than the rest. The eldest of the bunch, but still the runt.

"Saph drew this," I whispered, staring at their faces—faces I'd forgotten. I traced them with my finger.

Dex pulled up on the latch on the door.

"I'm going," I said, looking up at him, resolute.

And as he turned, a smile peeked out beneath his beard. "I know. Still a few days till then. Rest up."

He disappeared into the corridor. After a long while studying the painting, I carefully tucked the flower crown back inside and refolded the paper along the creases. Figured Iris probably wouldn't want me seeing that. I fell back into her pillow and dreamt of better times.

At some point over the next few days, when I couldn't stand lying there any longer, I sent Raindrop back to El with a cipher message letting her know we arrived at the flats safely: 6-6-1-8. Unfortunately, I couldn't give her a piece of my mind in the scope of four numbers, but I was sure as hell gonna let her have it as soon as we met back up.

When Dex saw me struggling to reach the hatch to let Raindrop out, he pieced together a makeshift crutch for me and started showing me around the Breacher. He was beaming with excitement.

Iris was nowhere to be seen in any of the other quarters. He said she'd locked herself up in the distillery on the lower level, and apparently it wasn't the first time she'd done so. She didn't drink the stuff, he told me. Just found the process of refining and fermenting therapeutic.

"She's not a drunk," he said. "I'm afraid that's her default demeanor—no liquid influence but the chemicals swirling about in her noggin. Not even when she first got here, all messed up and bleeding and screaming through the night."

He sighed. "It would have been a godsend to the both of us, but I think she wanted to feel it all, with the way she was blaming herself. Might be the first raincoat I've met that doesn't drown away their sorrows in dragon's-milk. I suppose I should just be happy she's not chugging away the extra fuel." He put a hand against the humming metal wall.

"This thing runs on dragon's-milk?" I asked.

"The internals and computers, but not the engines." He smirked. "That's a wholly unique mechanism of my own design. Dragon's-milk doesn't burn hot enough and won't produce enough energy for our needs. But don't you worry. My arc harness will do the trick."

During my recovery, he kept talking about the arc harness, seeming more pleased with himself with every mention. It had something to do with the spires outside. I didn't understand most of the technical jargon, but from what I gathered, Dex was using the storm to store remote power. When I compared it to our old broken generator at Commonhope proper, Dex waved his hands in offense.

"Much more complex than that old pile of junk," he said. "Took me nearly eight years just to build the darn thing. And the process wasn't some kite-and-key discovery. It might be the prettiest thing you'll ever see. Brighter than Christmas, and every inch crackles and chirps like a caged bird made of lightning. I'd say twenty of the cells should be full up by now. More than two-thirds of what we'll need. Few more storm cycles should do it, if they're severe enough."

I'd read about Christmas. Some solstice celebration. Big trees, lights, gifts—even music. If the arc harness was anything like that, I was excited to see it for myself. Though, considering the crudely built crutch beneath my arm, I had my doubts about Dex's genius.

That is, until he showed me the extraordinary machinery beyond the CONTROL door.

Inside, there was an amalgam of color unlike anything I'd ever seen—a panel of a hundred switches or more, all begging to be pressed. Dex was giddy and fast-talking, firing off descriptions of how everything worked and leaving me in the wake of my own ignorance. I functionally understood none of it, but that didn't dilute his excitement or mine.

Above the panel was a wide pane of thick glass covered in compacted dirt and rock. Three leather-bound seats faced the glass and control panels. When Dex had finally settled down, he took a seat, put up his feet, and seemed almost serene.

"It won't be long now. Soon, we'll fill this window with stars."

He stared through the glass as though there was a paradise only he could see. "Won't be long."

We spent the rest of the day in that room, fiddling with dark controls and talking about imagined worlds beyond our own. He told me the computers in that room were the result of centuries of research. There was supposedly an entire library, digitally coded, constantly running complex equations needed for interstellar travel. According to him, the Breacher was designed to break the atmosphere and travel to stars unknown. No other ship could do it, including the piercers.

"Any other books in that library?" Maybe there were answers—the ones El was still hiding from me.

Unfortunately, Dex seemed as tight-lipped as El about certain subjects. There was some thread tying their secrecy together, and he wasn't going to reveal it. "Nothing that'll wet your whistle, lad. But I've got my own collection if you're partial to romance."

"I'm…good." I kept one curious eye on the computer, but I had no idea how to use it. I wondered if I'd get a chance to sneak back in there and try.

The next morning, we took a ladder down to the second level. The corridor was a mirror to the one above, just tighter and shorter, and there was only one cabin and a room labeled STORAGE at the end. Harrow was busying himself in the cabin, tending to the eggs we helped him stash away. I couldn't see Crumb from the doorway.

"How're you settling in?" Dex rapped two knuckles on the open doorway before showing himself in.

"Too warm." He shook his head as bottled frustration fizzed out, huffing and puffing. "Too warm for egglings."

"Well, I'll just have to see what we can do about that." Dex patted him on the back. "Don't want to cook the little guys before they have a chance to hatch."

"No, we do not," Harrow confirmed earnestly, "Do not want to cook the little guys."

"Where's Crumb?" I asked.

"Sulking." Harrow leaned his ear deeply into the eggs, listening for mysteries that only he understood. Then he pointed up. Crumb was perched on an exposed joist. "Won't come down."

"I know someone just like that," Dex laughed. "What do you do when he's like that?"

Harrow was rushing around the room with his arms out in front of him, mostly ignoring us and looking for different ways to cool the eggs down. "When Crumb falls, I will catch him."

At that, Dex scratched his sides and nodded, "Hm. You're a wise old bird, you know that, Harrow?"

The bird keeper stopped at that, and his eyes darted around the room. His hands tucked into one another as he seemed to shrink. "Wise old bird."

I socked Dex in the side.

"What'd I say?" he grunted.

I put my hand out on Harrow's hunched back. "We'll get them back, Harrow. All of them. I promise."

I was starting to believe my own lie. I just couldn't stand that look in his eyes. It might disappoint him later, but I needed him to know someone else cared—that someone else would try.

He got back to work, fanning the eggs with loose aluminum. "Much too hot."

Dex gestured to the corridor, and I followed him out. "Let's go give Iris a bother," he said. "Maybe she's ready to fall."

He knocked lightly at first. We heard heavy things being scooted across the metal floor and shoved up against the door.

Dex banged on the frame with his fist. "Come on out of there, you stubborn—the universe saw fit to give you a brain! Put it to use before it rots inside that bald melon of yours."

Metal screeched as more objects were pushed toward the door. He cupped his hands around his mouth. "Ah, stay in there then. Sweat it out of your system, for all I care."

"I guess she's not ready," I said.

There was no smile on Dex's face. "S'pose not."

"Sorry."

"What in the world are you sorry for?" he asked. I wasn't even sure. I was just sorry.

"Sorry," I said again.

"Oh, hell," Dex ruffled his hair. "Don't get all mopey on me now. There's enough of that going on around this ship. Where's that fire in your belly from a few days ago? Hmm? Stay angry. Stay alert. We're gonna need that in the days to come."

"Sounds like you're expecting to run into Skavers or something," I joked.

His eyes squinted behind his wire-framed glasses. "Gaius," he started slowly, "let me be very clear. When I'm talking about Skavers, you'll know. I will have your full attention." He put both hands on my shoulders. "Do you really believe the Luminators taught you to run because of the storm?"

He waited for me to answer. I hadn't really thought about it. The training always seemed normal to me. But I'd been wrong about everything else. "I don't know."

"I do. Your regimen is a remnant of a time when we had no other choice but to run. If you find yourself in the company of such monsters, you show them ass-end of that training. You turn, and you run. You use every muscle, every bone, every book, every piece of knowledge to flee and survive. They weren't just stories, lad, and I won't tolerate jokes about it. Clear?"

He didn't sound like himself. I nodded. "Yeah."

"Alright." He cracked his knuckles. "Let's go see the secondskins."

As we climbed back to the first level, I tried not to think about the fear on his face. I didn't believe in monsters, but Dex had a way of making me believe in fantastical things. I didn't know much about where we came from or even the world I lived in. My own memories weren't trustworthy either. Part of me wished I'd never said anything about Skavers in the first place. Like it would've been better not to know—not to believe that something worse than Renner was out there.

We climbed back up into the room with the hatch.

"This used to be a galley," he continued. "But I don't cook much as of late. Neither does Iris. Too much to do. So now it's more of a work area. Well, a work area in-progress...a working...work area. Oh, just forget about the galley. This is what I really wanted to show you."

He waved me over to the other bulkhead door—opposite the cabin and control room. He yanked on the handwheel. It didn't budge or make a sound beside the squeak of his fingers on the metal. He yanked again and his fingers slipped off. He laughed and tried to wipe the ever-present oil off his hands, but all his clothes were equally greasy.

"I usually have Clark open this one for me." After one more futile attempt, he grunted and kicked the door. "Getting to be too many locked doors on my ship!" he yelled to no one in particular. "Well. Darn. Guess I have to show you this another time." He patted the solid steel door, seeming to appraise the frame as if the door was at fault. "I'm sure it's fine."

"How's the old Jack doing, by the way?" I asked. "Starting to miss him."

"Clark is predisposed elsewhere. Probably won't be back until the next cycle. But he's been fully repaired if that helps." Dex removed his glasses and tried to find a clean spot on his shirt to wipe them. "Truth is, there's smoke rising from new places every day. We need eyes out there. Varic must be in a rush over something, and he's getting sloppy, trying to uproot us all at once."

"About that. Renner mentioned something back at the mountain. He said this planet only has eight months left. Any idea what he meant?"

"Eight months? Hmm." He crossed his arms. "No data to suggest seismic, geological, biological, or astrophysical events that could account for an apocalypse."

"Yeah. Well, it wouldn't be his first lie. Doesn't matter anyway. We're stuck here."

He waved me back through the galley. "I know it's hard to do nothing right now, but rest and healing is the best thing you can do for anyone. We just have to leave the heroics out there to Clark. Time to get off that leg."

He was right. I was healing up nicely, but I wasn't gonna miss my chance to give Renner what I owed him.

A few days later, Raindrop flew in on the tail-end of a nasty storm cycle. Her cipher was sealed. El had spun her a new message for us: 3-0-1-8. Three-raincoats-safety.

She was making progress. We had to do the same.

CHAPTER 14 - SUN SISTER

On the eleventh day, Iris's cabin door swung open with more force than I had become accustomed to, waking Raindrop with a startled squawk.

I was met by a clean silver face and a familiar voice with a happy hum. "Up, Gaius." Clark's chin was high as he leaned his freshly minted right arm against the doorframe.

"Well, look at you." I crawled out of bed and reached for Kai's boots. "Is this what a hundred percent looks like?"

His eyes blazed extra bright beneath the hood of his freshly-tailored stormbreaker. "The storm has passed, and we are readying for departure."

"Any luck out there? Survivors?"

His grin couldn't hide the truth. "We will keep trying." He wiggled his bright new fingers like an elderly Luminator looking for the softest slice of mudmelon. "Now, I will assist you in your preparations."

"Hey, I might not have shiny new parts, but I'm good." I carefully tied the laces on my boots—not too tight. "Stitches are almost ready to come out."

"But…I have been tasked with preparing you for departure. I assure you, I am well-suited for this delicate task."

"Hey." I held out my hand to stop him. "I am not a delicate task. And I can tie my boots just fine, thank you."

"Very well." He retracted. "Shall I…assist you in equipping your pack, or perhaps—"

"—I've got everything under control," I said.

Clark fell silent, and his shoulders slumped. I know he wanted to feel useful, but his enthusiasm would translate to over-tightened pack straps or triple-knotted laces. Always better to deal with a sullen Secondhand Jack than an overzealous one, especially with the capacity to crush me with his pretty new hands.

I shook my head. "Fine. Can you make sure my pack is rationed?"

He snatched my bag from the shelf and rifled through its contents with apparent disinterest. I'd already rationed it the day before, but it gave him something to do.

"Rope. Blanket. Water. Oil. Dried meat." His voice trailed off with a thousand-pound sigh. "All is accounted for."

He relinquished my pack at the tips of his fingers.

I secured it around my chest and realized it was laying snug against my back, more comfortable than before. All my attire had been stitched and cleaned—purged of my runner's smell. Only Iris could've managed this. When did she sneak away with my things? Why didn't she talk to me?

Even my stormbreaker hung square across my shoulders and straight down to my knees like it was intended. I felt ready to run again. Needed to. Being cooped up in that cramped, sunless place was enough to drive any packbrat to madness, and the itch in my leg wasn't just because of the sutures.

"Dex is expecting us," Clark said. "Today is the day."

"Can't wait." I equipped my brela and followed him out.

We made our way back to the exit hatch in the galley. It was already open and flooded with morning light, and a small ramp had been extended down to the floor. We sure could've used that when we first arrived.

I whistled and Raindrop took off over the ramp ahead of us. Dex and Iris were silhouetted against a flawless cerulean sky, working around some massive machine.

We still hadn't spoken since she stitched me. Dex waved us over, but Iris paid me no mind.

We climbed up and out as my eyes slowly adjusted to the piercing brightness of the Looking Glass. They were prepping a vehicle of some kind. I'd seen something similar in Anansi's astronautics books. Looked like an old lunar rover but bigger.

It was large enough to seat Clark three times over—with two black leather seats up front, and a rear-facing bench behind. A steel support frame had been welded around the top to a short lip around the whole chassis, like a caged rowboat on wheels.

It had boxy, angled features, and its broad face was made mostly of mottled iron. There were gold and black reflective panels in tesselated symmetry on every up-facing surface. And the vehicle sat high on four rubber wheels, nibbed and treaded, which came up to my waist.

Still, the most impressive piece of work was an anchoring winch welded beneath the wedged front end. I recognized the torsion spring design, but it was easily five times the size of my old broken one. I could only imagine the firepower.

"Hell of an anchor," I said, admiring the contraption with a gliding hand across the surface.

"She's much more than that. Hop on up, lad." Dex wiped a greasy mask of sweat and oil across his reddened forehead. His eyes were squinted behind smudged glasses fixed at the tip of his nose as he extended his hand.

He pulled me up onto the iron monstrosity. It barely shifted under my weight. "What is this exactly?" I asked.

"A Sun Sister. Only one north of the canyon…with some modifications, of course. She drinks solar during the day and burns dragon's milk at night. I was wary of parting with the extra fuel, but Iris has been…busy cooking extra batches…at night." Dex muttered to the back of his hand, "Instead of talking to—"

"—try not to drink it all, packbrat." Iris shoved Dex aside to pack more supplies. "You talk too much when you're drunk."

"Oh. So we are talking," I said. She continued rigging canvas bags to the rear carriage without a response.

"Tempest won't be happy about you cheating across the desert," Dex said. "Not one bit. You'll be moving swifter than the wind. I got the storm cycles and shelters mapped as best we could, but you probably know the whims of the Tempest better than me. Keep your eyes peeled and ears clean."

"Where exactly are we going?" I asked. Dex hadn't told me the full plan. My part in it was mostly clear: Kill Renner. Oh, and get the key from Varic. But apart from that, I was still in the dark.

"Iris knows the spot." Dex handed her a large fold of gridded paper. "Titan's Grave separates the hemispheres, so there's no going around it. Gotta go over. Problem is, we don't know precisely what's on the other side."

He discreetly pointed out an area on the map to Iris. She acknowledged, folded the paper back up, and pocketed it.

"We have some educated guesses," Dex continued. "Varic, for instance. But the Luminators have tried to send raincoats over the canyon before. None came back. Which is what makes our timing here work, I think. Varic's getting desperate. He won't see you coming. His bloated ego wouldn't even consider the possibility."

"Renner might," I argued. "I basically told him I was coming. And he mentioned the canyon outright, like an invitation. Catching him off guard might be tough."

"Maybe," Dex said. "But we've got surprises of our own. They don't know about Clark. A Secondhand Jack bringing the hammer down on their house? Wish I could be there to see it."

"Wait, you're not coming?" I asked.

We all took our seats—Iris and I up front and Clark lounging among our supplies in back. Raindrop came down with a screeching trill to land atop one of the many bars.

"She's not either," Iris said. "Command her to stay."

"Absolutely not." I reached up to scratch the scruff beneath Raindrop's neck. "She's been with me through everything. We're practically family."

"I don't care if she's your left nut," Iris said. "This mission requires stealth."

Raindrop squawked as if to confirm Iris's point.

"I can keep her quiet."

"Untrue," Clark said. I should've known he'd betray me. "Red-tails do as they please. They only listen if it suits them."

"And apparently, you've picked up their habit," Iris added. "She stays behind or you both do."

I chewed the inside of my cheek. Having to choose between Renner or Raindrop felt like a raw deal. We were always together. My only companion in the wastes.

"Fine," I said through my teeth. "Come on, girl. You gotta stay. I'll be back before you know it. Keep Harrow company while I'm gone."

I removed the pearlescent cipher from her leg and pocketed it. Then, I pointed to the open bunker and whistled three short descending tones. She shifted uncomfortably on her perch, refusing my command.

"Now's not the time." I whistled more sternly and pointed with emphasis. She flapped up into the air with a defiant squawk and soared above us.

"Hate to say I told you so—" Iris started.

"—I really doubt that. She'll get the hint when I stop feeding her."

Dex smacked the side panel with a big smile. "Listen up. We don't know what the key to Heaven's Vault looks like. But we should assume Varic will keep it on his person. Find him, and you'll find the key."

He hugged Clark over the metal bars like it was his final goodbye.

"Stay underground," Clark said, tapping his repaired glaive on the warm metal bed.

"You're really not coming with us?" I asked again.

"Wish I could. Got other things which need my attention." Dex hopped up and rubbed Iris's head for good luck. She swatted at him as he swung off. "Be smart out there. See you when you get back."

The vehicle hummed with power as Iris began flipping metal switches on the panel between our seats. She slammed her foot on a small rubber lever on the floor, and we jerked into the expanse, smooth and swift.

I yelled back over the rumble of the wheels cracking salt and sand. "Take care of Raindrop. And keep an eye on Harrow for me. He won't say it, but he gets lonely."

Dex threw me a salute. "You got it. Oh, I nearly forgot—check the back, lad!" A wide smile faded beneath his mustache.

Clark poked his head into the front carriage and held out my old anchor belt, fully repaired. "Dex spent half a day retethering the line, improving the firing pin, and welding a new housing to keep out the dirt and dust. It should work more efficiently and reliably now."

I grabbed it and waved it in the air back at Dex as thanks. We were already out of earshot. Damn, this thing moves fast. I sat back down and hitched the anchor around my waist. I didn't realize I'd missed the weight and security of it.

The cool morning wind was a welcome passenger. As we passed through the rings of half-retracted spires (apparently, they were part of the arc harness, whose function still mostly eluded me), I recalled the chaos of the storm from days ago. My back was flecked in small scabs from all those shards of glassed salt. I didn't know a single person on Galilei without scars, but I was accumulating them at record speed. I needed to be smarter. Faster. Better. Or my luck would run out.

We were already into the Rustyard before midday, a distance that had taken us three times as long a couple weeks prior. And even though the Sun Sister slowed atop the red sand, it was still considerably faster than traveling by foot. More importantly, it took no energy to sit in the breeze with the sun on our faces.

Clark stuck his head through the exposed frame and let the wind beat against him as he pointed into the distance and rattled off information about the area every few kilometers.

"…currently over an ancient seabed…"

"…only four hundred eighty-four kilometers to reach the Titan's Grave…"

"…allows connivores to burrow deeper than any other mammal on Galilei…"

"…runs on solar energy with heat-resistant…"

"…four hundred sixteen kilometers to…"

Iris kept a tight lip, though she flexed her jaw at Clark's every utterance, and her brow was stuck in the furrowed position. When I got stitched, she seemed in a better mood, but even that was unpleasant. I won't push her.

Every time I looked back, Raindrop grew smaller and smaller in the distance until she was nothing but a speck in the approaching dusk. She couldn't keep up with us, though she certainly tried. When nightfall came, she disappeared completely. I'll be back, girl.

A secondary engine rumbled to life—much noisier than the first—and it smelled of burning oil. Four wide beams of light flooded from the nose of our vehicle as we drove into the night. We only rode for another hour like that.

"We should travel mostly by day," Iris said, slowing the vehicle to a sudden halt. "The fuel is for the return trip. Everyone out."

They'd packed sleeping bags, water flasks, and a drum of dragon's-milk. For food, we had dewroot sweetbread, morels, and mudmelon. No meat. No fresh thunderfruit. Iris didn't like complaining, so I kept that to myself.

We were heading two days out of the way to avoid the mountain range along the western ridge of the Titan's Grave. Our vehicle couldn't manage that terrain, so we'd have to swing around it to the far east. Plus, we needed the anchor to cross, so hoofing it wasn't an option.

Our old Nest was at the foot of those mountains. Right at the edge of the thunderfruit fields where the soil was rich from the mountain runoff. I wondered what was left of it. Is the ash and refuse washed away? Is there anything left?

In fifteen years, I never visited. Never wanted to. But the thought started itching inside my head like a scar that never healed quite right.

The blankets didn't keep out the cold that night, but I slept well enough. Iris finally spoke to me the next morning, just as we were packing up camp—while Clark was doing his morning stretches at the top of a nearby dune, the sun cresting behind him in ripples of orange.

"You know how to use that?" she pointed at the all-too-clean and entirely unsharpened brela at my hip.

I smiled, anticipating a dig or insult, but she just stared right back, waiting for an answer. She bit into more of that spicy-sweet, dried plant. Dex told me it was licorice root, and that I should never take it without asking.

"I guess it depends on what you mean by use." I pulled out the knife and fumbled it in my hand. "It's barely sharp, but it's seen the inside of a gravehound. That was sort of an accident, though."

"An accident—you accidentally stabbed a gravehound?" She popped another small piece in her mouth.

"It's not like I slipped in a puddle and oops'd my way into it." I sheathed the blade. "I meant to do it. It just kinda…happened, though. Sort of a blur. I'm sure you know how it is." I pointed to her own brela.

"I never stabbed anything I didn't mean to stab." She looked at me with genuine confusion, still chewing. "Certainly never stirred up the gravehounds for fun either. But hey, you survived mostly intact, and that's not nothing."

"I suppooose…" Again, I was waiting for the other shoe to drop.

"Show me," she said, dusting off her hands and spitting out the chewed up root.

In a second, she flipped the brela from her hip into her hand and held it blade-down in front of her face, just like Lars. Her legs were slightly bent, and her head was tilted with her eyes sharp, obscured just behind her blade.

"Uh. Show you what?" I took an unconscious step backward.

She quickly loosened up with a sigh and came up next to me. She put my hand on my brela and widened her eyes. "Show me."

"Alright, but it's not pretty. And I mostly just threw it around. Got lucky. And I wasn't trained like you. So, I'm not—"

"Enough. Show me."

She took her stance again, and I tried to mirror her, blade-down. Watching her now, I could see several things I had been doing wrong. I should've asked Lars for more advice. Like how to sharpen the damned thing. I bent my knees and lowered my head.

But before I was comfortably in position, she was on me, and my arm was twisted behind my back. My face plummeted into the sand with an oof as my blade sank into the dune next to my head. She scooped it up and poked it into my neck. For all my complaints about its sharpness, it sure seemed sharp enough in her hand, given enough pressure.

"Troof," I spat through the sand between my lips. "Truce."

"Is that what you're gonna say to Renner?" She lifted her knees from my back and released my arm. She helped me to my feet and extended the grip-end of my brela.

I brushed my clothes and picked the sand from my ear. "You've made your point."

"I wasn't making a point. I asked you a question. Have you given a single thought about how you're going to take down a trained killer?"

"Well. Yeah. I think about it every day. That's not—"

Clark came barreling down the hill. "Are you alright, Gaius?" Then he pointed at Iris. "And you. You would do well to remember why I am here."

"I know why you're here." She batted his finger out of her face and yanked my pant leg up to expose my stitches. "Were you there when this happened? Hmm?"

Clark didn't respond.

She released my pant leg. "Thought so. I'm not gonna coddle him. You know this wouldn't have happened if he could handle himself in a fight." She hammered her fist into my chest. "From now on, he trains at night. And he keeps his brela sharp."

With her eyes on me, I shrank. "Yes, ma'am."

Clark looked between us both and held his chin up. "Under my supervision." He planted Toothpick in the sand.

"You'll thank me when all three of us come back alive." She shielded her eyes from the sun. "Days are getting hotter. Let's move."

With the last of our supplies hitched to the rear carriage, we all piled in and started off into the morning heat.

During the trip, Iris handed me a whetstone from her pack and instructed me on blade care. The additional wisdom she added, however, left much to be desired.

"A dull blade is like a dull brain. You have to…you won't—shit. What did Doran used to say?" She scraped her brela across the fuzz on her head while she drove. "They both need to be sharp. That's the gist of it. Make sense?"

"Uhhh. Yeah. I get it."

Sometimes, the kids who grew up with parents would talk about this shared experience—some utterly human moment would reduce their parents from deity to dumbass, and they'd realize they were all just people. I think I finally understood what they meant.

Far above, I heard the distant kree-eee of Raindrop attempting to catch up. When I tried to turn and find her on the horizon, Iris caught my chin with her hand. She shook her head. There was no anger—just clear command: Don't.

I slumped back into my seat, and the pressure grew inside my chest. I'd only been apart from Raindrop when she was delivering a message. Please, stay safe.

Clark poked his head into the front carriage. "I would give the bird credit for keeping pace," he started, "if she were not acting in direct opposition to your instruction."

"And would you stay if I told you to?" I asked.

His head turned to me. Then, without a word, he retreated to his seat. After that, we let the soft hum of the engine lull us into a drowsy state—just awake enough to sit upright but comfortable enough to gloss over the uniformity of the terrain. Up and down. One dune, then another. Windward. Slip face. Sand, and nothing else.

If it weren't for the sun and stars, I'd never know where I was. The only changing feature on the horizon was the smoke. Whenever more rose far north, my legs twitched with an urge to run. But we needed to finish what we were doing, or no Nest would survive.

The two moons had risen over the flat peaks of the mountains on our right. We couldn't see the canyon, but it was there, on the other side. Dry heat still clung to the metal around us for another hour before we stopped to set up camp.

"Hydrate." Iris tossed me a flask without warning. "And when you're ready, I'll show you how to kill a man."

CHAPTER 15 - BRIN

Iris handed me a wooden training knife—probably for my safety, not hers.

"Speed, power, accuracy, misdirection. Combat isn't about cutting and stabbing. It's about reacting and predicting. Paying attention. Creating opportunity. Patience. I'll repeat that last part. Patience." She stopped and waited for me to acknowledge. I did. "And when the moment presents itself—" She thrust her palm into the left side of my chest. "You strike. Got it?"

"Conceptually," I said, although I knew it would only translate to more sand in my mouth.

"Show me."

We circled each other for a moment, but she didn't approach. The way she looked at me—like dinner—made me so nervous I struck with the knife out of pure nerves, right toward her heart, like she'd done. She swatted my wrist, knocked the training blade into the sand, and chopped my arm with her other hand.

"Your wrist is fractured, and your tendons are severed." She pointed to my imaginary injuries. "Were you paying attention to what I was doing, or were you thinking about something else?"

I picked up the brela. "Just let me try again."

She stopped and fixed my grip. "Make sure you cap the bottom with your thumb here. There are other grips I can teach you, but for now, consider this default. That pressure? That's how it should feel."

Is that why it's always slipping out of my hand? Maybe if someone had taught me that a few weeks ago, I'd have one less scar across my palm. "That feels better."

Her hand lingered a moment. She nodded and pulled away. "One more thing. Remember the thunderfruit fields?"

"Of course I do. It was—" She clapped in my face, and I jerked away from her. "What the hell…?"

"Yes. Just like that." She knelt down, bent my knee, and angled my foot toward her. "You've got good instincts. Decent reflexes too. But they need honing like your brela, or they'll go dull—oh…I just remembered that thing from earlier. Anyway. Forget trying to hit me for now. Just react. Be a thunderfruit. They don't need to be as quick as lightning. Because it's enough to react to the thunder."

I slowly nodded. With my grip fixed, the blade did feel steadier in my hand. I had leverage that wasn't there before. "Okay. Let's try it."

Over the next few hours, I don't know how many times she flipped me over, threw me to the ground, or knocked the wind out of me, but I never dropped the brela again. I never got close to striking her either, but a win was a win.

"You're bad at this now, but your body will start remembering it." She moved my limbs and showed me how to stretch after a session of training. "You'll notice it more tomorrow and more the day after that. Oh, and I think you should start practicing throwing. Any spare moment. Even if it's just the motion. Close quarters combat only solves one problem. You need to be versatile from any distance, and your anchor isn't a reliable weapon."

She took my brela out of its sheath and held it between her thumb and forefinger. I mimicked her with my training blade.

"Release from this distance." She slowly arced my arm downward, thumb on top. She pointed to a spot in the sand about five meters away near a rusted Secondhand Jack arm.

I practiced the motion as she continued.

"From this distance, you want a half spin—not more, not less—and your thumb should be pointing at the target at the end of your throw. Release too early or late and it'll bounce off or go wide. You'll have to learn to gauge the release. But that's about instinct. With practice you—"

I was listening, but it all seemed so obvious to me. Unlike melee, this felt natural. Just like sling-n-snatch. Keeping pace with a red-tailed hawk took precision, creativity, and an eye for trajectory and speed. Without thinking, I tossed the knife, and it stuck in the sand, slightly left of where she'd pointed.

She looked at me, then back to the knife with a cocked eyebrow. "Huh." She picked it up and handed it back to me. "Do that again."

For the next few minutes, I hit the mark—or close to it—almost every time. Even when she'd back me up a meter or two and make me try again. Throwing just made sense. Adjusting for weight, distance. Though, admittedly, I kept feeling the urge to whistle every time I threw.

Iris eventually insisted I try the real brela. "Maybe the wood's a fluke," she said.

But the heft of the metal was even better. They'd obviously been balanced for throwing. It was like an extra limb. My brain told it where to go, and the blade just went.

"I'll be goddamned," she finally said, with a smile in her voice. "Fair enough. Let's not waste another second on this. You're good. Damn good. Keep practicing your form during the day, but we'll focus exclusively on close quarters combat at night. Excellent work today."

"Thanks." I was really trying to hide my elation. I didn't want her to know how nice it felt to hear her say that. But her face went slack, and she tottered off toward our supplies without another word. She must've noticed.

I went to sit alone and nurse my bruises. Iris hadn't taken it easy on me, and my combat skills had only evolved to the stage of eating slightly less sand, but I was still pleased with myself. I kept flexing my fingers and staring at my throwing hand, like the answer had been hiding somewhere in my palm all along. Am I actually...skilled at something?

I grabbed Raindrop's sling-and-snatch bags from my pack, held them for a moment, rolling the three colors in my hand. I juggled them with one hand and half-whistled through my fingers. They fell at my feet, one at a time—each with its own unique thud, different sizes and weights. As I gathered them up and stared off westward where Raindrop had been following, I wondered what she must be doing. Hunting, flying, chasing us. Maybe she'd given up and gone back to Dex.

Metallic footsteps sifted the sand beside me, and a blue light cast across the dunes as Clark sat down.

"I just caught her smiling," he said.

My arm tightened with goosebumps. "Didn't think that was possible," I said with a smirk of my own. "And all it took was her beating the shit out of me."

"You know it was more than that."

I wasn't prepared to poke around in that wound just yet. "Maybe."

Iris called from the Sun Sister between sips of water and heavy breaths. "We'll follow the canyon tomorrow. There's a Nest on the way. Won't be on the registry. We'll shack up there for the next cycle."

A Nest not on the registry? To my knowledge, there was only one Nest in the direction we were headed—the one I'd been pulled out of fifteen years ago.

I'd been thinking about it constantly when I learned where we were going. I was curious if it would spark anything in me—maybe fill in some gaps.

"Get some sleep," she called. "Long day tomorrow."

I wanted to talk to her about it. Is it enough that we were both alive? Does she think about them as much as I do? Her face was just so hard to read. In an instant, she could go from neutral to boiling.

Most of the time, she didn't strike me as the kind of person who would lock themselves away for days at a time. She was volatile, but not fragile. Maybe I wasn't paying attention, or I wasn't asking the right questions. I sauntered down to get a sleeping bag.

"You know Dex pretty well, right?" I asked. "What's the deal? Why'd he stay behind? He made such a big fuss about going without me."

"He never intended to come," she said.

"But he—"

"He played you." She laid down on her pack with her arms behind her head. "A stiff breeze could kill that ginger old fart. You think he'd survive out here? Use your head. Before you two showed up, I was the plan."

He played me? Dex hadn't convinced me to do anything. Renner and Varic were already my targets, and I was going to find them with or without his help.

"I don't get it. What's the play?" I asked. "Why tell me he was going at all?"

"Don't know." She rolled away from me.

"Why would he—"

"I. Don't. Know." She pulled her pack over her ears. "Don't care. Sleep."

Clark came over and laid down beside me. He linked his hands over his chest, and he stared up at the stars. "Perhaps it was to convince himself." There was admiration at the edge of his voice.

"Of what?" I asked.

His eyes were slowly rotating. I wondered what he could see far off in the night sky.

"That his absence from the world was worth it." He ran a finger across his metal grin. "I like to think I know my creator well. And I believe his lie was a response to your indictment—that he was hiding away from the world and its troubles. I think he was trying to tell you; I would go if I could."

"Hmm." I thought about the smoke rising—how badly I wanted to run and check on them. And I thought about the decision I was making now. To ignore it. To do other work.

"Great. We solved the mystery of the world's least interesting man," Iris said from beneath her pack. "Now shut up and go to sleep."

Dex had done years of lonely work, knowing the world around him was coming to ruin, knowing smoke would be rising every day, and he'd be unable to help. Now, I understood how he must've felt, just letting it happen. It was starting to feel normal.

Life on Galilei could cause calluses to form. Those calluses were usually invisible, but they weren't immaterial. They protected us when an impossible decision demanded action—where tenderness or pain might get in the way. Because sometimes, to cut the head from the serpent, you have to ignore what the tail is doing. Even if it's choking you to death.

I fell asleep again with Renner on my mind. The night he took Saph. I couldn't shake the thought of what he must've done to her. Or why he even took her in the first place. I was the only person who saw what happened. Would it help to tell Iris what Renner said? About how Saph died, how he tortured her? Maybe we both had a lot to say, but no way to say it. How do I help her?

I decided I was going to try. When the time was right.

Iris looked like she hadn't slept a wink. She was quiet and nervous as we packed up and started the day, and she kept dropping supplies and huffing in frustration. I was about to approach, but she kicked the rubber wheels. Twice. Then a third time. Not now. Patience. Wait for the right moment.

The Sun Sister glided over the smooth rock of the southern mesas, right alongside the Rustyard. The mountains were shorter than those in the north but also wider, and there were no snowy caps or jagged peaks—just meandering slabs of smooth crimson stone, slammed against one another at varying elevations. There'd be no crossing them without heavy equipment, just as Iris had said.

We passed our old Nest early in the day. It snuck up on me. I could tell where it was, but not what it was. There was nothing left but a hole in the mesa walls. No ash or bones or refuse to remind us of what had happened or that people had lived there once—no memorial of our shared tragedy. I stood up and tried to see the flue, but it was impossible unless we got closer.

I thought I would feel something more profound. Pain, bitterness, closure. But I was just confused. Even the terrain looked nothing like I remembered. How odd.

I sat back down and turned to Iris to see if it had jogged her memory, maybe fill in some of my gaps or be an opportunity to reminisce. But her eyes were closed, and she was sweating profusely.

Her white knuckles squeezed over the wheel, and her arms were trembling. She suddenly veered hard to the north, away from the Nest, and gasped for air like she'd been holding her breath all morning. She was hyperventilating. We swerved back and forth.

I reached over and put a hand on the wheel to steady it. Iris turned to me with teary, bloodshot eyes and barely managed to choke out, "help," as the vehicle came skidding to a halt.

"Clark, take the wheel," I shouted. I had to practically peel her hands away from the wheel as Clark climbed into the driver's seat. "Come on. Sit here in the back. Take a drink."

She struggled to hold the water siphon in her hand, as she stumbled into the rear seat. "I-can't-breathe." She was scratching at her neck and gasping for air.

Clark started the rover back up and started driving us away from the Nest.

"Hey. Look at me," I pulled her hands away from her neck, but she resisted. "Come on. Look at me."

She shook her head. She was sobbing in high-pitched whines, muttering something I couldn't understand.

What am I supposed to do? I squeezed her hand and pressed my forehead to hers. "Come on. Talk to me. I'm right here. Iris."

She shoved me, hard. I held on. Clark turned back to me, and I looked at him for help, but he just gestured for me to continue. And do what?

"Hey, uh," I stuttered my way through. What can I say? How do I help you? "Remember when Rile brought that baby connivore home?"

She tried to pull away from me. I simply held her hand, just enough to not let go, to remind her I was there.

"I'd never seen you that mad. You said you'd cook both of them if he didn't put it back where he found it. Remember that? He said, yes, ma'am. You made sure we always called you ma'am."

Iris just winced in response, like the mere mention of Rile's name was a dagger to her heart. She leaned limply away from me, mouth half-open, moaning, still unable to catch her breath. She banged her head against the metal bar behind her, harder and harder, so I put my hand behind her neck and pulled her in.

"But he just stood there, and he started crying," I continued, "because he didn't know what to do. God, he was always crying, wasn't he?"

Her body was still shaking, and her throat squeaked as she inhaled.

"Do you remember what you did next?"

She pulled her hands in close over her chest and took some deep breaths.

"You told him you'd do it. Remember? And you took care of it. You brought that thing back to the hive all by yourself. He cried the whole time you were gone too. You were always doing stuff like that for us."

She squeezed my hand so hard. I didn't know if any of this was helping, but she was listening.

I squeezed back. "Back then, I was sure you did it because you were the adult. You had to take care of business. But I get it now. You just couldn't stand to see him cry. You were actually the biggest baby of us all."

She stifled a laugh that quickly turned to tears again, and she shoved me in the chest. But I could finally understand what she was saying. She was repeating, "I'm sorry," over and over.

"I never blamed you," I lied. Whether it was for her or me, I didn't know. "I just wanted you back. I needed you."

She broke under those words.

"Because I know who did it. I saw Renner's face, and I have his name. I even stuck my brela in his back. I'm gonna finish the job for Maksy, Rile, and Saph. And for you and me—for what he put us through and what he's still putting us through. But I can't do it by myself. I still need you. For the hundredth time."

Iris sniffled a few deep breaths and opened her eyes to check the horizon. We were past our Nest. A tearful sigh of relief. She wiped the dribbles of snot on her sleeve and rested her head against the metal bar, exhausted. She gave me the slightest nod.

"Good. Listen. Clark and I will manage for a while. Just rest up."

It took her a few more minutes to fully catch her breath again, but once she calmed down, she conked out and spent the rest of the afternoon snoring in the back.

I snuck a glance now and then to check on her. The Iris I knew was still in there, under the tough exterior, even if she bubbled out in unpredictable ways. I started to worry why I hadn't reacted the way she did—why I was so disconnected. Her reaction seemed natural, far more than mine. But I couldn't make myself be or feel those things, even when I knew I should.

"Look, Gaius," Clark pointed stormward, to the east. "Supercell is approaching at eight-two kilometers per hour. Faster than average. We must find shelter quickly."

I pulled out the map Dex had given Iris. The imagery was vague, drawn mostly in large, childish shapes. Was this Dex or Iris? There was another Nest nearby, but I couldn't tell how far away it was.

"Keep your eyes open, Clark."

Ominous clouds brimmed ahead of us over the eastern horizon, and distant rumbles belched out from the white-flashing smiles of the Tempest. We were making good time, but the days between storm cycles were growing longer again and less predictable. The longer the inhale, the greater the exhale. Three days at our speed, heading stormward meant about five days between cycles for everyone staying put. Three was the average. It was going to be ugly, but hopefully it would be enough to keep the fires at bay for a day. A rare silver-lining.

"There—hold on," Clark yelled as the dunes dropped out beneath us. We dipped several meters into a massive basin of mudrock with dozens of deep pits. Iris jolted awake.

The whole vehicle bounced violently back and forth as we skittered across the rock surface. Clark yanked the wheel to avoid the gaping holes, and I was losing my grip on the bar in front of me. Shit—

We came grinding to a halt, and I flew outward, tumbling across the mudrock in a barrage of skin and bones.

Ow. I slowly peeled myself up off the ground. The stitches on my leg had held. Small victory, thanks to Iris's skilled needlework. I rotated my limbs. Nothing broken, but everything hurt. I waved to them, to let them know I was fine.

Clark and Iris guided the Sun Sister down into a shallow pit, cranked stabilizing augurs down into the rock, and tarped the supplies.

I was watching the east where the storm was advancing. The clouds were expanding upward far more than average. I hoped Raindrop wasn't still following us. She wouldn't be able to get above a storm that size.

Clark bolted over to check on me, but he stopped short before one of the deep holes. He waved below. "Hello, little one."

I limped over and saw a chubby face and two eyes, girlish and scared. She stared up at Clark. The Nest was meager, perhaps meager enough to avoid unwanted attention. It was in the middle of nowhere, far too close to the canyon. They weren't on any packbrat route I knew of. I pushed Clark back.

"Don't be afraid," I said.

Iris pushed me away beside Clark. "Brin?" She called into the Nest. "It's me."

"Iris?" An older feminine voice called from inside. "What are you doing here?"

A woman came into the light. She was quite a bit older than Iris, with strands of silver coursing through her straight, lustrous, dark hair, which fell about her shoulders.

She pulled her child into the flowing layers of her graycloth as a cracking arc rolled over the dunes beyond. Iris hopped into the Nest, waving us in behind her.

"Please, make yourselves comfortable," Brin gave a curt bow, guiding her child away from the opening.

Clark hopped down and helped me inside. It was notably comfortable for a hole in the ground. There was enough space for us all and then some, even for Clark's head, and it was deeper than it appeared from outside.

The floor was sloped upward in the center and had two long water trenches along the walls, lined with fine sand, filtering into various pots and jars at the end. Inelegant but functional.

I'd heard the desert dwellers were mostly dewroot farmers, supplementing their diet with mushrooms and insects, but here, fish hung from the ceiling above dying cinders. We didn't have fish up north. Raindrop would love this.

Amid the stench of fish and smoke was an ever-present perfume of sweat and petrichor. It was cozy, and smelled of our people. A proper Galileian home.

Brin was sitting cross-legged over a coarse blanket at the rear wall where the water was filtering. She pulled the young girl onto her lap and followed Iris with sharp eyes. There was clearly history between them.

"Please, Brin." Iris took a seat against the right wall and removed her pack. Lightning flashed across the walls as Iris rested her eyes. She still seemed shaken. Maybe by the near-crash or our little trip down memory lane. "We're just here for the night. No need to speak to each other."

"I can speak in my own home," Brin said, "and you don't get to decide that here." She combed the toddler's curly hair through her fingers.

"Whas dat?" the little girl whispered. She pointed with her chubby fingers at our towering Secondhand Jack.

"My name is Clark." He bowed his head and extended a hand. "And who are you, little one?"

She hid in her mother's graycloth. Brin smiled. "This is Nello. Tell him how old you are, Nell."

Using both hands and biting her lip with concentration, Nello forced three awkward fingers together, which she held high above her head. She collapsed into her mother's lap in a giggle fit.

"She's actually four, and she knows that." Brin snuggled Nello. She looked at me. "Are you hungry, dear? You look practically starved."

"Oh, no." I hitched up my pac., "Thank you, ma'am. I've

had plenty." Though, I wanted nothing more than to try a piece of smoked fish.

"For a true raincoat, it's no trouble," she insisted.

She must've seen my brela. "Oh, I'm not—"

"—He's a packbrat," Iris said. "And he said he's fine. He'll survive—" but she stopped suddenly. The room grew cold. What is it with these two? Like walking on eggshells.

Brin's expression was more cheerful than her voice. "Don't stop there," she said. "You know all about survival. Don't you? Enlighten us. Should he be just like a raincoat? Strong. Smart." She shot her hand through the air. "Swift as the wind!"

"Brin, please," Iris said softly, finally looking at her.

"No, really." Her dark smile only convinced little Nello. "What kind of reckless idealism did you weave for this one? Did you tell him the same things? Or..."

She stopped and appraised Iris. Her gaze was unforgiving, cold.

"Have you changed? You did chop off all your lovely hair. Wearing some new scars too." She stroked Nello's hair with a stern look. "A shame really, to see what you've become. All that charisma. And that smile. Gone. Cole would be so disappointed."

"Cole?" Clark asked. "You were familiar with Cole—" Iris slugged him good in the arm. He nursed the metal there.

"Were?" Brin said.

"He's out there." Iris sat forward. "You know he was better than the rest of us."

"He is better," Brin replied, "and we'll be here when he finally comes back. Just like we promised. Right, Nell?"

Iris was probably spinning the same platitudes we'd all been trading with one another since the fires started, the same lie: that someone we loved could still be out there. I stole a glance at Iris. Only my lie had come true.

Cool wind howled through the Nest and flashes bounced from wall to wall in cadence with the cracking thunder. I could barely hear it rumbling over the tension in the room. I considered waiting outside.

Footsteps thumped above us, and we all reached for our

weapons. An older man, dripping wet, hopped down into the Nest. He looked as tall as Clark—taller even, and his head almost scraped the ceiling.

"Da!" Nello shouted with a bounce.

He slipped on the wet rock when he saw us. "Who the—"

His gaze fell on Iris. A grin stretched beneath his bushy mustache, and his eyes went soft and were full of life. He turned and reached upward to slide a makeshift gate closed, just enough to keep out the excess rain.

"Iris. It's good to see you." His voice was deep and slow, like rolling thunder.

"You too, Foss." Iris pulled her knees up to her chin and meekly stared up at him through them.

"So." He looked optimistic. "Any luck finding our boy?"

Iris hid her face between her knees. Foss walked over, crouched down, and rubbed her head.

"Hey," he whispered with a smile. "Don't worry. He's a raincoat." He got up and took his daughter into his burly arms, bouncing her with little effort. "Well, friends, the Tempest is stirred up tonight about something. Might be a while. You're welcome to stay as long as you need."

"Of course they can," Brin said. All the tension in her voice had melted away.

I didn't often wonder what it might feel like to have a living parent. It was common enough on Galilei to grow up without one. But when I saw how Brin softened, how Nello lit up—I recognized the appeal in having someone who could make you feel like everything would be okay. I remembered when Lars hugged me and the safety I felt. But falling too hard for comfort was dangerous.

Foss nodded to me with a twinkle in his eye. But he utterly ignored Clark. I found that strange. Not even a glance in his direction. He kissed Brin on the cheek and handed Nello over.

That's when we heard the sound. Heavy, piercing, and mechanical. A humming frequency separate from the storm. One flew over. Then another. And another. Seven of them, in perfect sequence.

I squeezed the handle of my brela. "It's them."

CHAPTER 16 - TRAINING

I awoke to Raindrop grinding her beak in my ear, daylight on my face. The sliding gate was open.

"Whoa. What are you doing here, girl?" I whispered with a groggy rasp.

I got to my feet and peered around with morning eyes. Foss was gone, but everyone else was still asleep. As usual, Clark looked awake, but I'd learned to tell the difference. His eyes wouldn't rotate when he was powered down. Iris had her hands tucked between her legs and her mouth was open and drooling as she snored. I allowed myself a smile at her expense.

With Raindrop on my shoulder, nuzzling me, I crawled out of the Nest on my tip toes. I ran down the dips and waves of mudrock up to the shallow pocket where we left the Sun Sister. Those augurs were exceptional. The vehicle was still in one piece and had only sustained minor damage—a dent here and there, some tears in the canvas, and a couple cracked solar panels.

Despite being thrown from the vehicle yesterday, my legs felt great. And it was nice to finally have something solid beneath my feet again. I hadn't run in quite a while.

Raindrop started to screech, but I hushed her. "Quiet, or we'll get caught." She shoved herself into my neck again and again, reminding me she was there. "I know, girl. I missed you too."

I scratched her head and got sling-and-snatch from the supplies. As soon as she saw the bags, she flew from my shoulder, gliding low across the surface. Then, like a spinning geyser of feathers, she shot up into the air and circled, waiting for my command.

I guided her out to the edge of the basin and with all my might launched the three bags in different directions.

Not yet. Not yet…

I whistled three quick cadences, each a distinct tone. She dove and spun, snatching the bags in perfect sequence, just as commanded. We hadn't lost a step. Before I could even whistle for her to come back, she returned, ready to do it again.

"She's smart," a voice called.

I turned to see Foss coming from the direction of the canyon, strings of fish hanging over his shoulder. My mouth salivated, and Raindrop's sable gaze was singularly focused.

"I didn't know there were so many fish down here."

He laughed. "The river is lively after the storm. Especially in the early morning. They practically swim right into your lap, almost like they want to be caught. You're welcome to take some."

He waggled a small one for Raindrop and tossed it high into the air. He blew a clumsy whistle. But she didn't even need the command. She darted off my shoulder and plucked it out of the air just above his head.

Foss ducked with a hearty laugh. "Whoa. And fast. She's a good hawk."

"The best," I said.

"The bird is a menace," Clark's voice called from behind. He was fiddling with the feather at the end of his glaive.

"And she obviously doesn't listen," Iris added. She looked rough—bags under her eyes and drool still stuck to her chin. "Get rid of her, or I will." She exchanged a glance with Foss for a moment, then looked away. "Let's get moving."

"It was good to see you, girl." I gently tugged on the fish in Raindrop's mouth. "But you got your meat, okay? Now head back. Go on."

I gave her a few extra scratches and an especially sharp whistle, and she flew back to the west. She always did listen better on a full belly. I'll sunbake her some mudmelon seeds when I get back. She loves those.

Before we left, Iris told Foss about Dex and the Looking Glass. He thanked her, but said they'd stay until Cole came back. I was worried about the risk Iris had taken. The Breacher was supposed to be the best kept secret in Galilei. I hoped her reason for telling him was more than just guilt.

Clark released the augurs, and Iris fired up the solar engine. We only had a few more days of travel before we reached our destination.

I spent most of the trip in the back, flipping my brela between different grips. I dropped it a couple times, but I was getting familiar with the timing and feel. Iris didn't seem bothered by my bungling either. I caught myself trying to impress her, but when I realized what I was doing, I felt like an ass.

What are you doing? Focus on Renner. On Maksy, Rile, Saph, Dim, Kai, and all the others. They required my full attention until the matter was settled.

With the storm cycles getting longer, we were safe to travel farther at night, but there were no more Nests to house us, and the area we were entering was outside the purview of Commonhope—unmapped terrain. We had to be careful. I was sure there were other elements besides the storm to watch for, even if I didn't even know what they were.

When we stopped for the night, Iris trained me on grappling. She showed me where human bones were most fragile.

"Enough leverage at the joint, and most snap like dewroot. Kinda sounds the same too." She was teaching me while her foot was on my neck, and my wrist and elbow were bent unnaturally behind my head between her knees. "But you don't want to be in a situation where you're on the ground, trying to break a bone. It's useful for disarming or disabling a single opponent, but try to stay on your feet."

"Got it," I grunted.

She gave me a chance to try a few of the techniques on her, always pushing me to apply slightly more pressure than I felt comfortable with. The gist of it was simpler than knife-fighting, but she was right. I'd only be able to take on one opponent at a time, and only from an advantaged position. I wasn't even sure if I had the stomach to snap a human bone. Renner? No problem. But someone else just getting in my way?

We spent a couple hours drilling more melee combat. She went slower, much slower. I was surprised to feel my body reacting. Not nearly fast enough to be useful in an actual fight, but I was making decisions—learning to be patient. I noticed things.

Her feet, hips, and shoulders moved before she'd strike. Her eyes watched my movements too, and I could play with her expectations. It felt like we were dancing. Her foot forward, mine back. Her hand up, mine to meet it. Lightning, thunder.

I feinted a left hook, noticed an opening as she ducked and moved in. I sidestepped her uppercut riposte, spun the training brela around my forefinger, and…it slipped. Shit. I braced to get flipped on my head again.

Instead, she picked it up and handed it to me. "What was that?"

"Sorry. I know. That was stupid."

"No," she said, flipping her own blade the way I did, but more skillfully. "I'm asking you: what was that? What was going through your head?"

"Oh. Um." I scratched my head. "You're fast. So I guess I felt like I didn't have enough reach with the downward grip. I thought if I could force you into that position and swap grips, it might take you by surprise."

She spun it around her finger again and smiled. "What you just did, that is the essence of what it means to be a raincoat. We don't fight the clouds, Gaius. And we can't stop the rain from coming. All we can do is expect the storm and prepare for it. We react. That's it."

It was starting to make sense. I couldn't believe it. I was beaming. Maybe I can do this. Maybe I am raincoat material. El would be shocked to see—

"Oh, wipe that smile off your face, packbrat." Her blade was under my chin in a heartbeat. "You still dropped your brela. Which means you're dead. Again."

We drilled until I couldn't stand. Clark watched from the top of a nearby dune the whole time, holding Toothpick by his side. I noticed him subtly dodging and parrying with his glaive.

When we were done, I was so exhausted Clark had to come down and basically carry me to bed. But I slept better that night than any I could remember.

The following day was grueling, hot, and long. By midday, it felt like the sun had stopped in the sky. All I could think about was getting back to training.

"What are we doing tonight?"

Iris threw a thumb over to Clark. "You're gonna fight him."

"What?" Clark and I shouted.

"It's idiotic to fight the same opponent over and over. Every person thinks and moves differently. You need to learn patience, not patterns."

"I have not agreed to any such thing," Clark said. "I am not adept at training."

"Besides, I'm getting the hang of it," I said, spinning the brela around my finger with relative ease.

"You're getting the hang—" She slammed on the brakes and turned back to me. "Do you actually understand what we're doing out here? What we're heading into? Do you? We're all that's left. No one's coming to save us. Which means we have to kill people." She paused. "They're gonna try to kill you too. And right now, they're a far cry better at it than you are."

That stung, and the training bruises all over my body were evidence in her favor, but I was improving every day. She wasn't giving me enough credit. Just like El.

"So tell me, how the hell can I trust you to watch my back if you don't even have the stones to fight Clark? What happens when it's a human being? Look at me. A man doesn't die like a gravehound, Gaius. He thinks and feels and begs for mercy. He screams for you to stop. When you kill him, you die right alongside him. Are you prepared for that?"

Even though her face wasn't hot with anger, her voice sounded cold and heavy, like lead. I didn't know what to say, but I wanted her to stop.

"And what if a woman comes at you? Huh? Can you take her down, break her neck, slit her throat? If you haven't already asked yourself those questions, then you don't have a fucking clue what we're doing out here. Say something that tells me you understand."

My heart was pounding with shame. I wanted to hide. I'd been such an idiot, caught up in celebrating the tiniest bit of progress. I forgot what our mission really was. "Yeah—yes, ma'am."

"Good," she said, driving off. "I don't hear you practicing."

That night, as I prepared to fight the world's last Secondhand Jack, I was in a fugue state. I just stood there, staring into the sand, hoping the ground would fall away and the world would swallow me whole. Clark drove Toothpick into the sand.

"Gaius, I have known you for many years, and I have witnessed your determination firsthand. The world in which we live does not abide weakness. Yet here you are. Still standing. A stone shaped by wind and fire." He made a fist and pressed it into my chest, then whispered. "Forward as always. Right?"

That was perhaps the least human thing about Clark—his ability to always know just what to say. I gave him a halfhearted smile. "Right. Don't take it easy on me."

He nodded, grabbed his glaive, and pointed the haft at me. I readied myself for the worst.

"React," Iris's voice was still heavy. She was sitting atop a dune with steepled fingers over her mouth. "Just react."

I breathed steadily through my nose and kept my peripheral focus on Clark's feet. She was right. He didn't move the way she did.

Without any anticipatory movement, his weapon whipped through the air and cracked against my shoulder. I almost dropped to my knees. I gasped like I'd been dunked in cold water. Goddamn, that's going to bruise.

"Are you alright?" Clark pulled away.

"Don't let up!" Iris stood up. "Our enemies won't." It was as if she was channeling El's voice. Sometimes I forgot that Iris trained under the Luminators too.

I steadied my feet under me. Focus. Okay. His feet didn't move at all, which means he has a reach and stability that Iris doesn't.

He also had no muscle or sinew, so his limbs could work without drawing strength from somewhere else—no tension or release, all independent movement. Those years watching him stretch and feign exhaustion—I must've bought some of the lie that he was made of flesh. But does this make him more predictable? Maybe I can just watch his weapon—

He swung, and I brought up my little wooden dagger to block the blow. Toothpick rebounded off my guard with a heavy twang. I stumbled back at the power of it. The strength he had was terrifying.

"Good!" Clark swung again. He's definitely taking it easy on me. I'd thank him later whenever Iris wasn't around.

"Watch his joints too." Iris was pacing along with us at the top of the dune.

I paid closer attention. His every swing was telegraphed milliseconds before the polearm moved—at the elbow and wrist, little lights would flare underneath his armored body, almost imperceptible. How much more was I missing that she could see? If it came to it, who would win? Clark or Iris?

It was thrilling—learning, adapting, improvising in the moment. I always wondered what it must feel like to be at the wrong end of Clark's glaive, but the truth was even more surprising: he's not invincible.

Duck. Advance. Connect. Sidestep. Feint. Misdirect. Deflect. Did he just take a step back? I just made Clark take a step back!

I swapped to an upward grip, stepped forward with my shoulder and hip, and jammed my weapon into his chest with all my strength. Wood cracked and splintered against metal, as my blade slid into the tiny rusted hole in his chest, right where his heart should be.

If he was human, and my brela had been real, he'd be dead on the ground.

Clark looked down at himself. His eyes were moving rapidly as he studied what just happened. He looked back up at me and tapped Toothpick on my shoulder. I could feel the smile bent into his face. "Once more?" he said excitedly.

I'd give him everything I had. "You got it, Jack."

We fought for another hour before I got a little too cocky and caught a stray swing across my temple. I came to consciousness sometime later with the taste of metal in my mouth. My pounding head was resting in Iris's lap.

"—and I cautioned you about my ineptitude in training," Clark shouted at her. He was pacing, and his hands were on his head. "I have killed him, and it is your fault."

"How does that make any goddamned sense?" she shouted back. "Besides, he's not dead. And I thought you were gonna take it easy on him? You were the one with the stick."

"It is called Toothpick! And you specifically told me not to!" His gears wound up at alarming speeds, and he pointed an angry finger at Iris. "You—if he should die, I will tie you to a rock and toss you into the canyon."

"Oh, I'd love to see you try, lugnut."

"You are the most infuriating woman—"

"So, I must be in hell then," I grumbled.

Clark immediately ran over and knelt beside me. "Gaius. You and I will never trade blows again. I promise. I will never let harm come to you in any way."

"Relax, big guy. It was a good lesson not to underestimate you—one I won't be forgetting anytime soon. Well…unless you broke my brain."

He held his fingers near his mouth.

"But you did surprisingly well," Iris said. "By my count, you only would've died thirty or forty times, and you would've taken a couple Clarks with you. Who knows…might've been more if you did some throwing."

She was stroking my hair. I didn't want to move or mention

it or remind her she was capable of softness. It was nice, reminiscent of another time—back when I'd gotten sick after eating rotten mushrooms. She'd stayed by my bedside all day, changing washcloths, keeping the hair out of my eyes, cleaning my puke bucket. Iris had always taken care of me. She still was.

"I'm so glad you're alive," I said. The words tumbled out of my mouth like loose stones down a mountainside; I couldn't stop them. I probably wouldn't have said it if I wasn't slightly concussed—at least not so sincerely.

She stopped stroking my hair and dropped my head on the ground.

Ow.

"Yeah. Well—" She stood up and slurred together a few nonwords before settling on, "You still need more training."

"Noted," I said, but I knew what she meant. I'm glad you're alive too, Gaius.

I didn't dream that night, or at least didn't remember if I had. Under different circumstances, I'd think it was the concussion. But recently, my nights had been calmer, almost serene. I wasn't used to not being haunted in my sleep. I could hardly believe it when I woke up. No lingering anxiety or stomach pain, just exhaustion in my muscles—the kind that felt like progress.

Iris was chatty, arguing with Clark about how to repack the supplies more efficiently. She looked more like herself.

"Today's the day," I said. They both turned to me.

"Yeah." Iris was chewing on more licorice root.

Clark lodged Toothpick between the seats. "Whatever lies beyond the canyon, we will face it together. Varic awaits."

CHAPTER 17 - TITAN'S GRAVE

It was good to be in the wind again, and the rover was moving well, drunk on the sun. As we crested past the last mesa, the Titan's Grave opened next to us like a scar across the world. We came to the edge where there was a sharp drop off into a thin, muddy-red river far away at the bottom.

The canyon was maybe fifty meters across at our current location but widened considerably farther east. According to Iris, our destination was a mere two hours away where the canyon was widest. My leg was bouncing. We were getting close.

I saw a hawk in the distance, maybe a couple kilometers behind us. It was soaring high on the summery winds. *That's not Raindrop. She'd be diving after us. It's bigger, older.*

"Clark, is that El's hawk?"

He stood and examined the sky, focusing hard on the small shape circling above. "Indeed, that is Derecho. The cipher also appears sealed. I wonder for whom it is intended, so far south."

"Should I whistle for him?" I asked. "Find out? We can always send him back. Reseal it."

"We're not stopping," Iris said. "If it's for us, he'll follow the scent. If not, we're just getting in the way."

"I put no credence in the bird either way," Clark said. "Though, I admit my curiosity is piqued. At least we know Luminator Eloanne is keeping herself busy. So too should we."

Iris bristled with incomprehensible muttering at the mention of the Luminator as Derecho faded behind wisps of fluffy cloud. I wondered how many raincoats El managed to find. Maybe I'll get to meet more than Andica.

In the hot afternoon, we arrived. Iris had not exaggerated. The canyon was at least three-hundred meters across and over a kilometer drop, with nothing but hard rock and river at the bottom.

As we all sat marveling at the sheer enormity of it, I turned to Iris. "Why here?"

"Those raincoats El sent down," she surveyed the other side. "They never even made it over. When they found the bodies, they'd been brutalized. I don't know the specifics, but Dex said they've probably got machines doing nasty work. Supposed to outposts across the other side of the canyon. Everywhere but here. At least, that's the hope, based on what little information Dex could gather."

"So this was always a gamble." I took a long drink of water under the piercing sun. Looking at the distance, I could see why. "I guess it doesn't make much sense to guard something that can't be crossed."

"Correction. What Varic believes cannot be crossed," Clark said. "Now we show him the error of his ways."

Iris carefully edged the Sun Sister to the lip of the canyon and pointed the nose perpendicular with the other side. We hopped out, and each of us manned one of three cranks—two in the back, one up front.

Clark finished before Iris and I, having hoisted the front end with a retracting bipod support, angling the nose by thirty or so degrees. The rear cranks bored the augurs straight down into the rock. Something cracked deep in the canyon wall, like too much weight on a frozen lake.

I turned to look at Iris.

She stared back and waited. When nothing happened, she breathed a sigh of relief. "Alright. We gotta do this now. In one go. There's no second chance."

We crowded behind the rover. Nearly a week lugging it across the Rustyard, but without a prior test, there was still no guarantee of success. Iris exhaled heavily as she lifted her hand.

"Wait." My back tightened. "Shouldn't we—"

She slammed the release switch. The Sun Sister kicked back and exploded with such kinetic energy that it cracked the stratum beneath us and scattered dust and sharp debris into the air.

The anchor erupted from its holster and whistled across the expanse carrying the carbon cable with it. After the backfire put us on our asses, we scrambled forward on all fours to watch.

The grapnel sailed through the air at an unbelievable speed. Just as the arc started to dip, it smashed into the opposing wall, piercing a full meter of sandstone, just below the lip.

I couldn't hear a thing besides the ringing in my ears. A haze of carmine dust sputtered from the far cliffside as the interior anchor opened and locked in place. The line twinged with slack as it came to rest with a slight sway in the wind.

"Whoa," my voice sounded hollow in my own head, until my hearing returned all at once, accompanied by the whooshing of blood.

Clark lifted me to my feet. "Whoa indeed."

"Now, the hard part," Iris wiggled her finger in her ear. She recoiled the tether until it twanged taut across the Titan's Grave.

"What if someone heard that?" I asked.

"Like I told you," Iris said. "No outposts around here. Gotta trust Dex. It's his plan. After we get over the Grave, we'll have to start improvising." Iris tugged and hung on the line to make sure it was secure. "You're up first, lugnut."

Clark stretched his knees and pulled his arms tight across his chest. He approached the cliffside, sufficiently primed, and reached for the cable. One hand over the next, he swung across the canyon without a second thought.

"Now you." She swung her head for me to go.

I wasn't quite as eager. I'd finally gotten on solid ground, and I was looking forward to using my legs for their intended purpose. Instead, I was supposed to hang myself over a hungry mouth like the last plump thunderfruit on a vine.

I stood at the edge, looking into the canyon below. Under different circumstances, you might say it was beautiful—a true marvel of nature—but I could only think of the color my corpse would be, floating down river like a cautionary tale to no one. Or the sounds I might make as I fell for a full ten seconds.

I let go of the cable several times before Iris laid a gentle hand on my back. "I'm right behind you."

That felt more like a threat than a comfort, coming from her. With an exhale, I grabbed the cable with both hands and pulled my feet up around it. I stared back at Clark who had nearly reached the halfway point. His humming felt out of place, but it wasn't the worst tune to go out on. My hands pulled my dragging feet, which were crossed and shaking.

The cable dipped as I came over the edge, and my stomach dropped.

"Don't stop." Iris pulled herself up. "And don't look down—"

"—I may as well let go now if you think I'm that stupid."

All I could think about was the river below. I was going to disappear in a hunk of boney clay, and they'd never even find my body. Titan's Grave. No. Packbrat's Grave. Gaius's Grave. Graveyard Of Idiots.

I pulled myself along in apprehensive strides as Iris closed the distance between us. It was either two minutes or twenty before I reached the halfway point, sweaty and slippery. The hot sun was beating down on me, and I had the uncontrollable urge to look down. My neck was tight with anxiety, my eyes were stinging, and my arms were getting tired.

"Don't. Stop." Each word fell out of her with its own heaping scoop of ire.

"Like this," Clark shouted from the other side, mimicking his own movement across the cable, which was plainly unhelpful in my position.

I grumbled obscenities through clenched teeth at every dip of the cable as Iris inched toward me. Then, before I'd even realized it, I was pressing my forehead to the rock face on the other side and looking up at Clark's brand-new hand—somehow the most inviting thing I'd seen all day. He pulled me up as if I weighed nothing at all.

Iris was right behind me, and her frustration was as palpable as the sweat beading across the bulging vein in her forehead. Clark pulled her over the cliff.

"Sorry," I muttered.

She shouldered me and stomped up the hill without a word.

Ahead of us, there were towering, narrow slot canyons of sandstone leading over a ridge. Some crags above balanced at a single point with nothing but their own weight to hold them there. We shimmied through the crumbling remains.

As we came through, over the top, a completely new world spread out in front of us, and the air in my lungs went still.

In hundreds of parallel rows running like green veins through shallow water, several kilometers of thunderfruit were being tended by a fleet of Secondhand Jacks, all polished, painted white, and gleaming in the afternoon sun. Clark's eyes waned as he took a step back.

My heart was thumping in my ears. It wasn't a mass of monstrous Skavers beyond the Titan's Grave. It was a civilization. At least, the makings of one.

"How…?" I turned to Iris for answers.

She'd hidden herself back among the crumbling crags. She wasn't panicking, but there was anxiety on her face—the same I imagined on my own.

What the hell are we doing here? I followed Iris's eyeline eastward to a pair of piercers hovering far off in the sky.

I suddenly felt very small. And scared.

Clark emerged and grabbed Toothpick. "Lies," he whispered and took off down the slope with purpose in his step.

Iris reached out to stop him, though half-heartedly, and he skidded down the slope without us. Dust and rocks tumbled in his wake. Iris pulled me into the shadows.

"What's he doing," she spat.

"At least a hundred Jacks down there, Iris." I looked at her until she felt my gaze on her. "You really didn't know."

Her silence and cheek biting said enough. Like me, she was searching for an answer. She leaned out to get a better view. "Dex told me about the outposts, but…this?" She shook her head.

We both got a good look from our vantage above the fields. As

Clark neared the bottom, the other Jacks showed no alarm at his presence—neither approaching nor retreating—only continuing to collect thunderfruit. They were talking to him, though I couldn't make out any words. He'd spend a moment with one and move onto the next and the next. His head stooped a little lower with every exchange.

It was his greatest honor to be named the last of his kind. The final triumphant survivor of the Secondhand Jacks. Yet down there he was just a rusty model number amid a hundred pristine automatons. Up until that moment, I always wondered why he took such pride in being the only one. But seeing him down there, among them—they were the last shiny new reminder that he wasn't really one of us.

"I can't leave him like that." I stepped forward, but Iris grabbed my pack.

"Careful," she whispered, one timid finger pointing up. "You hear anything buzzing or rumbling, and you get to cover."

"Yeah, I know."

She didn't let go. "Say it."

I pulled her hand off my pack. "If I hear anything, get to cover. Okay? Now, come on. There aren't any answers up here." I lifted her out of the shade, and we shuffled down the hill together.

When we reached the bottom, the Jacks just stared with taciturn disregard. As if we belonged there. It was an unnerving feeling. Clark was hiding under the hood of his stormbreaker.

"They insult me." His eyes rotated slowly.

Behind him, the others were bent at the hips collecting the lowest-hanging fruit. Like Clark, there was power and finesse in their movements, but no subtle smile had been bent into their jawlines, nor did they show any sense of personality. There was no sign of life at all.

The closest of them stood upright, triggered by nothing. "We will abide," it said, looking at me directly. "How shall we assist, keeper?"

"How shall we assist, keeper?" another asked, picking fruit.

Clark sighed. "They acknowledge your sentience, but I was repeatedly advised to withdraw to the harvest compound for restoration." He appraised his hands like they were foreign objects. "Which is a further insult, as they have declined to relay the location of any such compound."

I bumped him softly. "They're the ones that need restoration." His shoulders slumped a little less. I approached the nearest Jack. "We're looking for someone named Varic?"

Iris walked past us with her head tilted toward the sky, eyes flicking through the clouds. "Careful," she said.

"He holds private counsel with Luminator Bracken," the android responded. "How shall we assist, keeper?"

"Luminator Bracken?" I nearly shouted. "They've got Luminators? And who the hell is Bracken?" My question wasn't directed at the machine, but it answered anyway.

"Luminator Dario Bracken assists in governing Colony Six. He holds private counsel with Professor Varic Eshmun. How shall we assist, keeper?"

Professor? What the hell is going on? Why didn't they tell us any of this? What was the point?

"How much of this did you know?" I said to Clark.

"Very little," his voice was dispirited, detached.

"Dex, El—none of the Luminators know either?"

"I cannot say. A degree of privileged information was disseminated to me. But this," he gestured generally, "was not part of that discussion. I was certainly not informed that a society of people had settled here. I can only deduce that they are also colonizers from Heaven's Vault."

"What does that mean?" I asked.

"They're us," Iris said, continuing to monitor the sky.

"That's how they know about Dex and the Breacher," I said. "And that's why Renner knows El. When was she gonna tell me this? When I ran into one of my cousins? A goddamn uncle?"

"What does it change?" Iris turned to me. "Now we know. Knowing doesn't change our mission. Doesn't change anything."

"It doesn't change anything?" I laughed. "They let us believe a lie. Twenty plus years of my life. For what?"

Clark stepped forward. "Luminator Eloanne claimed it was

to protect—"

"—Well, maybe the kind of person who protects us from the truth isn't worth listening to," I said. "Whatever El's protecting, it's not us. Everyone died for her secrets, and we still don't know why."

Maybe 'Professor' Varic would know. With the right motivation, I could get him to elucidate some facts. But I still didn't know where he was or what awaited us between here and there. I didn't know a single thing about half the world. Dex was right. It was disorienting to turn on the lights.

"We need to move." Iris yanked me into the crop line. "Cover. Now." Her eyes were wild, not bothering with what was in front of us.

"How shall we assist, keeper?" one asked, too close for her comfort.

"Back off." She kicked it into the mud.

The android didn't skip a beat. "We abide." It rose to its feet with little effort, continuing to pick fruit as if nothing had happened. They stared at us with an eerie vacancy.

"We abide," another said as we passed.

"Where are we going?" I asked her. "We have no idea where we are. How are we supposed to find some key? It's a needle in a haystack, and we don't know what the needle looks like or where the haystack is."

"Qui-et," she whispered.

We crouched in the thunderfruit. I listened but didn't hear anything suspicious.

The perfume of nectar was on the breeze, earthy and sweet. Smelled like my childhood. At least there was that—something real. I carefully plucked one of the glossy green-turning-red fruits. They weren't quite ripe—still tart probably. "I wish Saph was here." I showed Iris the size of it. "She'd love this."

Iris shushed me and signaled us to crouch lower, her eyes fixed on the eastern sky.

I finally heard what she heard. Something was approaching, and fast.

"They will see us." Clark ducked his giant body as low as he could.

Iris put a hand on her brela (as if that would do anything), and in less than a minute, we heard them break the sky over us. The same mechanical thunder we'd heard at Brin and Foss's place. They passed over in the blink of an eye. Incredibly fast.

"We could probably do some damage with one of those," I said.

Iris pulled us deeper into the crop line. "Keep moving."

Every few minutes, we ran into another group of Secondhands who were ready to assist us or suggest repairs for Clark. We ignored them and skittered sideways through the stalks, which flapped in warm waves with the setting sun.

Nearly three hours had passed before we reached the end of the tall crop. I was still picking fleshy green fibers and seeds from my teeth as the daylight faded.

Between the first field and the next was a structure, flat and squared at the edges like a monument of pure-white. The building bore a single doorway at its center where golden light spilled out but had no other distinguishing features. Behind us, we heard the distant hum of flying machines careening over the horizon.

The Secondhand Jacks came filing out of the field from the same direction. Their heavy footsteps dredged up swirls of mud and murk in the shallow water. An android passed, and its eyes flickered at Clark as the top half of its body gyrated backward. "Withdraw to the harvest compound for restoration, designation CL4-K." It continued to walk while facing backward.

"Mind your own business," Clark whispered.

As the piercers flew overhead, I heard metal creaking inside Clark's palm as he tightened the grip around his glaive. "The sun is setting. If we follow their trajectory, they may lead us to Colony Six."

Iris gritted her teeth. "Fine. But we move slowly. Carefully. Never in the open."

We slinked past the Jacks and the compound as they carried baskets of fruit and seeds inside, filing in one after the other like clockwork. Is this what Clark was originally built for? That seemed offensive. I didn't want to imagine Clark as anything other than Clark.

I rested a hand on his shoulder as we ran through the fields.

"They're nothing like you."

He smiled at me—because he had no other choice—but I knew what was hiding behind it. "Thank you, Gaius."

Light peaked through the edge of the crop line ahead of us, but it wasn't the sun or moons. The source was just beyond a hill on the horizon. We came to the edge of the crop line and studied the night sky.

"Stay low," Iris said.

We crept to the ridge on all fours and looked below.

There were people, or rather, the sound of people—hundreds, maybe more—somewhere inside the mouth of a wide-open grotto, leading deep underground.

The cavern was swollen with laughter, yelling, babies crying, the murmur of conversations competing over one another to be heard. It came in waves, peaking and subsiding, though we couldn't see anyone.

"They're laughing," Iris said.

After everything they'd done to us, they were living in peace and safety. Thriving. Something sharp and hot roiled in my chest, swelled in my cheeks, tightened in my fist. What the hell was I angry at El for? They're the enemy.

Whatever doubt had lingered in my mind before our arrival, it melted away. Varic is going to die. Renner is going to die. Anyone who sided with them is going to die. I wanted Iris to ask me again—if I could do it. Slit their throats. Break their necks.

"Caution. Violence returns violence," Clark said. The feather fluttered from the end of his weapon. "It would be wise to complete our task and withdraw before it is returned to us."

No. I won't let them off that easily. Iris will understand.

She was calm, nodding to herself. "First, we take the key." She flipped her brela into her hand. "Then, everything else. They all die."

CHAPTER 18 - COLONY SIX

The entry to the grotto was empty. They clearly weren't worried about an invasion, but we stayed cautious as we crept inside.

It was the largest cave system I'd ever seen by a wide margin. Farther in, it fanned out like a delta, wider even than my field of vision. And somewhere—as if it was trapped in the walls or the ceiling—was the sound of rushing water.

Far off on our left and right were hundreds of cramped caverns that could lead anywhere. I couldn't make out any clear details. The underground was a labyrinth, much more complex than the mountains of Commonhope. If we weren't careful, we could end up walking for hours in the wrong direction.

A bundle of bright bulbs illuminated columns of knotted mineral deposits and cascades of brittle flowstones overhead, although half the bulbs were dead or dim. We kept under the rows of lights, which cast our shadows along pillars of smoky gray ore.

After a while, my eyes and ears started playing tricks on me—seeing figures approaching, laughing, sneaking up behind me. The cacophony of voices ebbed around us as we sneaked from one stalagmite to the next. With the sheer enormity of the cavern, it was impossible to tell where any of the sound was coming from, and no single voice was distinct enough to pick out—except for one.

A feminine voice, louder than the rest, was repeating a short message with robotic consistency, every half hour or so.

"Safety. Peace. Comfort. Community. These, Professor Varic Eshmun provides. Loyalty. Harmony. Duty. Self-sacrifice. These, Professor Varic Eshmun requires. None fall below. None rise above. All serve, so all survive."

"What a bunch of bullshit," Iris whispered.

We heard the message a total of six times before I caught a glint of metal— supports holding up a crenulated corridor. Man-made. It was all-too-welcoming. And as we moved closer, the lights converged into a single array, away from the corridor and deeper into the subterranean hollow.

I nudged Iris and motioned to the corridor. "What do you think?"

Iris waved Clark over. "Take a look, Jack. What do you see?"

His eyes whirred as he glared down the sculpted passage. His hand tightened around his weapon. "There are many voices, though I am uncertain of the precise—"

"—Then that's where we go." She walked ahead of us.

Clark pulled back his hood and addressed her directly. "We should advance with caution."

Iris disappeared around the passage, as though Clark had said nothing at all. I looked at him with a shrug and followed.

There was barely enough light to see Iris's shadow rising and setting across the walls. Even that disappeared around a sharp bend. As we rounded the corner behind her, a wave of unnaturally warm air rushed over us. It smelled of oil and burnt iron. She stood before the opening of a bright room. Clark pulled her back, out of sight.

I had to turn my head to see it all. The chamber was clean— spotless, almost as if it was separate entirely from the cavern. The structure was reinforced with shiny angled steel beams, and the walls were made of white mortar like the harvest compound. It was as wide and tall as it was deep, a massive box that housed twelve of their prized flying machines. A whole bay of piercers. They were lined up in perfect sequence, polished, and each one had COLONY 6 scribed in bulky letters—the same sort of lettering I'd seen inside the Breacher.

Nearly a hundred people skittered about, outfitted in white and orange jumpsuits. They operated complicated machinery and rolled steel tables from one side of the room to another. Others hooked and unhooked tubes and hoses from the ships or performed a dozen other tasks my eyes couldn't follow.

Everyone was shouting at each other over the chaotic buzz of the room, but they seemed to flow, constantly shifting to make room for one another. I could barely discern a word. Then that same feminine voice cracked overhead, but with a new message. Everyone stopped to listen.

"Second phase piercer recall complete. Boltslinger and Ember squadrons prep for phase three. Ashdiver and Uproot squadrons on standby for maintenance. Grounded raincoats fall in for briefing." The voice went silent after a scratchy chirp, and they all returned to work—busier than before. They looked tired.

"What the hell is happening?" I was dizzy and confused. There was no way Clark and Iris knew about this. No way that El knew.

Amidst the bustle, four men in black suits with full-face oculums exited an interior compound made mostly of tinted glass on the far right. They strolled across the open area with another man in a pale red suit. I leaned in. He was quite a bit shorter than the rest and walked in front with a loose gait, exchanging smiles with everyone he passed.

The sea of people always parted for them. The other four's faces were obscured, but I knew who the short man in front was, holding his mask at his side. I'd never forget that fiery hair. He and his men were heading straight for us.

"That's Deek." I pointed at him. "He burned Harrow's place."

Iris and I stepped forward, but Clark immediately grabbed and yanked us back into the tunnel. He pinned us to the wall with little effort.

"Are you really that keen on running to your deaths?" He held each of us with one arm. "Do not meet them on their terms. They are coming to us. Let them. We practice patience and wait for our opportunity. Those were your words. Remember?"

Iris turned her head and huffed.

"He might know where Renner is," I said.

"Perhaps he does, but that information will be difficult for him to disclose with this in his belly," Clark pushed my blade down. I couldn't even recall drawing it. "We may yet achieve justice and answers if we strike when the time is right. I urge you both. Patience."

Iris's face contorted as she muscled out of his grip, slipped under the swing of his other hand, and darted behind him. "He's right." She walked back down the tunnel. "Let's get into position."

Clark's eyes flared brightly. "They will reach us in less than a minute. Come."

We fled on light feet back into the open grotto where we cracked a few bulbs and hid behind a lightless stalactite. We waited and listened. They took their time coming out. But as the crunch of their footsteps drew near, we all held our breath—even Clark. Their five silhouettes converged through an adjacent cavern. They'd all removed their oculums, but I still couldn't make out their faces in the dim light.

"Are they armed?" I asked.

Clark shook his head. "It is unclear. One of them carries a device I do not recognize."

Iris darted off without a sound, skirting up to the tunnel entry.

Clark and I moved to keep up with her. He couldn't help cracking and popping the cave pearls beneath his heavy feet, but thankfully it was drowned out by rushing water and the commotion of distant people. The babbling voices were waning but still seemed to number in the thousands. I hoped it was an auditory trick played by the underground.

We followed Iris into the passage at a fair distance, never too far off to lose them and never so close as to be seen or heard. The mostly dead lights overhead buzzed with the sound of overuse as they hung from bundles of dirty wire. One of the men laughed in the distance. Something boomed and panged like hollow metal.

"It's now or never." Iris bounded into the dark with her blade out.

"Wait." Clark reached for her too late, then squeezed his hand into fist. "Vexing woman."

"We're losing her," I said. "Come on."

She was always so deft on her feet, and we were falling more than a step behind. As we came around a bend, I watched her sneak into a small rectangular room with the five men.

She jammed her blade into one of their backs. "Who the hell—!" A black iron door slammed closed behind her.

"Clark, the door!" I sprinted forward with him at my side.

He tried to drive the butt-end of Toothpick beneath its frame to pry it open, while I pounded against it. It didn't squeak or budge, but there was some mechanical winding behind it. The room was moving—ascending somewhere. Clark stopped when his glaive began to bend under the pressure. He tapped his fingers on the barricade, testing it for weak points.

"They have her." My throat was closing as I remembered what Renner had done to Saph. I was pacing back and forth. "Come on. They'll kill her. Get it open."

He rammed his shoulder into the door, again and again, grunting with every collision. It rang out like a hollow bell but seemed otherwise unaffected. Only silver smears from Clark's shoulder were scratched across the seamless iron.

I traced my fingers around the edges to find some mechanism that might release it. "Why didn't she wait for us?"

Clark didn't answer. He simply switched shoulders.

To the left of the door was a flat panel. I pried it open with my brela. There were several clear, blinking buttons inside. I hesitated, then pressed one, then another, and another, but nothing happened. I slammed by fist into them all. "We have to do something!"

"Gaius. Back away." Clark retreated down the hallway about ten meters behind me. The mechanisms inside his legs whirred with rising energy. He erupted toward the door and slammed hard against it. It shifted. Not much—but it shifted. We looked at each other.

I nodded. "Go, go. Again."

He backed up to rush the door, but as he turned to run again, he skidded to a halt. The buzzing and low rumble inside the walls started back up. The room was descending.

I drew my brela and held it as Iris had shown me—capped with my thumb, blade down. It was time to put it all into practice. If they hurt her, I'll hurt them. If they kill her, I'll kill them.

The walls vibrated for a few seconds before a boom echoed, and the room came to a stop.

"They will mean us harm." Clark came up next to me. "Harm them first."

The door shifted backward an inch with a cracking thump, then rose slowly. My muscles tightened, ready to spring at the first sight of them. The leather of my brela hilt creaked with tension. We inched forward. I held my breath. Patience. Wait for an opening. Pay attention.

Deek was standing at the center of the room, surrounded by prostrate bodies, gutted and bled out, their faces contorted in painful visages. He was looking smug but tired, and he made no sound. His teeth were gritted in a bloody smile.

I darted at him, "I'll kill you—"

Then, as though some invisible string was cut, he collapsed loosely to the floor.

Iris was standing behind him and the other bodies, hunched over and breathing heavily with a bloody brela in her hand. Her fatigues were charred and dashed with ribbons of red, and her brow was bruised, matching a swollen bottom lip. The walls of the room were also seared with blackened streaks as though a lightning storm had passed through it.

"You're okay," I said, loosening all my muscles.

"Alive isn't the same as okay." She kicked Deek in the stomach as hard as she could. "They were definitely trying to keep this one alive." Deek moaned as she yanked him by the hair into a sitting position.

"He's still alive," I said.

"Barely," Deek said, holding his severed pinky with his other nine fingers. He was faking a smile through pained grimaces. "This was my second favorite pinky."

Iris put the heel of her boot on his sternum and pinned him to the wall. "This room goes up to another level," she said, ignoring him. "There might be more like him up there." The rubber of her boot squeaked as it inched toward his throat.

"More like me? Not on this planet," he laughed. "But now that you mention it, I saw some just like you a couple days ago. They gave a spectacular effort. Even killed a few pilots before we contained them."

I exchanged an obvious glance with Clark.

"So you did know them." Deek eyed me. "Thought so. Oh, don't look so grim. We always take special care of our guests."

Iris cracked her boot across his face, knocking him unconscious to the floor.

"Wait—" I grabbed him by the collar, but he just flopped limply in my grasp. I dropped him. "Iris, come on. What if it was El? The other raincoats?"

She scoffed. "Just a few hours ago, you were up in arms over El's lies. Make up your mind. And we can't trust a word he says unless we see it for ourselves." She jimmied open another flat panel inside the room. "I think this is how they closed the door and got this thing moving. There's a long clean hallway and a pretty-looking door up top. Seemed important."

Iris popped more licorice root in her mouth. She looked at us with that same dull face—an expression that said she didn't feel the scorched flesh on her arm nor the gravity of the situation.

Clark stepped toward the bodies. "What is behind that door, I wonder?"

"Didn't get a good enough look. One of them was using this," she kicked a long tapering baton through the door. It was made of some reflective black metal and had three segmented gold rings around the top end.

I'd seen something like it before. Deek used one to ignite the ferno at Harrow's Nest.

"It hurts like hell," Iris said. "The thing shocks and shoots sparks and makes a real goddamn mess." She crouched and flipped the handle of her brela toward Deek, prodding his unconscious body. "And this little jackass shut the door on me before I could get through. He's shifty. I don't like the way he fights. And he's not too concerned with dying either. Tie him."

"I leave that to you, Gaius." Clark dragged away two dead bodies.

"What's the move here?" I pulled rope from my pack. "We don't know anything about this place, and if El got here first with a group of raincoats and failed…" I shook my head. Couldn't think about it.

Iris nudged the last dead body out of the doorway. "I doubt they had a mouthy little prick to leverage. If they need this one alive that badly, that means we can use him. Probably."

"We can't rely on that. Or their goodwill." I tied Deek's hands behind his back. "They murder children. I saw it happen with my own eyes. Renner did it without remorse. These people…they're—"

The message played again from a perforated metal box in the upper corner of the room. "Safety. Peace. Comfort. Community. These, Professor Varic Eshmun provides. Loyalty. Harmony. Duty. Self-sacrifice. These, Professor Varic Eshmun requires. None fall below. None rise above. All serve, so all survive."

"That's really starting to get under my skin," I said.

"Me too." Iris lifted Deek to his feet and slapped him across the face. "Look alive, shithead. Got some questions for you."

CHAPTER 19 - THE LABS

Deek was much more forthcoming about what awaited us on the second floor after Iris threatened to bring his total finger count to eight.

"It's just suits up there," he said. "Whites and grays mostly. Awful bunch, but they make the wheels turn. Especially the bald one. The Professor's a curmudgeonly son of a bitch."

Iris yanked his arms up tight behind his back. "Varic?"

Deek managed a sly grin. "Ah. Thought so. Man, you lot are easy to read. Tell you what, if you can get inside, I'd be happy to introduce you on one condition."

"You don't get to make conditions," I said.

"Be that as it may, I politely request that you don't kill him. Turn his teeth into a necklace or something. Take his fingers—you're obviously into that. Just don't kill him."

"He'll get what's coming to him," Iris said.

"I don't care what happens to Varic," he continued. "I mean, I really don't care what happens to him. I woulda put that geezer in the grave years ago if I could. Look, it's hard to explain without you freaking out."

Iris pushed a clear button on the steel-paneled wall, which started blinking as the door shut us in.

"Try," I said, my palm resting on my brela.

"You hear that message?" He nodded to the box above us. "It's been on repeat for over a decade. Professor Varic Eshmun provides. Most of these people think he's some kind of prophet, come to cure all the world's ails, which has the reasonable minority by the short hairs. Dissenters get exiled to the Cistern, and everyone else is either a goddamn sheep or too scared or smart to speak up. I'm the latter, obviously."

"I still haven't heard a good reason for not killing him," Iris said.

He continued. "Even if you succeed, he's got the devil in him. You'd still lose. If that man dies, things go tits-up in ways you can't imagine. And not just for us. I'm talking full-scale, planet-wide, screaming catastrophe. You're better off jamming that knife in your brain."

"Or I could stick it in yours for what you did to Harrow," I said.

He laughed. "Harrow? Come on, kid. The old bird keeper? He's nobody in the grand scheme. His neighbor gave him up almost immediately."

Clark tensed his grip around Toothpick.

We reached the floor above us, and the door opened and revealed a pristine hallway, lit from above with wide panels of bright light.

I stepped out. I couldn't believe what I was seeing. They really are us. Clear as day, painted right there on the far wall was the gold emblem of Commonhope—two interlocking stars—where the hallway came to a T.

Deek nodded down the corridor. "Up there to the right, a big iron door leads back outside. You want the door to the left, tinted glass, takes you to the labs. Varic is locked in a room up the stairs at the end of the hallway. But you won't be able to get in. Only Luminators know the code, and I'm not one of them. Cut off all my fingers if you want."

"If you insist." Iris shoved him with her boot, and he stumbled out. "Shout or sneeze or say anything I don't like—"

"And you'll cut off a finger," Deek wiggled his severed digit behind his back. "Got it."

She kicked him again as we sauntered down the stark hallway, which was so eerily quiet I could hear my ears ringing and whooshing.

It sort of washed over and disoriented me.

"Where is everyone?" I whispered. "This doesn't feel right."

"You got lucky," Deek said, "Varic has the rank-and-file scrambling to find your Breacher. He's in a real panic over something--but you know, now I'm curious. Is old Harrow still alive?"

I gnashed my teeth. He clearly enjoyed antagonizing us, but I wasn't going to give him the satisfaction.

"No, I'm just saying," he continued as we turned the corner to the left. "Good for him. Dangerous times we're living in. Fires and whatnot. Will you let him know I'm keeping an eye on his owls? They're mounted right above my bed."

Clark tapped his fingers impatiently against his side.

"Anyone got something for his mouth?" Iris sighed.

Deek turned around and threw her a lecherous smirk, "I can think of a few things—"

Two of Deek's teeth went scattering across the floor as Clark's fist connected with his face—his face, which then connected with the wall, and subsequently, the floor.

"I can abide much," Clark said, lurching over Deek's crumpled body, which was lying on the floor drooling blood and groaning in pain, "but that sort of licentiousness directed at my dear companion merits a broken jaw. I suspect this is a lesson you will only need to learn once?"

Iris put her boot on Deek's back. "That wasn't rhetorical."

He nodded slowly, painfully. All the humor had gone out of his face. Good. He deserved worse. And he'd get it once we were done with him.

At the end of the hall, there was a tinted glass door with no handle or latch. It spanned from floor to ceiling with no visible seam, button, or panel.

"I…have seen this before," Clark said. "Though, I do not know where."

He approached slowly, then pressed his hand to the glass. An orange dial glowed and spun at its center. With a twist of his wrist, the door hissed and slid into a recess in the wall. Clark articulated his fingers and studied his hand. "Curious."

"That's an understatement," I said. "Maybe we don't need you after all, Deek."

He didn't make a sound.

On the other side, the hallway expanded in the same manner, but there were six more doors, three on each side, and a stairway at the end, just as Deek told us. Everything was still, dead silent—not even the buzz of electricity.

"The labs, I presume," Clark said.

Deek nodded.

"What's inside?" Iris asked. Deek shot her a look and moaned something indiscernible. He nodded his head to the door at the end of the hall. Iris smiled. "Something you don't want us to see? Well, let's take a look."

I pulled out my brela and readied myself. "Do your thing, Clark."

He opened the first door on the right in the same way.

Inside, I was reminded of why I started this journey—not for a key or information or even uncovering the lies I'd been told all my life, but for retribution.

At the center of the room, caked in dried blood and surrounded by metal trays full of sharp, violent instruments, was an empty reclined chair, the design of which could only be described as torturous. There were red-stained braces and thick belts for the neck, chest, wrists, legs, and ankles. Iron creeped through my nose and down my throat.

And in the far corner, in a chrome bin, barely large enough to fit Clark, was a stuffed-beyond-capacity collection of corpses in various stages of decay.

Vomit pushed through my teeth, as I leaned over a bucket filled with viscera and chunks of skin.

When I looked up, I saw her face. I wanted for it to be anyone but her. Anyone. She had plans in motion. They were going to fight back. And we were going to rebuild. She was supposed to be made of steel. I trusted her, then I hated her, blamed her, and spat on her legacy. But I loved her too.

"Eloanne," Iris whispered.

"It's not her," I said. I grabbed Deek by the collar and slammed him into the wall. "It's not her. Say something. Tell me it's not her. It's not El."

He just looked back at me with a smug, crooked smile. A throaty laugh bubbled up over his broken jaw.

"Say it. Say it!" I slugged him in the stomach, and he toppled over. "It's not her." I kneed him in the ribs. "That's not El. Say it."

He fell to his knees sputtering and laughing.

A cold metal hand came to rest on my shoulder. "She was gathering the remaining raincoats," Clark said. "We must assume they are also dead."

"No. I…I sent Lars back home. Clark, I sent him back."

"It is not your fault."

He was right, but the anger, the helpless frustration burrowed under my skin and seethed there. There was only one person I could direct it at.

"I know whose fault it is." I spun Deek around on his knees and put my blade to his throat. "Fix his jaw," I said to Clark. "I want to hear his last words."

Iris slapped her palm against the wall. A map of northern Galilei hung there with red circles drawn around familiar locations—Nests, granaries, fisheries, and the mountains.. "It could've been any one of us in that chair. But it wasn't. They interrogated her, tortured her, and found out who she truly was."

She ran her hand along the markings.

"Look at this," she said. "Do you see what I see? I see the Lady of Steel up there. Along with every good Galileian who knew how to keep their mouth shut. Look."

She pointed to the northern mountains where 'BREACHER???' was written in red.

"They still don't know jack shit, thanks to El. Which means we can finish the job. The one she gave you. So, get him up and into the next room."

"We don't need him," I said. I kicked Deek to the floor. "Clark can get us through any door."

"You don't know that." She walked over. "And you're not thinking straight. Ask yourself what that awful woman would tell you right now."

"She came here for blood. This is what she wanted—all of them dead."

"She wanted a future." Iris batted my blade away. He brow furrowed with confused anger. "Did you not know her at all?"

I swallowed the lump in my throat and stared her down. Of course I knew El. Why is she defending her? Iris should hate her more than anyone. And she should understand why I wanted to put Deek down.

I sheathed my brela and stormed out into the hallway. The ringing in my ears was growing louder. I couldn't think. What would El want? Why was she even here? She told me to follow Dex's plan to the letter. Find Varic. Get the key. Don't get sidetracked. Damnit.

Clark and Iris spent a couple more minutes in that room. I kept hoping they wouldn't find Lars. He shouldn't be in there. If I hadn't sent him back. Maybe he didn't get back quick enough. Maybe they left without him. Maybe he escaped.

"Andica and Karrigan are dead, along with some others I didn't know." Iris came out toward the first door on the left. "Didn't see Lars. But we'll check every room. Maybe someone survived."

Clark opened the next door, and I readied myself for the worst. But as it slid open, I just stood there, staring at the floor. I couldn't bring myself to pass the threshold, like seeing it would make it real.

Iris came back out a moment later. "Same sort of room but no bodies or blood. Nothing useful." She whispered as she passed me. "Come on, Gaius. We need you. Next room."

I was in a daze as we checked the next three rooms. The first was some sort of horticulture research lab. There were seeds and sprouts sealed in glass dishes. Dissected thunderfruit, dewroot, all kinds of fungus and local flora were set under some kind of examination device I'd never seen. Nothing helpful to us. Most notably, no Lars.

The next room contained a series of desks and chairs in front of machines like the digital library Dex showed me inside the Breacher—flashing screens with indecipherable numerical data, topographical imaging, and a buzzing blurry image of a man. The screens seemed to respond to touch. I flicked my finger over the blurry image, and he began speaking incoherently.

"This…Prime Lumarch So…Commonho…Ganymede. We r…distress beacon…Gali…twelve years…expect full cooperat…arrive…my command. The dereliction of duty…presence of…Skaver…catastrop…urvival…species. Cain Proximity is paramou…urvivors must also…cleansed."

Clark scratched his head. "I…do not know how I know this, but The Cain Proximity—that is an old colony protocol executed to extinguish all human life within a certain radius."

There was a date below the message: January 8, 2545.

"He said twelve years…" I tried doing the math in my head. "Clark, what's today's date—in Gregorian standard?"

His eyes rotated for a moment. "May 6th, 2556."

"So…eleven years and…four months from this date," I pointed at the screen. "Meaning…something is happening eight months from now? Clark, that's what Renner said to me. He said we only had eight months. This has to be why Varic is panicking, why he's rushing."

I sat down in the chair.

Iris touched the screen next to mine, and a massive visual projected across the wall behind us. There was a bird's eye view of a sea of people in an underground city—some part of the grotto we hadn't found yet—thousands of them. Living blissful, peaceful lives. I threw my brela, and it sunk into the wall up to the hilt.

I retrieved it and got a closer look at them. I wanted them all dead.

Clark sidled up next to me and watched. "We do not yet know the depth of their complicity. Power consolidates and obfuscates. Remember, even Luminator Eloanne hid the truth. These people may not know. We have more yet to learn."

He was right about that, but unfortunately, for the wrong reasons. In the second to last room, whatever hope I had died with the man strapped to the chair.

Lars.

He had been brutalized beyond recognition. There were bruises around the straps that held him in place. He'd struggled against his restraints. His lips and tongue had been removed, and much of his exposed skin was blistered with chemical burns.

I held his hand. "Why? He couldn't speak. He couldn't even tell them anything."

Iris shut his bloodshot eyes. "It wouldn't have mattered. He wouldn't have revealed Dex's location." She whispered to him. "Gentle giant. How did they catch you?"

"Iris, he was the one who pulled me out," I said.

"Lars did?" She ran distressed fingers over her shaved head.

"After the fire. It was him. And again at Reaper Springs. Why are they doing this? For a goddamn ship? What did he do to deserve this? How can they hate us this much?"

"Hate doesn't explain this. No reason would justify it." She took his giant hand from me, removed his restraints, and rested it across his chest

His limbs were still pliable. Did we only just miss saving him? I started to think back on how long we'd spent sleeping every night, how much time we'd wasted bickering and training, instead of getting there.

"One more room." Iris looked back at Deek. "Who did this? And I better believe you, or you're going in that chair next. Clark, his jaw."

"With pleasure." Clark grabbed the back of Deek's head and jammed his chin back into place with a crack and a yelp.

"Ah." He swiveled his jaw back and forth, clearly trying to hide his pain. "Look, I admit I'm a bit of a bastard, but I don't have the stomach for torture. There's only one man capable of that. Renner."

Of course it's Renner.

Deek continued. "There's something not right about him. He always follows orders. Always. It's like his rule or something. I heard he gets dangerous when he's bored. We all just stay out of his way."

"Cause you're just an innocent bystander?" Iris said, pushing

Deek back out into the hallway.

"I've killed my fair share. But I never did anything like that," he threw his head back toward the room with Lars. "And I saw what you did on that lift. Your hands aren't clean either."

"Shut up," Iris said.

I didn't stop Renner when I had the chance. I had the drop on him, but I wasn't good enough. And others paid the price. Bodies in a bin. And I still couldn't shed a single tear. Something's not right with me either. I could only muster fury, violence.

I remembered when Lars held me. I felt something then—like a pinprick of warm, inviting light. But I couldn't feel it now. There was just a gravity at the center of me—pulling at all my edges, making me thin. And Lars and his light were gone.

"Come." Clark opened the last door, and my stomach coiled tight.

Inside was a wide pane of transparent glass bisecting the room from one wall to the other. There was a warmly lit space on the other side. Bespoke paintings hung on the walls, and there was a bed and a writing desk covered in books, drawings, and scribblings. There was also a tray of half-eaten food resting on a u-shaped slit in the glass. Uniform markings covered every wall—dashes, more than I could count.

A young woman, around my age, maybe early twenties, was sleeping on the bed amid a huge mess of her own hair. She looked peaceful but frail.

"What the hell is this?" Iris spun Deek around to look at her.

"Hell if I know," he said. "I'm just a pilot. Never been here. Never seen her before."

"So I guess you were taking that lift up here for fun?" She got in his face. "No, I think you had business up here. Business you're used to conducting." He turned away from her and kept his mouth shut. Iris scraped her blade over his other pinky. "I guess nine fingers is still too many."

The young woman stirred in her bed. She rolled over and stretched her legs, groaning with fatigue. "Is that you?" she muttered, picking the sleep from her eyes. She stretched her limbs and yawned.

"Did you bring it? I'm tired of reading about old men and fish. Less Melville and Hemingway and more Austen, please." She looked in our direction but didn't react, as if we were invisible.

"I don't think she can't see us," I whispered.

"Luminator Bracken?" the young woman called.

"Who are you?" Iris asked her.

At the sound of Iris's voice, she stood up and pressed her hands against the glass, trying to peer through. She was thin, too thin, wearing loose-fitting garments—a soft material, pale pink with long sleeves and pants—though nothing on her feet. Her overgrown hair was bunched up inelegantly behind her. I didn't recognize her face. Maybe she's a raincoat.

"Has something happened?" she asked. There was hope in her voice. "Who are you?"

"Your name," I said firmly.

"Everyone here calls me Miss Innes," she said. Her mouth hung open. A single bottom tooth was amiss.

Iris inhaled, as if she'd just fallen into an ice bath.

"But my name is Saph."

CHAPTER 20 - SAPH AND VARIC

Renner had taken her. I saw it with my own eyes. If I knew a single thing to be true, it was that these people didn't take prisoners. Is she working with them? Did they manipulate her? She's familiar with Bracken. No. She's locked away. What is this?

"Please," she said, trying to look through the slit. "Tell me who you are."

"Saph, it's me. It's Gaius."

Her hand went to her mouth as her eyes welled with tears. "Don't—leave me alone! I don't believe you." She started muttering to herself. "I don't believe you. It's another trick. It's always another trick. He was—" Her eyes studied the glass in front of her. She approached slowly. "I never told them about you."

She rushed forward and squeezed her arm through, knocking the food tray and some brittle plastic dinnerware to the ground. She reached for us.

"Gaius, is it really you?"

I ran and grabbed her hand. Her skinny arms had long-healed burns, and her wrists were marred with thin crisscrossing scars.

"Yeah. It's me," I said. "I can't believe it. You're alive. I'm here with Iris and Clark. And we have one of their people hostage. We're gonna get you out."

I turned back to Deek and gestured for him to open it.

"Do you see a door?" he said. "If there's no lock or key, then it wasn't meant to open."

Iris started unlacing Deek's boots and yanked them off his feet.

"What are you doing?" he asked.

She ignored him and walked up to the glass, tapping the hilt of her brela on it. "Saph, get back against the wall, sweetheart," Iris said. "Clark's got a key to every door. Don't you, Clark?"

As Saph released my hand and backed away, Clark rolled up the sleeve of his stormbreaker.

"I always keep a spare on hand." He drew his fist back and wound up at the waist. "Cover your eyes, Saph."

Like releasing an anchor, his waist spun back as he fired his fist into the glass at the center. The sound rebounded with a heavy thwap as a huge crack spiderwebbed from the center. Then the whole wall came shattering down in tiny pieces.

Iris handed me the boots, and Clark and I rushed in, but Saph jerked away from us. Her movements were slow and confused.

She nearly collapsed into the bed. "Sorry. I haven't seen anyone in…a while." She held a hand over her eyes. "It's a lot. Your faces… look sort of…odd."

How long has she been in there? What have they done to her? I covered my face with my oculum. "How's this?" I asked.

She nodded. She was a bit wobbly as she took my arm.

"Here, put these on," I said, handing her the boots. "Careful of the glass."

"Thanks." She slipped them on—a couple sizes too big. "Sorry. I don't know why, but it's confusing to look at you. I feel like I'm dreaming, or…I don't know. Like I'm going crazy."

"Don't worry about it. You look so different," I said. "I didn't recognize you at first either."

That didn't seem to comfort her. She was refusing to look at me, and she was putting on a brave face, with a shaky, failing smile.

"It's gonna be okay, Saph," Iris said as she pushed into the bedroom, getting a closer look at the markings on the wall. I looked around. Tally marks. She was counting days. Thousands of them.

Iris shot me a look that said, get her out of here.

"Come on." I gently led Saph back into the hallway. She felt so light on my arm, like she would shatter if she fell. I hated seeing her like that.

"It's so bright out here." She was squinting and covering her eyes. "I can't believe you came for me."

"We didn't," Iris said, following us into the hallway.

"What she means is we didn't know you were alive." I corrected Iris with my tone. "But we're glad we found you. We're actually here for a man named Varic. He has some kind of key."

Saph shivered and pulled away from me. "No."

Deek shifted in his binds. "See. I told you. That's the reaction of someone who knows exactly what Varic is."

"Don't do it." Saph pulled weakly on my arm. "Let's just leave."

She had no idea what we'd been through to get to her, or that the corpses of her people, our people, were a door away. But we didn't know what she'd been through either. We were strangers.

"We can't leave," Iris said. She was looking up the staircase at the final door. "It's true that we didn't come for you, but we never forget about you either. Did we, Gaius?"

I shook my head. "No, we didn't."

Iris turned back to Saph. "And the Saph we knew was hell on a stick. A clever little girl who wouldn't take shit from anyone. I bet you made a lot of trouble for them, didn't you? That's why they had you in there. In that…room."

Saph nervously pulled up the collar of her shirt, like she was trying to cover something. She wouldn't look any of us in the eyes, but she was nodding at everything Iris was saying.

"I'm sorry we didn't come sooner." Iris laid her scarred hand on Saph's shoulder. "You did good. You held on. The hard part is over. Now, all you gotta do is watch. That's it. Let us take these assholes down and make sure they can't hurt anyone else. Then we all go home. Easy peasy."

Saph mouthed the words silently, then muttered, "O-okay."

"Good. Now. Any last words before we breach that door, Deek?" Iris said with a boot kick to his ass.

"I already told you," he said. "I. Do. Not. Have. The. Key. And even your Secondhand Jack isn't gonna be able to punch through half a meter of polycarbonate. That room is hermetically, magnetically, and microelectronically sealed with a forty-eight-digit alphanumeric code. Three people know it. Renner, Bracken, and Varic. Nothing is getting through that door apart from the damned apocalypse."

Iris handed Deek over to Clark and peeked up the steps again. She motioned for us to step back into one of the side rooms as she rustled through her pack.

"You know, Dex was right," she said. "You smug pricks are all so smart. With your fancy doors and your big bright lights and your flying fucking whatevers." She slowly pulled out a pocked lead cylinder about the size of her forearm. It was capped at both ends with crudely welded crowns. "But you built this place to protect yourselves from other smug pricks. And I'm the dumbest motherfucker you've ever met."

Deek skidded in protest as Clark dragged him away from the stairs. "And what the hell is that exactly?"

She carefully twisted one end, and the metal started hissing and creaking. She tossed it up the stairs all the way to the glass door. "Everyone get down!" She ducked back into the room with us and plugged her ears.

Two more seconds passed in silence. Then, with a rush of hot air, the entire room shifted, and we all fell to the floor. I'd only heard the initial crack before the explosion. I was confused, and I felt unbalanced.

When I pushed myself off the floor, the lights were flickering sporadically, hanging from hinges and sparking wires, and heavy black smoke was barreling down the hallway. Iris was gone.

Amid the chaos, Deek slipped through Clark's grasp and rushed out into the smoke on bare feet. Clark started to go after him but saw me struggling on the ground. He rushed over to me and was saying something, but I couldn't hear him. I just shook my head and pushed past him to find Deek, but I couldn't see anything in the smoke. Clark helped Saph into the hallway, and we all climbed the stairs. Iris was just ahead of us.

As we neared the shattered door at the top, I heard two

sounds—one like the ocean, rushing all at once inside my ears—the other was a high-pitched blaring, up and down. Warning lights flashed inside the room ahead of us.

When I noticed Saph coughing, I drenched my scarf with water from my pack and wrapped it around her neck and face. "Breathe through that." I was probably shouting, but I could barely hear my own voice over the blaring.

Up ahead, muffled human agony competed over itself—one scream overtaking another, amid moans of pain and dying. My hearing was slowly returning. Glass and rubble crunched under my boots as I coughed and lumbered past the worst of the smoke into another lab.

It was clean from top to bottom, just like the hallways, but the explosion had charred a third of the room near the entry and filled the rest of it with smoking detritus and sparking overhead light. There were large and complex devices—giant Secondhand Jack arms, stationary and spraying oily lubricant from busted rubber hoses. There were also flat displays, beeping information in heartbeat-rhythm and cold metal beds half-slid inside threatening, tomb-like machines.

Dead bodies littered the floor, a dozen or more—people wearing graycloth and whitecloth. Two were barely conscious, dragging themselves across a trail of their own blood. They'd be dead soon.

"Renner!" I yelled. I didn't see him. Much of the room was obscured in smoke and steam venting from the walls and ceiling. The flashing lights made everything worse in the haze.

Against the far wall to the left, a woman with a deadly head injury held a decapitated body in her lap. She was catatonic. She probably knew about Saph. Everyone in this room knew.

I could see Iris at the opposite end of the room, battering an older bald man. His eyes were jaundiced, and he was pinned to the wall by a twisted shard of steel—it had pierced all the way through his chest and shoulder and was suspending him on his tiptoes.

He was yelling something desperately. My ears were mostly back to normal, but I still couldn't hear his voice over the hiss and crackle of the destruction around us.

His body was connected to a host of medical equipment, the

majority of which was no longer functioning. Tubes and wires extended from him, snaking all over the room to more machines, pumping, billowing, beeping, dripping, flashing—as if he were the sole purpose for this room's existence, as if he were another machine.

His skin was oddly translucent, and his veins were far too blue, almost inky.

Clark left Saph with me and stepped toward the old man. "Varic, return what you have stolen." His voice was different, commanding.

"You're the captain's," Varic coughed. His face was brutalized from Iris's blows. "It's been over twenty years, CL4-K."

"I have no memory of you," Clark said, opening his hand. "We are here for one reason. Give us the key, and you will die quickly."

"Like hell he will." Iris grabbed him by the collar and pummeled his face.

Varic laughed, coughing onto the back of his hand. He was struggling for air, having to push up on his tiptoes for every breath. "Renner, if I die, Initiate Cain Proximity."

Iris drew her brela and turned to us with wide eyes, "I have him. If anyone moves or tries to leave, kill them—"

A boot whipped through the smoke into my peripheral vision. It smacked into my palm first, but I'd only barely reacted—my backhand collided with my face and knocked me to the floor.

Clark crashed to the ground next to me. Sparks surged over his rigid body as Renner withdrew his jolting baton.

I rolled away and stood in front of Saph with my brela out. Renner was between us, Iris, and the door. He brandished a crackling weapon like the one from the lift.

"There you are," I said.

He squinted at me. "Who are you?"

I didn't play into his hand. He knew who I was. But Clark wasn't moving, and the light in his eyes was fading. "What did you do to him?"

Renner had the same emotionless expression in his dead, bulging eyes. "Oh, I remember you now," he said. "The untrained pup.

Looks like someone finally taught you how to hold a knife."

"She taught me more than that." I flicked the hilt of my brela around my thumb and gripped it, blade-down. "Want me to show you?"

Varic cried out in anguish.

Iris was resting one boot on the metal shard in his chest. "Everyone shut up," she said. "Where's the key?"

"You already have it." Varic tilted his head toward Saph. "It's the girl."

"Wrong answer." Iris kicked his feet out from under him, and he wheezed and swayed from the metal spike in his chest. "You gave that up too easily. Where is it really?"

He grabbed the fragment with both hands and lifted himself to his feet again. "It's the truth. She's the daughter of Gabriel Innes—former captain of Heaven's Vault. Without her, the ship won't move or operate."

The back of my stormbreaker went taut as Saph tugged on it. "We need to get out of here," she whispered at a high register. She was terrified.

Iris scanned the room with her boot still on him. "I don't buy it. Why give her up? There's something you're not telling us. What's—" Her gaze stopped on a row of glass cabinets. "Wait. Does that say…Panacea?"

She slid her blade under Varic's chin and lifted his face toward it. There were hundreds of sealed glass dishes inside—samples of some kind of—labeled PANACEA and MALH with various dates.

Iris repeated. "Does that fucking say Panacea?"

"It's complicated," Varic said through his bloody teeth. "Far more than you illiterates can comprehend. Look at my skin. Look at me, you damn fool." He held up his arm. "Did you not already see it? Do you not understand what's happening here—what happens if you kill me? You're making a mistake."

"That's impossible," Iris muttered. "You'd be dead—we'd all be dead."

"What are you all talking about?" I asked. "Someone tell me

what the hell is going on?"

Iris turned back to me. There was dread on her face, and she was struggling to find the words.

"He's a Skaver."

CHAPTER 21 - SKAVERS

Rumors. Bedtime stories to keep children from running off. Scare tactics to deter us from the Titan's Grave. Nightmares and superstitions. That's what they were. But Iris was telling me we were standing right in front of one. In the form of a pathetic dying man, begging for his life.

Varic took shallow breaths. "I'm not a Skaver. Not yet anyway. I'm a hematopathologist—" Iris pressed her blade closer, and he grit his teeth. "—it means blood doctor. I have a rare and aggressive form of cancer. The same one that was killing my daughter, Circe. It's called Mynard's acute leukemic hematopoiesis."

"Big words aren't gonna get you anywhere with me," Iris said.

"Listen to me," he continued. "This is important. More important than anything you're doing here. I discovered two cures. Panacea, administered in small doses—it was a miracle, and it was working until her father," he pointed to Saph. "He threw my little girl out an airlock into open space. Before I could finish my work."

"So—what, Panacea is an illness?" I asked.

Iris's face was disgusted. "It's what makes Skavers. He's telling us he turned his daughter into one."

"No, I cured her!" The frustration was growing in his voice. "That's what I'm trying to tell you. Instead of overtaking the body, they attacked each other. The cancer acted as a counter to Panacea and vice versa. It would've kept Circe's condition in stasis, like it has mine for two decades. That's what all this was for—engineering a cure to Panacea and eliminating the Skaver threat. For good."

Why had I never heard of Panacea? But Iris had? The Luminators never described Skavers as an illness.

He gestured to the room and the equipment loosely attached to his body. "Except you destroyed it. Now, I have to begin again. You must understand, if I die, so does the hope for humanity. And I become the Skaver you so fear."

"You're lying," Iris said with desperation in her voice. She bent the metal shard with her foot and screamed in his face. "This is a trick. You're just afraid."

His veins pulsed erratically as he squirmed. "If you hadn't killed all my physicians, one of them could've confirmed it. But you—you animals just destroy everything."

Renner pointed his weapon at me. "Give me the order, sir. I'll put them down."

Saph squeezed my stormbreaker even tighter and pressed into my back. She was hiding from Renner. Just as the rings on his baton started crackling with electricity, his feet were swept out from under him by Clark. He slammed to the ground and dropped his baton.

Clark gyrated wildly at the joints as he stood up. Something was wrong with him. His head was twitching, and he leaned and wobbled in place. The left side of his body didn't seem to be working either. He grabbed the baton with his right hand and yelled unintelligibly at Renner. Two voices were fighting for space in his head. He looked monstrous as he teetered in place, yelling nonsense.

Renner was quick to his feet, though he was unarmed. I stepped to attack him, but Saph was still tightly holding onto me. Shit. I can't do this with her on me.

"Clark, you okay, big guy? Can you keep Saph safe?" He turned and trained the weapon at me. I threw my hands up in surrender. His one functioning eye was locked on me and spinning rapidly. "Whoa, it's me," I whispered to him. "It's Gaius."

I couldn't understand the garbled response he gave me, but it sounded less threatening, and he lowered the weapon ever so slightly.

"Give me the order, sir," Renner repeated. "I'll get the key and put it back where it belongs—"

Saph stepped up beside me. "I'm a person! Not a key…not a thing…" Her weak voice cracked, and her lips were quivering. She was staring daggers at Renner. I held her back for her own safety. "Five-thousand, two-hundred, and fifty-six days. I'll die before I ever go back there."

Varic lifted himself to speak. "Go then, girl. See what the world outside is like. I did everything in my power to make you comfortable. You wanted for nothing. Books, clothing, food, optimal medical care. Even company twice a day. Miss Iness—"

"My name is Saph. And when I refused your food, you forced that…that tube down my throat." Her hands were around her neck. "And when I tried to—"

"—all done to protect you," Varic said with a convincing smile. "From yourself. You don't know what you're worth. You're not like these people. They can't protect you from what's coming. They have nothing left. You want to go home? Where? Out there, you'll realize this is all you have."

"No," she screamed, thrashing in my grasp. "They didn't put me in there. You did. The only thing I needed protection from was him." She pointed at Renner. "You let him…you let him…"

My blood boiled, my fingernails drove into the skin in my palm, and my eyes burned a hole through Renner. Whatever he did to her, I'd give him worse. I tried gesturing subtly for Clark to take Saph, but he was still trying to get his feet under him.

"You owe us your life," Varic said. "Without us, you'd be ash and bones like—"

Iris silenced Varic with the blade against his throat. "I don't care what you are. If I hear another lie from you, I'll cut you a new mouth—one that only tells the truth." She turned to Saph. "Go ahead."

Saph pulled down the collar of her shirt to reveal old scars—soft branches clawing up her chest. "I kept them with me. Right here." She pushed one finger into her marred skin. "I never forgot who I was or where I came from. And neither did they."

He stared at her, wheezing and laboring. There was sincere confusion on his face. "How do you not get it?" he whispered, mostly to himself. "I thought you were intelligent. You and I, we're the only ones that matter. We have to survive above all else. None of them matter. The others weren't even worth the fire we spent on them—"

"They were children!" Iris screamed and slit his throat. "Piece of shit!"

Renner leaned forward to attack her, but Varic shook his head at him even as blood drained from his neck. Varic's eyes went wide as he gargled the words, "C-Cain Pro-oxim-mity." He spat and thrashed, reaching at Iris as the death throes set in. She slapped his desperate hands away and beat his body until, slowly, he drowned in his own blood. He went limp and still with a bubbling sigh.

A beeping sound slowed, then held out in a long monotone. We all waited for something to happen.

"No." Saph's voice was soft with fear. "Iris, what did you do?"

I half expected a devil to rise from his corpse. And while there was no movement in his limbs, his veins shivered, brighter and brighter.

"You people just couldn't leave well enough alone," Renner said. He shook his head and laughed. "Look." He pointed at Varic. "That's what the end of the world looks like."

The skin on Varic's neck was stitching itself back together, machine-like, one tightening blue thread after another. Renner kicked a hot conduit off the wall, spraying a cloud of hot steam in our direction.

Clark haphazardly hurled the baton in response, and the wall showered with sparks above Varic's corpse. Iris charged Renner, going low to sweep his legs, but inside the steam, his knee came up and connected with her chin. She went limp and tumbled across the floor. I flipped the brela in my hand to throw. Clark kicked Renner in the chest and sent him flying the length of the room. He smashed into the wall by the doorway.

Saph yanked on my stormbreaker. "Gaius, please. We need to get out of here now," she said.

Renner fled the room on a limp, one hand on his stomach. Damnit. I had him. "Fine," I said. "Grab Iris. We're going."

Clark had a hitch in his step, but both his eyes were functioning, and his voice clarified. "Quickly," he said, as he lifted Iris's unconscious body onto his shoulder.

"Don't leave me here," a voice called. I barely recognized it. It was throaty and inhuman. Like a bad impression.

We all whipped around. Varic was very much alive—more so than before—and bending the steel that held him against the wall. It straightened under his grip with little effort. He was channeling the strength of a Secondhand Jack.

"Don't worry," he said through the closing wound on his neck, "I can help you, if you take me to the Breacher."

"What the hell…?" I tripped over a dead body on the floor.

Varic was slowly inching over the shard of metal as if pain had no effect on him, and his skin was fusing over the lacerations. I backed away on my hands, slipping on blood and glass.

"Get up!" Saph lifted me to my feet.

"We can work together to save humanity," Varic said. His body moved like Clark—unnatural, as if on hinges and hydraulic mechanisms instead of joints and muscle. A sparse cloud of tiny lights exhaled from his throat, glowing and pulsing with the same color and cadence inside his veins. It was funneling toward the nearby dead bodies, disappearing inside their injuries and open orifices.

We all raced out into the hallway. A cold sensation rushed up my spine as I ran. We made a mistake. We made a mistake.

We skirted past the rooms with Lars and El and the other raincoats and back into the T-shaped hallway. I turned the corner just in time to see the elevator door shutting with Renner behind it, taking our escape route with him. He looked utterly calm. As always.

"This way," Saph said, pulling us away from the elevator. She pointed at the far end of the long corridor where there was a large iron door—the one Deek mentioned. "I think that leads into the commons. But there will be a lot of people."

"The Skaver must not get through that door," Clark said as we ran.

"And how do you propose we stop him?" I asked. "I just watched him bend steel with his bare hands. I don't think a metal door is gonna hold him."

"I will figure something out." Clark seemed mostly himself again, apart from a few sporadic twitches. "We have little time. Varic initiated the Cain Proximity. If possible, Renner will destroy the grotto and all human life on Galilei."

Less than an hour ago, that would've seemed extreme.

"Is that true," Saph asked. "Everyone?"

"I'm afraid we are beyond questions of morality," Clark replied without hesitation. "This is now about survival. That room was not simply designed to treat him—it was designed to contain him—perhaps destroy him if possible. Whatever failsafe they might have had, it was likely destroyed when Iris blew open that door." Clark hitched Iris higher on his shoulder.

"If they've got an entire system in place for this kind of event, then it's happened somewhere before," I said. "Dex told me my training wasn't about running from the storms. I get it now."

Clark nodded. "A plausible conclusion."

"No doubt Renner's gonna save himself," I muttered. "Saph are you okay to do some running?"

"I'll try," she said, Deek's boots clomping under her feet. "But—"

"Come back," a voice called, as we reached the iron door at the end of a long hallway.

Varic's warped body was lurching down the hallway after us. He was dragging that huge hunk of steel behind him, still stuck in his flesh. His expression was blank, and his eyes moved independently.

We barreled through the door and slammed it behind us. On the other side, Clark lowered Iris to the ground and shook her awake.

"Huh? Where are we?" She held her head and stood up. "What's happening?"

"No time. Go," Clark said, pressing his full weight into the door. "I will delay the Skaver. Evacuate as many of these people as you can."

"What about you?" I asked.

He hesitated. "Only humans are affected by Panacea." There

was genuine disappointment in his voice.

I put a hand on his shoulder. "Clark, thank you. Get out as soon as you can. We'll meet you outside."

He didn't nod. "Do not stop running until you reach the Sun Sister."

Saph and I helped Iris get her bearings. We appeared to be in the massive subterranean city I'd seen on that giant screen. It was easily twice the size of the hangar, though almost perfectly spherical in scope.

Hundreds of colorful geometric domes lined curved walls, decked in lights and green hanging plants. More green than I'd ever seen. They also had pens of livestock and hundreds of cages of poultry—goats, sheep, chickens, even cows. I'd only seen such animals in pictures.

At the very center of the hollow, the largest pillar housed a multitude of pipes, pumps, and rumbling, steaming machines. The noise was overwhelming and chaotic—bleating goats, crying children, growling machines, laughter, banging laborers, and general clamor.

We stood high at the top of two descending pathways in a half-moon, leading down into the common area. It was so full of people that I first mistook them for water, in the dim light. Our shadows stretched across them.

Iris flipped her brela. "There's more of them." Even though she was a bit wobbly, she looked prepared to kill them all, one at a time.

Saph stayed her hand. "They didn't know."

I was surprised at that. Saph had as much reason, maybe more, to hate them and want them dead.

Iris sneered and bit her swollen lip as we sprinted down the path into the crowd. At the bottom, worry-faced people in tailored graycloth and dark jumpsuits gave us dirty looks.

"They deserve a chance to flee," Saph yelled over the noise.

Iris leaned into her ear, "If we cause a panic, we're all dead. We wait till we're clear, then tell them."

Even above the commotion, I could hear metal pounding and bending up the hill behind us. Clark was struggling to keep the door closed.

People were starting to gather at the base of the path we'd come from. They were watching Clark, pointing and mumbling in disquiet to one another.

"You all need to get out of here," Saph yelled at them as we waded into the crowd. Her thin voice didn't carry very far.

Iris put her hand over Saph's mouth and began carrying her ahead of me.

"What'd she say?" a nearby stranger asked.

We were getting squeezed by the agitated crowd, as they all became aware of Clark. I almost lost sight of Iris, but she shoved a few people and made an opening for me to catch up. There was sweat on her brow, and her eyes were shifting from me to the crowd behind us, then toward the top of the incline. I turned back to see what she was looking at.

There were dozens of people clinging to Clark, trying to pull him away. The door was wide open, but I didn't see Varic. Clark wasn't hurting anyone, though. He just grappled them and held as many as he could.

People were yelling, scrambling over one another toward us. A cloud of blue dispersed into the air around the mass of panicked people.

"Skavers!" someone shouted. They all started screaming, shoving, and running.

"Run, Gaius!" Clark growled from beneath a pile of Skavers. He was buying us time.

We shoved our way through the crowd. The people of Colony Six were running alongside us. They were scared and confused.

"Is it true?"

"Is it really Skavers?"

"How?"

I ignored them and ran as hard as my legs could carry me. My sutures started to itch. Saph wasn't doing well either. She needed food, water, and rest.

We made it out of the densely populated area, through some narrow caves, and back into the wider grotto entrance. We followed the string of lights until I could see morning light peeking over the lip of the cave mouth.

We'd made it. But not all of us.

CHAPTER 22 - ESCAPE

It was eerily quiet as we trekked up the hill out of the grotto. The screaming had subsided, and the ones who'd managed to escape with us were scrambling ahead into early daylight. The fallen rain from the night before was evaporating in ghostly threads—maybe it really was spirits of the dead. Anything seemed possible.

At least the storm missed us. Hard to call that a silver-lining considering the circumstances we were in.

"Of course that piece of shit was a Skaver," Iris said.

I shook my head. "No. He wasn't. But we made him one."

Saph's hands were on her knees, and she was trying to catch her breath. She was either going to pass out or throw up.

"Even in death, he's managed to be the worst thing on this goddamned planet," Iris said. She pulled Saph up over a sheer ledge. "It wasn't us. It's not our fault."

"I don't know," I said. "Deek warned us. He told us not to do it."

I looked northwest, toward home. My heart was heavy with longing. And I was tired and scared. Renner was still alive. He'd be coming for us. We had the key, but we'd lost Clark in the process. If our mission was a success, then why doesn't it feel that way?

"I can't believe I'm saying this, but we should've listened to him," I muttered.

Iris reached down to lift me up. "Not a chance in hell. They picked a side. Even if they didn't know." She glanced at Saph. "They knew enough. We stick to the plan. We just need to get back to Dex and—"

A sudden blast of hot air erupted from the cavern behind me and sent us all flying out into the dirt. I could feel the warm gust suck back underground, echoed by an aftershock of explosive debris. The entire grotto dropped by several meters as a mushroom cloud of smoke and fire erupted from its center.

Renner.

I pushed myself up onto my knees as adrenaline thundered in my veins. A hunk of metal crashed a few meters away from us, skidding and spinning across the dirt. When it came to rest, and the dust settled, it slowly stood amid the rising vapor with a glaive as support.

"Clark," I yelled through a cough.

He ran over, spattered in ichor. "Do not stop."

"What happened? I asked.

"Renner did as he was told," Clark said, as we helped Iris and Saph to their feet. "The Cain Proximity. Maybe the only good thing he's ever done. But it will not be enough to stop them. They were… strong beyond belief. I would not have escaped without Toothpick."

Saph was holding her side in pain. Her eyes were bloodshot. "That man will destroy everything. He doesn't think the way we do." She looked down at the grotto with remorse in her eyes. I couldn't understand how she still had compassion for them after what she'd been through.

"We have little time," Clark said. "I told you not to stop until we reach the other side of the canyon. Can you all manage?"

Iris shot me a skeptical glance as she eyed the crimson blot seeping through my pant-leg. I must've lost a stitch.

"I'm fine," I said. "Your stitches were good. And they're almost healed. It's nothing." She held my gaze, looking for a crack in my resolve. She found none.

We both nodded at Clark. But no one was in worse shape than Saph.

"Just focus on your breathing," I told her. "In through your nose, and out through your mouth. I won't leave you behind. I promise. Just keep in step with me."

As we sprinted away from the grotto, hundreds of Secondhand Jacks converged over the hill ahead of us, jogging with heavy steps.

"How shall we assist, keeper?" they asked. But they did not wait for an answer. Their torsos rotated toward us as they ran by, descending into the hell we were just fleeing. I caught them digging through the rubble just as we cleared the horizon. Clark's face was hidden away in his hood. He said nothing.

We rushed into the edge of the thunderfruit fields with Clark as our guide, retracing much the same route as the day before. The leaves were still damp from the storm, leaving a trail of moisture on Saph's clothes, and the protective outer shells of the tender fruit had already begun peeling away.

Saph looked back at me with a weary smile. She didn't have to say anything, but I understood. It was her first time seeing thunderfruit again. When this was all over, I'd make sure she'd get to play and clap in the fields again.

A sudden gust was whipping through the crops in waves, and water droplets flicked from the leaves. Thunder boomed nearby, despite the clear sky. Iris pulled the back of my shirt.

"The storm's already passed," Iris called over the noise.

"It is not the Tempest," Clark replied.

"It's them," Saph cried, ducking into the crops as half a dozen piercers flew overhead.

"Go!" Clark turned and ran off behind us, as flinging debris shot up in violent eruptions of mud and shredded vegetation.

Fire showered the field around us, and the fruit shells snapped shut in response. I dashed through the tattering stalks with Iris ahead of me. The heat was too much. I turned back to make sure Saph was keeping up. She was a few meters back, cowering with her hands over her ears as the hailing blasts thundered around her, screaming at every explosion.

There were figures moving through the crops behind her. Skavers. Clark was dealing with them. I called out as I doubled back toward Saph, but she didn't respond. The Skavers were walking calmly—eerily so—voices talking over each other, and I watched as they fell one by one to attacks from Clark and the zigzagging piercers above. But they each stood again, a pulsing glow growing in the shade of the vines.

I slid through the muck next to Saph. Her eyes were closed and weeping. I shook her, but she wouldn't open them. Her legs were shaking more out of exhaustion than fear. She wasn't going to make it. I tightened my pack as much as I could, knelt down in front of her and lifted one hand from her ear. "Get on," I said. She peaked one teary eye open to see me. "Come on. Up."

She nervously climbed onto my back. She barely weighed more than a full pack.

With Clark behind us, I carried her for what seemed like an eternity, keeping our heads low beneath the crop line and staying our course toward the canyon. Flames were erupting not far off, and I could feel their warmth on the wind. Saph stayed silent, just breathing in her nose and out her mouth. Good.

When we'd traveled far enough from the noise of the piercers, she patted me on the back. I stopped to get a better look at her. "You okay?"

"I'm fine. I can handle it from here. Really."

I set her down. "If you need help, just ask. Okay? I told you. I'm not gonna leave you behind. Never again."

Her eyes welled up at that. She wiped them and nodded.

We slowed enough to catch our breath as we passed the harvest compound and shuffled into the next field. The area looked barren without the Jacks doing their work, asking how they could assist.

Blasts started to sound like an echo—far off and moving away like a retreating storm. Iris was waiting, ducked at the edge of the field where the hill led out to the canyon. Just beyond that was our escape.

"We have to keep moving." Clark came tearing through the vines behind us. "I bought very little time."

Iris was distant as she watched the sky from her hunched position, eyes bloodshot and baggy. It had been a full day since we slept, and even I was struggling to catch my breath. We were being run ragged.

Saph was holding her shoulder and failing to hide obvious pain.

"What happened?" I asked her.

"Oh, um. I don't know," she said, pulling her hand away, covered in blood. "It must have happened when those things flew over. But I don't even feel it. I'm probably okay. Right?" Her eyes darted between me and Iris for confirmation that she was okay.

"That's the adrenaline," Iris said. "Lemme see."

Saph turned, and the entire back of her shirt was wet and sticky with blood. I started to panic. If she dies, this was all for nothing. We'll lose Saph and the key—no, don't think of her like that. Iris just pulled Saph's collar back and inspected the wound.

"It's not an artery, or you'd already be dead." Iris cut the sleeves off her fatigues and began ripping them into long shreds and braiding them together. "We'll get it properly dressed as soon as we have a moment. For the time being, try not to move your arm. And if you start getting dizzy, say something." She pulled the cloth tight around Saph's shoulder and tied it off.

Saph winced, then nodded.

"You'll be fine," I assured her.

"None of us are fine till we're out of here," Iris said.

Clark pointed up the hill toward the canyon. "We will be utterly exposed moving forward. No matter what happens, do not stop." He combed the sky for any incoming piercers, then waved us forward.

Saph sprinted up the incline with a wet wheeze, dripping a trail of blood as she went. I went after her. The sky was mostly empty but for a single circling piercer far off in the direction of the grotto. With their speed, it wouldn't even take them twenty seconds to reach our location if spotted. Iris caught up and we ran together, side by side.

I only turned back to keep an eye on the sky, but I saw tons of shadows barreling through the field, tousling the thunderfruit trellises like fingers reaching through a head of green hair. I quickened my pace. Clark bounded past us with ease and overtook Saph at the top.

As we climbed under the archway of sheer rock walls and came out the other side at the edge of the canyon, Clark was pacing and mumbling something to Saph who was too busy trying to catch her breath to entertain his anxiety.

"Is the tether still attached?" I shouted, sliding down the sandstone bank with Iris in tow.

"Looks like it," Saph shouted back.

"Why aren't you already going across?" I yelled to Clark.

"We were waiting to make sure you were—"

"Just go!" I shouted. Clark looked back and forth like he didn't know quite what to do. 'They're coming. Skavers,' I mouthed to him.

Clark immediately hopped down and helped Saph over the cliff. Her shoulder was going to be a problem. She wouldn't make it on her own.

I turned to Iris. "How much concentrated weight can it support?"

"We're about to find out," she replied. "Clark, you'll have to carry her across. Be quick about it."

"Sorry," Saph said.

"Not at all." Clark held out his hand for her. "I am happy to escort you across."

She took it and climbed onto his back for transport. He started hauling them both across the tether. His pace was slower than before, and I could hear the anchor in the wall buckling with every swing of his arms as the line bounced under their weight.

"You first," I said to Iris. "I'm right behind you."

She took less than a second to realize we didn't have time to fight about it. "You better be," she said, as she nimbly scaled the cliffside. She stepped down onto the anchor, then wrapped her legs around the line and started pulling herself across.

I looked over the edge. A mistake. My stomach leapt into the back of my throat. I can do this. I already did it once. Come on.

Scampering footsteps pitter-pattered from the hill above.

Shit. Oh shit shit shit. It's now or never.

I didn't even bother looking behind me as I shakily slid down the rock face toward the anchor. Watch your step. Be careful. Don't—

My foot slipped, and I toppled over the edge off the canyon wall. For a moment, there was nothing but air beneath me. What scared me the most was the overwhelming sense of relief. Is this what I hoped for? Is it easier if—

My arm suddenly snagged on the Sun Sister's anchor cable, and I squeezed a hug around it to keep hold. No. I gotta get her back. Hang on. I swung upside down as my legs wrapped tightly at the ankles. All of us bounced. Saph screamed.

The sediment cracked around the anchor, and the bending metal whined from the other side. The Sun Sister was bending.

The tether pinged with tension as Clark continued gliding his way past the middle. Iris wasn't too far behind. I pulled myself as fast as I could, ignoring the depth beneath me and the pursuers behind me—instead fixing my eyes on the cliffside ahead of us.

"Gaius. Gaius," Iris said with increasing concern and volume. "Gaius, look."

One after another, Skavers started to emerge near the anchor. My heart pounded as I pulled as fast as I could away from the canyon wall. "Go!"

The anchor pinged loose by an inch, shooting shards of rock and dust into the air. We all stopped and held on tight, waiting for the line to stabilize. A Skaver sauntered to the edge of the cliffside and stared down at me as I clutched tight to the cable. His head rolled from side to side, studying me.

"Where's Dalia?" he said. "Have you seen my daughter?" Then he leaned too far over the edge and fell head-first into the chasm. His eyes were locked on me as he fell. He struck the tether and flipped violently down below. The cable whipped about as the wall cracked again. With my eyes closed and my grip tightening, I listened, waiting for it to snap.

The line held.

"Go," I yelled again.

My eyes opened at the sound of the thud below, to which Saph screamed again. Another leaned over the edge and plunged into the canyon—then another and another—each slamming against the cable with their arms outstretched before falling into the valley below. Their movements were awkward and slow.

The anchor yanked farther from the wall with every strike. It was almost free.

Across the canyon, there was a cacophony of grinding stone and warping metal. The ground that held our escape plan in place was curling upward from the excess weight and pressure.

"Get Saph across," I yelled. "Get her across."

I scrambled forward as the line pulled again. The Skavers started to dive a couple at a time. One of them managed to grab hold of the line. It hung for a second before its fingers slowly gave under its own weight.

"Help me up," it said, no emotion on its feminine face, glowing shivers spiking up its neck in deep blue waves. Then it slipped away, eventually becoming just another thud in the distance.

As three more bodies came toppling over together, the line shrieked and snapped. My body plummeted, weightless, my stormbreaker flapping upward in the wind. I squeezed hard on the line to get a better handle, but it was sliding between my fingers, and I was spinning uncontrollably as we swung rapidly toward the other side. Hot friction split the skin on my palms as I slammed into the canyon wall.

The wind was knocked out of me, and I dropped a couple meters before coming to a stop again, only able to take short, gasping breaths. Then the weight of Iris's boot came down on my knuckles. She'd fallen down the tether to my position.

She growled angrily, and I peered up to see her squirming by one exposed arm, shaking under the burden of her whole body. There was something off about her other arm. Looked broken.

"Can…you…slide…down?" I croaked.

But I only heard crunching steel far above as the line dropped again. The Sun Sister was giving way.

I felt Iris slipping over my body, grunting in pain with every inch. The mud and sharp pebbles in her boots scraped down my arms as she scooted down. She was unabashed about putting her boots on my shoulders for support.

Together we started sliding down the tether toward a perchable slope halfway down the canyon. The sound of thudding bodies grew more frequent. The Skavers were now running and launching themselves toward us from the other side, plummeting, devil-may-care, to their deaths.

Clark yelled something from above as the rover started to bend over the edge, raining crumbling rocks and dust onto us. My fingers loosened, and we slid down to the bottom of the tether where Iris finally lost her grip and flipped backward over me. I reached out and grabbed her boot with one hand and wrapped my other around the tether. She was heavier than I imagined, and the mud on her boots was slick. Clark suddenly dropped down and landed on the slope below with Saph still on his back. She yelled in pain as they landed.

It was still a six-meter drop from the bottom of the anchor, but Clark reached up for me to drop Iris to him as Saph climbed down. Iris shook her head at me, the veins bulging at her temples as she ground her teeth, but I didn't have a choice.

"I'm sorry," I said, trusting Clark, and let go.

Clark leapt up to catch her as the cable dropped, sending me into a five-meter freefall. I landed on my feet next to them, popping another stitch as I scrambled away as fast as I could.

The Sun Sister crashed beside me in an explosion of distorted iron and dust, before plummeting the rest of the way to the bottom of the canyon.

We all held there for a moment, trying to catch our breath. But the wet smack of bodies hitting the ground, and the cracking of bones and tearing flesh reverberated from one canyon wall to the other.

Brown streaks of dusty tears ran down Saph's cheeks as the pile of bodies grew. I could feel it under my boots—their bodies slamming into the dirt nearby.

"We need to get to the bottom," I said. "It's not over. Go."

As we climbed down the rest of the way, there was movement among the disfigured corpses. Just like Varic, they were still alive. They seemed unkillable, like the stories I'd been told. They were only a few hundred meters away.

"Why didn't you use your anchor?" Iris slugged me in the arm.

Goddamnit. I shook my head and failed to find a better answer than: I forgot.

"I have no idea how the hell you ever survived out here," she said as we slid down the slope.

We backed into the wall next to Saph and Clark. I couldn't look away from the growing corpse pile. The Skavers that hadn't splattered on impact were trying to slither to us on exposed bones, and others were stuck in violent convulsions as their limbs cracked and popped back into place. But as more of them continued jumping from the ledge, landing on those who had leapt before them, the injuries of the ones on top became less and less severe.

Clark pulled Saph's hands away from her ears despite her screams. "Where can we flee? Quickly, now."

"I don't know." She shook her head and closed her eyes.

But Clark pushed. "Every moment we linger could mean the difference in life or death. Did your captors disclose any operations within Titan's Grave. An outpost. Anything."

"No, I don't know. I don't know."

"Think," Clark said. "If you know nothing, we die."

"I don't—" She was in the midst of shaking her head again when she suddenly took a sharp breath. "Wait. Um. The Cistern," she said. "Bracken said something about it. He said exiles are sent there. It's in the valley of the Titan's Grave."

"We need to move," Iris forced through her teeth. She was in a lot of pain. Her shoulder was dipped and out of place, hanging limply at her side.

"Did they say anything else about it?" Clark said, as his eyes scanned the canyon. The Skavers were moving quicker. Their broken bodies were mending themselves. They'd be on us in less than a minute.

"I don't know," Saph said. She was panicking. "It's—it's underground."

"Good. A cave system?"

"I don't know!"

"There," Clark said, pointing westward, a couple hundred meters away. "Run!"

As we ran parallel with the canyon wall, the Skavers followed suit, first hobbling in our direction, then nearly matching our pace, then gaining on us. Their voices carried in the valley. They yelled about family members, about needing help, about their injuries—all a ruse.

Clark pulled back to bring up the rear. "Just there," he said. "Inside, quickly."

We ducked into a cavern and hurried deeper inside as the Skaver voices bounced around us.

"Don't leave me behind."

"I'm so scared."

"I'm not one of them."

Clark crashed down and shoved us all away from the entrance as Skavers swarmed the opening. He slammed the blunt end of Toothpick into the cave ceiling, collapsing the entry in a plume of rock and stale talc.

CHAPTER 23 - THE CISTERN

We were all coughing, wheezing, and stumbling around each other in the dark.

"Is everyone alright?" Clark's glowing eyes brightened the narrow passage, which was supported by iron braces.

Iris shoved him against the wall with her one good arm. "You're the only one in here who can see well enough to know I'm not alright!"

"I am indeed aware of your physical injuries," he said. "I was querying your emotional states."

She sneered. "I'm not worried about my goddamn feelings—"

I could barely see them, but I heard him grab her bad arm and shove it back into the socket with a pop.

Her breath hitched with pain, then relief as she slid down the wall. "...Thanks."

"Do not mention it," Clark said.

Scratching and muffled voices pushed through the rubble. The Skavers were right outside, separated by a few meters of heavy rock. If they'd survived the collapsed grotto, they'd get in eventually.

Clark turned to us. "Forward as always."

Iris slowly rotated her shoulder. "Aimless wandering? That's your plan?"

"It will not be aimless. We already have our bearing." He pointed down the only direction available to us. Then he turned to Saph. "Do you know the function of this place? Where an egress might be? The layout? Any of the people who were exiled here?"

"I—no, not really. Um, it might be for water treatment?

Wait…I think I heard Bracken say something about electricity." She paused, picking at her elbow. "I'm sorry. I don't think I'm going to be any help. They didn't really trust me with that kind of stuff."

Clark suddenly stopped his frantic questioning and took a knee in front of Saph. "I…apologize. I have maligned you as one of them, and in my haste to secure an escape, neglected to reassure you of our position. Let us be clear, so you know." He gingerly took her hand in his. "You do not have to be useful to be of value."

Saph looked him in the face for the first time, her eyes reflecting the azure glow of Clark's gaze.

Iris leaned into me. "The same doesn't go for you, packbrat. If you don't make yourself useful, I'll leave your ass in the lurch."

I leaned back, "Says the one who needed me to catch her."

An exhale passed through Iris's nose. Was that a laugh?

"Come," Clark said. "We have a long day ahead of us." He led us deeper in, leaving the voices and digging behind us.

We still hadn't slept. What made matters worse, was that the path was as stagnant as the air. Every so often Clark would stop and turn back, eyes flaring down the long shaft behind us as we all sat in silence, waiting for him to give the go ahead. I nearly fell asleep leaning into the wall. I was spent. Even the best packbrat runners had their limits.

The farther we went, the more the tunnel seemed to buzz and grumble with energy—with electricity. We were heading toward some massive machinery.

The passage soon opened up and out into a large cavern with a basin of still water. I couldn't see far enough to the other side in the darkness, but stacks of rumbling machines, valves, and hissing steam vents snaked in silhouettes around the bank. I could hear the flow of pumping water somewhere beyond. High above us, there were a dozen or so headlamps intersecting over a series of interlocking bridges and metal stairs.

"Well, I'll be," a voice called ahead of us as another headlamp came on. "Fresh rooks? Welcome to the Cistern."

A figure emerged and approached until he was flooded in

Clark's blue light. He was skinny, shirtless, outfitted in heavy, raggedy working clothes half tied at his waist, and had a puff of thick black hair.

"Twigs, grab a bundle of headlamps for these sootless softies," he yelled.

"Come on, Moss. I'm on the coils," someone called back from a metal walkway above us. A new headlamp shined down on our group, "Can't you get Grisham on it? He's been grinding ferno all month. Probably needs some freshers. Or send 'em to the east sink."

"You owe me, Twigs," Moss mumbled. "Alright. Listen up, you shiny-fingered rooks. That way leads down to the east sink." He pointed to our right into what only looked like complete blackness. "There's water and food in it for you if you sweat like you're supposed to. But it's up to you if you want to work. Don't, and you go hungry. It's that simple. We make most of our own rules down here, but we're fair. Fairer than Varic, at least. First, see Grisham. He'll take good care of you. Just follow the tunnel—"

Iris pushed into his face and grabbed the sleeves tied at his waist. "You listen to me. Skavers are coming. Everyone in here needs to run as far and as fast as they can."

He scrutinized her for a moment with his sunken eyes. Then, he unfurled her fingers. "Well, aren't you imaginative. Skavers don't come from that direction. Everyone knows they come from the North." He pointed behind him.

"She's telling the truth," I said.

"Uh huh. You know, now that I'm looking, there's something off about the whole lot of you." Moss flicked his dim headlamp at each of us before focusing in on Clark. "Ah. That's what it was. First time we've had a Jack sent to moil the Cistern. No paint job either. Curious looking fella." Then he cupped his mouth and shouted into the bridges above. "Ay, Youngest, lift the eclipse for the rooks."

"Will do, boss. Ladies and gents, put on your dimmers," a young man called. "Flashes in ten."

Iris didn't appreciate being ignored, but it didn't seem like Moss could understand a word we were saying. I had no idea how long he'd been down here, but judging by his hollowed features, probably a while. Maybe the dark made them all a bit mad.

Moss pulled thick, shaded glass down over his eyes and smiled a dusty grin.

"Flashes in three...two...one. Happy Sun-Day."

A thousand bulbs turned on in unison, saturating the subterranean world in false sunlight. I had to squint at first.

Nearly a kilometer wide and half as high, the cavern was filled with sweaty, dirty people. There must have been a hundred workers standing across the spans of vertically staggered footbridges, pausing to bathe in the muted, throbbing light.

Metal stairs and walkways hung from the ceiling by precarious wires and converged in multiple intersections above the water. At the apex of the chamber was some sort of reservoir, like a giant waterskin, sagging through the ceiling. It was connected to a series of pristine pipes and pumps drinking cool water.

Moss was still smiling at us, pointing down a tunnel to our right as a couple bulbs shattered in the distance. "Soak it in while you can, rooks. We only get this kind of sunshine once a month. Now, off you scoot. Later, we can swap stories about how you pissed off Varic."

When it was clear we wouldn't make headway with him or any of the cogs in his well-oiled machine, Iris huffed, and we headed off toward Grisham.

We kept an ear on the distance, awaiting the inevitable. I kept getting a shivering sensation crawling up my back, reminding me what we'd done. It didn't feel real. I wondered what was going through Iris's head. Does she even care? Does she understand the reality of what we've done? I'd barely had a moment to process El and Lars. I just wanted to stop. To breathe. To sleep.

It wasn't long before the lights slowly dimmed again. My eyes tried to adjust, but I could barely see the tip of my nose. Clark was our only light source.

I could feel my heart rate increasing, but it took me a moment to realize why. There was a smell in the air—something I recognized, a chemical element like clay and fermented fruit. Ferno. We began to see purple blazing in a far chamber, casting great shadows across the wall.

There was shouting ahead of us and the sound of igniting fire. As we entered the chamber, a burst of brilliant violet flames lit the far wall. There were two men in vertical half-suits next to a collection of weeping barrels and walls of crumbling rock.

The men continued their work without interruption as we approached from behind. Their heavy fabric and metal suits were rigid and bulky, protecting them from the front but exposed at the back.

The barrels oozed with the slimy ferno, which clung to their gloves like inky mucus. They slathered it across the rock in front of them in dripping globs, then struck their batons across the ground, sparking blinding flames that slithered up the path of ferno and pulverized the rock and clay like breadcrumbs.

Our collective gasp was enough to finally grab their attention. "Hey, back away from the barrels," they warned, stepping backward out of their shielded suits, which stayed upright where they left them.

"What are you doing here? New cookers?" the larger of the two asked, wiping his hands on his undershirt and flicking his headlamp on. His broad body glistened with sweat from the dying flames.

"Moss sent us this way to meet Grisham," I said, "but we're just looking for a way out."

"Way out?" the other laughed through his thick mustache. He was a wiry fellow, and his ill-fitting undershirt hung loosely over his bony shoulders. "You hear that Grisham? This new lot of rooks is full of hopefuls. Might make me sad if it wasn't so goddamn sweet."

"Are you saying there's no way out?" I tried not to sound as anxious as that made me feel. I wanted Saph to feel safe.

"Course there is," he replied. "Lots of ways out, but nowhere to go once you get there. If it's back to Colony Six you're thinking, you can cork that bottle. They don't take exiles back. Not ever."

"We're not going back," I tried not to lose my temper with them. Information would be harder to get if they were on the back foot. "We just need a way out."

"A way out to where?" he laughed again. "North? Nothing but Skavers. I mean, be my guest, if you got a death wish. But you're better off accepting your fate with us. Trust me, kid. None of us wants to be here. The sooner you get used to that, the better. And, hey, it's not all bad. Tell him, Grish. We get enough to eat as long as the water keeps moving, and we've got all the clean drink your bladder can stomach."

Grisham placed his massive hand over the man's head like it was a piece of ripe fruit to pluck from the vine. "Flint, look at them, you dimwit," he said. "They're northerners." He paused and appraised us. "What's really going on?"

"Good news. Varic's dead," Iris said. "Bad news. It's because he's a Skaver. And more are headed this way." They both stepped back. "You were lied to. The North isn't what they said it was. We have to get there now. With whoever will follow."

Flint scoffed. "Skavs won't come into the Cistern. They don't know about it."

"You can tell them that when they get here," I said. "We saw it happen. Everyone in the grotto, starting with your leader. They were screaming and scrambling over each other. Maybe a handful made it out alive. Less after Renner scorched the fields."

"It's the truth," Saph said. She wouldn't look them in the face.

Grisham crossed his arms over his brawny chest and sighed like he was preparing us for disappointment. "Even if I buy your story—and that's a big if—Moss and the rest won't. They've been down here too long. They speak a different language."

He looked over at his partner with a high brow.

"Flint and I have only been here a few years. Came down together. We can show you out, but it takes a few days. If you're wrong about this, I expect you to pick up our shifts next week. And we get your nosh."

"There's no faster way out?" I asked.

"Unless I'm mistaken," Grisham started, "it sounds like you came from the canyon. Which was the only other way out. So, no. Do we have a deal or not?"

He stuck out his hand for a shake, and I took it. "Fine. Now let's get moving."

"If there's really Skavs waiting out there," Flint said, "we should stay put. Fill the tunnel with Ferno or something. Send the devils right back to hell."

Grisham flicked him in the nose with his giant finger. "And bring the whole Cistern crumbling down on us?"

"Ow, you big lunk. If we're really going, I ain't gonna leave Moss and Snags and the rest," he said, rubbing his nose.

"We already told him what's coming," Iris said. "He didn't care. We need to move."

"The Skavers will eventually get in," Clark said, "and when they do, we will be out of time."

Flint nearly jumped out of his skin. "It talks," he said. "And has ideas."

"He," I corrected. "And you'll be glad he's with us if things go poorly. Or when, more accurately. Trouble tends to find us."

Flint smacked the sides of his face and yipped. "Well, let's not just stand around then. Hitch up. But we're telling the others on the way." He pointed an accusatory, loosely bandaged finger at Grisham.

"Fair enough," Grisham said.

"Wait. You have medical supplies?" I asked. "We need to bandage her shoulder."

"Him too," Saph urged them, noting the blood soaking through my pant leg. "Even if he tells you not to."

"Grab the kit," Grisham said to Flint. "Make it quick."

Most of their medical supplies were for burns, but they still had what we needed. Grisham applied some sticky liquid to our wounds and dressed them tightly. The bleeding stopped, and my pain was gone. Almost immediately. Whatever he'd used, it certainly worked better than drinking dragon's milk.

They grabbed their batons—what they called strikers—and took us down an adjacent tunnel which poured out into the far edge of the first basin where the miners were producing a chorus of singing, laughing, and banging in the dark. The dissonance wasn't unpleasant. It was alive. I wondered if we could've lived like that if Varic hadn't burned away any sense of peace.

Flint climbed a short staircase nearby and flicked on his headlamp. I couldn't hear what he was saying over the low, powerful rumble of nearby machinery, but his conversation with Moss went as we imagined—punctuated with laughter which spread to a few nearby listeners. Flint turned and lumbered down the staircase, dragging one foot.

When he reached us, he just muttered, "Don't say nothing." Grisham put a large hand on his shoulder and squeezed.

Flint led us through the north end of the chamber, which was riddled with winding tunnels. He told us most of them led to housing modules—not unlike our Nests.

We stayed the course for hours. Without the sun or stars, time felt meaningless. Iris kept telling Flint to stop dragging his foot. He said it was an old connivore injury—took part of his knee—which naturally garnered zero sympathy from a scarred, cut, bruised, and broken ex-raincoat.

But when I showed him the scar on my thigh, he gave me a surprised smile.

"It still hurts," I told him. "Worse when it rains."

"Mine too," he laughed. "I thought I was doomed when I got sent to the Cistern, but being down here actually helps with the pain. Plus, Grish does most of the work, if I'm honest."

Eventually, we had to sleep. The day was approaching late afternoon or evening—probably forty or more hours of restless chaos. Clark stayed up and kept watch. We only allowed ourselves a couple hours before we had to move on. Saph was looking worse for wear, and she slumped into a different kind of quiet. Those oversized boots probably didn't help.

We reached the next basin of water at the peak of our exhaustion—the east sink. It was nearly the same size as the first, but with half the workers. Flint dropped his striker and flicked his headlamp on, flourishing the beam through the chamber like a slender, golden spoon stirring a bowl of midnight soup.

He cupped his mouth and shouted "Snags? Snags, you up there?"

"That you, Flint?" a smoky voice called back.

"Come on down," he called back. "It's me and Grish. We just come from the south sink."

"Naw. Why don't you come up?" she called back. "You know my legs. Besides, I'm on smears, and the pistons are always sticky in the summer. Might be a while."

He looked back at us with a face that demanded our silent compliance. "Just…" he started, holding up one finger.

"Skavers are coming," Iris yelled back into the void.

The shifting of busy workers halted. Their headlamps all shined down on our group. Then they all went right back to work.

Iris huffed and flexed out her fingers in frustration. "We tried," she said through her teeth.

Undeterred, Flint cupped his mouth again, but we heard nothing but screams from the tunnel behind us.

CHAPTER 24 - THE DARK

Clark turned and darted away, Toothpick-first. "Get them to the exit. Keep them safe," he called back, his voice trailing as he went.

"Who's he talking about?" Flint asked.

"These two," Iris said, hurrying me and Saph. "Just move. Go."

In a scramble of crisscrossing headlamps, nearly half the miners descended and ran off into different tunnels. Many stayed right where they were, too dulled by their curiosity or exhaustion to gauge what was happening.

"Get out of here," I yelled to them, "or you're dead."

As we sprinted alongside the basin, we nearly collided with a short, elderly woman. She was halfway between us and the group of disappearing lights at the end of the cavern.

"Snags," Flint sighed with relief, wrapping his arms around her.

"It's really Skavs, then?" she asked through too many teeth and a wrinkled face. Two white braids hung over her back—somewhat hunched from difficult work.

Flint nodded.

Moss was first out of the tunnel behind us, looking much too frightened to pass for a Skaver. No shivers under his skin either. Behind him, two more came barreling out. He sprinted toward us, electing a few profane words as confirmation of our fears.

"Don't stop," Iris cut in, waving us forward. "Move."

I kept one eye behind me as we ran. A flickering headlamp came rolling out of the tunnel onto the ground. The miner it belonged to crawled after it. It was a Skaver—yelling for help in a breathy voice, deadweight legs dragging behind him. Grisham flicked off his headlamp, as did Flint.

"Help me," it called, its voice detached and toneless, as if its tongue wasn't working quite right. "They're coming. I'm scared. Please." It rolled over on its back in moans of despair, the voice growing more emotional, more believable with every word. "They'll kill me. Please, don't leave me. My legs."

Flint slowed, but I pushed him on. "That's what they all sound like," I said. "Do not stop, no matter what they say."

He gave me a disconcerted look but limped alongside me as dozens of blue pulsing figures swarmed into the east sink.

We were nearing the far side where a number of interior caves led in all different directions. No one approached or took the bait of the fallen Skaver. Its legs snapped back into place, and it hopped up and darted in our direction as though it was never injured.

In the reflective gloss of Grisham's helmet, I could see headlamps behind us being snuffed out, followed by the sound of muffled cries. But I couldn't see much else without Clark guiding us.

My foot struck something soft—the back of Saph's boot—and my center of gravity flipped. In the darkness, I felt a rush of musty air on my face before my chin struck the ground, and I skidded to a halt, Saph tangled underneath me.

"Ouch—" she huffed before I covered her mouth.

They're too fast. We aren't going to make it. We have to hide. I tried to focus, to find somewhere, anywhere to hide.

I dragged her back against the wall as she squirmed, the pain in my chin thumping, and I squeezed us beneath a shallow alcove. We had to slide on our bellies to fit, with barely enough room to breathe. She was out front. There was nothing I could do about that.

"Shh," I whispered. "Don't move or speak."

Beyond her silhouette, flashes of ferno turned to pandemonium as clouds of the Skaver infection settled and took over new hosts. The laborers were fighting back but losing.

What the hell are those things? I was glad I couldn't see exactly what was happening. It already sounded horrible enough—screams cut off with choking sounds that went quiet—desperate wrestling drowned in cries for mercy.

Saph was stifling her cries.

"Just look at me," I whispered. "Don't watch."

She turned to face me. So scared. She was looking to me for reassurance.

I'd been here before—stuck in the wall, hiding. Helpless. Watching as everyone else died. But this wasn't like last time. We'll survive. I'll make sure. I needed her to see it on my face. I locked eyes with her, calmly put a finger to my lips, and nodded. She nodded back.

Shadows scurried past us in palpitating blue, and we held our breath. Saph closed her eyes. Her hand found mine and squeezed.

Past her, I could barely see the water where the glow of Skavers exhaled luminescent clouds into the faces of hapless miners. There was no fight. They took out the easy ones first, the slow and elderly, then began searching for stragglers. We waited for a long time.

Several minutes would pass until the Skavers found another—others hiding in the east sink with us. Some would make a run for it when they thought the coast was clear. They always got caught.

I gently squeezed Saph's hand to tell her it was okay, to remind her I was there. And for me. They're not going to find us. I've always survived. They're not going to find us.

I don't know how long we laid there, side by side, listening, holding our breath as something passed. Sometimes, a phantom voice would call out.

"It's alright now," one said.

"They're gone," another said.

"Is it safe to come out?"

"We took care of them."

"Someone help me, please."

We stayed until there was nothing but the settling hollowness. The voices and footsteps faded completely, scouring the Cistern for whoever remained. I realized, even with the sleep we'd gotten, that the exhaustion had finally taken its toll. Despite all the death and loss she'd suffered, or perhaps because of it, Saph had fallen asleep. Like seeing a yawn, I succumbed alongside her.

I jolted awake—what felt like seconds later—to clanking footsteps barreling into the chamber with us. Clark's familiar figure and glowing eyes passed by us. I almost mistook him for a Skaver.

"Clark," I whispered from the back of my throat, waking Saph in the process. He skidded to a halt as we both shimmied out, our joints cracking.

"Are you both unharmed? Where's Iris? The others?" he asked, gripping Toothpick, which was bloody and damaged. He reeked of a putrid metallic aroma. I'd never smelled anything like it.

"It's just us," Saph said, sweeping the dust from her bandaged shoulder.

"Grisham mentioned heading northwest," I said. "Iris was with him when we got separated. Can you get us out, Clark?"

"Yes, but that is the least significant obstacle," he replied. "I am unable…I cannot protect you from Panacea. The mode of infection appears airborne, though limited in range. So, if I tell you to run, you must do it without question. It will take more than strength and vigilance to survive. Luck may be our only saving grace."

"The one thing I seem to have in abundance," I said, grabbing Saph's hand. "But we're still running blind down here."

"For now, stay together. We must manage in the dark."

We both kept behind the outline of his stormbreaker. For at least another day, we traipsed through the underground in silence. Eventually, Clark had to carry Saph, then I did. But the path was slow, monotonous, and maddening. Quiet was too consistent down there, so I could hear my ears ringing again. I would lose myself in it, forget what I was doing.

The labyrinthine caves that cast off to our left and right would resound with intermittent screams. But it was the anticipation between screams that truly had my attention—the waiting.

And I was still worried about Iris. Is she alone again? Hiding, running…worse? Our people were dwindling by the hour. I can't lose her too.

Clark hushed us and pulled us against the wall. With his hood down over his eyes, he kept his cold steel hand across us. I held my breath, listening. A pair of Skavers sauntered out into an adjacent tunnel without a word. One of them dragged their foot as it walked. Flint? I couldn't tell. If they got him, maybe Iris…

We waited several minutes after they disappeared. We'd already learned the Skavers would sometimes linger, only pretending to move on. Once Clark was certain, we continued on, slower than before.

It was a while before we felt wind on our faces, blowing in from somewhere unseen. I was taught never to consider the open air a comfort, but just this once, I allowed myself to breathe it deep. Safety. I'd much rather take my chances with the Tempest.

Ahead of us, light poured into the tunnel like drips of honey. We rushed out into the blinding dawn. No storm. And we were back across the Titan's Grave, just outside the Rustyard—nothing but dunes and rock. It was a red morning, though. Not good. The storm would reach us by midday.

As my eyes adjusted, Iris came sprinting over the dunes, wide-eyed and desperate. Relief washed over me like cool water, and the hair on my arms stood on end.

She rushed down the sand with a genuine smile, but her gait slowed when she came down to meet us. She started to reach up to touch my arm, but reconsidered. Some words were forming between her lips, but they never found their way out. I was searching for my own and failing.

"You're alive," I said, instead of the other hundred things I wanted to say. What have we done? Is this all our fault? I kept Saph safe. Are you proud of me? I was worried about you. I'm glad you're okay. I needed you to be okay. Don't ever leave us again. Don't—

"She made us wait for you," Grisham said, as he and Snags came out of hiding. He was nursing his arm. "And she's a lot stronger than she looks."

Iris shot him a look, and his eyes drifted to the sky.

Moss was also there with several filthy miners I didn't recognize. He shook his head at us. "Well, at least they're not Skavers."

And dragging his foot just behind them was a downtrodden

Flint, waving us over with weary enthusiasm. "What took you so long?"

CHAPTER 25 - FOUR WORDS

Across the horizon, thin wisps of smoke were rising, likely more distant Nests, burned away by Renner's squadrons. There wouldn't be many of us left now. Whatever survivors El had gathered were buried in the grotto of Colony Six, and I'd never know why she did it. Was it to buy us time? A distraction? Did she even know we were heading there? Did she know anything?

It didn't matter. She kept her motivations a secret until the very end, and that's probably how she wanted it. But I could still do what she asked of me. I was going to deliver my last commission—Saph Innes. The Key to Heaven's Vault.

Our haggard group of weary travelers were due some rest. The Tempest was already scaling the eastern horizon. We must have been underground for three or four days. We wouldn't have much time to find proper shelter before the next cycle hit, and Skavers would be on our heels. There was no sign of them on the surface, though, and the Tempest might keep them at bay.

With the hot wind on my face at the top of a high plateau, I looked over the rolling desert of the Rustyard and toward the Looking Glass somewhere far beyond. It would take us twice as long to get back without the Sun Sister, maybe longer with elderly now in our caravan. The North was about to become the living nightmare some of them believed it to be.

Our descent into the dunes was rife with the muttering and passive finger-pointing of the Cistern workers who hadn't felt sunlight in years. Moss took little joy in his freedom, choosing instead to blame us for all his grief.

But even if he didn't know the whole truth, he was right. With one frenzied decision, we doomed thousands of people. Iris did the cutting, but I would've done the same in her position.

There were children at Colony Six. I saw scared, confused faces. The same sort of faces I saw fifteen years before, from the inside of an oven. So, why did I feel so little sympathy for them? I'm nothing like him. I regret what we did. Renner wouldn't care. I tried to conjure an image of them in my mind—to prove to myself that I regretted their deaths, that I felt remorse. I'm not like him. I'm not.

For most of the day, we trailed the cistern workers to keep pace with the slowest of them and to keep an eye on the shadier ones.

"Peace and quiet till they showed up," Moss said to no one in particular, ruffling sand from his puffy hair. "That's all I'm saying."

"Imagine that," Iris shouted back. "Peace and quiet? Boy, I'd sure love to know what that sounds like."

A nervous laugh spilled out of him like an apology. He kept his voice to a murmur after that.

The stench of old sweat and grease was in the air at the back of the group. Saph walked between them and us, like an exile from both sides.

I sidled up next to her. "Can I ask you something?"

She slowed and turned toward me, keeping her eyes on the ground. "Of course. But I'm not sure I'll be much help."

"No, nothing like that. I'm…" I wasn't sure how to say it. "What happened? All this time. With them. You don't have to tell me, if you're not ready."

She walked next to me for a while. Her far-off stare scoured the sand. "I'd been there a couple years, I think, before I learned what Renner did. I was about ten when I tried to kill him. Almost died in the process." With two fingers, she pulled back her collar and showed me the severe scars down her neck and collarbone, long healed over. "Tried to do to him what he did to you all. Just burned myself instead."

"I'm so sorry," I said.

Part of me wanted to show her my scars—evidence that I understood. But that wasn't quite true. Iris's pain wasn't the same as my pain, and Saph's wasn't either. We'd all lived completely different lives, even if we shared some losses. I didn't know what else to say or do. Maybe she noticed.

She gave me a curt smile and brushed her fingers along the ridges of her scars. "I don't regret it. This is where I kept you all. I think it made surviving feel less…I don't know. Like, if I was hurting too, it meant I knew how it felt to be—" she stopped and covered her mouth. "Oh, I'm so sorry. That was horrible."

No," I said, reassuring her. "You did what you had to. We all did. I'm always thinking about what happened. What I could've or should've done differently. Blaming myself, then forgiving myself again. Just stuck in this cycle. I try not to think about it. Because sometimes it feels like drowning. Like I can't breathe. And I want to run or tear off my skin."

I felt I should stop, that I was sharing too much. But I just wanted to get it out. To tell someone who would understand.

"You know, Maksy saw me that night," I said. "She didn't say a word. Just looked at me." I tried to picture her face. "She was so scared, but she still didn't tell them I was there."

I swallowed my anxiety and continued.

"And I've always wondered. What did I look like under there? What did she see on my face that made her keep quiet? How scared did I look?" Heat coiled in my stomach. "And then they took you. And I'll never forget what you said. You said it's gonna be okay."

Iris walked out of earshot at that. We both watched her go.

I brought my voice down, "God, Saph…how the hell did you do it?

"What do you mean?" she asked.

"I don't know how else to say it. How did you survive? How did you stay this way—yourself?"

She shook her head with a knowing half-smile that said she'd asked herself the same question. "You are who you are." She shrank into herself and pulled at the edges of her clothes. "After Varic built… that place for me—sorry, actually, can we talk about something else?"

Her hand tarried around her neck, and she was breathing more rapidly.

"Of course. Sorry," I said. "Hey, you know what." I handed her my oculum. "Why don't you try it on? It helps a lot with the sun."

She slid it on, and I adjusted the straps around her head.

"Well?" I asked.

She looked around and kept a nervous hand up to hold it in place. First she scanned the sky, her mouth lulling open—that one tooth still amiss—then at the horizon ahead of us, and finally at me. She smiled wide and nodded.

"It's yours," I said.

"Mine? To keep?" she exclaimed. "I couldn't."

"I insist. Just take care of it." I dusted off some of the gunk that had built up over the last week. "It's been through a lot with me."

"Of course," she said earnestly. "Wow. I haven't had something that was mine in a long…thank you."

"You're welcome—"

Clark came barreling down the dune ahead of us. "Derecho," he said, pointing into the sky behind me. "The hawk is still circling."

The bird was in the same place we'd seen him days before. I whistled short and high. As he tucked back his wings and swooped down, I held out my arm for him. He furiously flapped to a halt and landed on my arm. Clumsier than Raindrop. His leg cipher was still sealed. Was this meant for us?

As I slid the iridescent shield up to read the numerical code, a small piece of rolled paper slipped out and drifted into the sand. I snatched it up and unrolled it.

As I read the four words on the page, I couldn't breathe. The space behind my eyes swelled hot with tears, and I could feel the ghost of Lars's arm squeezing me, like I was collapsing in on myself. I gripped my chest.

"What is it?" Iris asked. I handed her the piece of paper and collapsed into the sand.

"El," I said, holding an arm over my face.

Iris read it to herself and then handed it back to me with a long sigh. "What an awful woman."

I sat there staring at El's handwriting. It was scratchy and stiff, just like her, but the message underneath…goddamn her.

Weeks ago, in my naivety and anger, I'd asked El how she could justify sending so many people to their deaths to save just one person. She gave me an answer, but I didn't understand it at the time. It didn't seem like enough.

I loosened the pack straps across my chest, but the tightness didn't go away. As Saph and Iris stood next to me—very much alive—and I held El's last words in my hand, I finally understood her answer.

"What does it say?" Clark asked.

I had to try.

CHAPTER 26 - RUN

It took us nine uneventful days to finally reach the edge of the Looking Glass. I talked to Saph a lot during those days. She told me that a Luminator named Dario Bracken had come and given her books from time to time. He wasn't exactly kind to her, but every couple weeks he'd come to admit things to her, things he'd ordered others to do or done himself that he was ashamed of. Saph had comforted him, though she couldn't explain why—perhaps some way to stay sane, to pretend what was happening to her was normal. Maybe to convince him to let her go.

But she never even saw his face.

I told her about El and Lars and everything that had happened. Slowly. Every conversation only lasted a few minutes before she needed space, but she'd always come back, curious about Commonhope, the twins, Raindrop, or what happened to Iris (who also warmed up to Saph after a few days of sulking). I wondered what they were talking about. Iris was looking slightly less glum. It almost felt like old times, until I remembered the three of us were the only ones left. But those briefly saccharine moments were still heartening, even if Saph preferred Iris's company.

At first, I thought I must've said something wrong, maybe pushed her too much, made her uncomfortable. But after a while, I noticed she would only talk openly with the woman. I realized it would take more than a few conversations to heal the wound of only ever knowing cruel, repugnant men. It might never heal, even with time, patience, and gentleness. I decided to wait for her to come to me. And

I was glad every time she did. It made the desert feel much warmer on cold nights and much more forgiving in the heat of the day.

In the interim between conversations with Saph, Clark and I kept each other company. And I finally got him to spill the story about the feather hanging from Toothpick.

"I can't imagine the explanation is actually interesting enough for you to have kept it to yourself all these years," I said.

"Interesting?" he replied. He shook his head. "Intrigue is not essential to significance. Even if I tell you, it may not mean to you what it does to me."

"Doesn't matter what it means to me. I'm asking because I want to know what it means to you. Come on, Clark. You really gonna take this to the grave?" I nudged a rusty Secondhand Jack leg sticking out of the sand.

He reached up and stroked the hawk feather dangling where the marbles clinked together. After seeing the other androids across the canyon, I wondered how much of Clark was Dex's engineering, and how much was his own experience. He was truly one of a kind.

"This happened when you were quite young," he started. "For a brief period, I was permitted use of a hawk of my own, for communicative purposes."

I laughed. There was no world in which I could imagine that. "You had a hawk? No way. What was its name?"

"Crumb," he said. He put his hand up as I opened my mouth to ask. "Yes. The very same. And before you ask anything else, please have the sense to recognize that many of your questions will be answered by virtue of allowing me to tell the story in full, and that it is difficult for me to recount."

I gestured for him to continue. Though, I indeed had a million questions. "By all means."

"He was ornery even as an eyas. No one else wanted to train him. The aviary almost abandoned him to the elements. But for a reason I cannot ascertain, despite sincere reflection on the matter, Crumb showed great affection for me. Naturally, I trained him myself, and he took to it the way a hawk should: once given an order, he saw it through. Without fail. Though, he was also partial to stealing table scraps, hence his namesake."

Clark stared up into the cloudless sky. "During the first fires, I had already been deployed by Luminator Doran to investigate other goings-on near the Titan's Grave. When I observed the rising smoke, I released Crumb with a warning to Commonhope. It was likely that I had been first to notice, so I knew we could not waste a moment. But—" he paused, resting a hand on his brow as if to block out the sun from his eyes.

His voice wavered between apologetic and frustrated, like he was trying to convince me of something. "It is true that in my haste, I neglected to assess the severity of the storm that was descending on us. And yes, Crumb took to the sky at my instruction. But you must believe me. When I realized my mistake, I signaled for him to return. Many times. The birds, they never listen when you need them to—when it is most important. They cannot be trusted."

I rested a hand on his back. "Tell me what happened, Clark."

He continued. "Crumb looked so small up there. I had witnessed such agility and grace from him, and he could fly with unequaled speed and purpose when it suited him. In his prime, he could compete with Raindrop." His hand dropped from his face. "So, to watch his little body simply fall from the sky, it was as if the world had turned upside down. It was…wrong. I whistled for him to return, but he would not listen, Gaius. He would not listen. He just kept falling."

I grabbed his arm and stopped him. "It's okay, big guy."

His head dropped. "He had been struck by lightning. He fell into the Rust Yard. I rushed to him, but it was too late."

"It wasn't too late. He lived," I protested. "Crumb's alive."

"Alive," Clark said incredulously. "Yet the bird has no memory of me. No recognition of my smell. No connection to the years we spent together. No acknowledgement of our bond. No affection for me at all. I was his singular attachment in this world, but when it came to it, he defied me, and in so doing, destroyed the greatest friendship I ever had. The birds are stubborn and cannot be trusted."

"Clark, what happened wasn't Crumb's fault," I said. "I'm sure some part of you knows that, but it bears repeating. So I'll say it again. It wasn't his fault. It was precisely because he trusted you that he kept flying. I mean, he flew straight into a storm, just because you asked him to. And he didn't even hesitate. It's okay to be angry at what happened, but it was an accident."

He was ignoring me, but I pressed further.

"And I think it's even more important for you to realize what you missed in all this. You reacted emotionally in a moment of desperation and made a mistake. Everyone has. After all, to err is human."

He lifted his head and turned to me. The smile bent into his face seemed so distinct in that moment. "Human…?" he repeated, just on the edge of silence.

"That's right," I said. And I leaned in to drive the point home. "So of course Crumb doesn't like you. Because he doesn't like people."

His shoulders went back, and his frame stretched up an extra inch or two. "Curious. I never considered that." He flicked the feather with one long finger, and it twirled in the wind.

"Thanks for finally telling me," I said, patting him on the back. "You're a good friend."

Clark only nodded in acknowledgement. Maybe he'd finally start believing what I already knew about him.

I rode that feeling all the way through the Rust Yard. And I think Clark did too. He told me he was going to try to win back Crumb's affection the old-fashioned way—patience, presence, and persistence. The same way he'd won me over. His new attitude and motivation certainly made the trip easier.

The cistern workers were also doing their fair share. Setting camp, staying up for watch, gathering food and water. It was nice to rely on them, even if both our groups had reservations about the other. They tended to keep to themselves, and so did we.

We found shelter during the first two storm cycles, but that was the least of our worries. Renner and his squadron of piercers were looming, always on the horizon. It kept us slow and weary, always one anxious eye on the sky. Eventually, we had to start traveling at night just to keep ourselves concealed.

But we'd finally made it. Nine days on the surface. The Tempest was fast approaching behind us as we stepped onto the salt flats, and the rain had already started.

Clark and Saph were up front with a couple miners. Snags had practically become Clark's traveling companion when Grisham wasn't carrying her—chatting him up about Dex. Apparently, they knew each other years ago. Friends even.

That made me miss Raindrop. I wondered if El had run into her before they stormed Colony Six. I whistled, just to make certain she wasn't nearby.

No answer. Good. Dex probably has her.

"Run," Moss yelled as he scrambled past me, tripping over himself in panic. "Skavers."

Red sand whipped into the Looking Glass, biting the already raw skin on my neck. As I turned back, I saw a legion of human forms crawling over the spraying dunes behind us. Farther beyond them in the sky were six piercers riding the waves of the storm, weaving between developing cyclones as they dropped streams of fire and chaos down onto the mob of Skavers.

The Tempest screamed in bursts of lightning and thunder and breaking clouds, blotting out the sky above the dunes with swirling funnels. She swallowed a piercer whole.

"Cole is still out there," a familiar voice cried over the storm. "Iris, don't leave him to die."

Iris stopped in her tracks next to me, but didn't turn around, rain pelting her. I saw Brin crossing the threshold of the Looking Glass with Foss and Nello in tow.

"I know he's alive," it croaked over the storm. It reached out its hand to Iris from fifty or so meters away, a cool glow shivering beneath its skin. "Let's find him together."

"It's not her," I grabbed Iris's arm and dragged her toward Dex's hideout. "We don't have time."

Iris resisted for a moment until she turned around to look for herself, slowly backing away. "Cole's dead," she called to the Skaver. "I found his body twelve years ago. You were right, but…he wanted to be a raincoat. So I won't ask for forgiveness. Because he'd hate me if I did. And Brin never would've offered it."

A whirling swarm of particles surged from Brin's throat as it held out a hand for Iris to approach.

"Run," I yelled over the turbulence. We rushed away, and the Skavers charged after us. They were fast, but the storm was faster. The rest of our group was nearing the arc harness spires.

Thundering over the assaulting wind, Renner's ships blasted toward us. The storm was providing some cover, but not enough. If he recognized any of us out of the group, we'd be targeted. I wrapped my scarf around my head and was glad Saph had my oculum. Clark would protect her with his life.

Flowering explosions peppered the flats as piercers burst through the storm in a hail of haphazard fire. They bombarded the edge of the Looking Glass behind us, and I could feel the heat expanding on the wind at my back.

It felt like running underwater or in a dream—slow, with little progress—and the rain was carrying upward back into the clouds. Red sand swirled and tried to nip at me, but my stormbreaker was finally the right size for me, thanks to Iris. I guess this is what it was always meant to do.

A pummeling explosion from a fly-by knocked me forward—then I was drawn back by the inhaling appetite of the Tempest. Iris reached out and grabbed me, just as Skavers were clawing at my heels through the prevailing winds.

"Stay on your damn feet, packbrat," she yelled as we sprinted into the first ring of spires.

The spires worked as footholds when we reached them, but the lightning was beginning to focalize. The rods were just another death sentence if we didn't move. With each arcing bolt that spread and flowed into the ground, the flats erupted in fragments of hot glass, scattering to the wind. I didn't want more scars in my back, but Iris was inching ahead of me, little by little.

My stormbreaker was getting perforated with glass. Blood flushed from my bad leg. Just move forward. Just keep moving. Iris couldn't do anything to help now that the storm was right over us. Her eyes never drifted from me, though. She kept shouting at me, but whatever encouragement or insult she was slinging was lost in the tumult.

I felt another burst of heat at my back. I was flung ahead and bounced across the hard, wet sand and salt. My chest careened off a spire, and I slid face up in aching pain. I stared into the sky through my scarf as the surging crest of sand and lightning blended into a grotesque behemoth—the Desert and Tempest fighting over who would devour me.

My body shook as I tried to get up. I'd barely had a moment to breathe in weeks. It would be so easy to just let the storm take me. Let it end. But I couldn't.

I had to try.

Her voice filled my mind. I flipped onto my stomach. The Skavers were converging on me, but those that inched too close to the spires were shocked and scorched black in an instant.

I closed my weary eyes and pictured the scene again. Her frail, charred fingers reaching for my face, the same dogged assurance behind her eyes, even after what Renner put her through. I couldn't hear anything but El's voice.

Don't get distracted. Run, Gaius. Hide. Survive. Try. Mantras she'd beaten into me.

I was so tired. Down to my bones. I didn't want to run anymore. But I struggled upward onto my knees. With my body level, I aimed my anchor at the terrain beyond my field of vision.

Bite down and don't let go.

I punched the anchor, firing the grapnel into the distance. It caught something. I hoped it wasn't a person.

The pain in my leg meant I was still alive. I grabbed the tether in front of me and pulled with all my might. The burning in my lungs meant I was still breathing. I struggled onward, inch by inch. My shaking arms meant my strength wasn't spent. I hauled my body through the deafening maelstrom on blistered toes.

I screamed all my exhaustion into the storm.

My legs convulsed as the tether was suddenly yanked forward by someone unseen. My voice cracked as I cried out and held on with what strength I had left. I was dragged through the scattering glass and biting debris until I saw the familiar glow of Clark's gaze ahead of me—the image of safety that had always been rooted next to me—pulling me into the Breacher.

CHAPTER 27 - ASCENSION

I tumbled inside as the hatch clanged and hissed shut. The musty interior of the Breacher was the sweetest air I'd ever tasted. I pulled my scarf away from my face and gasped for air.

I looked around. Everyone had made it. Saph was cowering in the corner with her hands over her ears. The Cistern workers were pacing and muttering to each other, and Clark and Iris had my anchor cable in their hands.

"Thanks," I heaved, cranking the retractor.

There was pounding on the hatch above us, like animals trying to get in. It wouldn't hold them for long. Our only chance was to trust the Tempest would deal with them.

As Grisham helped me to my feet with his giant mitts, Dex came barreling out of the left bulkhead door. Snags hid behind Flint as soon as Dex entered.

"You certainly know how to make an entrance—oh." He eyed our motley crew with suspicion. "Right. Uh, Iris, go double-check the bolts on the arc harness, would you? These oiled sausages aren't what they used to be. And Clark, boot up the navigator, or we're flying blind." He looked at me. "Please, tell me you got the key?"

I went over and took Saph by the hand. "Dex, you're looking at the Key to Heaven's Vault. This is Saph."

Saph nervously brushed the hair away from her oculum.

"Is it indeed?" He pulled his glasses off and held them against his chest. "Oh, of course you are. How about that, aye? There's a mountain of things I want to tell you, lass, but we only have a few minutes before the eye of the Tempest is on us. We can't miss our window." He wiped grimy fingers on his shirt and squeezed her arm gently. "You go with Iris now, dear."

"You're with me, Saph," Iris said, dragging her along. Clark ran ahead of them.

Dex pointed at Grisham. "You, big man. Ever work a heat-sink release?"

"It's Grisham. Can't say I have," he replied.

Dex made a crescent shape with his hands that swiveled at his wrist. "Looks like this. Hotter than hell. Drinks tons of water."

"Doesn't sound like fun work," he said. "But I'm used to it."

"Appreciate it." Dex thumbed the door. "Go on and head through the door at the end and climb down the ladder. Ignore the warning on the wall. The siphons and hose are temp-automated, but we need someone to muscle the spout a bit when you see it going into the red. Make sense?"

"Simple enough. But don't blame me if we all go up in flames." Grisham dropped his striker and ran off down the corridor.

"Dex, we have a bigger problem," I said, leaning hard on my good leg. The banging above us was still going.

"Just a minute. Need to flip the…there you are." Dex attempted to part the sea of miners huddled around the room.

"You talking about this?" Moss flipped two red-handled levers upward. A wry smile crossed his face as a whirring noise surged the length of the entire bunker.

Dex shooed him out of his way. "Keep your hands to yourself unless I ask you." He pointed two fingers at Moss. "This ship is the only ticket out of here, and it doesn't include any plots, coups, or revolutions, got it?"

Moss backed away with his hands in the air. "Just trying to help. I got a mind for machines, is all. You need a switch flipped, just pass the word."

Dex stared Moss down with a finger poking into his sternum. "I've made note of your skills, switch-flipper. And I know which side of the canyon you lot came from. So get to the cabin, strap in, and stay there until I say otherwise."

Snags nervously covered her face. I thought Dex was an old friend.

"Alright, alright." Moss surrendered himself with the rest of his crew into the corridor. "Come on people. Outta his way."

"Dex, we've got a problem," I repeated.

He grabbed me by the shoulders and moved me aside as he frantically flipped more switches and checked quavering dials. "Go ahead, then," he said. "What's eating you?"

"Skavers," I said.

He snapped a look at me. "I told you I won't have jokes—"

I pointed to the banging hatch above us. "When the storm passes, they'll still be out there. I've seen what they can do. They can bend metal with their bare hands, regenerate skin…pretend to be human."

He was calculating something in his head. Then he continued his fiddling. "Then let's not be here to greet them."

"Dex." I probably already knew the answer, but I had to ask anyway. "What about the others on the surface? There are still people on Galilei."

He didn't look at me, but his face went grim. "No, lad. There aren't. We stick to the maxim, or we all die." He pushed a button on the wall and leaned toward a small box. "Clark, how's the nav and reserves looking?"

Maybe the Skavers wouldn't find Hollis out in the springs. Maybe the sub-granary was hidden well enough to keep Kwendani safe. But I doubted it. They'd found Brin, Nello, and Foss after all. Did we really doom them all for our petty revenge?

"Trajectory still calculating. Cells are at eighty-nine percent and falling at nought-point-one per second," Clark's voice called back through the radio. "Even without the increased weight burden, we are below a nominal energy threshold."

"Don't fret," Dex said. "I already knew we'd need another boost before we broke atmo. We'll catch some lightning on the way up—one more drink for the road. Iris, how's things looking?"

"Arc harness recoiler is as secure as I could make it," Iris chirped over the radio. "But this is some shitty work, Dex. I mean, real shitty. I'm heading to control now, but if this thing falls apart, I'll break your godda—"

"—Thanks for the report," Dex cut in. "Clark, retract the rods and empty all cells into the engine ports. As soon as Her eye is on us, we're scooting off this rock."

"Wait. Where's Raindrop?" I asked. My stomach dropped. She hadn't come flying to me when I'd arrived, and I didn't hear her squawking or calling for me. "Did she make it back—"

"Don't worry, lad. She's with Harrow."

"You're certain? She could've got out. You saw her yourself?"

"Calm down," he said with a nervous laugh. "She's here. I'm as certain as the sunrise." He waved me toward the bulkhead. "Come on. I'll take you to her. But let's be quick."

I breathed a sigh of relief as we left the galley and followed the corridor down to Iris's room.

He pulled the latch up and swung the heavy door open. Harrow was sitting on the edge of Iris's bed with Crumb perched atop his hood. He was stroking Raindrop's head with one finger.

"Master Gaius," Harrow said with a start. "The fast one has not eaten in days."

Raindrop flew straight into my chest and flapped her wings wildly with a screech. I could barely contain her excitement.

"Hey, girl." I lifted my forearm under her and pulled her close. She clicked her beak and pressed her head into the bottom of my chin. "I missed you so much. Come here. Ah, I'm glad you're okay."

It didn't take long before she hopped up on my shoulder and started digging in my pack. I didn't have any meat left, though.

Dex nudged me. "Alright, lad? Come on."

I whistled and extended my arm toward Harrow. "Thanks for taking care of her. I owe you one."

"Nothing owed, Master Gaius." He held out a sliver of meat, and Raindrop hopped over and happily took it. "I have enough treasure."

Dex and I retreated to CONTROL. The door was already open. Inside Iris, Saph, and Clark sat in brown leather chairs facing the pair of glass bay windows, which were compacted with dirt on the other side. I'd been in there before, when Dex was telling me stories about the stars. But now there was a lively, blinking rainbow of buttons on a control panel humming beneath their fingers.

"What were you doing?" Iris said. She was sweating and exasperated. "Her eye is already on us."

"Good. Punch it," Dex replied.

Iris's hand hovered and shook over a palm-sized green button that read ENGAGE. Dex rested his hands on the headrest behind Iris. "Well? Get on with it. We'll lose our window."

She bit her lip and looked back at him, then at me, her chest rising and falling. "What if it doesn't work?"

I couldn't muster any nuggets of wisdom, mostly because I had little idea about what the hell was going on. I was at a loss.

Dex rubbed Iris's head. "It'll work. I've got my good luck charm."

I was surprised she didn't swat his hand away. She just pursed her lips and exhaled three times in rapid succession.

"Fuck it. Here goes nothing." She closed her eyes and slammed her hand down on the button.

Electricity crackled inside the hull of the Breacher, and the walls rattled and croaked as if the whole ship was about to collapse in on itself.

"And now, for the real show," Dex said as energy exploded beneath us with enough force to drive me to my knees. The sound was like thunder and fire and the howling of an elder gravehound all at once, amplified by a magnitude of ten.

Dirt and salt crumbled away from the bay windows, exposing the serene, sun-soaked world outside. Dex wasn't crazy. We were flying. Into the sky. Just like he said. Awe crept across my face and stayed there.

We were right in the eye of the storm, in the calm. I hated to admit it was beautiful seeing the most powerful force on Galilei from the safety of our metal bunker, but I couldn't deny the view.

Not far off, piercers were diving in and out of the storm's eyewall like sleek, black fish in a sea of sand and lightning.

Superheated air bellowed beneath us as we rocketed over the Looking Glass. Iris closed her eyes and squeezed the life out of her rattling seat as everything creaked and strained. Saph smiled with a big, open mouth and leaned over the bay window to see what was happening outside.

I suddenly felt very heavy, like my body was being sucked into the floor.

"You should get that rebandaged, lad," Dex said, pointing to the small pool of blood accumulating on the metal grates beneath me.

"We have exceeded the nominal weight burden," Clark said.

"Ah, it's just our merry band of freeloaders." Dex waved a hand. "No worries. Just push her for all she's worth. I told ya, we'll ride the storm on the way up and catch some of her anger."

"Incorrect. I have calculated the approximate weight of the additional crew, sodium, and soil accumulated on the hull from takeoff, but it does not account for the disparity. There is additional weight elsewhere. At our current rate of acceleration, we will not reach the necessary velocity to—"

A Skaver suddenly tumbled down over the bay window and flung off into the flats below. We all waited for a moment.

"Well, that answers the weight question," Dex muttered.

Iris kept her eyes closed. "What the hell was that?!"

"Nothing, Iris. You just keep focusing on, uh…not focusing." Dex anxiously ushered me out of the control room. I followed him into the corridor where he averted his gaze and itched his head. "I hate to put this on you, bleeding leg and all. But it looks like we got some uninvited guests."

"What do you need?" I asked.

"Bless your tenacity, lad," he smiled, relieved. "Can you hop on the thumper? Clark and I will be busy keeping us afloat and enroute, and I wouldn't trust the newbies with a damned wrench, let alone a weapon of that size."

"Just point me in the right direction." I'd barely learned how to handle my brela over the last few weeks. I had my doubts I'd be able to wield anything but a slightly bigger knife with any degree of competency.

He pointed down the corridor. "There's a hatch behind the stairwell. I'll walk you through the details on the intercom when you get below. Just make sure you strap in."

I turned and hobble-hopped down to the stairwell. My body was twice as heavy as I remembered.

"Gaius. Make sure to strap in," he repeated with emphasis. "Got it?"

With a thumbs up, I slid behind the stairwell where a looped leather strap was connected to the floor around a metal ring. I yanked the loop and released the square hatch. It flung open against the wall, and I climbed down some wrought iron ladder rungs into an unlit, spherical room with a seat hanging in the center.

As per Dex's instructions, I pulled myself up and strapped in to the best of my ability. It was like wearing a giant pack.

"You buckled, Gaius?" Dex said on an overhead radio.

"I guess," I said. "But it's dark in here. Can I get some light?"

"You may regret that phrasing," he said, as two massive steel panels peeled away from the floor and walls, revealing a glass pod.

My stomach leapt into my throat, as I tried to scoot away from the glass window around me, clawing at the top of my seat as the room burst with outside light.

"Flick the blinky switch and grab the handles," Dex said.

"The goddamned floor just opened up," I screamed back.

"In hindsight, a warning might have helped," he said. "Just trust me—that glass won't break without tremendous force. You're safe, relatively speaking. I mean, safe as any of us. This whole thing could come dropping out of—"

I heard Iris shout something at him and the intercom cut out.

"Dex? You there?"

"Ow. Sorry. Just flick the switch like I told ya," he said. "Point the barrels, and just squeeze when something's in your sights."

I settled into the seat, double-checked the straps crisscrossed over my chest, and tried not to stare into the abyss below me. When I was sure the harness wouldn't give, I flicked the switch and two rounded handles swung down in front of me.

The grip of the right one was flashing red. I grabbed them both and my seat swung downward to face the surface. Two short metal pipes followed my movement like an extra set of arms, and I had full 180-degree rotation.

The eye of the storm was drifting away from us, and we were about to hit the inner wall of the maelstrom where three piercers were pursuing from below.

Spires and carbon tethers were dangling, needle and thread, underneath the Breacher, which Skavers climbed toward me.

I rotated the barrels and took aim. *There's the dead weight.* I squeezed the flashing right handle. The pod quaked with enough force to compress my ribs, as a flash of red-hot, rusted shrapnel—nuts, bolts, nails, and scrap metal sprayed out.

The spray caught two of the Skavers in the face, and they scattered into blue chunks and swarms spinning off and plunging below.

Two more climbed the last segment of cable toward the hull.

"Take care where y…aim th…thing," Dex called over the ringing in my ears. His voice was crackling and distorted. "One… shot pack…punch, and you've only…a few. Just m…sure they're… close enou…to count. And don't blow o…the cables or rods. We st… need 'em."

"Got it," I yelled back. *I think.*

The left trigger started flashing yellow. I squeezed it and felt an internal mechanism rattle as it drew in more ballistic shrapnel.

The two Skavers reached the hull as a twisted zap of lightning reached out and roasted another still climbing, sending his cooked corpse into the jaws of the Tempest. The lightning continued to arc up the spire, through the tether, and hummed as it entered the ship somewhere in the wall near me. *Dex is still gathering energy.*

We suffered a generous spray of fire from a piercer as it flew by. I tried to close in on them, but they were too fast. The thumper obviously wasn't built for aerial combat.

Skavers were crawling along the hull in my direction from opposite sides. I turned to meet the closest one and pressed the flashing right trigger, sundering its body into plummeting hunks of flesh. It was still trying to piece itself back together on the way down.

I clutched the left handle to replenish the shrapnel, but the other Skaver was already at the edge of the glass pod. It began striking the glass repeatedly with its free hand. I swung the thumper down and smeared its body across the hull. But as I lifted the thumper, it held onto one of the barrels with a broken arm. I fired into the abyss, hitting nothing, but violently jolting the Skaver into a freefall.

Three more came crawling over the same side of the ship. I loaded up again and spun to meet them. My next shot shattered pieces of the hull, shredding them all into an unrecognizable mess. The Breacher rumbled as something...important looking came loose and flew off.

"I told y...to watch th...hull," Dex called. "It's the only thing kee...us from burning alive...mosphere."

We took another spray of fire as our ship collided with the storm and collected an array of lightning through the tethers. I squeezed the reload trigger and spun myself around to face the fleeing piercer and fired into the sandstorm. They disappeared unscathed.

As I clenched to reload, nothing happened. The handle wasn't flashing. I squeezed it again. Nothing.

"Dex," I called out. "It's not working." I got no reply.

The ship was swaying in and out of the eyewall of the storm. There was another shadow out there. Another piercer? Something else? I hit the handles repeatedly, trying to knock something loose.

A pulsing hand slapped over the pod, and a shredded visage came over the edge, the bones of a feminine face exposed. Its one vacant eye stared past me. It was talking to me—probably trying to convince it was human, but I couldn't hear it.

I desperately squeezed the trigger with both hands. Nothing. I tried to swing the thumper around to crush the Skaver, but the Tempest was fighting me, pulling the barrels away. I pushed myself up and yanked down hard. The barrels missed, clanging against the hull like a low bell. They caught on something—wouldn't move.

The Skaver's skin was peeling back and reforming as the whipping sand lashed it away. It reared back and smashed its head into the glass. Again. And again. And again. It's not gonna break. It's not gonna break.

The glass cracked. I yanked at the handles. They wouldn't move. I looked around for something. Anything.

The window cracked again. Small pieces sucked out into the wind. The pressure went out of the pod as I held my breath. I struggled with the latches holding me in place, trying to scramble backward. But my seat was facing toward the surface, and there was only a cracking window and a Skaver below.

"Dex, help," I yelled. "Someone, please."

The crack split across the edges of the pod. I couldn't unlatch. Couldn't shoot. Couldn't move.

The Skaver pulled its head back as far as it would go and smashed straight through the window, shattering the glass into a thousand pieces. It slid back down the barrels, a cut-up mess of shivering flesh.

I pulled up my scarf as the sand and debris came flying into the pod. My oculum sure would've been helpful.

The Skaver climbed up the thumper and started to pull itself into the ship. I screamed and scrambled. I had nothing. My anchor would just pull it toward me.

Dex was crackling over the intercom, but it was incomprehensible in the wind. The Skaver opened its mouth. A cloud of tiny particles emerged but was sucked back out into the storm—the only favor the Tempest had ever done me.

It stood on the frame of the pod to get closer. I grabbed the back of my seat to pull away. We were about to break the clouds—the storm was waning. Half the tethers were gone, most of the others were fried or damaged.

I couldn't even hear my own voice over the screaming wind and roaring engines. I could only sit and watch as the Skaver slowly advanced.

Something flew past my head—a very large wrench, which collided with the Skaver's head, knocking it clear from the ship, down among the cables of highly conductive spires. And with all her spite, the Tempest reached out and struck it in a blaze of fury.

I looked up, past the hatch.

Saph was looking down at me through her oculum, holding an armful of Dex's tools. I'd never been more glad to see her. I waved halfheartedly. I still needed to get out.

The iron doors started to shut under me, but the latches of my seat were cutting into my skin. I was stuck.

Your brela. You moron. You absolute goddamn idiot. I almost died with my weapon still secured to my hip. How the hell did I forget it was there? Iris had trained me to reach for it instinctually. Over and over.

I took it out and cut one strap open and slipped out of the chair. My free hand caught one loose strap, and I watched the blood drip from my leg, one bead at a time, through the closing doors. Without Saph, that would've been me.

I achingly pulled myself up on top of the seat and leapt to the ladder above as another heavy tool plinked into the ladder above me and careened just past my head. I looked up. Saph was giving me an apologetic hand wave as she put the rest of the tools down. The wind faded with each reluctant step upward.

"Ge...ou...of there!" Dex's voice was still static as I reached the top.

"No shit!" I screamed back.

Saph lent me both of her hands, and weakly pulled me back into the corridor. I sealed the hatch shut behind us, and the howling wind ceased all at once. We collapsed on the cold steel floor in heaving breaths.

"You did it, lad," Dex's cheerful voice came through a box above us. "We made it. Breached the storm and caught enough juice on the way up! Brace for atmo."

Cheers rang out through the corridor as the ship rattled beneath us. I laid there on the grated floor next to Saph. I could hardly catch my breath. Everything seemed to shrink around me. There was suddenly nowhere to go. Nowhere left to run. And no one could follow us where we were going.

I stared up at the ceiling. The ship slowly stopped shaking, and the stillness returned. And the silence. My ears started ringing again.

"Sorry about the second one," Saph said.

"Yeeeah," I said. "Almost killed me."

I smiled, which turned into a slight chuckle. I shook my head and turned to look at her. My oculum was still strapped to her face, and Deek's oversized boots were on her feet next to a small pile of tools. She looked ridiculous. I couldn't contain my laughter. She'd just saved my life looking like that. It was all so sincere. Too sincere.

She cracked a nervous smile. "I really am sorry," she pleaded.

"I know," that made me laugh even harder.

I heard the CONTROL door open and footsteps approach. Iris stood over us. "The hell's so funny?"

I just put a hand up and shook my head. "Nothing. You seem okay now."

She kicked me in the arm. "Shut up. Just come and look. You too Saph."

I took the deepest breath my lungs would allow and rolled over. I snorted one more good laugh as I lifted Saph to her feet. She shouldered me with a snicker as we followed behind Iris.

I've missed this.

The CONTROL door squeaked open, and Dex spun in his seat and waved us inside.

"Welcome back to the endless night," he said with a smile, leaning back and staring out the bay windows.

"Whoa," Saph whispered.

The stars glinted across the infinite horizon, wet reflections in a sea of ink—each one as distant as it was beautiful.

When I was younger, if I stared at the night sky for too long, I'd get this sense of dread, like I might just fall off the face of Galilei if I couldn't shake the fear. But here, with my feet against the sky, it was as if the freckled face of the cosmos was smiling at me. No malice. Just an invitation: Where do you want to go?

The Breacher slowly spun toward a single golden glimmer in the distance. A torch beckoning us onward.

"There she is," Dex whispered. "Home."

CHAPTER 28 - HOME

Heaven's Vault was colossal. It looked like a long, black-stemmed flower, half-bloomed at one end and gilded with silver thorns and fractal petals. The stem comprised most of the craft and was a slender, many-sided prism—pristine and glassy. I'd never seen anything so beautiful or complex in all my life.

The empty space around it was tinted in bronze light from the panels jutting under the belly of the ship in dozens of fins, illuminated by the sun. Nine windowed levels in height, and more than ten times that in length, were sealed in tinted glass which was framed in thin chrome.

Over the apex of its bulbous, rounded nose was the double-crossed emblem of Commonhope in white. However, the grandest display of opulence fanned out behind the ship, eclipsing the vessel with flared flower petals, all bright, reflective gold.

And though the ship hung suspended in such a brilliant spectacle, it seemed more wilted than alive, like a moon, shining but producing no true light itself. There was no movement inside either.

As we floated closer, the size of it filled the windows and eclipsed our sun. We were just a speck approaching one of a dozen uniform docking bays—the thorns—riddled across the highest two levels.

As the Breacher slowed, our feet lifted from the floor. Dex unlatched from his seat and pushed up into the air, patting Iris on the shoulder on his way up. We were weightless.

Saph grabbed my hand as she lifted herself out of the seat. She giggled. All those times in the thunderfruit fields, clapping and watching as one tiny mystery of the universe unfurled itself—not in our wildest dreams would we have imagined something so impossible.

"Take us in, Clark," Dex said. "I'm sure Iris is itching for some solid ground. Let's see if we can't get the Vault spinning for her. Dock seven should do the trick. The ship's been soaking in the sun for over twenty years now, so I'm sure there's more power than we'll know what to do with."

"Looks dead to me," I said.

He scratched his beard and muttered to himself. "In a manner of speaking. No one's been keeping up with maintenance or working the oxygen scrubbers, which means there won't be much for air, if anything at all—likely clogged with the dust of those who stayed behind. Hmm. I don't much fancy inhaling what's left of my comrades. We'll have to prime them ourselves."

"How do you propose we do that with no air?" I asked, then realized, after years of hearing him mimic human breathing, one of us didn't actually need to breathe. "Oh. Clark."

"He'll be coming with us, yes." Dex floated to the doorway and unlatched it. "But we'll be working on different ends of the ship, and he can't do both."

"Mooring at dock seven in twelve-minutes eight-seconds." Clark was focused. He didn't seem himself. It was as if he was part of the ship. I didn't like it.

"Gaius is hurt," Saph said. "Can't you take Grisham?"

"Grisham?" Dex belly laughed. "That two-legged monstrosity wouldn't fit in the secondskin if we cut him at the knees. And before you go suggesting anyone else, you should know I didn't expect most of those black-lunged bumblers to survive the ascent. It's a miracle they did." He smiled at Saph and looked at her over the rim of his glasses. "Don't worry. You're coming with us. Without you, none of this works."

She turned toward me for confirmation. I smiled and nodded as if that was information I already knew. For the first time in years, someone was looking to me for answers. Damned if I wasn't going to fake it.

Dex ruffled the growing fuzz on Iris's head. "Keep the control room clear of those squatters."

She swatted at him and found herself floating away. Her hands shot back under the seat and gripped tighter.

I watched orbs of my blood drift by. "Uh. Saph's got a point," I said. "My leg won't be good to walk on."

"Who's asking you to walk around on it?" He waved his arms in big circles. "The only gravity up here is the situation we find ourselves in, which I'll add, isn't all that grim compared to what we just left behind. So, quit wasting our air on grievances and get in tow."

He grabbed me by my pack and pushed me and Saph through the door down the center of the corridor. As we passed by Iris's room, I caught Harrow, Crumb, and Raindrop lazily floating through the cracked door. Harrow was smiling with his eyes closed.

His feet never did belong on the ground.

We came back through to the galley and Dex pulled up a stool. "Take a seat. Saph, help him get that old bandage off, will you?"

"I thought you weren't good at this kind of work." I sat down and removed Kai's boot.

"I'd have Iris do this," he started, "but I'm sure you saw her. She needs a minute. Just bear with me, if you can."

"Is she going to be okay?" Saph asked as Dex went to work redressing. "She looked really scared."

Dex and I shared a glance and a smirk. "She'll be fine," I said. "And definitely don't tell her that."

Thankfully, the wound didn't need stitching again, but Dex's hands had none of the soft care Iris had initially given me. He wrapped it twice as tight as I would've preferred, but no bleeding.

He nodded over to the over bulkhead door when he was done. "Finally got it working," he said, floating over.

He spun the handwheel open with ease. It hissed, and dim lights pulsed on above. The room was narrow and tall with a circular hatch at the end. There were three large figures hanging from the ceiling by their necks.

Dex called them secondskins. They looked somewhat like the

ferno-suits Grisham and Flint wore—open at the back to allow us to step inside, but these could be sealed from behind. They had glass face masks tinted with a gradient of cyan to brown. The torso and legs were shielded in metal and thick white canvas, which was highly rigid but for some malleable areas near the joints for mobility.

"Bay six primed for docking." Clark startled me from behind. He floated through the air with ease, as if he'd done it before. "Iris seems to have settled into a manageable state of anxiety. It is worth noting that she was able to take control of the ship with open eyes."

"Told you," Dex reassured Saph. "She's reliable."

"Indeed," Clark agreed. "I assume you still require my assistance aboard Heaven's Vault."

"That we do." Dex drifted through the open doorway. "Need you and Gaius at opposite ends of the ship to prime the O2 scrubbers. Can't take care of it myself, as I'll be heading up to the bridge with the captain's girl here. Gotta restore secondary and ancillary power before you can prime them, or the air'll be too damned cold to breathe. No point jumping out of the fryer and into the freezer."

We all followed him inside. He took out a wrench and began adjusting the suits according to our sizes.

"By the way, you two won't be able to wear your oculum or anchor inside the secondskins," he said, as he finished adjusting the joints on one suit. "Here, Gaius. This one's for you."

I took off my anchor and stepped inside. Dex swung the hinged back. He motioned for me to keep an eye on his movements as he closed six latches. When the last latch clicked tight, I was sealed inside with a fwish as lights twinkled inside my suit. All that rigidness disappeared. I could move as though it was my own body, just slower, heavier. Cool air flowed against my neck as I waved at Dex.

He was saying something, but it sounded like he was underwater. I could only hear my own breathing. Clark helped Dex and Saph into their suits and double checked each latch.

Dex spun his suit around to face me and pointed at his other hand, which had his thumb pressed into his palm.

"Press your thumb like this when you want to talk to us. Do it again when you want to end the transmission" His voice was all around my head. "We're on the same frequency as the Breacher, but these radi-os are short range, so I'll walk you through the basics before we dock."

He told me the oxygen scrubbers were a lot like the suits we were wearing, but on a massive scale. They needed to be manually reset after years of neglect. All I had to do was prime some levers a few times and push a big button to restart the system. Sounded easy enough. After a few minutes of explanation and triple-checking the seal on our suits, Clark hitched the three of us into harnesses across the wall and took his own position across from us.

Iris came over the radio. "Shit. Uh, hold onto something." A moment later, the Breacher slammed into something. We jostled about in our harnesses. I turned toward Dex, waiting for bad news.

When everything finally stopped shaking, Iris came back over the radio in heavy breaths. "Okay. I think that worked."

"So much for her open eyes," Dex huffed. "All she had to do was make sure the light stayed green."

"I can hear you," she shot back.

"Right. Well, good job…and all that. But how about we turn 'I think' into 'I'm sure.' I'd prefer to end up inside Heaven's Vault than waving a long, lonesome goodbye."

After the silence of a much-too-long moment, and a lot of wide-eyed head turning, Iris calmly came back over the radio. "I'm pretty sure."

Dex pursed his lips and looked at me through his helmet, as if to ask permission to kill her.

"Iris would never let us get hurt," Saph chimed in.

"You're ruining it," Iris replied.

Dex sighed with relief. "Glad we brought you along, Saph. You're a ray of sunshine." He waved his hand toward the port door. "Okay. Clark, go ahead and depressurize."

Clark detached our harnesses and sealed the entrance behind us. He flipped a switch, and I felt my suit tighten ever so slightly.

We all crowded around the circular hatch. It was only large enough for one of us to fit through at a time, so Dex took the forward position. He spun the handwheel at the center until it stopped and turned back to us for one last look before whatever the hell was about to happen.

He pushed a big glowing button beside the door, and the whole room jerked forward as the hatch swung out into the darkness.

"In we go," Dex whispered.

I followed close behind him and Saph as we came out over a suspended, aluminum-grate bridge, a little more than a meter in width. Dex reached up behind his head and two bright lights flashed on at the top of his helmet. Saph and I turned ours on as well.

Floating dust particles glittered in the swallowing shadow. I peered over the edge. It was a long way down, mostly empty space except for other walkways leading to other parts of the ship. However, the walkways didn't make sense—they were angled away from us but all flush with the hull. Odd.

Dex pointed to both ends of the bridge. "Oxygen scrubbers are that way and that way." Then he pointed up. "Just follow the ventilation shaft. It'll lead you to a lift. Once the lift terminal lights up all green and pretty for you, take it down to level five."

I looked up, and my helmet illuminated a massive, black cylinder running the length of the interior, farther than my lights could see.

"I imagine it's gonna make a real mess outta this place when the vents kick open and the air starts flowing," Dex said. "So don't be surprised by a sudden dust storm. Should clear in a few minutes. Saph and I are off to the bridge. Just take it slow and radio me if you need anything. We're in no rush."

He nodded to me and leapt right over the edge of the bridge and floated into the nothing below.

"Stay safe," Saph said. She took a few moments to gather her courage, then less-gracefully jumped after. I watched them through the grates for a minute—just two suits, slowly disappearing. Clark gave me his customary shoulder squeeze and turned away, heading off to do his half of the job. When all their lights were gone, I took a deep, cold breath and pulled myself along the railing.

My movements were slow at first, but I gained momentum as

I got used to the secondskin. I had to consciously think about what I was doing, or I might go veering over the edge.

To my left and right, about every fifty meters, gangway ramps led to other bay doors exactly like the one we'd come through.

My ears started ringing again. They were probably permanently damaged. I started to wonder if I'd ever hear true silence again. I started humming to shut it out. In through your nose, out through your mouth.

The only sounds were those inside my suit. My breathing. Humming. My shifting discomfort. My teeth grinding inside my head. I could even hear myself blinking. And my heartbeat. I'd never been so bombarded by quiet in all my life.

"Just breathe," I muttered. "Think about something else. For once, nothing is chasing you."

How old are these suits? Is it actually safe? What if it leaks? Would I even know? Am I going to suffocate? Am I breathing? I can't breathe. I'm going to die. No one will find my body.

I was fogging up the glass of my helmet. "In through your nose," I said. "Calm down. You're okay."

I heard a crackle in my ears.

"You know, I knew your parents," Dex said.

I realized my balled fists had relayed everything through the radio.

"They were something special," he went on. "One of the few who stayed behind. Botanists. Worked with plants and such. You know that's where your name comes from?"

"Really?" I asked.

"Yep. There used to be more green here than you can imagine. Very little of it made its way to Galilei. Shame." He hummed a soft laugh to himself, like he was remembering something.

"What were their names?"

"Seamus and Clarity Pomona. Clare had you right in the middle of the arboretum. I mean, just right in the moss and shrubs like a chubby head of lettuce." His laugh scratched inside my helmet. "Quite a scene, you can imagine. And you were smaller than usual. Worried the doctors, but not your mom and dad. They just kept on working, like the lights would go out if they stopped."

I wondered why Dex hadn't told me about them. Maybe secrets were for Galilei. "What were they like? Were they good parents?"

"If I'm honest, you didn't change their world much. I don't mean to say they didn't love you. Far be it from me to suggest the Pomona's didn't love their tiny lettuce. But they just kept working. Wasn't uncommon those days. Even when things went sideways. Nothing could slow them down. Forward as always."

I liked the thought. Maybe my stubbornness, my affinity for the world and distance from people, came from them. And no wonder I was so bad in a fight. I came from two gardeners. "What happened to them?" I asked.

"Oh, I wish I had a satisfying answer to that," Dex said. "All I can say is, the day we left, they swaddled you in a green blanket like one of their little peapods and handed you over to the Luminators. They stayed behind, knowing they wouldn't survive, and went right back to work. I promised them I'd keep an eye on you. And I did, as best I could."

"We can both agree you could've done better," I said. "Didn't meet you until a couple weeks ago." Then I realized. "Wait...Clark?"

He chuckled. "The programming wasn't even the hard part. It was getting that darn smile just right. Took twice as long. Too much, and he'd look insane. Not enough, and he's just any other Jack."

"Well, it's safe to say he's not just any other Jack. He's your best work."

"And you were theirs," Dex said. "They'd be so proud. You made it, kiddo. Back to Heaven's Vault."

The radio clicked in my ear and everything went quiet again. The silence felt different after that.

CHAPTER 29 - INTRUSION

I reached the lift and had to wait in the dark for a few minutes, contemplating Dex's words. I thought back on El and how she must have known my parents too. But she never told me. I understood some of her reasoning for withholding certain things now, some of the lies—hiding the identities of the raincoats, the Breacher, the truth.

It was all to keep Varic and his ilk out of Heaven's Vault. I just didn't understand why we couldn't know where we came from, or why the older generations decided to keep that from us. They all knew. They'd lived up here and went down to the surface together, but I knew nothing about it.

And there wasn't a single slip of the tongue in twenty years? Maybe there was, but I didn't realize it at the time—words or phrases that didn't quite add up. The missing volumes and torn-out pages in Anansi's library certainly started to make more sense. Maybe that's why all the Nests were so far apart, why we used birds to communicate. To minimize risk.

"Alright, people," Dex said, slightly fuzzy in my helmet. "Here comes the juice. Hold on to something."

The interior started spinning slowly clockwise. I held onto the rail. Some dust kicked up but settled after a moment. I was getting heavier—being pulled downward.

A button flickered on in front of me just like Dex said it would, pretty and green, reading: 10. I pushed it, and a slatted door slid upward, revealing an enclosed lift. I toe-hopped inside. This looks just like Colony 6. Same technology.

The rest of the lights came on, and I studied the panel inside and pushed 5. The lift moved down as my feet lightly settled onto the floor. A small display above the door blipped with descending numerals. 10 - 9 - 8 - 7 - 6 - 5.

The lift slowed, then the door opened without any input from me. The fifth floor was a long, angular hallway washed in pale light from a narrow ceiling, and nearly every surface was covered in a fine layer of dust. My secondskin was growing heavier and my bouncing steps were slowing, so I relied on my good leg.

When I reached the end of the hall, it split to my right and left. To my right, another hallway—twice the length of the one behind me and riddled with doors on both sides. To my left, a tinted door with bold letters reading O2 MAINTENANCE. Just like Dex said.

The door automatically receded into the wall as I approached. Beyond was a square room with a soft, rubber floor, and hundreds of slender steel cylinders lining the side walls. There were also snaking pipes and valves above me, but it wasn't chaotic like the Cistern. Everything was organized and their purposes were defined by clear labels or intuited by the mechanisms they sprung out from.

In the center of the back wall was a series of four y-shaped levers in the down position, ready to be primed. I dragged myself over and pinched my thumb over my palm. "I'm here, Dex. About to prime the scrubbers."

"Go…head, lad."

Levers one and two went up and down with ease, but levers three and four gave me some resistance. I used the weight of the suit to pull them, and they slowly clicked into place.

A terminal lit up below them with a big inviting button. I pressed it, and the chrome cylinders started pumping in syncopated rhythms next to each other like pistons—down into the floor or up through the ceiling, slowly at first, then progressively quicker. My suit reacted, loosened. After a minute, a little light in my helmet blinked from red to yellow with a low blip, then slowly from yellow to green with a pleasant ding.

"Great...ob, lad!" Dex crackled in my ear. "Clark...ox...evels...

rising. Shoul…be…saf…"

"Should be?" I asked. He didn't respond. I crossed my fingers. "Please, don't die." I reached up and put my fingers over the top latch of my secondskin. "Please. Please, don't die."

I closed my eyes, flicked it open, and the helmet hissed. I peeked an eye open.

"I'm not dead." I took a deep breath of relief and slowly released the rest of the latches. I wouldn't call the air fresh, but it was breathable.

I stepped out onto the rubbery floor, bent the thumb of my suit, and poked my head into the half-open helmet. "Dex, I'm heading back to level ten," I said. "I can't bring the suit with me. Weighs too much."

He said something, but all I heard was crackling as I walked back out into the corridor. The hallway was filled with a dense dust storm, but it was nothing compared to the Tempest on a good day. Nothing would be. I pulled up my scarf and strolled through it.

As I stepped onto the lift and pressed the blinking 10, I allowed myself a true smile. Like relaxing a muscle after fifteen years, a sense of relief washed over me in pinpricks and goosebumps. We'd really done it. I wondered what kind of future my parents had imagined for me. And where would we be off to next?

A feminine voice, like the one we heard in Colony Six, rang through the corridor as orange lights pulsed, "Unauthorized access to docking bay ten. Unauthorized access to docking bay thirteen. Unauthorized access to docking bay nineteen. Unauthorized access to docking bay twenty-four."

"Get back up top, and find out what's happening," Dex's voice came over the same external radio system.

"I'm going," I shouted back at him, but there was no response.

The lift stopped at level ten. As the door buzzed open there was a heavy fuming dust storm illuminated by distant overheads. Some loud whining sound pulsed with the throb of warning lights.

The voice repeated the warning over and over as I ran. Perpendicular gangways alternated on my left and my right every few meters, with ascending numbers that were barely visible in the haze.

"Unauthorized access to docking bay ten."

I passed docking bay five. Then six.

"Unauthorized access to docking bay thirteen."

I continued running past seven and eight where the Breacher was docked, but I couldn't see far enough to know if anyone was ahead of me. I heard docking bays hissing and cranking in the distance to my left and right. The overhead voice swelled and faded as I neared and passed each jutting walkway.

"Unauthorized access to docking bay nineteen."

I slid to a halt at bay ten and flipped my brela into my hand with the blade facing down, capped the handle with my thumb and angled it in front of me. React. Patience. How the hell was I supposed to react if I couldn't see anything?

I tightened my grip on the leather-bound handle and breathed deep, watching down the walkway for any shadows in the haze. The docks beyond were shifting and unsealing.

Long before I heard or saw anyone, I felt the rumble of footsteps approaching from the distance on my right. Is that from the Breacher or one of the other docks? I lowered my body but kept my eyes forward on bay ten. There was a hiss and pop down the gangway in front of me. I inched backward to react as footsteps plowed forward.

A figure tackled me in the ribs and slammed me to the grates. But I still had my brela. I threw my elbow across their chin and yanked my blade back toward their head. But they pinned my arm across my neck with both arms, choking me. They were stronger than me. And bigger. I wasn't going to be able to lift them off me.

I dropped my brela into my other hand and thrust it up under their ribs and drew it across their belly. I felt warmth rush over my hand as I pulled it out.

They growled, swung me around, and squeezed the crook of their elbow into my neck until green dots popped in my vision. Iris had done that to me before. Push a thumb into the soft spot beneath the jaw. I squirmed in their grip and swung wildly for their face.

There. I got my thumb underneath their jaw and jammed upward as hard as I could. A beard. Renner? He cried out and loosened his grip only enough to sock me in the face a few times. I spit blood and skin up into his face. He lifted me like I weighed nothing and slammed my spine down onto the metal floor. Deal with the pain later.

I wrapped my legs up around his muscled arm and yanked backward as hard as I could until I heard a snap. It does sound like dewroot. He didn't cry out. Instead, he drooped over me like a sack of meat.

Did he pass out? I kneed him in the stomach, but again, he didn't react.

There was something weeping down my arms as I shoved him into the railing. I flung off my scarf and rolled away, giving him a solid kick to the ribs as I stood. When he slumped over, I saw the damage my brela had done.

His guts were hanging out, and there was blood everywhere. All over my arms, clothes, and boots. Far more than I'd ever seen. One cut in the right spot, and a man had bled out in less than a minute.

My knife was sharp. Sharp enough to kill. It went in so easily. I didn't think it could do this much damage. I tried to rub the blood off, panicked, and slipped backward onto the floor. I dropped my weapon. I couldn't move. It was everywhere—what I'd done. He was already dead when I'd kicked him, when I'd snapped his arm. The thought made me ill.

Do all men die like that? He was just here a moment ago. He was going to kill me. I had to do it. Will I die like that? Am I—

Iris ghosted through the dust with no sound and squatted beside me. She assessed the scene for a moment. I couldn't look at her. I wanted to hide it—the body and the blood.

She sighed. "I know. This is what I meant." She picked up my blade and handed me a cloth from her pack. "Clean your brela, raincoat. It's not over."

She grabbed my bloody hand and lifted me to my feet. A moment later, she disappeared back into the fading cloud ahead of me toward bay eleven. I could barely even remember standing. What did she just say? Everything was processing so slowly.

Raincoat? The word washed over me—everything I'd wanted to be, from the only person left with the authority to grant it. Is that still what I wanted? Does that even matter now?

I clumsily wiped down my weapon and looked at the two stars on the hilt, stained with blood. I wondered if El would disapprove or be impressed. Maybe this was why she told me I wasn't meant to be a raincoat. She knew I was the son of two gardeners. I'd finally proved her wrong, and it didn't feel the least bit satisfying.

I wanted to stop. But more work still needed to be done.

The dead man next to me wasn't the one I was looking for, but he was a piercer pilot, which meant Renner would probably be among those infiltrating Heaven's Vault. How the hell did they make it up here? The Breacher is supposed to be the only ship that can break the atmosphere. Did they ride our wake? Was that just another lie?

"Unauthorized docking in bay nineteen."

As best I could, I wiped off the rest of the blood and ran down the walkway after Iris in a daze. I couldn't feel her footsteps ahead of me, and there weren't any sounds of fighting as I reached bay thirteen and turned down the platform. I could just barely see the door, a few meters away. Where is she?

There were alternating lights signaling the intrusion. Then, one after the other, they shut off, and the bay door slid upward. A short-statured man with greasy red and white hair hopped out and waved at me.

"You people owe me a pair of boots, two teeth, and a pinky," Deek said.

He pulled a striker from his waist and sparked it across the railing as he advanced on hopping feet, back and forth. He was mocking me. A shower of sparks scattered across the walkway in front of me. He was less than two meters away.

"I'm not usually good with kids," Deek said, still hopping. "Don't suppose there's any chance you'll surrender?"

My arms were still dripping with blood. "I asked your friend the same thing," I lied, flicking the blood at Deek. He didn't need to know I was sick over what I'd done.

"It wasn't Vikas, was it? Big guy? About yay high?" He lifted the crackling baton over his head. "That's a shame. I liked him. Always laughed at my jokes."

I stared back at him with no answer. He wanted me distracted. Focus. Patience.

"Well, well, well. Maybe you'll make a good dance partner after all." He sprung one foot to feint, smiling as I jerked away on instinct. "Good. Follow my lead. Left foot next." In a blink, he was on me with a swipe of the baton, sparks scattering from the handrail as he struck it. "Now, take my hand."

I countered his striker with my brela, but a stinging pain jolted up my arm as I connected. My hand started tremoring. It felt like I'd been struck by lightning. I could barely hold the blade.

"Next, a pirouette," he said.

He was fast—much faster than me—and he had a longer reach with his weapon. His eyes were different than when we had him tied up—that smile was an act. Iris said she didn't like the way he fought. I understood what she meant now; Deek only pretended to play. I wondered how she'd got the better of him back at Colony Six. Did she just get the drop on him, or is she really this good? He's too close for throwing. Should I create some distance? Should I—

He scraped the striker, flinging indiscriminate sparks in my direction. "Box step. Very good."

I could only cover my face, back away, and try to keep a squinted eye on him. Wait for your opportunity. He wasn't giving me any room, and the rail behind me was getting close. I wouldn't have anywhere to go soon. Maybe I can grapple him to the floor. He's shorter than me.

Again, he barreled down with the baton, but I sidestepped hard, catching myself against the rail with nowhere to go. Shit. I flicked my brela to my off-hand and flailed my left arm in his direction. I was surprised to feel it hit something soft. He dropped his weapon and headbutted me in the nose with a crunch. I stumbled back onto the floor, piercing pain in my eyes. My nose was broken.

"So you're a southpaw," he grimaced, pulling the blade from

his arm and tossing it aside. He switched the baton to his other hand. "Me too."

I scrambled to my feet as he scraped the floor and shot more at me. Again and again. I backed away; my arms raised. I had to close my eyes. He had me. I couldn't fight what I couldn't see, and certainly not without my knife.

"And now the finale—" he said.

A sound whizzed by, and I heard a slicing thud against the far wall by the bay door. I looked up to see Deek's striker at my feet. He was skewered through the chest and pinned to the wall with Toothpick

He struggled and twitched as his weak, scared hands reached up to pull out the massive glaive. Then, all at once, his body went limp.

Across the ship, five levels down, were two glowing blue eyes staring back at me through the dust.

"Get to bay nineteen! Iris needs you!" Clark shouted over the still resounding sirens.

"Thanks," I yelled back.

If Iris needed me, it had to be him. I grabbed my brela and ran off toward nineteen. Stop dropping the goddamned knife.

The overhead light had finally broken through the haze, and I could see Iris's back about a hundred meters away in a brutal fight with Renner. They'd already been at it for a while. Both were nursing minor injuries outside bay twenty, but Renner was on the back foot, barely dodging her quick swipes.

On my best days, I could span a hundred meters in under fifteen seconds, but a lot could happen in that time. I was a packbrat first, a runner. I put everything into my legs and sprinted.

Renner noticed me. "Finally, backup," he shouted.

In the briefest moment that Iris turned to see who was coming, Renner clocked her in the temple with a right hook. She wobbled and swung wide. He easily caught her again on the chin, and she fell to the floor in an unconscious heap.

"Perfect timing," he said with a salute. Eighty meters. Seventy meters.

He battered her unconscious body with kicks to the ribs and

stomach, but he wasn't hitting her hard enough to kill.

"I'll kill you," I screamed. Forty meters. Not close enough.

"You keep saying that," he yelled back with another kick. "And I'm still here."

"Then fight me." I was only twenty meters away. Almost.

He didn't respond. He knew I was helpless to watch as he repeatedly kicked Iris in the face. The only sound after my voice went hoarse was the wet smack of his boot. Ten meters.

"Too late," he said. He drew his foot all the way back to end her.

Now. I flipped the blade of my brela between my fingers, and with everything I had, hurled it at Renner.

It stuck. Right in his thigh. He reeled back, limping away with a hand on the hilt sticking out of his leg.

"You little shit," he had the same unmoved look on his face as he pulled the knife free with a spurt of blood. Does nothing affect him?

Iris was a mess as I slid next to her. Her left eye was purple and swollen and her lips were like muddy clay—wet, cracked, and smeared with blood. But her chest was rising weakly, and I could hear the wheeze of life through one of her nostrils. I leaned down and took up her brela in my hand.

"What did I tell you, Renner? I said you'd make another mistake, and I'd be there. Didn't I?" I looked down at Iris. "And this was your last goddamn mistake." I squeezed her blade. "Look at her. You're gonna get what she got twice over. I promise you that. You're a fucking dead man."

He waved a flippant hand. "I can't even remember how many of you have looked at me the way you're looking at me now," he said, monotone. "And they were all stronger than you. Including her."

I continued toward him, shaking my head. "No one knows that better than me. Everything I've tried to do has been a brutal reminder that I'm not what I thought I was. I'm not the strongest, the smartest, or the fastest. But I just keep on living anyway."

It was more than that, though. I was a survivor. El had said that to me once. Maybe it was time to start listening to her. I know who I am. I'm not like him. I would never do what he did to Lars. What he did to El. What he did to Saph. To Maksy and Rile.

To Iris.

She was still alive. We'd made it through everything else. Renner wasn't a storm or a monster or ghost. He was just a man, and he could be killed.

I pointed her brela at him. "It stops now. With me. Just like I told you it would."

I'd never seen him show any emotion whatsoever, but there it was on his face, for the first time—the smallest crack. Fatigue. He couldn't hide it. Not from me. Because I knew what a bad leg looked like.

He sighed. "You sound just like she did. I'll never understand you people. You make everything so personal. If my orders were to protect you, I would've done that too. Without question. Sentiment only gets in the way. You ended the world over your sentiment."

"El was right. I'd pity you if you weren't such a piece of shit. You've never a had single thought of your own."

"You're boring me. It's over, kid. You're alone, and you're not good enough."

"Wrong again." I gripped the blade hard. It won't slip out of my hand this time. "One cut is all it takes." I bent my knees. Patience.

He looked at me, shook his head, then spit a glob of blood on the floor. "Whatever you say."

We circled each other, both of us favoring one leg, but I had more experience with poor mobility. He charged me, arms crossed in front of him. With an upward grip, I thrust my brela into his guard. Now that I knew how much damage a sharp blade could do—why isn't he dodging?

The blade clanked against something inside his sleeve, and he parried my strike away with ease. Shit. He's wearing some internal armor. As my blow went wide, he kneed me in the gut. I keeled over, trying to catch my breath.

Before I could even react, his elbow cracked down on the back of my skull, flattening me to the floor. My world spun as I rolled over onto my back.

It was so fast, so powerful. I was seeing double. El had warned me not to fight him, but I was utterly outmatched, and it wasn't even close. Why is she always right? What do I do? Do I run? Iris is right there. He'll kill her. Do I try to pull him away? Can I even stand?

For a moment he stood over me and gawked. "You're not even half the fighter she was." Then he hobbled over and picked up his striker, flipping it in his hand with skill.

I was reeling from the pounding sensation inside my head and the frustration welling up inside of me.

Be clever. Use your legs. Patience. You don't have to be fast as lightning. It's enough to react to the thunder. My hands felt weak, and I could barely hold the brela. Am I really gonna drop this thing again?

He swung the baton down, and I lifted the blade to meet it. I closed my eyes as an array of sparks singed my face. He swung again and again, striking me in the shoulder, then the leg. It was painful, but he wasn't aiming for my vitals. He was toying with me. Just like he did with Iris. We were nothing in his eyes. Just play things. Just orders.

He believed he had already beaten me. Fine. Let him believe. As he struck me again in the side, I went limp, dropped my guard, and my eyes. The baton came down on my shoulder. I clenched my jaw and took it. Wait. React. Use your legs. The pain means you're still here.

"No. I'm not done with you yet," he said. "Wake up!" He brought the baton up with both arms.

I cocked my good leg up to my chest and plowed the heel of Kai's boot up under his knee. The joint crunched and popped. He cried out in pain and fell forward onto his other knee.

I brought my brela up toward the soft flesh under his chin, but he thwacked my wrist with the baton, and the blade clattered onto the grates behind me. Goddamnit. He jammed the hot end of the baton into my chest.

No more games. He was trying to kill me. The striker burned through my stormbreaker and instantly cauterized my flesh. I screamed out, gasping, legs kicking as I tried to force him off of me.

He leaned into my face with blood dribbling from his lips and put all his weight on the baton. "Maybe the two of you could've taken me. But alone—"

I heard metal scrape against bone, and Renner gasped for air, stumbling backward off me. His face was contorted. There was a brela sticking out of his ribs. He shakily pulled it out and held it in his off hand, confused.

Iris stumbled in front of me. She was up, in a manner of speaking—peering through a bloodshot, bleary eye, her bruised arms shaking limply at her sides. Still so light on her feet.

Her breaths were shallow, but so were Renner's. He wobbled somewhat to his left where he'd been stabbed and had his knee shattered.

Iris's fists shot up as she came in low to dodge a haymaker and hammered him in the throat. He teetered backward, choking. But she pulled his shirt in for more. She wrapped an elbow around his wrist and tightened her hold, cracking the bone to retrieve her brela.

He groaned and brought his forehead down and she brought hers up to meet him. The sound was like rock against rock. He staggered into the railing.

I clambered to my feet in blinding pain and slid along the rail after them. The lights were dancing as I picked up my brela and followed.

She dodged a desperate swing from his baton and perforated his lungs with her blade. One, two, three, four quick stabs. He bled in short, steady spurts.

With a desperate wet choke, he said, "wait," as he dropped his baton and turned to stumble away toward docking bay twenty-one. I came up next to Iris, and we stayed in step with him.

He threw backhanded swings, weaker with each attempt, and we riddled him with holes and shallow cuts—the thigh, shoulder, forearm, calf, a finger. He reached bay twenty-one at the end of a long trail of blood. Nowhere left to go. He couldn't speak, but his weary eyes and shaking curled lips were full of the emotion he'd gotten so good at hiding.

I thought back to that day I first saw him, squatting in front of

Maksy and Rile, asking a question I never understood. "Now do you know what they were afraid of? Now do you get it?" I yelled. With a grunt, I kicked him against the bay door. It slid open and took a smear of his blood with it.

Iris nudged him inside.

The three of us stood there, glaring hate at one another. I recalled the names of everyone I could remember. Everyone we'd lost because of his goddamn orders.

"They were children," Iris whispered. It was almost a question, rife with all the whys Renner could never account for.

He said nothing.

She turned to me with her one good eye and looked at me, really looked at me. We held each other's gaze. No one else would understand what that man had done to us. She reached over and held my hand in hers—the same hand that had taught me how to cook, sew, and kill.

"For Maksy and for Rile," she said.

I slammed my fist on the red RELEASE button.

The door in front of us slammed shut, and the outer hatch of the docking bay blew open. Renner jettisoned into open space. His skin boiled and burst as his blood froze and shattered. His screams were silent and quick—much quicker than he deserved.

Iris's breaths were growing more ragged and mournful as we watched our greatest enemy float away. Tears and blood fell from her split, quivering lips, and a guttural scream emerged from her mouth, deeper and more profound than anything I'd ever heard.

We didn't cry like that on Galilei. It betrayed our maxim. Dwelling led to pain, led to hesitation, led to failure and to death. Survival above all else. Forward as always.

But at the sound of her excruciating courage and her willingness to remember—to dwell—an old pain swelled in my chest. I allowed myself to feel the loss, the aching I'd rejected, the gaps in my heart where the shapes of people should be.

Maksy and Rile were gone. And El. Lars. Dim and Kai, Shanna, Anansi. Brin and Nello and Foss. So many more. Others we'd left behind. No justice or thoughtful remembrance would bring them back. No matter how profoundly they were missed, it made no difference. They were gone the same way Renner was gone. I couldn't reconcile that, so I didn't try. I just felt it.

As the shadow of his broken body eventually faded into the night, Iris and I slid down the wall.

She sobbed, and I laid my arm across her shoulder. Her cries were wet and messy—muffled beneath the pain of serious injuries and the weight of a regret she'd carried for most of her life. The tighter I held her, the harder she wept.

I wanted to tell her it wasn't her fault. That none of us blamed her. But all I could think about was the fact that we were alive, and the others weren't. And I missed them so much. It wasn't right. None of it. They should be here.

"That night," she whimpered, voice as cracked and broken as her body.

I leaned in to listen.

"I was at the springs," she said. She barely eked out the next words. "...picking flowers."

Flowers? Of course. The crown in her room. That's where she was fifteen years ago. She must've come home to nothing but smoke and death, flowers still in hand. She was no more than fifteen years old, digging through smoldering ashes to find us. A child searching for dead children. Just what had we gotten used to down there? Iris didn't deserve to live with that guilt, and I'd never know why El let her.

I couldn't do a thing about the blame she held onto, but I could at least remind her why we did all this.

I gently pulled her in. "There's still time," I said. "Saph's still with us. Give her the one you kept. The one in your room."

She turned to look at me, surprised I knew about it. "It's old and smashed."

"So are you," I said with a smile. "And she likes you plenty."

I was surprised when she didn't slug me. She just sunk into me. Iris and I stayed like that under the flashing orange lights and echoing warnings until the dust completely cleared and we had no more tears to shed. We saw the others exiting the Breacher from far down at dock seven and struggled to our feet.

We stole one last knowing look at each other. I wondered how I looked to her. Does she still see that kid from fifteen years ago?

I rubbed her head.

"Your hair's grown."

CHAPTER 30 - CAPTAIN INNES

Together we hobbled down the walkway back toward docking bay seven where Moss and his crew had poured out. We met at bay thirteen.

"Well, this is something else," Moss said with squinted eyes, nudging Deek's impaled body. "Flint, get your peepers over here. I'm not imagining this, right? It's Deek. That curly crown of fire is hard to mistake."

Flint dragged his foot over. Then spat. "That'd be him."

"Thought so," Moss said, looking at me. "Guessing he gave you lot some trouble."

"A bit," I said, half-glancing back at the blood-smeared door of bay twenty-one. "Not as much as Renner…who's also dead, if that means anything to you."

"Varic's little puppet?" Moss laughed. "Most of us were buried in the Cistern because of him." He tapped Clark's glaive with his finger, and it squished in Deek's body like a stick in the mud. "Nothing but death suits men like them."

Snags scanned the ship with relative calm. She was smiling and leaning against the rail like she belonged there.

"You," Iris mumbled through her swollen lips, pointing to Snags. "You're familiar with this place."

She lovingly stroked the railing with a chuckle. "I never thought I'd see this old bird again."

Iris glared down the walkway where Clark was stomping out of the far lift. "Where's Dex, then?" she said.

"Well." Snags parted the crowd. "I spent most of my time in the guts, but if memory serves, the bridge is thatta way." She pointed toward Clark. "Take the lift to level two."

"This place have an infirmary?" Iris cocked an eyebrow.

"The other way." Snags thumbed toward the lift I'd used earlier. "Level eight? Seven or eight. Ah sorry, I didn't spend much time there either. Doc said I've got a good ticker."

Moss pointed to Iris. "Grisham, can you get her to—"

"Keep your hands off me," she said.

"You bunch sure are testy. Thought you were suggesting it for yourself," Moss said, trying to deflect. "On account of you teetering like a drunk toddler."

"Maybe you wanna see the infirmary for yourself?" she said.

"Well, that's…" he started. Then, he shut his mouth.

Clark came up beside us and pulled out Toothpick, dropping Deek's body onto the walkway with an unceremonious flop. "Dex is on level two," he said, his eyes fixed on me. "The bridge is open to us. Come."

"Information we already had, Jack," Iris said. "And we really could've used you in the fight."

Clark looked down at Deek's corpse on the floor, then at his bloody weapon, then over at me. And finally, back at Iris. "But I killed this small awful man."

"For which I am very grateful," I said. "Don't mind her. She's punch-drunk."

Iris just stumbled off toward the lift, leaving a thin trail of blood behind her.

I looked through the rest of the group. "Where's Harrow?" I asked. "We can't just leave him on the Breacher."

"We tried," Flint chimed in. "He said, and I quote, 'the birds will tell me when they're ready.' Cryptic fellow."

"Yeah," I sighed. "I guess that's fine for now." Dex needed our more immediate attention.

We all took the lift down to level two together. There was a subtle wane in power as we descended, but we still reached our destination in seconds. As the door opened and the room expanded before us, a hushed awe came over the group.

The bridge was like a massive eye—a concave room of multi-paneled, dark amber glass, beyond which were countless stars and a familiar set of moons. A dozen curved, leather seats were staggered around as many terminals, vastly more complex and sleek than the Breacher. Some terminals were powering on, others were cold and dead.

Saph was spinning in a chair next to empty secondskins while Dex was tinkering with a flickering pedestal at the center of the room. There was a transparent man made of light standing at the center. He was very well dressed in some fitted-military fatigues. His hair was tight and short, and he had sharp eyes and a sharper jawline. He was saying something I couldn't quite make out amidst all the crackling and broken speech.

When Saph saw us, she stood up and ran over. "Are you okay?"

"Sweet Sunday, Iris." Dex poked his head out and winced at her injuries. "You alright?"

"Doing better than Renner," she said, flopping into one of the chairs and popping a piece of licorice root into her mouth.

"That's wonderful news. And I'll do you one better. Our girl here is the genuine article," he said, wrapping one hand around my shoulder and the other around Saph. "This staticky fellow is Captain Gabriel Innes. Her father. He commanded Heaven's Vault during our journey from Commonhope Ganymede."

As we all circled around the image, it stopped flickering and grew louder and more distinct. "Here we go," Dex laughed with satisfaction.

Saph didn't move. She just watched with bated breath as the image began to speak.

"...as of July 29, 2538 we have neither the energy nor the manpower to maintain primary systems aboard Heaven's Vault. We've taken measures to direct all tertiary power to the astral arboretum. The nearest star is too distant for a new viable solar orbit before our life support systems shut down, and even if we were to break our current trajectory, the colonizers on Galilei would perish.

"The climate oscillators were successfully installed at the two points of polarity, but due to unexpected limitations in planetary resources, they will require a constant satellite supply of ancillary energy from Heaven's Vault in hopes that the atmosphere stabilizes. We have no way to control the density of this energy, which has overloaded the rotational governors.

"As it stands, this malfunction has created an untenable surface life with supercell storms rotating in severe three-to-five-day cycles. While the ground team remains in good spirits, referring to the storm as a vengeful Tempest..."

He paused for a moment. "In short, the ship will be drained of primary power within eleven months, and those of our crew who chose to stay behind will be dead. Our distress beacon to Ganymede will take eight years to reach them. However, previous terraforming operations have succeeded under poorer conditions.

"It is our hope that with diligence and courage, the remaining crew of Heaven's Vault can still create viable conditions for survival in the interim before Commonhope sends aid. We've lost contact with Archimedes and Gna's Progress, but I trust they will reach their destinations, and I can only hope their planets are more forgiving."

He flickered away. Then returned, less immaculately dressed. Saph leaned in, watching his face closely.

"...climate oscillators are drawing more power than we anticipated, and they appear to be gravely malfunctioning. Contact with those on the surface has now proven impossible, and the sheer mass of the supercells is visible even from orbit. By the end of the second month the storm will reach a sustaining severity that will make survival on the surface of Galilei unlikely. Before then, our remaining crew will be dead."

He moved his hands behind his back and exhaled heavily through his nose.

"It has been eight weeks since Luminator Varic instigated his mutiny. Ninety-percent of the crew dissented with him when I enacted the Proto-Cain Proximity. Shivers were apparent on the arms and neck of a young girl named Circe, as was consistent with Panacea infection.

"Varic suggested that she showed no signs of Skaver behavior, that he had cured her, but I assessed that the risk of spread was too great. I released her...his daughter, from the airlock of bay seventeen on the 23rd of June. When the crew mutinied on the 25th, I was compelled to seal off the bridge and deny access to the Breacher. I sent CL4-K, my Secondhand Jack, to mediate.

Clark approached the pedestal with a hand over his chest.

"I had hoped my message of peace would deter them enough to see reason. To my surprise, they recklessly seized all piercer and mobile landing vessels along with the industrial colonization units. Due to the thin atmosphere, most of their ships survived the descent, but many died. They have taken up residence underground, a few kilometers south of a large canyon, near the only known sources of fuel, below-surface-shelter, and fresh water.

"Those of us still onboard had to make assessments for survival. Ultimately, a decision was made to load the Breacher beyond capacity and send it to the surface. There were several infants onboard. My..." He paused again. "My daughter, Saph, is with them."

Captain Innes lifted his chin slightly and swallowed. Saph made no sound, but her eyes were locked on him as he cleared his throat and continued.

"Given that the nature of our mission has been distilled down to survival, those going to the surface will raise the children with no knowledge of where they came from, nor knowledge of the others living apart from them. There is little hope that they will ever return here, and a life lived and a future imagined should have meaning on its own merit, even one hoped for in strife.

"We have done what we can for them. What rations Varic left behind have been distributed equally among those of us who stayed. I must make note, however, some chose to yield their rations to the Breacher crew. Those brave souls have since passed, and their sacrifice is documented."

His image flashed away, then reappeared sitting down. He was gaunt, and his eyes were sunken.

"This is Captain Innes. It is the 12th of September. This will be my final log. Of the eighteen who chose to stay behind, only seven remain onboard Heaven's Vault. With some good fortune and great difficulty, we managed to unfurl the solar belts, and we will continue to draw power as lead engineer, Dexan Altrose, advised before he boarded the Breacher. If, by some miracle, anyone is able to return with the Key, we have prepared your means of survival in the arboretum. Good luck to you all. Forward as always."

When he disappeared, we all stared wide-eyed at the pedestal.

"Odd. There's another message," Dex said. He reached out and swiped at the top of the glowing pedestal. A different transparent figure appeared.

He was standing much the same way—his hands at the small of his back and his posture rigid. His hair and eyebrows were thick and gray, but his face was clean shaven. The uniform he wore was adorned in a myriad of decorations. It was the same man I'd seen on the screen at Colony Six.

"Oh, no," Dex whispered.

"This is Prime Lumarch Soren of Commonhope Ganymede. We received your distress beacon and have departed for Galilei on the 8th of January, 2545. It will take us twelve years to reach you, and I expect full cooperation when we arrive. The colonization of Galilei has been reassigned to my crew of the Somerville Connexion, and your assets will be discharged into my command. The dereliction of your duty and the presence of the Skaver calamity aboard Heaven's Vault will invoke catastrophic obstacles to the survival of the human species. Therefore, the dissenters will be dredged from the surface, tried for sedition, and cleansed. As adherence to the Cain Proximity is paramount, the remaining survivors must also be cleansed."

Then he flashed away.

"I'm definitely not interested in being cleansed," Moss said.

"Oh, no need to worry about that," Dex said. "In case you weren't listening, you lot would be tried and put to death for sedition before they cleanse the rest of us."

"To hell with that," Moss stumbled back into a dead terminal that came to life under his touch.

"That's why Renner said we only had eight months," I said.

"Mmm. Assuming it's twelve years to the day..." Dex trailed off, pulling at the hairs beneath his chin. "Soren is an exacting man. I imagine he'll arrive right on time."

"Then we just tell him we came to an understanding," Moss said. "The Skavers are stuck down there. We're up here. All's peaches and cream, right?"

"Don't expect sweetness from the likes of him," Dex said. "You won't get any from me either. I remember what happened up here, and I know what side you stood on."

"What are you gonna do, toss us out into space? There's more of us than there are of you," Moss sneered.

Clark tapped his glaive against the floor. "Your arithmetic is flawed," he said. "I would count again."

"Ah, we're not tossing anybody anywhere," Dex grumbled. Then he slumped into a leather chair and began scratching at his sides with crossed arms as he stared into space above us. "We made it. We're here. Damned if that wasn't enough."

Iris peered through her swollen eye at me and gestured toward Saph. She was still staring at the pedestal. "It doesn't make any sense," Saph said. "Why kill the survivors? We're innocent."

"It's not about innocence," Dex said. "I told you he's an exacting man. It's just math to him. He'll zero out the equation, get rid of variables. The Cain Proximity is his little invention. There's a part of me that might even respect the consistency, if it wasn't at our expense."

"I'm the Captain's daughter, right? That has to count for something. Maybe if I just explain," Saph continued.

"It's not enough, lass," Dex said, still scratching, thinking. "It was out of our hands from the moment your father sent the beacon. He meant to save us. Just couldn't look past protocol. It's the same thing that happened to Circe and started this whole mess. Following orders."

Renner was the same.

Saph slid down against the pedestal and pulled her knees up

to her chin. Iris seemed disinterested in the whole thing, biting at the dried blood on her bottom lip. And Dex was lost in the stars, watching the universe spin above him.

"Come on. We're all thinking it." I stepped up to the pedestal. "Aren't we?"

Saph looked up at me. "Thinking what?" she asked.

"We make a go of it," I said.

Dex leaned forward in his seat and chuckled. "A fight? Are you nuts? We wouldn't last five minutes against them. This is a colony ship, not a cruiser."

Not a fight," I said. "We have eight months to make this thing move, right? Somewhere they can't find us? Anywhere but here." I leaned in toward him. "Is that enough time?"

Dex stopped scratching, "Won't take them long to track us."

"Fine. But is it enough to buy us more time?" I asked.

He stared at me with two sharp eyes, cocking his head slightly and not giving me an inch to look away.

"There have been worse ideas," Moss said. "Snags taught us most of what we know about romancing a machine, and I told you I can switch levers that need being switched. The rest of these grease-fingered idiots have worked tech maintenance for the better part of the decade, and they did it in the dark."

"I can teach them the basics," Snags chimed in. "With a helluva lot of luck, and a few blisters, we might get the old bird moving again. And I'm happy to report, she's breathing real good."

I looked around the room at the eager eyes—eyes waiting for permission to hope. Dex remained silent.

"Better than doing nothing," Iris said.

"The probability is quite low, but no lower than our chances of standing here right now," Clark added.

After a moment, Dex stood from his chair and laid his rough palms down on the pedestal. He slowly looked around the room at hungry faces until his sharp eyes locked on me. A gap-toothed smile reluctantly crept across his face. He nodded.

"Youth," he chuckled. "You gotta be sure about this.

Won't be easy."

I rested a hand on the brela hanging from my hip. It was no longer a symbol—it had become something else, like me. From the moment I was pulled out of the ashes and asked to run, I knew the answers wouldn't be behind me. And every person in the room around me knew what it meant to survive and what was necessary to achieve it. Everything we did came at the cost of lives. But we didn't stop. We didn't go back. We'd forged a path to the stars, against all odds, because there was only ever one direction to move.

"You know the maxim, Dex. Let's get to work."

THE END.

ABOUT THE AUTHORS

JAKE SIDWELL

Jake Sidwell was a writer, producer, and composer for the sci-fi animated hit, Final Space (TBS). He is currently studying to complete his MA in professional media composition with Thinkspace Education through Arts University Bournemouth.

He lives in Oklahoma with his partner and their three dogs.

The stories he finds most compelling are those about reluctant heroes, found family, and shared trauma. When asked about this psychological pattern, his therapist responded: "That is privileged information under the Oklahoma Statutes Title 43A. How did you get this number?"

Jake is also disabled due to chronic illness, which makes him, among other undesirable things, an *inspiration*, despite the fact that he mostly just plays Baldur's Gate 3 and watches long form video essays.

OLAN ROGERS

Olan like Reese's. (slams club on table)